BATTLETECH:
THE PROLIFERATION CYCLE OMNIBUS
A BATTLETECH ANTHOLOGY

EDITED BY **JOHN HELFERS** AND **PHILIP A. LEE**

This is a work of fiction. Names, characters, places and incidents either are the products of the author's imagination or are used fictitiously, and any resemblance to actual persons, living or dead, business establishments, events or locales is entirely coincidental. The publisher does not have any control over and does not assume any responsibility for author or third-party Web sites or their content.

If you purchased this book without a cover you should be aware that this book is stolen property. It was reported as "unsold and destroyed" to the publisher and neither the author nor the publisher has received any payment for this "stripped book."

The scanning, uploading and distribution of this book via the Internet or via any other means without the permission of the publisher is illegal and punishable by law. Please purchase only authorized electronic editions, and do not participate in or encourage electronic piracy of copyrighted materials. Your support of the authors' rights is appreciated.

BATTLETECH: THE PROLIFERATION CYCLE OMNIBUS
Edited by John Helfers and Philip A. Lee
Cover art by Eldon Cowgur
Design by David Kerber

©2021 The Topps Company, Inc. All Rights Reserved. *BattleTech & MechWarrior* are registered trademarks and/or trademarks of The Topps Company, Inc., in the United States and/or other countries. Catalyst Game Labs and the Catalyst Game Labs logo are trademarks of InMediaRes Productions LLC. No part of this work may be reproduced, stored in a retrieval system, or transmitted in any form or by any means, without the prior permission in writing of the Copyright Owner, nor be otherwise circulated in any form other than that in which it is published.

Printed in USA.

Published by Catalyst Game Labs,
an imprint of InMediaRes Productions, LLC
7108 S. Pheasant Ridge Drive • Spokane, WA 99224

CONTENTS

INTRODUCTION — 5
JOHN HELFERS

BREAK-AWAY — 9
ILSA J. BICK

PROMETHEUS UNBOUND — 65
HERBERT A. BEAS II

NOTHING VENTURED — 112
CHRISTOFFER TROSSEN

FALL DOWN SEVEN TIMES, GET UP EIGHT — 170
RANDALL N. BILLS

A DISH SERVED COLD — 216
CHRIS HARTFORD AND JASON M. HARDY

THE SPIDER DANCES — 266
JASON SCHMETZER

THE TRICKSTER — 329
BLAINE LEE PARDOE

INTRODUCTION

I've been working at Catalyst Game Labs for more than a decade now, but just when I think I know practically everything there is to know about the company and what's been produced during its tenure with *BattleTech*, the folks who have been here since the company's founding still manage to surprise me.

Take this omnibus, for example. During the frenzy that was the *BattleTech* Clan Invasion crowdfunding campaign, when the fans were blowing past stretch goals like an *Atlas* through an infantry platoon, one of the things that was thrown up to stay ahead of the crowd was something called the Proliferation Cycle series. As the main fiction editor for the past several years, I *thought* I'd known just about everything CGL has produced in fiction, even the stories that had been created on BattleCorps, the predecessor to *Shrapnel* and the current fiction line. That turned out to not be the case.

Back in the BattleCorps days, someone (probably Loren) had come up with the idea of telling a story of how the first BattleMech was created. If I know these guys, someone else (probably Randall) then blew it out into a series of novellas about how the rest of the Inner Sphere schemed to get those plans however they could. This resulted in a six-part series written by six excellent authors, each one taking one of the Great Houses:

"Break-Away" by Ilsa J. Bick: During the final trials to find the first pilot for the Terran Hegemony prototype *Mackie*, the contest is infiltrated by a deadly enemy who wants to ensure that no one survives. It's up to the last remaining Terran candidate—and a scientist struggling to perfect the human-machine interface that controls this new war machine—to save Terra's BattleMech program from those who wish to destroy it.

"Prometheus Unbound" by Herbert A. Beas II: To acquire BattleMech schematics, the Lyran Commonwealth is about to employ one of the oldest strategies in the book: if you can't beat 'em, steal from 'em. A crack commando unit is assigned their most perilous mission yet: infiltrate a heavily defended Terran world and steal the BattleMech plans. Besides the odds being stacked against them, the leader of this team has his own demon to deal with—one that stands twelve meters tall, and shakes the ground when it walks...

"Nothing Ventured" by Christoffer Trossen: The Federated Suns is trapped between the Terran Hegemony and its fielded BattleMechs, and the Lyran Commonwealth, which has just acquired the plans to build its own war machines. Beset by enemies on all sides, Prince Simon Davion employs his most cunning weapon—a diplomatic envoy sent to Tharkad to gain access to the stolen BattleMech plans. But when diplomatic niceties are unable to accomplish this goal, subterfuge and deception will have to win the day...

"Fall Down Seven Times, Get Up Eight" by Randall N. Bills: The Draconis Combine will do anything—*anything*—to possess BattleMech technology—even grind its most loyal subjects into useless husks to gain the information the Dragon so desperately needs. Two brothers. One an intelligence analyst and deep-cover operative, the other a leader in the Combine's commando unit. Both with the same goal—recover the BattleMech plans—but with very different ideas on how to do so. But only one will survive and emerge triumphant...or will the Dragon's machinations destroy them both?

"A Dish Served Cold" by Chris Hartford and Jason M. Hardy: The Free Worlds League is fighting for its very existence against the encroaching Lyran Commonwealth and its new weapon, the BattleMech. With a new, untested leader on the throne, a precarious plan is hatched to gain edge needed to repel the invaders. Using guile and seduction, a small team of infiltrators plans to take the information the Free Worlds League desperately needs, and the men who possess it, into their arms in one fell swoop…but how can they create a scenario where these technicians will come over of their own free will?

"The Spider Dances" by Jason Schmetzer: There are three ways to accomplish a difficult objective: Be first. Be smarter. Or cheat. The Intelligence Directorate of the Capellan Confederation, otherwise known as the Maskirovka, is well-versed in all three. But when the first two methods do not achieve the desired results, they have no problem resorting to the last one. And when a covert team gains the plans they are willing to die for, that resolve will be tested to the limit as they try to escape the Free Worlds League planet they have infiltrated, matching wits with one of the most feared intelligence officers the FWL has to offer…

Thanks to some swift action behind the scenes by my co-editor, Philip A. Lee, we managed to get all of these stories proofed, reformatted, and distributed to the backers during the campaign.

Naturally, my first thought afterward was to collect them into an omnibus volume. But as I was assembling it, I felt that, as terrific as all of these stories are, the cycle wasn't quite complete. I wanted one more to finish the evolution of the BattleMech, to go beyond the *Mackie*, and realized I needed a story about the creation of the OmniMech over on the Clan Homeworlds.

I reached out to Blaine Lee Pardoe to tell a story about a Clan that hasn't gotten a lot of screen time, Clan Coyote, and their creation of the *Coyotl*. Blaine came through as usual, and created a story that was both what I wanted and unexpected at the same time.

Last but not least, I wanted a new image of the venerable *Mackie* for the cover, and artist Eldon Cowgur came through in a big way. This is his first official *BattleTech* image for us, and I look forward to seeing many more from him in the future.

Now, the cycle is complete.

—John Helfers, Executive Editor
Catalyst Game Labs
May 2021

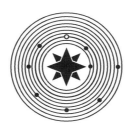

BREAK-AWAY

ILSA J. BICK

"Naw, naw, we got that beat. Battle of Tybalt, Amanda and me did this break-away thing. Snuggled up real close. Meter, maybe. But, see, when you get painted, you look like one guy on GCI, right? So we're going speed of heat, and then just outside visual, Amanda slid out and did this roll, pulled real hard into a split-s, ninety degrees, and she's booming, peeling angels, and I'm playing the music so the Capellans lose the bubble. Then when I yell "Go!" she does this righteous bat turn. Thing of beauty: one-eighty roll, wings-level pull-out, hooking into their bellies, and then I'm loading angels, and the Capellans are loading angels, and they're so busy looking up at me, they never see her coming from below until she rips them a new asshole. Wingman vaporized and the lead bails, but no nylon letdown we could see, poor bastard.

"Anyway, yeah, break-away. Crazy damn stunt. Never works twice.

"But you know? You live for that kind of shit."

—Colonel Charles Kincaid,
as overheard in the Double Ugly,
Terra, 19 October 2435

**SIGNAL MOUNTAIN
TERRA
22 DECEMBER 2438
2030 HOURS**

Hackett took sixty seconds to die, ten more than the colonel expected, and he bled like stink: twin ropes of dark blood spattering on icy rock, like water gurgling on concrete. Hackett's eyes went glassy, and as his knees buckled, the colonel stayed with him, playing a wash of yellow light from his flash over Hackett's face: the star in the spotlight of a terminal drama. Wisps of blood steam curled in delicate fingers, misting the chill night air. Hackett's mouth was open, gawping like a fish as he tried to breathe, but the cut was deep and had sliced his trachea in two. A saving grace: he would suffocate long before he drowned or his body drained of blood. He would lose consciousness even before that. Then, Hackett toppled face-first and very hard. A dark red pool bloomed, spreading like dark machine oil chugging from an overturned bottle. Then the flow of blood dwindled as Hackett's heart failed. Stopped.

The colonel released a slow breath that coalesced in a miasma, a kind of giving up the ghost. His knife hand—the right—was tacky, and he caught the scent of wet rust, like the bed of an old wagon left in the rain. The knife was a standard-issue Hegemony Armed Forces KA-BAR, black on black, with a straight edge seventeen centimeters long, and oily with blood. He cleaned his hands and then spent five minutes on the knife, cleaning and then applying a thin film of boot oil to the blade. When he was done, he slipped the knife into a sheath riding his right hip and secured the thumb break over the black-leather grip. His fingers lingered over incised initials on the KA-BAR's bolt butt: *C. K.*

Squatting, he searched Hackett. The man didn't have much, but this was standard for a Level-C SERE exercise: Survival, Evasion, Resistance, and Escape. He took the major's rations, a jackknife. Didn't need the axe or the major's KA-BAR. Instead, he peeled back the collar of Hackett's parka and then his BDU tunic, thermal, and olive tee. His flash picked up a glint of chain. The chain was blood-slicked, but Hackett's identifier tags were a metallic blue, like the color of aluminum exposed to a flame. Unzipping the parka, the colonel jerked the tags from Hackett's neck, then dropped them into a radio-opaque pouch that nestled against his own thermal tee to keep the tags warm. The metal *chinked*.

Thumbing off his flashlight, he fitted a pair of night-vision goggles over his eyes. He'd made excellent time these last few days, but had kilometers to go before he slept. He raised his left wrist, depressed the stem of something that looked like a wristwatch but wasn't. In an instant, there was the glow of red digits. He tapped in a command and received more numbers, a bearing.

So he set out, slipping in and out of shadow, here and then as quickly gone: the avatar of a gathering storm.

**YAKIMA PROVING GROUNDS
TERRA
24 DECEMBER 2438
0800 HOURS**

The hot, humid air of the inner habitat was musty, with a lingering, ripe stink of feces mingling with mashed jackfruit. The smell always reminded Dr. Carolyn Fletcher of a cross between a New York City sewer and a cow barn.

A slow rivulet of sweat trickled into the hollow between her breasts. She'd been at the target range first thing that morning; popped off two, three mags from her Prestar-Glock 90 just for something to do. Pretty darned cold outside, and she'd worn her black cashmere sweater, jeans, and black cowboy boots: exactly the wrong clothes for the inner habitat. She felt wilted.

Her boss, Dr. Htov Gbarleman, had given the entire neuroscience staff a week off. Christmas, and all that. The military guys skedaddled like they had rockets attached to their butts. Unfortunately, her only standing invite was San Antonio and a ninety-year-old aunt with purple hair from a bottle. So, after tossing the PG-90 in its case into the well behind the driver's seat, she opted for the lab. Data to collate, neural inputs to study. Yada, yada, yada. Busywork.

The neurohelmet worked. No question. But the system made her nervous. Tricking the brain into churning out more neuropeptides than required... She hadn't liked it before, when the assistant director—a military type, natch, but hell of a good-looker—had strong-armed Gbarleman into the augmentation loop seven months ago.

The colonel liked it just fine. Kincaid racked up a slew of kills; got a real hard-on in the sims—hooting, hollering and carrying on like a bronco-bustin' cowboy racing after the steer that got away. A shoo-in for the *Mackie*. Best man. Hegemony Special Forces Sniper Champ and all that crap. (Someone said there was a whole bunch of very pissed-off Blackhearts; just totally ticked that one of their own hadn't won. Seemed kind of dumb to Carolyn; if the Blackhearts didn't want anyone winning but HSF, they shouldn't open up the competition to every branch. Dumb. But that was another one of those military-intelligence oxymoron things.)

Call her sexist, but Carolyn was rooting for Major Cunningham. Not that she knew the pilots more than just to say hello. (Carolyn was hired help: a simian neurophysiology specialist, and pretty much invisible.) Amanda Cunningham's numbers were darned good, and she was more under control emotionally. Racked up kills but without the hoo-hah swagger, joy-of-killing crap. Kincaid might be the best man, but Amanda was a better woman. Except there was all kinds of politico mumbo-jumbo going on, Jacob Cameron's fingers in the pie, the Kincaid family in all kinds of industries, most of which had spent a pretty sizable chunk of change on the project, blah, blah. The final decision would be like, you know, really fair.

So, Carolyn had been in the central lab, scrolling through numbers, blah, blah blah. Not really paying attention but eyeing her reflection: chestnut hair tacked to her scalp in a sensible bun with a forest of bobby pins; the illusion of a heart-shaped face accentuated by a widow's peak. Thinking maybe her eyes—large, deep brown-black—were her best feature, and about how if that's all you got going it's, like, hopeless.

Then sounds seeped into the periphery of her awareness the way water bleeds into paper. She pulled out of her slouch, listened hard. The sounds were screams, but not from people; not a *person* screaming; the screams were...

Oh, my God. She tore out of the lab and clattered down an access corridor, boots banging linoleum like gunshots, but by the time she keyed in her combination code, did the retinal scan and cracked the seal for the inner habitat, the screams had stopped.

Now, she glanced over at the females huddled on a wooden platform three meters above ground. Lucy, Betty, Shana. They were still wild with fear; their brown eyes were wide, whites all around, rolling in their sockets. Tongo, Shana's infant and Jack's son, looked like he was trying to melt into his mother's chest. Linus, an easygoing adolescent male and Shana's firstborn, was high in one of two sycamores that topped out near the removable ceiling grates. That was wrong.

Jack was wrong, too. The alpha male, Jack wasn't a huge chimp. Sixty kilos, a little wiry. Very sociable. Always came over for a hug. Not that aggressive, but smart. The way he'd gotten to alpha male, for example. Instead of an out-and-out fight, Jack had scrounged three plastic jugs and charged the dominant male and his buddies while screaming and juggling the plastic jugs, making a hell of a racket. The other males scattered. Pretty smart chimp. Today, though, Jack was jammed in a corner like he'd been sent to time-out. Hadn't looked around, hadn't made a sound. Wrong.

Normally she never approached the chimps. Better they come to her. So she was cautious. Moved slow, made sure she had a straight line to the door. "Jack," she said, from about a meter away. "Jack, what is it, boy?"

This time, for whatever reason, Jack answered. No, strike that. He cried: an owl-like hooting, a call Carolyn recognized but didn't believe because it made no sense.

Chimpanzees cry, but they do not weep. Their sorrow is vocal: *Hoo, hoo, hoo-hoo-hoo.* Jack's was a slow crescendo that built in volume and frequency, crested. Fell. Eerie.

She reached for him, blindly, the way a mother consoles a child. When her fingers brushed his coarse, dry fur, he shuddered like she'd sent an electric charge sizzling into his bones. His fingers moved in a palsied tremor that was oddly, uncannily familiar. And then Jack pulled his head around, and she saw his face. That's when everything went to hell. When all her assumptions went out the window.

Because Jack was weeping.

SNAKE RIVER
TERRA
24 DECEMBER 2438
0845 HOURS

Job one after the kill? Get rid of the frigging body.

Major Sarah James did everything by the book. Take sniper shots. You had to clamp down on every little twitch no matter how bone-cold you were, or that your nose was icier than a brass button. (Thank heavens, the weather was freakish, and snow hadn't arrived in the Tetons yet.) So she kept still, let her heartbeat slow. Tried not to think about the way her stomach was one big, sharp, ripping cramp, like a cat's claw snagged on skin. Plus, she reeked. Hadn't seen a hot shower for three days, and was pretty sure her BDUs would stand up on their own.

None of that mattered, though, because there was the colonel on the west shore of Snake River and looking one-eighty in the *wrong* direction. Charles Kincaid: HAF Certified Rock Star with a head of blond curls and blue eyes to die for—and the one to beat. She was dying like hell to whip Kincaid's tight little ass.

She peeked through her scope to double-check. Watched as her targeting crosshairs glowed crimson and her IFF read the identifier tags:

KINCAID, CHARLES
SERIAL# 11031902
FOE

All right. Figure, maybe, seven-three-oh meters. James emptied her lungs, the warm moist air jetting from her nostrils. Waited for the pause between heartbeats.

Beat. And...*Amanda Cunningham, eat your heart out...* Beat. She fired.

A mosquito whine and then the ruby red of laser fire cut a seam in the air. The laser needled the colonel's back, and Kincaid flinched, jerking like a fish flipped out of the water. And he went down.

And the crowd goes wild; they are celebrating in Times Square tonight. James waited a few seconds, then trotted over.

Kincaid was facedown, left arm flung to one side, his right folded under his stomach. His laser rifle lay just beyond the outstretched fingers of his left hand. As a precaution—and because she knew every little thing counted—she kept her weapon at the ready and gave the body a wide berth, kicked the rifle to one side, out of reach.

The colonel was playing it to the hilt. Rules said to fall down and play dead, not hard to do when you'd been pretty much semi-Tasered. Not as bad as the real thing but still laid you out a couple seconds. She shouldered her rifle then nudged Kincaid's right leg with the toe of her boot. "All right, Colonel, show's over." And then she grinned, because she was *that* much closer to piloting the *Mackie*. "And if you don't mind my saying it, sir...you is one *dead* mother."

In response, the colonel stirred. "Naw, not me," he said. He rolled left, and then he was on his feet, hood flipping back, his right hand moving up in a single, smooth arc—and James's mind did this little stutter-step of surprise because now she was staring into the huge black *o* of the business end of a silencer.

"But you are," he said, and fired.

The slug rocketed at a speed of a half klick per second along eleven centimeters of barrel plus silencer and zipped the scant ten centimeters between James and the muzzle before the *pfft* ever reached her ears.

But, by then, well...her skull had exploded.

**INSPIRATION POINT
TERRA
24 DECEMBER 2438
0850 HOURS**

Major Amanda Cunningham perched atop a hummock of granite called Inspiration Point that overlooked Jenny Lake, directly behind and to the east, and the craggy, snow-covered peaks of Grand Teton and Mount St. John due west. She wasn't admiring the view. Instead, she was whittling a fishhook out of a supple whip of stripped aspen. She didn't need a new hook; it was just something to do. She'd snagged a fair-sized brook trout out of Jenny Lake just as the sun was coming up. Best time to ice-fish, first thing in the morning. She bled, scaled, scooped out all the fish guts. Buried the guts as far into the frozen earth as she could (not much) because of animals, and if a squad came by, to make it look like no one had been around. Couldn't make a fire. Smoke was a big no-no, kind of empirically obvious if you were trying really hard not to get caught. So she ate the fish raw. It was okay. Hey, people paid a lot of money for that stuff and called it sashimi.

Raw fish, whittling hooks, watching her ass: what SERE was all about. Big field manual on the thing. Playing by the rules, Amanda ought to be on the move, heading for Death Canyon, twenty-odd klicks southwest. (There was probably some irony there.) Up at Death Canyon, there was a radio she could use to vector in a rescue chopper. Deadline was midnight December twenty-fifth, and a Merry Christmas to you, too.

That same manual also said that come daylight, you get a move on. She bet that's what Hackett and James and Kincaid were doing because whoever got to Death Canyon first won. The trick was not getting captured, and staying alive.

But this was the fubar part. Not only were there enemy squads gunning for your butt, *you* could take out the competition. Show you had grit, and all that crap. Taking out your own people was stupid, even if you were competing with them. Amanda hadn't survived this long playing by rules that made no sense. It wasn't like she wasted a lot of time and energy feeling bad about doing her job. She was a soldier and a realist. Some soldiers gazed at their navel, wondering if killing the enemy was like, you know, moral. Screw morality. You think the enemy's getting all existential? Don't want to kill people, be a writer.

On the other hand, some rules existed because only some people could break them and not end up vaporized. Like Tybalt three years ago, that break-away, a stunt you bragged about in a bar. Won 'em a couple of medals, and then she and Kincaid had celebrated in bed for a solid day, giddy with relief and tickled to be alive.

At the thought of Kincaid, a whiny little voice seeped up from some dark Neanderthal crevice of her brain: *That's what's really eating you, isn't it, sweetheart? Hard enough Kincaid's got his eye on the* Mackie, *but having to train with him, watching him ace those simulations. Not enough that he knows more about slug-throwers than any guy living and has the medals to prove it. But seeing him do it with that kind of weird energy he gets so you know that he's happier shooting almost than flying...got you going, huh, baby doll?*

"Shut up, you moron." Suddenly furious, she jabbed a knothole with the tip of her jackknife and twisted, popping it out like an eye. "You think the two of you would live happily ever after? Not when there's a Cameron in the picture, right?"

She remembered the day everything went to hell. This year, a Thursday afternoon in early July: the heady, too-sweet aroma of day lilies swirling through an open window and over their bodies on the warm fingers of a gentle wind as smooth and soft as velvet. She'd been his wingman for four years, and his lover for most of that. They just fit together. In bed, out of it, and when they made love, she could pretend that Colonel Charles Kincaid wasn't destined for great things—and that one of them wasn't Isabelle Cameron, the Director-General's third cousin.

They'd lain in a tangle of sheets, Kincaid on his stomach along her left side, thigh to thigh. He was a leftie, and that was his side of the bed because he hated reaching across and fumbling around the nightstand for something. As much as she wanted him, she had to know. Call it perversity. Or maybe self-defeating. But she said, "So you're marrying her."

She expected him to be angry. Maybe that's what she wanted. Nice big fight, maybe break a couple things. Then losing him wouldn't hurt so much.

Instead, he rolled up on his right elbow. Kincaid's eyes were very blue but dark, like the sky at twilight. "You know I don't have a choice."

"You have a choice. Just say no."

Kincaid sighed. "Amanda, we've been over this and over this. My family has connections…"

"Who cares which uncle served under whom? I know your family's been in service to the Hegemony for a long time."

"That counts for something. I'm not narcissistic enough to believe that Jacob Cameron would fall if I don't marry Isabelle—"

"Jacob Cameron's an idiot."

"Being an idiot and Director-General aren't mutually exclusive. Even if we leave out my family's military connections, there are quite a few Kincaids with a vested interest in seeing this very expensive project through. I don't think my relatives or their friends would be very keen on seeing, oh, billions go up in proverbial smoke. There's a lot riding on the *Mackie*, including the future of how you and I will fight our wars."

"And the Kincaids are keen on that, too, I suppose? More war?"

"I could say that war is a business."

"It is."

"Yes," he said, "it is. A very expensive business that we can't afford to let go bust. So if this doesn't work, or the Camerons are perceived as weak, then the Capellans, the Federated Suns, or even some our oh-so-loyal disgruntled nobles won't hesitate to stake their claims and carve us up. Then little things like Tybalt, all that suffering…our people will have died for nothing, Amanda."

"Don't pull that guilt shit." Her voice went watery, and she didn't want him to see her cry. "Damn you. I hate you, you know that? And I really hate her."

"It's political, Amanda. It's economic. The marriage is only one factor in a very complicated calculus that's about as cold and hard and mathematical as the equations governing life and death. This is an alliance my family wants and the Camerons need. You know I don't love Isabelle."

"I know *that*," she said, more sharply than she liked. Reaching over, she laced her fingers behind his neck and rolled onto her back, pulling him down then crushing his mouth with hers, and...

"Stop." Amanda fisted her hands. The whittled point of her rough fishhook bit into her left palm, but that was okay. Mooning over some guy who was going to get married come February just as soon as he piloted the *Mackie* for its test run...

Now, *that* was an interesting bit of defeatist thinking. She unfurled her fingers and stared at a bead of bright red blood welling up in her palm. Was she trying to lose to spare herself the humiliation of Kincaid's being chosen *because* he was Kincaid? Even if she really was better?

Nothing was certain. There were, for example, three possible outcomes between now and midnight December twenty-fifth. One: she could win. Make it to the radio, vector in the chopper, and exit right into the *Mackie*'s pilot couch.

Two: she might get captured. She'd managed to avoid two separate squads over the past three days only to nearly walk into one yesterday near dusk. Sidestepping her way down a slope, she saw movement out of the corner of her left eye and ducked back in the nick of time. Three of them, tiny as ants, making their way around Hanging Canyon, maybe a good thousand meters away and too far to tag with her target laser. She watched them long enough to figure that they were going to be between her and the pick-up coordinates the rest of the way. So they might snag her unless she figured a way to take them out of the equation.

Or, three: she could get herself "killed." There were three people running around with the go-ahead to eliminate her if they could, by using nonlethal weapons to knock her out of the competition. One was Brian Hackett. Another was Sarah James. And the third was Colonel Charles Kincaid.

With deliberate care, Amanda broke down her jackknife, slipped it into her pocket. Then she wormed her fingers into her tee and pulled out her tags, the ones that signaled friend or foe. She dangled the metallic blue tags, watching how they spun then unwound in a blur. They chinked like tinny chimes.

Everything came down to this: Would she pull the trigger on a man she loved and hated in equal measure? Even if it was pretend? She didn't know. But she was sure of one thing. If Kincaid found her first?

"Pow."

**SNAKE RIVER
TERRA
24 DECEMBER 2438
0846 HOURS**

The back of Sarah James's head erupted in a fine pink mist of blood, brain, and bone. The impact knocked her back a half-meter where she crashed to the shore, her body leaving a bloody smear like the track of a large snail.

He waited a moment, watching, listening. A pity about the silencer, but in a wilderness this quiet, an anomalous sound carried for kilometers. Oh, he had a perfectly serviceable rifle. He'd even used it twice this week already. But he still had work to do. No point alerting the remaining contestants.

Still, he really enjoyed a truly well-made handgun. His SIG Pro-SP 2022 was a thing of beauty, an antique passed down through his family for generations. The pistol was very blocky, with a stippled grip plate that fit his large hand. The frame was finished in a gray-black matte, though the barrel was left bright and the metal anodized. Virtually no recoil, fifteen rounds to the magazine. It would've been so nice to hear the boom.

He looked down at James. She'd died in a nanosecond. Her hands were rigid with cadaveric spasm, the fingers curled and arms flexed until her balled fists nearly touched her shoulders, as if daring him to put up his mitts. Her unfocused eyes bugged from their sockets and her mouth was still open, her features frozen in that last moment of surprise. A baseball-sized chunk of skull a little below the crown of her head had blown away, leaving a red-black crater.

Unscrewing and pocketing the silencer, he snugged the SIG-Pro into a concealed-carry holster riding under his waistband over his crotch. The barrel was still warm, which was, all things considered, very pleasant. Then, he bent and pocketed his brass, because you never could tell.

He levered James onto her back, rolling her like a log. He struggled with the zipper of her parka. The dispersion mesh—a conductive layer sandwiched between Taslan nylon outside and an inner waterproof layer laminated with nylon tricot—made the material stiff. The zipper gave, grudgingly, with a chattering metallic sound. He slid his fingers down her thermal shirt, reeled up a pair of ID tags, and deposited them into his specially lined pocket.

Then he hooked his hands beneath James's armpits and dragged her body away from the river's edge to the gear she'd stashed behind a tumble of boulders. He debated about covering the body with stones. This had been glacier country back in the last ice age, and the landscape was littered with tumble-down heaps of boulders alternating with streamlined drumlins. On the other hand, this was also mountain lion country; there were grizzlies; there were small animals eager to drag off a foot, a finger, a hand. Without her tags, they wouldn't find James, or what was left of her, for a long, long time, and likely not all in one spot.

He took a moment to search her pockets. Virtually the same gear as Hackett. James's only weapon was her target laser: a nonlethal variant of the Mauser 480, the HAF standard, with a built-in IFF that pinged the identifier tags. But he discovered a pleasant surprise: a stash of cello-wrapped ration bars. Perching on a boulder, he ripped open one promising to taste like peanut butter and chocolate, but didn't.

While he ate, he tweezed out a photograph from his left breast pocket. The photo had been taken at MacBeth shortly after the Battle of Tybalt; he recognized the onion bulb of the spaceport's control tower. And, of course, there was Amanda. She was willowy and very tall for a pilot, easily two meters. She stood, bulky helmet tucked under her left hand, her right hand on the cockpit ladder of her fighter, her right boot perched on the first rung. She wore an olive flight suit that highlighted the fiery cascade of her hair around her shoulders and accentuated her eyes, which were a deep green, like the depths of a forest. Cool, welcoming yet full of mystery and absolutely maddening. No matter how long he studied the contours of her face and the curves of her body, she remained elusive, like a half-remembered dream.

He chewed the last of the ration bar, swallowed. He took a long pull from James's canteen. The water tasted like tin from the purification tablets, but was so cold it hurt his teeth, an ache that rivaled the physical tug he felt every time he looked at Amanda. Desire vised his chest.

Abruptly, he slipped the photograph back into his pocket. He squeezed his hands together, waiting for his pulse to slow. Then the colonel stood, turned his back on James's body and faced due west toward Death Canyon. Aptly named, because that was where he knew Amanda must and would head.

There was a method to his madness, and it was this: he'd saved Amanda for the last act—the last act *here,* at any rate, and oh, what a drama awaited the Director-General; how the Hegemony would feel his wrath. He wanted her, and he would have her: Amanda's neck between his hands, her blood in his mouth. Amanda's *life*, and his face the horror she would take to her death. He hungered for all of that, and he wanted it, up close.

But first they would play a little game. Cat and mouse. A cat was a study in patience, knowing when to pounce and how to maim without killing so the fun could go on and on. And then, when a cat tired?

Smiling, he straightened his right index finger, cocked his thumb: a classic gesture children throughout the universe knew.

"Boom."

**YAKIMA PROVING GROUNDS
TERRA
24 DECEMBER 2438
1030 HOURS**

"Parkinson's disease?" asked Colonel Nathan Powers. He stood behind Carolyn's left shoulder and when he leaned down to get a better look at her screen, Carolyn caught the scent of a subtle musk aftershave and sweat. "It can't be."

"I'm just saying it's a possibility." She was anxious, his being so close. The flight surgeon was one of the most attractive men she'd ever seen: black wavy hair cropped close, dark brown eyes, and the faintest suggestion of a swell to his lower lip. He was dressed casually in a biking outfit: navy-blue one-piece, insulated jacket, gloves, hat, biker glasses on a strap. The outfit was very form-fitting around the bulge of his calves and thighs, and she was having a hard time remembering not to stare...

She quickly turned her attention back to her screen. "I'm not sure. But this clip—" She pressed a key, and the deflated, slouched figure of an old man firmed up on the screen. "That guy fits what I saw."

The clip had obviously been taken in a hospital of some sort. A splash of fluorescent overheads turned the man's papery skin a sickly off-yellow. An anonymous cotton hospital gown, also off-yellow, drooped open at the man's scrawny neck. A glistening track of saliva dribbled from his lower lip. Carolyn pointed. "There, his hands, see how they're shaking even when he's not reaching for anything?"

"I know what a pill-rolling tremor looks like," Powers rapped. "I'm a doctor, remember?"

"I know that." A wave of heat crawled up her neck, and that made her angry. *Damn these military people; they're all so self-righteous, like they're the only guys with brains.* "And I know I'm just a stupid-ass simian expert, but let me tell you something, Doctor. Chimps don't get Parkinson's. They don't get malaria or AIDS or Huntington's chorea. They may be our closest relatives genetically, but there are a lot of things they don't get unless we help them along."

Powers scowled. "Yeah, but then you're talking surgical ablation, drugs. We didn't give them anything."

"Oh, come off it," she said. Powers was drop-dead gorgeous, but she wasn't about to go brain-dead because of a pretty face. "You know perfectly well what I'm talking about."

"Yeah, yeah, I know." His tone was clipped and his brown eyes had turned flinty. "You're trying to blame some abnormal chimp shit on the augmentation loop that you just so happen not to like."

"I'm not blaming you or your precious loop. But the reality is that the loop does feed into regions of the brain most associated with attention, focus, and concentration. These just so happen to correlate with dopamine-rich neurons, like the basal ganglia and frontal lobe, and dopamine depletion—"

"Then how do you explain that when we checked the chimps' neurotransmitter levels three months after we discontinued testing, their dopamine levels were normal?"

"Maybe we didn't follow them long enough."

"Yeah, you think?" He sagged back in a chair. "I'm sorry, that was uncalled for. You did right calling me. Hell. Kind of fits, too, like that crying jag. People with Parkinson's can be pretty volatile. Loss of emotional control, stuff like that." Then he scrubbed his close-cropped hair and blew out. "We're debating in a vacuum. We need a vet. I'm a people doc."

"He's TDY. In Sydney, for God's sake. I called the communications people and they said they couldn't authorize contact unless I had command approval. You're command approval."

"I'm assistant director. Gbarleman's the boss."

Uh-huh, and that's why Gbarleman caved when you wanted the loop. "He's civilian. Anyway, he's in Tel Aviv somewhere. Hell and gone."

"Figures." Powers eyed her. "By the way, why aren't *you* gone? I checked Gbarleman's paperwork a couple days ago. You're supposed to be in San Antonio."

It crossed her mind to wonder why he cared, but she really didn't feel like getting into it. "I...change of plans. I had work. Like collating all the neural input data from the sims we ran on Kincaid and the rest."

"That couldn't wait?"

"Well, I don't mind being alone. I like when it's quiet," she lied. Then she told a truth: "Went shooting. I like that, too."

"Yeah?" Powers looked at her with new interest. "What kind of laser you got? Sunspot?"

"No, semi-auto pistol." She told him about the PG-90, and he asked a couple questions about that, like where she got ammo, and while she was kind of enjoying this and he really seemed interested, she said, "Look, we can bond over slug-throwers later. Right now, we have to get moving. Get the vet, run tests. Maybe then, I dunno, bring the pilots in."

"Over Christmas? Make a big brouhaha because a chimp's got the weepies? No way. Anyway, Kincaid and the others, they're out on some exercise."

This was news, but it tallied. Being a civilian and relatively low on the totem pole, no one told her anything. "Where?"

"I don't know. They don't keep me in the loop about stuff like that."

"So what do we do?"

"You want my opinion? I say we close up shop, turn off the lights, go shoot, and then I'll take you to lunch."

She did a double take. "What?"

"Shoot. You, me. Then eat. Couple of beers. C'mon, it's Christmas. Forget the chimps. Let it go for a couple days." Then at her incredulous look, he said, "You wanted a command decision. Well, that's it. We go at this one step at a time. You know how hard it is to change around orders?"

"No."

"Hard. Plus you got to double-check, lick the base commander's hairy ass. In this case, that would be General Coleman, and I'm not hauling him away from a Christmas party or shagging his old lady because some chimp's having a bad hair day. I could be at this for hours, maybe *days*. Then, ten to one, turns out to be a big zero, and I've got me a salmon day." At her mystified expression, he sighed. "I'll spend all day, maybe two, swimming upstream only to get screwed and die. It's not happening."

It was not the answer she expected. "Well, gee, I'm sorry. Silly me, I thought the assistant director might be, you know, interested—"

"Whoa, whoa." He held his hands up. "Just a sec, lady, how about you beam back to reality—"

"Don't blow me off! I don't have the authority to get anything done that needs doing. So, if you would—" She broke off suddenly. "Oh, Jesus, not again," she said, pushing up from her workstation.

"What?"

But she was already moving for the door. "The chimps, the chimps, can't you hear them?" Then she punched the door open, and a cacophony of screeches and yowls billowed in a solid ball of sound. She took off at a dead run. "Come on, come on!"

It was like running down an echo chamber filled with sounds that banged around and around, and sent gooseflesh rippling up and down her arms and legs. *Jesus.* She bent down to key in her combination code, cursed when her fingers slipped. *Got to get in, got to...*

But then Powers was there. "Here," he said, pushing her aside at the same time. "Command override." He punched in a code, and as the door hissed, he grabbed the edge with both hands, forcing the hydraulics into a whine of protest. "Go, I'm right behind you. Just go!"

She squeezed through the door and then skidded to a halt so abruptly Powers ran right into her. The impact forced the air out of her lungs and she nearly fell. But he snagged her by the arms, hauled her up and against his chest.

And then they just stood there, speechless.

EN ROUTE TO DEATH CANYON
TERRA
24 DECEMBER 2438
1230 HOURS

Amanda spotted the vultures first, a big black funnel cloud cartwheeling to the southwest. She didn't think too much of it. Things died in the woods all the time. But when she started her ascent to the ridge running around Phelps Lake and onto the pass for Death Canyon, she realized that the vultures were close, nearly overhead. Again, it could be a trick of the eye. Distance was hard to judge here. But then she smelled the blood and knew something was very, very wrong.

She'd been too keyed up to sleep. The feeling reminded her of a palomino she had when she was about ten, eleven. Rex, very original name: every time that horse caught sight of the stable, he'd flat-out gallop no matter how hard she hauled on those reins. So, she was like Rex, dashing for the barn. Bad survival tactics, maybe; the manual said you kept a steady pace, you rested. She couldn't.

The first stretch along Cottonwood Creek was due south and easy, just wide open. Frozen prairie and meadow and, thank Christ, no snow. But no people either. Not even a close call, and that was weird. She'd thumbed on her target laser, carried it like a real weapon: strap around her neck, stock clamped to her right side, trigger finger along the guard. She couldn't kill anything with it, but the targeting IFF had a range of about 730 meters, 1,100 on a really good day. But, no Hackett, no James. (Forget Kincaid; fine, let him win. She just had to be so close behind he'd think she was tattooed to his butt.) Weird.

She didn't catch sight of the squad either, and that almost worried her more. She'd already figured that she couldn't just shadow them, but had to get around them somehow. Problem was how and where. She'd soaked in those briefings and studied maps so long she knew them better than her own name. When she cut west and headed for the mountains, there was a lot of up and down over heavily forested moraines before Phelps Lake, where she'd hook west around the lake's northern edge. From then on, she didn't have much choice but climb to Death Canyon, dogleg south, and then circle to the Shelf and the radio. The way up to Death Canyon was steep, the elevation changing in a hurry the first third of the way. The trees thinned halfway. The rim, while very high and overlooking steep jagged cliffs, was all sagebrush, sparse Douglas fir, and rock. Dropping into the canyon wasn't an option. With very few exceptions, there was no way to get up and down without climbing gear.

She chewed over that problem when she stopped to rest. Tried to come at it from a different angle. Not how to evade the squad, but how to thwart those guys. If she could confiscate their weapons, that made it ten times harder because then they had to get right up close. Couldn't just point and shoot and set off an electric tingle—not the almost Taser-like shock associated with a kill but a little zap that let you know you'd been made, courtesy of the mesh incorporated in her parka and BDUs. (No choice but to wear the clothes, the cold kind of negating the option to run around butt-naked. Course, she could cheat. Take off the identifier tags. Although there was a failsafe: the tags relied on body heat. Take the tags off for more than two hours, they changed color and wouldn't revert back. Sort of a dead giveaway. Anyone found with black tags was immediately disqualified.) So, thinking out of the box, she figured it boiled down to doing the unexpected: go right down their throats. Slip in. Grab the rifles. Get the hell out of Dodge. The only thing was to find them.

The moraine cradling Phelps Lake was one massive carpet of dark-green lodgepole and white-barked pine, and the thinner, denuded limbs and peeling white trunks of slender aspen. Sunlight bathed the frozen lake behind her and set up a glare, making the vultures' black wings glisten like slick oil and giving her sun-dazzle that left her blinking away spots. She had a sense that things were going to open up soon and her cover would give out. The gaps in the canopy were wider, the trees smaller, a little stunted, and farther apart, and the air definitely colder.

But then two things happened at once. She glimpsed the straight edge of a frame tent—and caught the unmistakable odor of spent gunpowder and blood.

She stopped cold, then ducked behind a pine. Crouched, waited. When she heard nothing, she glanced around the tree. Nothing moving and now she picked out two tents: one dead ahead facing west, and the other slightly off-center opposite, looking east. The flaps of the east tent were cracked a smidge.

But that was all. The blood smell was still there: heavy, a little...gassy, like blood got after coagulating.

She eased back behind the tree. Chewed her lip and tasted dead skin. Darted a glance at the vultures. Thought long and hard about what she was going to do. Because no question: something dead up ahead. She'd been a soldier too long to forget that the unexpected happened, constantly.

And that's when she thought of an alternative explanation: this, too, was a test. Would she act on self-preservation and detour without checking a site that obviously screamed for a recon? Or would she investigate, but carefully, without getting captured or eliminated herself? Certainly, a new wrinkle. She tried to remember if command had said anything about scenarios that would involve simulated casualties, and could recall none. But shit happened. Assuming, as she did, that Kincaid was ahead, she wondered what he'd done, and then got mad she was even thinking like that.

She looked right, left, behind. The tents were maybe three hundred meters away. Studied the layout of the trees, how they petered out to the left and thickened to the right. Going right was the only obvious choice and, despite being obvious, the best. She moved with care and varied her rhythm, pausing now and again, darting quick looks around and behind. The silent vultures skimmed air. She edged up to the closest tent, the one opening west and away. The canvas was stiff and smelled cold. She levered right, keeping the tent on her left. She waited, listened. Smelled blood.

Go on. She shifted her weight to the balls of her feet. *You've come this far, just do it.*

Holding her breath, she edged around the corner.

The colonel tracked her with his scope and from a vantage point nearly five hundred meters due north and straight up, in a tree. He would have preferred a hardwood, not a pine. He didn't like the stink of resin, and the needles were sharp. But they did possess the distinct advantage of excellent cover.

Before Amanda arrived, he used the time to check his rifle, yet another antique, a bolt-action Barrett M468. The barrel was forty centimeters long with a muzzle brake to both blast expanding air up, as well as down and back at a forty-five-degree angle to reduce recoil. He'd given the weapon a thorough going-over before, but he was a stickler for detail.

While he waited, he snapped out his magazine and pressed his right thumb on the first shiny bullet and then eased up, checking the return for hesitation. Ten bullets to a magazine: full metal jackets, each 6.8 millimeters, tapering to a sharp, blood-red point. He had three such magazines, more than enough. He eased the magazine back until the catch clicked.

Scanning the area around the tents, he saw movement, braced his right foot on a limb and then his rifle on the hump of his knee and raised his scope to his eye. The scope had not come with the weapon; he'd had it custom-made so he could see who he was shooting, right up close. And there she was: a blur framed in the small circle, like a religious medal. He thumbed the focus and her face firmed. She'd thrown her hood back; her head was cocked a little to the left, and he read her tension and, he thought, a little bit of fear. Her skin was very pale, and this made her remarkable green eyes even deeper. He inhaled a quick breath. She was the incarnation of the beauty he remembered and the one he recalled in dreams.

When she paused at the edge of the tent, when he knew she would have to look, he was ready. He watched her tense, then pivot. Then she flinched, straightened in shock, and he dropped the scope's crosshairs on her back, left of center and over her heart, just as she let out a short, sharp cry of horror.

YAKIMA PROVING GROUNDS
TERRA
24 DECEMBER 2438
1232 HOURS

"Oh, my God," Carolyn said. Her knees went water-weak, and she suddenly understood what being numb with disbelief really meant.

There was blood, everywhere. Or maybe that's just the way it seemed. The females—Lucy and Betty—still screamed from the safety of their platform. But Shana wasn't screaming. Instead, the chimp sprawled in a loose-limbed heap of congealing blood. What was left of her throat was raw, ugly, ripped wide open. One clouded brown eye stared fixedly at a point behind Carolyn's left shoulder. She'd been bitten in the belly repeatedly; dark-red liver and bluish-pink loops of intestine spilled over her side, and Carolyn had an insane, horrible image of a child's piñata split wide open.

Where's Linus? Where's Jack? And the baby, what about the baby? She dragged her horrified gaze from Shana, probed the habitat, finally spotted Linus hunched in a nesting den. Maybe the baby...

Powers touched her shoulder. "There." His mouth was close to her ear, and she felt his breath tickle her cheek. He pointed to a spot above her head. "In the tree."

Jack perched upon the tallest sycamore. His mouth was wide open, his lips peeling back from teeth stained burnt orange with blood. Every time the females screamed, he answered with a roar. But as strange and awful as all that was, this was worse: dangling from Jack's left hand was the limp body of his son, Tongo.

"No," Carolyn said. Her vision went blurry with hot tears, and she turned her face into Powers's chest. "No, no, no."

"Come on." Slipping an arm around her shoulders, Powers nudged her toward the door. "Come on, let's get out of here."

She balked. "No. We can't leave. We have to *do* something!"

"Like what? The baby's dead, right? That other chimp? You can't do anything for either of them."

"But, Jack..."

"Yeah, what? You're going to climb up there?"

"I could try to get him down..."

"No."

"But I have to do *something*!"

"Staying alive is good. What makes you think he won't rip you apart? You wanted a command decision. Well, here it is. Let's get back to the lab where we can hear ourselves think."

She rocked back on her heels when he tugged. "What about the other chimps?"

"He hasn't bothered them, has he? He only took out that one, and the baby. You think they'd still be alive if he didn't have some kind of internal control?"

He had a point. So she let him lead her away. But the screams chased her, all the way back to the lab.

EN ROUTE TO DEATH CANYON
TERRA
24 DECEMBER 2438
1245 HOURS

Amanda let out a small cry before she was aware that she had. Then training took over. She ducked low and now she transferred the useless target laser to her left hand and then flicked the thumb break over her KA-BAR and withdrew her knife in one smooth movement. Her heart galloped and her lungs worked like bellows. Her vision swirled as she hyperventilated. *Slow it down, slow down, one step at a time.*

She didn't look at the men, not closely. Time for that in a minute. First, she had to make sure there wasn't anyone waiting for *her*. She slid along the tent she'd rounded, nudged the flap with the point of her target laser and quickly swept the flap back, her knife at the ready. Empty. Just duffels ripped open, two bedrolls. Same thing in the second tent, but just one bedroll and duffel, so probably the squad's chief master sergeant's gear.

She sheathed her knife and stepped back to look at the men. Part of her wanted to run screaming in the other direction; the other knew that she had to be thorough here if she wanted to stay alive.

The men were seated in a line: backs against the tent, the second and third man listing so their heads touched—a comical effect, if it hadn't been so awful. Single shots to the chest from a slug-thrower, large caliber. Very accurate. Whoever had killed them wanted to advertise because the men's parkas were unzipped and sagged around their shoulders. Their shirts were slit down the middle and folded back like the covers of a book so she could see each single, neat hole drilled six to seven centimeters beneath the left nipple and a little off-center. Right through the heart. Just a dribble of blood coagulated like a frozen tear. Not enough to cause the blood smell.

The reason for the smell: their necks were slit. Ear to ear. The heart, even one that's been shot, beats an agonal rhythm for a minute or so. A quick swipe of a knife left to right, and more than enough blood drizzle.

But cutting throats was overkill. Like lining them up as if they were spectators to a play. Unless...she took a few steps back then scoured the ground with her eyes. There, to her far right: a KA-BAR stabbed the ground. Two sets of tags coiled around a black-leather handle slicked with dried gore. When she bent down and yanked the knife, she saw the initials on the bolt butt: *C. K.* She cradled the tags in her gloved hand. James. Hackett. The tags were black.

The small muscles of her jaw clenched. She didn't believe for a second that Kincaid had killed these people. Okay, he was a champion marksman and yeah, he was competitive. But she knew Kincaid as a soldier and a man. If the killer had Kincaid's knife, Kincaid was dead. She was surprised that she didn't feel grief. Maybe that was because, at core, she was a soldier, and a soldier grieved when there was time. Right now, she had to stay alive.

Everything here screamed that she was the only one left. Meaning this little spectacle had been arranged for her to find by someone who knew she had to come this way. *And if he set this up...*

"He did it so he could watch my reaction," she said suddenly. "Oh, shit."

And as if to also prove that the killer was telepathic, her left leg exploded in a single burst of white-hot pain.

YAKIMA PROVING GROUNDS
TERRA
24 DECEMBER 2438
1330 HOURS

"Hold up a minute," said Powers. He still had her hands, and now he leaned forward so their faces were less than a half meter apart. "Let's think about this. Maybe this is a good thing."

"What?" Carolyn jerked her hands away so Powers clutched air. "How can you say that?"

"Didn't you just say that this could be normal?"

"No, I said it's not unheard of for a male to kill an infant, even his own. But this is something Jack has never done."

"Which doesn't mean he couldn't. How do you know that this kind of aggressive behavior isn't just nature asserting itself?"

She blinked. Her eyes felt scratchy, and her nose was stuffed from crying. Jack, a killer? A cannibal? Chimps could change on a whim: docile one moment, murderous the next. They also hunted, usually in packs, for fresh meat to supplement their diets. But the chimps in the habitat were fed a carefully balanced diet; they were given chunks of raw meat at monthly intervals in an attempt to prevent just this kind of behavior.

On the other hand, she knew that chimps, like humans, murdered, and for many reasons: to establish dominance, to exact revenge, and sometimes because they liked it. She said all this, then added, "Let's say for the sake of argument that Jack's behavior is normal, that he killed Tongo out of jealousy or something. What about Shana? I'm not aware of any report of any *male* killing both mother and infant at the same time. Females usually do that. Jack was being...sadistic."

"You're anthropomorphizing. You have no idea what's motivating Jack, right?" When she didn't answer, Powers continued, "Maybe it's plain old aggression. From where I'm sitting, that might be really good."

She gave a bitter laugh. "Explain that to Shana and Tongo."

"I'm a soldier, you're not. When you send troops out, you don't want them being swayed by subjective factors. What they should or shouldn't do. Soldiers are trained to kill.

You want them to do their job without hesitation. So if this augmentation loop not only focuses and sustains attention and concentration with no fatigue *and* heightens aggression... then that's perfect."

She gaped. "Are you...you're...you're serious, aren't you? How can this be good?"

Powers gave a horsey snort. "Come on, think about it. We're not chimps. You remember Kincaid. Remember what a kick he got? How much better he got? Now *that's* a soldier. Knows how to keep a lid on it, that's all."

"No." Carolyn stood, drilling him with a look. "I don't agree. But since I'm not the project director and Gbarleman is, I'm going to let him make that decision. I'll get through to him somehow, even if I have to bully my way to some general's office to do it. The worst they can do is fire me. So, either you're coming with me, or you're not."

He stared up at her for a long moment. She couldn't read what he thought. He had his neutral expression firmly slapped in place. Finally, he pushed to his feet. "All right, I'll come. Gbarleman needs to hear both sides. That way nobody panics."

It was on the tip of her tongue to say something about covering his ass, but she bit that back. Instead she said, "We won't know anything until we can run more tests."

"And that's a damn good thing." He looked down at her. "I don't apologize for thinking the way I do. If you were in my position, you might have exactly the same response. From my perspective, this is a potential windfall."

"Mmm." She stared right back. "Well, then thank heaven I'm not."

"And *vive le différence*," he said, without irony. "We'll go to command communications. You drive."

They pushed out of the lab. Neither spoke as they circled around back. The sun was behind clouds. The air had a metallic smell and was so cold her nose hurt.

At her car, Powers pulled up. "Aw, hell. I forgot my jacket. Look, you go on ahead; just let me run back. I won't be a sec."

Carolyn didn't need encouragement. Shoulders hunched against the cold, she trotted to her car, aimed the remote, popped the doors. When she hauled back on the driver's side, the metal was stiff, and the hinges squalled. She dropped in, slammed the door.

The vinyl upholstery was frigid. Turning around, she reached behind to the passenger seat. A wedge of her sheepskin jacket was beneath her gun case still in the well; she snagged a corner, reeled the jacket in and then shrugged into it. The leather creaked with cold.

"Heat," she said, cranking the engine and pushing buttons. "Heat, heat, heat." Cold air blasted her face, and she jammed a control that sent the chill lapping her ankles. She cranked her defrosters to max, waited a few minutes, watched as her breath bunched and balled.

She was just beginning to get impatient when Powers crunched up, his bike in hand. Knocked on her rear windshield, mimed putting the bike in her trunk. She depressed the latch for the trunk, waited as he took off the front wheel, folded the bike to fit and slammed down the trunk lid.

"Sorry," he said, popping the passenger's side door. A blast of cold air billowed in. He dropped into the passenger's side, slammed the door. "Got hung up shutting down one of the computers."

"Yeah?" She popped the brake, dropped the car into reverse, pulled out then shifted into drive. Her gloves were in back; she wished now that she'd thought to put them on. The steering wheel was like a block of ice. "I was positive I shut them all down."

"Guess not," said Powers, reaching around for his shoulder harness. "Jesus, if it's cold here, Kincaid and those guys have got to be freezing their asses off in Wyoming."

"Wyoming?" Frowning, Carolyn shot Powers a quick glance then faced forward as she pulled to the stop at the end of the exit. She hit her right turn signal then swiveled her head left to check for traffic. "I thought you said you didn't know where they were."

"Yeah?"

She looked back at him. "Yeah."

Powers's face was unreadable. "Mmm." Then, lifting his chin to indicate something to her left, "Jeep coming."

She turned back, spotted the jeep. "I can make that."

"But you want to go left."

She twisted back to look at him. "No, the communications—" she began. Then stopped.

Carolyn Fletcher had seen a lot of slug-throwers and more than a few lasers in her life. She liked to shoot. So she registered that the weapon was a laser pistol, standard military issue, and easy to flick from single to continuous burst depending on whether Powers wanted to drill a hole or burn a track along her chest.

"No," said Powers. "You really want to go left."

EN ROUTE TO DEATH CANYON
TERRA
24 DECEMBER 2438
1330 HOURS

Watching Amanda's reactions through his scope—her horror shading to disbelief and settling on intense calculation—filled him with a certain pride. Yes, that was the Amanda he knew, the confident wingman, the consummate soldier. She turned north because he'd buried the knife up to the hilt, and far enough away from the bodies so she had to face forward. The sun spilled over her shank of fiery red hair and made it glow like copper. A glint of metal in her hand: the tags. And then he saw her study the black butt bolt, read the initials—and then her head jerked up and she seemed to look right at him.

He exhaled, brought his targeting crosshairs over her heart. Waited for his to beat. And then he squeezed the trigger.

Amanda felt the bullet before she heard the shot. There was the flash of pain as the bullet sliced through her left thigh before exiting.

She shrieked. Her knees folded, and she tumbled down hard on her right. By the time she was falling, the sound of the shot—a startling *BANG*—clapped against her body and bounced off, echoing along the hills, a sound that would carry for kilometers.

As much as she hurt, instinct and training kicked in. She hit and rolled right behind a nearby pine. Stayed sprawled on her stomach, head down. No point in pulling into a crouch for a shot; she didn't have a weapon worth shit anyway. She listened for the report of a second shot. Heard nothing but her heart banging away. She held her breath a second. Still nothing. Her left thigh screamed with pain. She was already sweating from the shock, and her stomach knotted.

Take it easy, can't afford to lose it, just hold on.

After a minute when nothing came, she crawled to sit, back to the tree. She still had the tags and Kincaid's KA-BAR. She tucked the tags into her parka, laid the KA-BAR alongside her right thigh. Pulled off her gloves and gave her left thigh a quick once-over. Her skin jumped beneath her fingers, and a fresh wave of nausea had her sweating and tasting sour bile. The shot was through and through, lateral aspect of her left thigh. How much damage the bullet had done would depend on whether it had a lead core, how much it yawed or fragmented. No way to tell any of that, but the entrance wound was small and dimpled, the material from her trousers dragged in with the bullet. Couldn't see the exit wound. Her fingers came away slicked with blood, but she hadn't felt the gush of a pumper. So that was good. Fumbling her buckle, she stripped her belt from around her waist, threaded it under her thigh, and cinched it down hard above the wound. She'd still bleed, but that would buy her some time.

High velocity, lots of kinetic energy, sniper shot, something with a really long barrel. Mac 2176, maybe a Ruger-Barrett RLR 7000, and very far away. Didn't hear the shot until way after I got hit.

That meant something else. Two things, actually. That far away, her sniper had a scope. If he had a scope, he knew what he was hitting and where he was aiming. The only way to hit her at distance was to aim high: heart-high. Or he could be a lousy shot. Somehow she didn't think that was it. So he'd meant to wound, not kill.

That was like toying with her, personally. No toying with those guys lined up at the tent, and she bet James and Hackett died quick. So that meant the sniper was someone she knew, really well.

There were a lot of good snipers in the universe. But as far as she knew there was only one that mattered. Couldn't believe it, but she didn't see a clear alternative.

And then she remembered her target laser; flipped the IFF and cautiously swept the weapon north. The IFF beeped, and she looked—and that's when her world crashed down around her ears.

Kincaid.

He could see the tail of her parka and a fold of hood. He thought about firing again but gave her several minutes to absorb the situation and realize the implications. His shot had been perfect. He needed the mouse alive. He was also confident she would move soon. She could not afford to stay in one place.

She did not disappoint. After perhaps ninety seconds, he saw her use the tree for support and pull to a stand. She wobbled, righted; through his scope, he could see how white her knuckles were, the way they tented skin as she clung to the tree. Then she pushed off, staying as low as she could, her walk a shambling lurch.

Excellent. Slinging his weapon, he swarmed down from the tree and took off in a jog to flank her right. He would, he decided, squeeze off a shot from time to time to herd her where he wanted her to go.

Run, little mouse. He moved in an easy lope, and he felt fine, better than he had in three years. *Run.*

YAKIMA PROVING GROUNDS
TERRA
24 DECEMBER 2438
1400 HOURS

They drove northeast in silence, Powers with the laser below the dash and aimed at her gut. The Manastash Ridge was north and west, the humps of the Saddle Mountains almost dead ahead. Carolyn knew the proving grounds were big, almost 1,300 square kilometers of rolling, dun-brown, tinder-dry shrub-steppe and chaparral bounded by the sheer basalt cliffs of the Yakima River to the west and the Columbia dead ahead. If he wanted, Powers could kill her in the middle of a lot of nothing and dump her anywhere.

And he won't even need the car because Iron Man's got the damn bike...

Then she remembered her PG-90, wondered if she could worm her left hand round, slip the catch, take out the weapon. Tight fit against the door, but she thought maybe she could. She waited a sec, then let her hand fall to her lap; waited a second or two more then eased her hand to her seat...

"No, no," said Powers. "Here, I'll get it." Keeping the pistol trained, he stretched his long arm behind her headrest, reached down and came up with her case. "Looking for this? We'll use it soon enough. Both hands on the wheel."

"What do you mean *we*?" When he didn't answer, she glanced right. "You want to explain? This can't be about that damned loop."

"Not the way you think," he said. His tone was neither hostile nor amused. Just there. "Eyes on the road, please. We wouldn't want an accident."

She did what he said. "You went back and wiped my data, didn't you?" A hunch, but it made sense given his protestations, then trying to talk her into waiting, and finally, when she wouldn't, the need to erase her data—and her. "What I can't figure is why."

"Don't worry about it. Instead, let's talk about you. Did you know you've got a depression problem?"

"Huh?"

"Pretty woman on a base alone over Christmas. No boyfriend. No family. Sounds depressing. You think that somebody's going to think it's abnormal when I talk about how intense you were and kind of down in the dumps? Lonely? Distraught about Jack? We talked shooting, and you said you were going out with your PG-90 to do some shooting, and

I offered to go with you, but you refused, and now I feel so guilty...well, you see how shrinks will go for it."

"Holiday blues? What, I'm going to shoot myself over Christmas?"

"No, *I'm* going to shoot you. The story is embellishment."

"Why are you doing this?"

A pause. Then: "I'm sorry, but I really can't tell you. Just drive."

She fell silent. She drove. She watched the road unfurling like a broad black ribbon and wondered what in hell to do. It scared her when her mind just kept turning over the same information again and again: *He's got the pistol; he's got my PG-90; all I can do is drive...*

They were on a stretch of road now that bent in a gentle curve south toward North Fork Lummuma Creek. The creek was on her right, and ahead she saw that the road dead-ended in another road running roughly north and south.

All I can do is drive.

Carefully, she slid her eyes right. The creek had iced over; the banks were sloped like a culvert and the entire width of the creek was about ten meters and not very deep. She had a half klick, she figured, before the road veered away.

All I can do is...drive.

Powers said, "Up ahead, where it dead-ends, take a right."

"Uh-huh," she said. Then, before she could talk herself out of it, she jinked the wheel right, hard, and hammered the accelerator.

A lot happened at once and in a split second. There was a squeal of rubber, the sizzle of asphalt and then a grate of gravel as the car went off the road. She felt a giddy swirl of motion; flashes of blue sky and brown grass whizzing past her windscreen; the feel of her harness biting her stomach. The sudden swerve jolted Powers left; he had enough time to give a startled shout, and Carolyn had an impression of arms flailing, the laser jerking right. The PG-90's case went bumping off Powers's knees, jamming into the passenger's side well, and the case popped open. Carolyn's fingers itched to grab the gun, but she hadn't let up on the accelerator and now here was the creek and a black gap and then the car's front wheels grabbing air and a sensation of catapulting forward, falling; a smashing, splintering sound as the car rammed into ice and rock and hard earth. She felt herself hurtling forward as the car bammed to a halt; there was a *bang* as her driver's side airbag deployed. Her harness locked as momentum threw her body against the straps so hard she'd be black and blue for a month. Her face smashed into the airbag then rebounded like a hockey puck careering from a slap shot. She was dazed, seeing stars; her neck shrieking, but she was fighting now, angry at her body, ready for blood. Powers was jammed by his airbag, too, and he'd lost hold of his laser pistol, which had catapulted into the back seat.

The airbags began to deflate, and she was ready. Unsnapping her harness, she lunged forward, pushed the limp passenger's side airbag aside and scrambled for the PG-90. But he was right there, his knees pushing her down and forward. Her arms scissored; she was jammed up against the glove box; the transmission lever stabbed her abdomen. He couldn't both pin her and grab his pistol, but she couldn't get her gun either. So she twisted around, saw nylon-sheathed pant leg and bit down, hard.

She tasted wet nylon and salty blood as her teeth tore at his skin. Roaring with pain, Powers jerked away, and then her fingers brushed metal and she had the PG-90 in her left hand and she was pushing back, knowing she had to get out of this cramped space or he'd wrest the gun away—

She transferred the gun from left to right, simultaneously fumbling for the door release. But her fingers skittered and then it was too late because Powers's face twisted with black fury and he lunged.

So she shot him.

DEATH CANYON
TERRA
24 DECEMBER 2438
1630 HOURS

The sun was slanting down directly ahead, yellow light painting the rock brassy and much too bright. Amanda was nearly out of energy and time. She was close to the canyon. And then? Her head spun and her skin was clammy, cold. The butt of her target laser banged against her right hip. Her left leg was one steady, aching throb and, with all the walking, still bleeding. Her left pant leg was black and smelled like a wet penny; she could feel blood oozing into her sock. Her boot squelched.

He was driving her. She knew that, figured it out when she tried circling back to find a place to hide near Phelps Lake. She had some half-formed notion of stealing back to the squad's tents, going through their rations, taking a bedroll, maybe finding a radio. But every time she made a move, there was a crack of a rifle and the high ping of bark chunked off a tree by a bullet. The fact that the two events were closer meant he'd gained ground, too, not hard when Kincaid had two good legs.

But how could he smuggle in a rifle? He's good, but he's not...

She thought about defying him, forcing Kincaid to show himself. He wasn't ready to kill her just yet. The more she thought about it, the more it seemed clear that he was keeping her alive. But why? Her brain kept snagging on that because it didn't feel right. Kincaid, why would *Kincaid*...

Then a light bulb flash in her mind: the men lined up against that tent flap, their throats ringed with bloody necklaces... Something wrong there, but what? Not the bullet holes. Not the clothes. Their necks, yes; something wrong... Then she glanced down at her own knife and the answer burst on her brain.

Of course, of course, it's the only explanation.

Twisting round, she looked down the pass and spotted him: a dark speck, growing larger. She tried using her scope, but she was shaking so badly from fatigue and blood loss the image jittered and she gave up.

Instead, she waited, not sure what she would do when he reached her. But she was through running.

Because she knew something else now.

When she stopped moving, the colonel was momentarily nonplussed. A new wrinkle; he disliked wrinkles. It was very important that she get up to the rim of the canyon. It was important that she not miss the show because he did not think they had much time. But when she stopped, he peered through the Barrett's scope, saw her hair plastered to her sweaty skin and the purple shadows bruising the hollows of those eyes.

Saw her mouth form the words: "*Come get me, asshole.*"

Well, well. When he came to within three meters, he was disappointed not to see shock or even horror. Horror he would have understood. In fact, horror was what he preferred. But she only nodded as if confirming some wager she'd made with herself.

She said, "You need to study up...is it Colonel? Or however you say 'colonel' in Mandarin?"

Excellent psychological tactics: get in the first word; ask the questions; assert dominance. Well-trained; a spitfire. Defiant even in a hopeless situation. "Colonel will suffice."

"I was present during several debriefings after Tybalt." Her eyes raked him from head to toe, and he felt her gaze, laser-bright, linger on the taut, shiny scar that swept like a scimitar from his left brow to right jaw before diving south beneath the neck of his parka. Only he knew that the scar continued to the level of his heart, spreading like the filaments of a web. He had refused plastic surgery. Let his body bear witness.

So he knew what she saw: the scar was as pink as the skin of a newborn rat and pulled down at the left corner of his mouth so that his lips were always slightly parted on that side, a slick of drool always there. The burns had singed away his left eyebrow to the pores and his nose had been foreshortened until his nostrils resembled the black pits of a sand viper. His left eye had boiled like an egg, and the orbit burst. He saw no need for an eye patch. So the socket was a wizened, pink crater.

She said, "You've obviously compensated for your left eye. Shooting, I mean."

"Indeed. Depth perception was problematic, but I have mastered myself. One only requires a single good eye to shoot." He cocked his head, studied her expression. "So, you knew. How?"

"I didn't at first. Then I remembered that squad." She nodded at the Barrett, its sling drooping over his right shoulder. "Kincaid's a leftie. A leftie wouldn't begin his cut under the left ear, but you cut those guys after you'd propped them up, and you did it standing behind each man. The cut's deeper under the left ear and tails off to the right. No way a leftie can do that. You had me going for a little while, though. So," she said, "where's Kincaid? You killed him, didn't you?"

He answered with a jerk of his rifle, remaining well out of her reach. She might be wounded; he knew she was physically weak. But this was a formidable adversary who had more than proven her mettle in battle. "Up there. Above Death Canyon."

"I asked you a question."

"And I'm not prepared to answer, nor are you in a position to argue."

In response, she eyed him for a second then lowered herself to the ground—awkwardly because of her leg. "I'm not going anywhere. And I don't think you'll gun me down here. You want me alive and up there. Why? What's this about, revenge?"

He grinned, awkward because of the scar. From experience, he knew the effect was ghoulish. "You are the sauce. A...how shall we say it? My reward? I am looking forward to it. For you, I have very special plans. But you are not the goose."

"Then what's the goose?" she asked, straight-faced though he detected a narrowing of the eyes and knew that, of course, she *did* know but couldn't say because this prototype battle machine was supposed to be secret. Why else assassinate the machine's pilots?

He was about to reply when he heard something not... right. Explosions. No. Thunder? He saw that she heard it, too, and then he looked left, due north. The sound came again, more distinct, and now he recognized it: the low, rhythmic *wop-wop-wop* of a helicopter, a big one from the sound, perhaps a Desert Cobra or an HAF Redhawk gunship.

They are early. How? Who alerted…?

Still too far away, however, to be a threat. He tensed fractionally, waiting to see if the chopper vectored for them or turned for the decoys he'd planted along the way. Circling, circling…he let his breath go as the sound faded. But it would be back.

He looked down to see her deep-green eyes sparkle with triumph. "You don't have much time."

"No," said the colonel. He whipped around, his booted foot whirring in a roundhouse kick that caught her on the right temple. Crude but effective. Her head snapped left, and she crumpled without a sound. He waited a moment, knelt, pressed a finger to her neck and checked for a pulse: thready but there. This close, touching her…he was tempted. But, instead, he shouldered his weapon, bent, grabbed her limp forearms then hoisted her over his left shoulder. Her target laser slewed to one side, the strap pinned between his back and her chest. She was much lighter than he expected. This was a good thing because he still had a kilometer or two to go.

The chopper was not good. It was early, and this meant something had been…compromised. He shot a glance left to the expanse of the shelf that opened up in a few hundred meters and quickened his pace. He did not wish for the helicopter to find them until he was done—with both of them.

With Amanda—and Kincaid.

Kincaid knew bad. A fighter in a flat spin, him and a Capellan in a knife fight in a phone booth—these were all bad. Battle of Tybalt was worse. But the situation now was beyond bad. The situation—Capellans in the Hegemony, Capellans infiltrating Terra, and one of the most secure bases *on* Terra—was damn near catastrophic.

Kincaid had had four days of Capellan hospitality to assess and reassess the situation. Three days ago—when they'd shot him and then he'd come to as hands fumbled open his parka and ripped his tags from his neck—he'd gotten a firsthand look at just how really, really bad his situation was. They could've killed him; should have. But he knew when he saw the colonel—that pink web of shiny scar instead of a left eye—he knew they were keeping him alive for a very special reason.

"I've let you live for now," the colonel hissed, so close Kincaid felt spittle against his face. Face purple with fury, lips quivering, the colonel fisted Kincaid's shirt in one hand and twisted until Kincaid's air choked off. "You'll live," he said, as Kincaid writhed, felt the blood thudding in his temples, his chest burning, "until I find her, and then I will enjoy watching you see her die. But I will do it slowly until you beg me to end her agony, and then you will know suffering the way I suffered as I watched my *wife*!"

The colonel let Kincaid go, and then as Kincaid doubled up, sucking in air, the colonel aimed a vicious kick to Kincaid's wounded left side. He laughed when Kincaid gargled a scream. Then the colonel went away.

One thing for sure: that guy was nuts. Kincaid suspected the colonel's men knew that, too. But they valued living. Or maybe living long enough for a transfer.

There were two guards, one a pretty nice guy as Capellans—and probably Maskirovka—went. The other was a fairly grim schmuck, also a Maskirovka agent, who was much more par for the course. They kept him alive. One, the nice guy, dressed his wound, peeling Kincaid's blood-soaked BDU tunic, thermal, and undershirt like soggy wrapping paper. The bullet had punched a hole just above Kincaid's left hip. The nice guy sponged the wound, fished out a red-black plug of blood clot. That started more blood flowing, but it didn't pulse. The exit wound on his back was about half the size of his fist. Kincaid tried to remember if there was anything vital there, but his thoughts were woolly, and it felt like someone was jamming a red-hot poker through his side. Then the nice guy made him swallow pills, persuading him with the business end of a laser pistol. One was a painkiller; he drifted in and out of a fog for most of the day.

That must have been when they moved him, because when he came around again in the middle of the night, he felt cold stone leaching through a bedroll, smelled damp, reached up a hand, grazed wet stone and knew: a cave. Looked around, still too groggy to do much, but saw the orange glow of a cigarette suspended in midair that seemed a thousand meters away, but was probably more like fifty.

Come morning, he was with it enough to take stock. Light filtered in from the entrance to his right and splashed the rock a muted silver-gray. The cave wasn't large. Maybe thirty meters long by fifteen wide, with a shape like the track of a bullet with a lot of yaw: a narrow opening high enough for a man to hunker down and crabwalk his way in. Then a stretch where the cave gradually opened up before the roof soared away in the center and a man could stand and move comfortably. Then a dip again as the cave tailed off, ending in the cul-de-sac where he lay.

That day he hurt a lot, so he didn't move much. He spent his time observing and figured after five minutes that he could take both these guys without too much trouble. Question was when and how, plus he had to get healthier. One thing he knew from experience: wait long enough, everyone relaxes. He spotted his target laser propped against the far left wall in the widest part of the cavern. He tried hard not to think about Amanda, because every time he imagined that colonel hurting her, his skin crawled, and the reality of what they were up against made things seem...not hopeless. Just daunting. So he shoved that down, boxed it. He couldn't help either one of them if he panicked.

And who was the goddamned mole? That *really* nagged at him. Couldn't figure who the asshole was who sold them out. Obviously, someone on the inside and pretty high up, because the SERE was classified, the project itself beyond top secret. Sure, there were a lot of people on the project, and it was hard to account for all of them. But for the Capellans to both know who the *Mackie*'s prospective pilots were and, more importantly, *where* they were...that narrowed the field.

Someone in command, or maybe one of the project directors, someone who deals with us on a regular basis;

someone who doesn't mind if the Hegemony falls and a whole bunch of us get killed...

The second day two things happened. One: they cuffed his hands behind his back. Nice shiny metal cuffs, and both the nice guy and Grim had a key. Two: the nice guy pestered him to get up and walk. It wasn't just to prevent a blood clot from going to his lungs. Because of the cold, the air flow into the cave wasn't great, and Kincaid's peeing into a jug made it smell like it was raining piss. Kincaid made a big show of reluctance and moved extra slow, just enough to make Grim impatient, complain about the stink, and gripe about wanting a cigarette.

The cave mouth opened onto a ledge about two meters wide. A rocky dirt track that Kincaid judged was about nine hundred meters doglegged north and then east back up to the canyon rim. The track wasn't steep, but Kincaid took his time, not just because he was in pain, but to scope the terrain. They were in Death Canyon, he knew; the craggy teeth of the Tetons haloed by clouds were visible north and a little east, and looking west he could see clear across the canyon. Damn close to the radio, but he figured if they knew about him and everything else, they knew about the radio. Halfway up the trail, they passed tangled clumps of dry sagebrush clinging to the canyon walls and the dark roots of Douglas fir like wiry black fingers. When Kincaid looked up, he saw that grass lipped the canyon rim to a knot of fir.

Because they'd cuffed him, he had to concentrate on keeping his footing on the track. The rock was slippery. Kincaid saw that the nice guy still had the laser pistol. Grim prodded Kincaid along with his pulse laser. Once they got far enough from the cave, Grim stepped back and looked at him expectantly.

Still cuffed, Kincaid peeked over the edge and then stared back. Paused for effect.

Grim uncuffed him; Kincaid unzipped, did his business, and they cuffed him again and retraced their steps.

By the middle of the third day, he got their routine. First off, they had contact with the colonel three times a day. Radios: no words but tapped codes that were scratchy with static. Bad. That meant he had to take both soldiers, pretty much at the same time, and between radio contacts. Plus, the way those guys grinned at each other after the evening message, Kincaid figured things weren't going well for his side.

That also meant the colonel was damned efficient. Knew where to go and who was there. So, yeah, someone on the inside, someone on the project. The fact that the colonel had his tags and parka meant he could play the SERE, pretty much trick anyone into thinking he was Kincaid. *Probably let himself get tracked by those squads.* The jolt when someone hit you with the target laser wasn't totally incapacitating, but it was damned unpleasant. So the colonel must be wearing some nonconductive material under the parka, and Kincaid knew he was a damn good shot. So things weren't just bad for his side. They were a disaster.

Second, the nice guy only had a laser pistol; Grim had both a hand and pulse laser rifle, and neither liked the other much. This was good. In fact, Kincaid didn't think the nice guy bought into the mission at all: weird for a Maskirovka, but maybe he had that nutso colonel pegged, and that was better. For one thing, he was way too...well, nice wasn't the right word. Humane, though, like Kincaid was a homeless mutt. Kincaid asked for painkillers; the nice guy handed them over. But he was sloppy because he was a Maskirovka, not a real medic. Didn't check Kincaid's mouth, didn't stick around so the painkillers, if Kincaid was mouthing them, would dissolve. Sloppy. By the middle of the third day, Kincaid had a stash that could probably put down an elephant. But then he had an excuse to always look groggy, pretend to sleep. He stumbled around a lot when they let him up to pee, or when the nice guy said he had to walk. (Actually, some of it wasn't acting. He hurt like hell.) He didn't even consider doping their coffee or something stupid like that. Dope in coffee tasted like battery acid. Dope in anything other than coffee tasted like poison and stank like crushed beer cans. But he played up the groggy stuff.

Grim wasn't nice. Grim was a Maskirovka who liked action. Grouchy. Glowered a lot while the nice guy changed his bandages. Kept that laser pointed in the right direction. Griped about having to take Kincaid to the toilet. And he liked to smoke.

By the fourth day, the nice guy and Grim were bored and sick of each other. A lot of glares back and forth. Grim smoked like a fiend. Took a smoke break about every five minutes; planted himself right at the entrance to the cave, rifle on his knee. The colonel called in that morning, but not in the afternoon, and the air was electric with tension. Kincaid was moving better, but he was still stiff. The day was bright, the cave mouth glowing like a milky eye. By midday, the sun had warmed the air in the canyon enough to set up a breeze.

Around midday, Kincaid heard a rifle shot. Didn't flinch but worried. Then, every once in a while, another shot. Random. Getting closer. The nice guy and Grim flicked looks.

Then they all heard the chopper. Kincaid caught only the dull boom of it, but he saw Grim roll back and duckwalk into the cave. After a few seconds, the thumping faded. Grim and the nice guy looked at one another, and something wordless passed between them because then they turned to look at him. When Kincaid stared back, the nice guy looked away first.

Bad. It was then that Kincaid knew he'd better get gone.

Lunch or early dinner or whatever, maybe a last meal kind of thing, was some chunky stew-muck: unrecognizable hunks of meat slicked with gray-green grease and something that passed for carrots and potatoes. The nice guy brought the food in a rations tin along with a fork, a spoon and a mug of sour coffee. By then, they'd let Kincaid sit up, hands in cuffs behind his back when he wasn't eating or pissing. Despite the fact that they hated each other's guts, the nice guy and Grim did the handcuff thing right: Grim with the rifle while the nice guy unlocked the cuffs. Then Grim went to smoke.

Kincaid forced down most of the food, chased it with sour coffee. Asked for another cup which the nice guy, being essentially a nice guy, brought without question.

All of a sudden, Kincaid stopped chewing in mid-mouthful. "Oh, Jesus."

"What?" The nice guy squatted two meters away, laser dangling from his right hand.

"I don't know." Then Kincaid groaned, doubled over. "Aw, Jesus, aw, I got to take a dump. Man, I got to go like right now!"

At the mouth of the cave, Grim ducked his head and looked around. Cigarette screwed into the corner of his mouth. Scowled. "You'll have to wait." Cigarette dancing.

"We should take him," said the nice guy.

"I'm finishing my smoke."

"Jesus." Kincaid exhaled, closed his eyes. Grimaced against a faked stomach cramp. "You want me to shit my pants? Come on, for Christ's sake, I can't help it if I..." Doubling over, grimacing. "Aw, God, that hurts."

"I'm taking him," said the nice guy.

Grim grunted. "Do it by yourself then. You can wipe his ass when he's done."

"Christ." Kincaid showed his teeth in a grimace and his face got frantic. "Aw, no, we got to go, we got to go, we got—"

Two seconds later, the nice guy's features shaded into shock. He started waving his hands. "Stop, stop!"

Grim was on his feet, cigarette dangling, smoke spiraling in a vertical curlicue. "*Hell* he doing? Man, don't let him do that!"

"Wait, wait!" The nice guy getting up fast, probably thinking he'd be the one stuck with cleanup. "Come on, I will take you!"

"Damn it." Kincaid averted his eyes. "Just a sec..." Doubling over from a cramp. "Give me a sec." Palming the fork. "*Christ*..."

"Will you get him the hell out?" Grim. "Just get him *out*!"

"Come on!" The nice guy, at his right elbow. Hand on his shoulder. "Come, I will take you, I will—"

Kincaid shot up, grabbed the nice guy's right wrist with his right hand and jammed the fork into the nice guy's eye with his left. The nice guy screamed, dropped the laser, clawed at his face.

Kincaid swept up the fallen hand laser with his right hand, danced right, crouched, saw Grim hunkering down for a shot—and blasted Grim just as he got his rifle set.

Screaming, Grim flinched back, slammed rock; his laser discharged, burning a seam that skimmed a few centimeters above Kincaid's head. Then Grim rebounded right and disappeared.

The nice guy was still shrieking. Kincaid spun him around, then smashed his left forearm into the nice guy's throat. Felt the brittle cartilage of the larynx explode and then the nice guy stopped screaming, fell to his knees, clawing at his throat, trying to get air through a fractured larynx, but only making bubbly choking sounds. Kincaid pressed the muzzle of the laser to the nice guy's temple and pulled the trigger. A flash, a sizzle. Stink of roast meat. The nice guy stopped trying to breathe.

Winded, Kincaid staggered to the mouth of the cave. He looked down. Wheezed. Grim had burst like a blood-filled balloon an easy fifty, sixty meters below. His rifle was nowhere to be seen.

Damn. Kincaid sagged against the cave wall. His wound had opened up; his side roared with pain, and blood was seeping down his side. The air reeked of charred pig. He went back, took the nice guy's hand laser and grabbed his target laser. Tugged his BDUs back on. Slung the target laser over his right shoulder. Thanked Christ he still had his parka and, in the parka, his gloves. He ducked down, duckwalked to the entrance and turned north onto the track.

If I can make it to the rise. He stepped as quickly as he could, but he was wobbly from days of immobility and unsteady on the rocky trail. *If I can just make it to the rise, I can find someplace to wait for the colonel; he's got to come this way...*

There was a faint thumping sound now, echoing in the canyon, and he realized that it was the chopper still north but closer. He was still too far below the rim to see the chopper, but if he could get up there, signal it... *Because something's happened; now they've sent people out to find us.*

And then he had an idea. Scuttled to the halfway point, when the lip of tinder-dry scrub and sagebrush was nearly even with his right shoulder, and he was still a good seven hundred meters shy of the rim. Laser thumbed to full burn, he played the stream of light over the sagebrush and gnarled roots.

Instantly, the grass flashed, sparked; there was a crackle and a sputter, and in a few seconds, there was gray smoke and orange fire racing for the rim. The updraft from the canyon floor brought oxygen and the flames flared up hot and bright. He saw the fire eat its way up the hill. Smoke billowed and swirled, and as the crackling fire spread to that trio of squat Douglas firs, there was a bright flash as the trees ignited.

Like sending up a flare. He started forward again, the whoosh and roar of the fire in his ears. *They got to see it...*

Then he looked up, and his stomach bottomed out.

Smoke, and now the colonel knew something was very wrong. Even with Amanda slung over his shoulder, he'd made adequate time, and she had not regained consciousness. The trail had come out above the tree line, and was much wider now as it headed west, worming in an *s*. So as the trail looped out, he saw the smoke first, and then he broke into a rough jog. Another 150 meters, and he saw the Maskirovka agent's body draped over crimson rock—and then he spotted Kincaid.

No, you won't steal this from me, not now! Cursing, the colonel stooped, tumbled Amanda from his shoulder and pivoted with his rifle in his right hand, dropping into a crouch. In the next moment, as he scanned the path through shrouds of smoke, he almost laughed out loud. Kincaid was perhaps six hundred meters, an easy shot, and had only a laser pistol and that pitiful target laser. He judged Kincaid was too far along the track to run back to the safety of the cave, where he would be trapped in any case. Kincaid's hand laser didn't have the range. So the only thing Kincaid could do was vault the edge—which he couldn't because the track was sheer.

Not exactly what he'd had in mind. He would have to torment Amanda alone. The colonel unhooked his rifle from his shoulder. It would be a pleasure among many to come.

Kincaid saw them both, the colonel and Amanda; saw the left leg of Amanda's BDUs saturated with blood; saw through the thickening smoke how the colonel slid Amanda from his shoulder to the ground where she lay, unmoving. He knew without looking that he could not go back or over the edge. So he did the only thing he could.

Jamming the hand laser into a pocket of his parka, Kincaid transferred the rifle from his right to his left hand and scuttled up the track.

One chance. I get one chance, and then it won't matter because I'll be dead, and the chopper might make it before he does anything to Amanda. God, how bad is she hurt? Did he...?

Kincaid's mind balked, and he concentrated now on scrambling along the ridge, wincing as his side bunched and caught. A thickening gray veil of smoke hung between him and his opponent. But that meant his opponent couldn't see him either...

His head snapped up as he caught the rhythmic *whop-whop-whop* of the chopper. *Yes, yes!* He was on the move, crouching, duckwalking. The chopper was closer because the pilot had seen the fire and smoke, and they would be in time to save Amanda; that was all that mattered, just get Amanda safe—

Suddenly, Kincaid's left boot crunched gravel then skittered to one side, and he slipped. The maw of the canyon opened on his left.

Amanda crawled to consciousness. The inside of her head felt like someone had thrown in a cherry bomb and clanged down the lid. A headache blistered her brain behind her eyes, and the pain along her skull and neck was bad enough to momentarily overshadow the persistent throb in her left thigh. She was aware that she was on the ground; dry sagebrush pricked her cheeks, and the taste of bloody grit was in her mouth. She heard something that sounded like cold cellophane being crinkled, but then she smelled wood char and began to choke against smoke. She propped herself up on her elbows.

They were on the rim of Death Canyon, and she saw the colonel, ahead and to her left: facing away, his rifle in his hands, thick gray and black smoke swirling over his body, the ground on fire so the colonel looked like a devil rising from a pit. She pushed up to sit, silently groaning as she did so—and felt the strap of her target laser drag over her right arm.

No! Kincaid swayed over the edge. His boot skittered on rock, then shot to the side. Crying out, he threw himself right, flailing for a handhold; he banged down, his chest punching rock, his belly slithering over hard pack—*can't lose the rifle, can't lose it!*—and then, at the last possible second, his right hand snagged rock. A shower of pebbles sluiced by, but he held on, digging in with his elbows and the toes of his boots, and pulling in air that tasted of smoke and hot ash.

It had taken all of five seconds, and when he dared to look again, he found that he'd slipped two, perhaps three meters from the ridge. *Take too long to climb back up.* He shot a quick glance at the smoke. The wind could shift direction at any moment, and he had to be ready. And then it struck him that having fallen this far was a blessing.

Because he won't have to compensate for gravity as much; if anything, he'll have to aim a little higher.

But he had to get closer; moving away wasn't any option. His eyes darted left, searching for any toehold. There was one, not more than a meter away, and not really a ledge, but a spur of rock that formed a natural saddle and it was perfect. It took Kincaid fifteen seconds to make it to the saddle and another two to drop into position. Then he blew out, trying to get his heartbeat to slow, searching for that calm place he needed to make his last shot count.

The colonel was so enraged that his anger choked him nearly as much as the accursed smoke! Eyes stinging with tears, he hunkered down as the wind whipped a dark funnel cloud. He heard the crackle of dry sagebrush igniting, saw flames licking the trunks of the firs. Smoke boiled over the ridge, and then just as suddenly the wind shifted again and the smoke thinned, and now he could make out the canyon's far rim, the flat butte of a distant pass and then, much closer, there was Kincaid.

For an instant, the colonel was so surprised, he nearly whooped for joy. Fallen from the track, trying to save his lady love? Well, Kincaid had failed in that as well. The fool had slithered down the slope. A pity he hadn't broken his neck, but now look at him: curled on rock, a target laser no more deadly than a child's toy in hand.

And thank you for making my job that much easier. With Kincaid closer, the colonel wouldn't have to worry about gravity as much, though the wind would be a problem. Five hundred meters, perhaps. A trivial distance.

Another billow of smoke, but the colonel was not bothered. He released a breath, dropped his crosshairs even as he heard the heavy bass rumble of the chopper, knowing that nothing mattered more than this instant toward which he'd been rushing these three long years.

Because I will kill him and then I will kill both her and myself and it will be done and what has been set in place may yet succeed in toppling Cameron and this accursed Hegemony.

Waiting for the smoke to clear, judging the wind gusting east, and seeing now that his aim was perfect, his crosshairs centered on a spot just above Kincaid's left ear.

His heart beat—and paused. And in that dead space, the colonel held his breath as his finger tightened on the trigger.

It was the moment Kincaid had been waiting for.

He was barely conscious of the chopper's thumping, the roar of fire, his own pain. Every distraction dropped away like a tree shedding the last of its leaves. The smoke thinned, parted, cleared, and Kincaid saw the white blur of his opponent's face appear then firm in his scope, because he had judged the distance just right. His focus was tight enough that he saw the colonel's shoulders give a little flinch of surprise, but his opponent had taken aim, had his scope to his eye...

And then Kincaid squeezed the trigger and took the shot of his life.

A searing red flash spiking the center of his crosshairs, and then his right eye erupted in a starburst of pain. Roaring in agony, the colonel flinched back, stumbled, lost his grip on his rifle, which went skittering over the edge. It discharged, and because it was so close, he heard the blast at the same time something hummed past his left ear. He heard the squeal and pop of gravel beneath his boots. His eye screwed shut; tears squeezed from beneath his right lid. The pain was so bad it was as if Kincaid had driven a white-hot poker directly through his eye and into his brain. He was afraid to open it, imagined that the eye had burst and he was afraid, he was afraid...

Blind! His thoughts came as jagged as shards of glass: *Laser...magnified...scope...blinded...my eye...*

Crying out in fear and pain, he twisted, bent at the waist, swung right. *Have to get up, more level ground, have to get away!* But he was too afraid to open his eye, and he couldn't see, he was blind...!

There was a rush of something whirring just behind. He heard it cleaving the air just before it barreled into his back with the force of a sledgehammer.

There was smoke and fire, and the ground vibrated from the basso rumble of the chopper, but she was on her feet, the target laser's barrel tight in her hands. She'd lost the feeling in her left leg, and the limb was numb; it was like trying to walk with a badly fitted peg. She limped forward, dancing on her right leg, trying to cover distance before the colonel could fire because she knew without having to see it that Kincaid was down there and she had to get to the colonel, she had to stop him!

But before she made it, the colonel's back went ramrod straight. He screamed and then his hands flew up, the rifle twirling away like a baton. She heard the crash of a gunshot, and then he staggered back from the rim, his hands clapped to his right eye. He stumbled back on his heels—and was just close enough.

Amanda uncoiled, swinging the target laser like an axe with all her might. There was a high whistle as the butt sliced air and then bammed against the colonel's back so hard the barrel tried to jitter out of her hands. The blow sent the colonel reeling forward a step, then two, and then—he was gone. All except his scream.

Kincaid saw Amanda lurch for the colonel, her laser cocked like a bat, and he roared with joy, cheered her on. She was a beauty. She was fire, with her red hair and taut, savage grimace. She was Death—and he never loved her more than he did at that moment.

He saw her swing and connect; he watched as the colonel rocketed from the blow, plummeting from the rim, falling away, screaming. He saw Amanda sway, take a step; saw the laser slip from her fingers and then he watched, helpless, as she folded in on herself and collapsed as a Redhawk rose into view, parting the curtain of fire and smoke and bellowing like a beast loosed from the throat of hell.

**EVANS MILITARY HOSPITAL
TERRA
10 JANUARY 2439
1825 HOURS**

Amanda regained consciousness by degrees. The first time, there had been a gabble of voices, the pinch of a needle, and the more deliberate pain of a catheter being inserted into a vein of her left arm. Someone shouting: "Major, we're gonna medevac you, do you understand? Major, you hear me, squeeze my fingers!"

She struggled to focus, and must have managed to do what he asked, because then someone was slapping an oxygen mask over her nose and mouth. A sensation of being swaddled, lifted; a roar of rotors and then the ground falling away. Or maybe that was her mind.

The next time, there were bright lights and a great deal more pain but all over. Her throat was very dry, and there was something hard in her mouth snaking to the back of her throat. She panicked, couldn't get her breath. Then there was the voice of a woman telling her not to fight the tube; a blurred image through gummy eyelids, and then the rush of something very cold along her forearm...

More blackness. More sleep.

She awoke for the third time in a bed with aluminum rails in a room that was dark except for a dim lamp on a night table to her right. Her mouth was terribly dry, and when she tried to swallow, it hurt. When she slicked her lips with her tongue, she discovered that they were fissured and chapped, and that reminded her of that moment on the mountain right before she rounded the corner of the tent...

She must have made a sound, because there was a rustle of fabric on fabric and then Kincaid was there. She was so overwhelmed her lips trembled and her eyes burned with tears.

"Amanda." He cupped a hand to her left cheek, and she felt his thumb wiping away the wet. "'Bout time you woke up, girlfriend."

She got weepy, and that embarrassed her, because she didn't want him to think she was crying because of *him*, even though she was. Her voice came out in little hitches: "I'm...I'm so...stupid...to...to...cry."

Kincaid's lips curled in a grin. "Don't worry about it. The doctors said the painkillers might do that, and even if they didn't, you've been banged up pretty bad. Go ahead, cry. I know you're glad to see me."

"You wish." She gave a weak, half-hearted laugh then winced as her throat balled. "Thirsty."

Kincaid fed her ice chips, and she never thought she'd tasted anything as wonderful. She felt a wave of relief that was as much a physical unclenching of her muscles as emotional. When she'd slowed down, he said, "Are you ready to hear what's going on?"

She nodded. "How did they find us? Why did they even come looking?"

"One of the docs back at the project called in the alarm. Name of Fletcher, works with the chimps."

"Doesn't ring a bell."

"You know her. She's one of the team but, you know, who pays attention?" He told her the story about Powers, then added, "She capped Powers and then took his bike. The problem is no one knows if Powers and the Capellans planned this as a joint operation—you know, having two prongs of attack in case one failed—or if Powers was working for somebody else."

"Break-away," she said. "So busy looking at one guy, you never see the second."

He nodded. "All they found for Powers was the number of an unlisted account way the hell off-world. No idea who paid him. So it could be just the Capellans, or the Capellans and Federated Suns working together, though that doesn't compute. For that matter, it could be any one of a number of nobles, someone figuring they have more right to rule the Hegemony than Cameron. The way I'd do it? Steal the *Mackie*, take out the pilots, turn Cameron into a grease smear, and throw the Hegemony into chaos as the *coup de grâce*, then waltz in and put on the save. Be some pretty damned grateful businesses out there not really keen on losing out billions on an investment."

"I thought you said your relatives own some of those businesses. They wouldn't turn."

Kincaid eyed her askance. "Don't be so sure. Business is business. Any of my family gets in the way, they get eliminated and someone more...easily *persuaded* takes over."

"Then thank God it didn't happen."

"Yet." Kincaid paused. "Whoever he is, he has plenty of balls, patience, and organization. He'll be back."

She couldn't resist. "Might be a she."

"Christ, no." Kincaid grunted. "Probably just like you, and then I know we're in deep shit."

They grinned at one another. Then Amanda said, "So they fixed the helmet?"

"Well, what they *said* is that they'd gotten rid of the loop. Whether the same thing might happen to us months down the line...who knows? They did tests on me. You, too, except you were out. So far everything's okay. Fletcher's assistant director now, and Gbarleman said there shouldn't be a problem. Far as the HAF is concerned, this never happened."

"I don't know if I like the sound of that."

"Why tell anyone? You know how many people get killed when they're testing new systems? Happens all the time. You just don't tell John Q. But how are you going to win if you never fail?"

"Don't tell me this is one of those risk-is-our-business things."

Kincaid shrugged. "Well, it is. Sure, we could pull out. We could try to raise a stink. But someone's got to take the risk. That's why there are tests and pilots willing to fly prototypes knowing they might crack up. You accept it as part of the job, or you move on."

She had to give him that. He told her about James and Hackett, then about the squads. Then she asked what she'd been putting off because she wasn't sure she wanted to know. But she said, "So what's wrong with me?"

"You had a pretty solid concussion, a non-depressed skull fracture, not to mention losing a couple liters. You've been out for a long time."

"How long?"

"Try almost three weeks."

She gawped. "Three *weeks*?"

"Yeah. It's almost the middle of January. You were in ICU for New Year's. The nurses threw a little party, put one of those pointy hats on your head."

"I don't believe you," she said, laughing, wanting to take a swat at him. The image was pretty silly. But next year; it was next *year*. "When can I get out?"

"Now that you're awake, probably end of the week. But you'll have to take it easy. Where you got shot was pretty nasty. They couldn't close it, it had been too long. So they just washed it out good and loaded you with antibiotics. Let the thing heal by itself. They said you'll have a hell of a scar."

She blew out. "That's the least of my worries. What about you?"

His lips quirked into a grin. "They kept me a couple days, then got tired of listening to me complain. The Maskirovka did okay by me, so mine wasn't as bad." He paused, and she sensed the shift in his mood. "There's no easy way to say this," he said.

She read it in his eyes, and didn't need to say it but she did anyway. "You're piloting the *Mackie*." When he nodded, she said, "Okay, makes sense. It's the only logical choice now. So, yeah. Right." She forced a smile to her lips. "Congratulations. I guess the best man won."

"Thanks." Kincaid cocked his head to one side and regarded her for a moment. "Actually, I pretty much refused."

"What?"

"You heard me."

"Yeah, but I don't believe it. The hell you do that?"

He lifted one shoulder, let it fall. "Because I was just the guy left standing."

"What happened to all that rah-rah Hegemony crap? Don't tell me the Director-General isn't, you know, pissed."

"No, he's pretty insistent. So are all my relatives who've tied up capital in this thing. They want the test run on the specified date, no delays. So, you know, family on my back, nag, nag. I finally agreed to think about it."

She was amazed when the words came out of her mouth: "What were we just talking about? Someone's got to pilot the damn thing. Might as well be you."

"And not you?" He frowned. "What? Why?"

"Because then everything will have been for nothing," she said. "Hackett, James...*this*. I don't know about you, but I came pretty close to dying. Even so, I accept that because I'm a soldier. Like you said, it's the job. So do your goddamned job. Show the Capellans, the Federated Suns...hell, show 'em all that we're pros. They can't keep us down. If you don't pilot that thing, then Cameron looks like a fool and we look like jackasses. Remember what you said about Isabelle?"

"I remember."

"Well, it applies. I don't like it. But I accept it because there are some things you have to do, and that's one of them. So if you can marry a woman you don't love because that's your duty, then you sure as hell are going to do this for me. Besides, how am I going to watch your ass in a *Mackie* if you don't park *yours* in that command couch and prove that hunk-of-junk works?"

He was silent, his dark-blue eyes steady on hers. Then his lips parted in a slow smile. "You watching my ass has its attractions."

"Count on it, Kincaid. I'm your wingman," she said simply. "Always have been, and always will be. Because put you and me in a couple of badass *Mackie*s?" She found his hand and held it tight and knew she'd never let go. "The universe is in for some serious shit."

PROMETHEUS UNBOUND

HERBERT A. BEAS II

**TERRAN HEGEMONY BATTLEMECH COMPLEX
HESPERUS II
LYRAN COMMONWEALTH
7 FEBRUARY 2455
1903 HOURS TST**

Thuh-whump!
Ever since accepting this mission, even before five months of intensive training, the dreams—the nightmares—had haunted Colonel Simon Kelswa nearly every night.
Thuh-whump!
They played out like some horribly scripted holovid. The hyperrealism of the dreams—with vivid colors, echoing noises, even the icy chill of the wind—all magnified in his mind. Enhanced. Fused with importance. Ensnaring his thoughts while at the same time telling him they were not real. Not real at all.
Thuh-whump!
But this time, the colors were half-cloaked in shadows. The echoes came from the distant rumble of explosions and wailing sirens. The wind carried heat, fire, smoke, a stench of burning chemicals.
Thuh-whump!
But now the thumping was real. Far more real than even the holovid intel reports he saw years before. Real enough

to shake the earth and rattle windows. Now, in the midst of a burning complex, the memory of those first images faded, replaced by the mind-blanking numbness that anchored Simon to a patch of rubble-strewn pavement. Stranding him in the midst of massive buildings wreathed in fire and smoke.

The monsters were coming!

Even Simon's nightmares failed to compare. The pounding, clanking symphony of death heralded an avatar of metal, one he had hoped never to see this close, even when he accepted this assignment.

Thuh-whump! Thuh-whump!

Each footfall of the lead monster shook the earth, raising a cloud of dust from the ground all around him. Larger bits of debris danced to the rhythm. The sound reverberated across the manmade canyon of office buildings, stopping Simon's heart with every world-crushing impact. Over the din, he was dimly aware of someone shouting at him, calling out his name in angry, urgent tones.

But it was too late.

The monsters were upon them.

Thuh-whump!

With one more bone-rattling footfall, the first monstrosity of metal, its desert-mottled hide harshly outlined in orange light, finally rounded the corner. Backlit by licking flames and flickering streetlamps, with its legs and lower torso wreathed in a low-hanging cloud of gray-black smoke, it looked for all the world like a titanic wind devil, emerging from the Inferno itself.

Simon's eyes, dry and stinging, bulged at the sight. Of their own volition, his lungs drew in another gulp of searing Hesperan air through clenched teeth, mindless of the choking taste of scorched metals and ozone.

The monster's shoulders brushed past three-story office buildings and warehouses as casually as a man strolling through a crowded parking lot. Its head, a bulb of metal atop a mountain of armor, presented a round portal of infinite ferroglass blackness for a face, an eye that swept across the grounds as it turned.

That eye of gleaming darkness, seeking prey, froze Simon in place like a Tharkan gazelle in the headlamps of an oncoming hovercruiser.

It sees me!

MARIA'S ELEGY SPACEPORT
TERRAN HEGEMONY COMPLEX
HESPERUS II
LYRAN COMMONWEALTH
1 FEBRUARY 2455
1137 HOURS TST

> *"Highness, you don't need to remind me how bad it looks out there, but is* this *really the answer? The Combine and the League are pressing us hard enough, and the armchair generals we have running the show have their hands full—no offense intended. This plan of yours…I mean, do we really want to risk opening a new front now?"*

Six days earlier, as he and his team took their first steps down the creaking, metal ramp of the drop shuttle *Firebringer* and into the blazing heat of Hesperus II's Terran Hegemony–owned spaceport complex, Simon's conversation with the Archon still echoed in his mind. He buried it at once. Here—for the moment, at least—there were no colonels or Archons. Just another group of semi-skilled off-world laborers sent by Commonwealth Mining Corporation for their Hesperan outpost, CMO 7.

Naturally, they had not rated the first-class, air-conditioned accommodations of the more connected executives and VIPs at the primary spaceport. Instead, a pair of dark-blue, dusty and dented ground trucks met them at their remote landing pad, far removed from the main buildings. Escorted by a couple jeeps, all four vehicles bore the three-star logos of Maria's Elegy Spaceport Security, as well as the more familiar solar-system insignia of the Terran Hegemony. Their crews, of course, had come to subject all twenty-five of Simon's men to a cursory weapons and contraband scan before shuttling them off to the outer terminals and the CMO-provided taxis beyond—security and welcome wagon all rolled into one.

Time for the show to begin.

> *"Colonel—Simon, you know the score, as well as I. We've lost a fifth of the Tamar Pact to the Dracs already, and Marik is pressing us hard. We need any advantage we can find, and one is sitting in our backyard as we speak..."*

True to security protocols, the guards ordered Simon and his crew well clear of the relatively cool shade provided by the *Firebringer*, their boxy, aging, 1,000-ton shuttle. As the Terrans performed their duty, never once cracking a smile or engaging the Lyrans in anything approximating conversation, Simon felt a burn slowly spreading across his bald scalp. The harsh, Hesperan sun seeped into his skin, drawn by his naturally dark complexion.

Chewing on a wad of sour tobacco, he waited, feigning indifference and scratching at the side of his broad, clean-shaven jaw, while his deep hazel eyes measured up the security troops and reviewed his own men, handpicked by the Archon himself only five months earlier.

All of them—male and female alike—maintained the perfect show of professional discourtesy one might expect from a bunch of roughnecks. A few even enjoyed it, and Simon could tell which just by the looks in their eyes, that genuine gleam of cruel mirth as they shot back curses and glib replies to a battery of standard questions. Johann, the shuttle's pilot, gave his female inspector a lewd wink as she approached with her metal detector, and made a point of thrusting his groin forward just as the wand reached mid-level.

"Drekking low-life," she grumbled back.

> *"But, this is a straight infiltration mission, Highness. Surely, this is a job Intelligence can—"*
>
> *"The Corps has had its shot, Colonel. They've had many shots, in fact. And they've cost us fifteen years of wasted effort. This plan calls for a team capable of bulling its way past any obstacles while simultaneously minimizing casualties all around. They need to be able*

to fight with maximum effect, but only when absolutely necessary."

"A surgical strike, then?"

"Yes. A surgical strike."

"Name and badge, please?"

It had to be the fifth time someone had asked him that question since the *Firebringer* arrived in system, and with each repetition, Simon wondered at how it verified anything at all.

"Look, *jefe*," he growled at the guard, "How many times you gotta ask us this shit? Ain't the logos and thumbscans we supplied you enough already?"

The Hegemony officer stood easily a head shorter than Simon and weighed probably all of forty-four kilograms dripping wet (not counting the thin sheen of sweat already pasting the tips of sun-bleached hair to his forehead). His iron gaze, delivered by emerald daggers, however, spoke of equal willpower—if not physical strength—to the man now looming over him.

It was enough to earn a notch of Simon's respect—not that he could afford to let it show.

"We can stand out here a few more hours if you like, Mister," he shot back. "I'm paid by the hour, and I need to work on my tan anyway—whereas I reckon you and your smart-ass buddies here haven't even punched in yet."

Outwardly, Simon sighed with exasperation and spat the last of his tobacco onto the charcoal gray of the tarmac ferrocrete. Steam rose from the splatter.

Inwardly, he took note of the guard's name, and applauded his audacity. "For the twentieth freakin' time," he snarled. "The name is Lorenzo. Augosto Lorenzo. And the badge is Charlie-Michael-Charlie zero-three-four-one-six-freakin'-Baker."

The guard—Daelun, according to his dusty blue fatigues—smirked back, briefly exposing a set of gleaming white teeth as he recorded the numbers and snapped shut his noteputer. "Well," he said. "That wasn't so hard, now, was it, Mister Lorenzo?"

"I've already picked out the best men for this assignment, Colonel. Frankly, I can think of no one better to lead them than you, a man who knows the

> value of human life, a soldier who can still be subtle in combat. The proverbial phantom in the mist."
>
> "I'm honored, sir, but a mission like this, without adequate intelligence—"
>
> "God's sake, man! Give me a little credit, would you? Although I have little faith in their ability to carry out an operation like this on their own now, I did see fit to give you one man who is an expert on this particular objective."

"Hey!" a voice bellowed, filled with indignation and outrage. Simon looked over to see Kirkpatrick a few steps closer to the DropShip's ramp. A harsh and soulless glare from the dark pools he called eyes now focused on the hapless guard who had dared to reach for his duffel. "That's private property, you Terrie *Schweinehund*!"

An involuntary belch rumbled up the back of Simon's throat at the sound of the man's voice, mixing the aftertaste of tobacco with stomach acid and last night's stale MRE. The burn inflamed his mouth and nostrils, and he swallowed hard.

Kirkpatrick's gaze promised certain death for any who understood it, and after months of training with him, Simon understood it well. He had that combination of the veteran's thousand-meter stare and the hungry, eager gleam of a predator stalking prey. Chosen by the Archon for a mission that demanded as little bloodshed as possible, Agent Brian Kirkpatrick had the highest kill ratio of his team in each training exercise.

> "He's the only operative who ever got inside the Hesperus facility. Gave us a basic map to go by, likely targets for the mission. The Hegemony sniffed him out eventually, but we pulled him out before they could make a capture. Since then, he's been...reconstructed, transferred to CTD."
>
> "CTD? Highness, I dealt with some of those thugs before. They're pure killers, agents of chaos!"
>
> "Heh. Well, Simon, I won't argue with you there. But to pull off this plan, you may need a little chaos to cover your tracks. And, as I said before, this man knows the

terrain. You'll need him, but you'll also have to watch him very closely."

Why did the Archon's "expert" have to be from the Corps' Counter-Terrorism Division?

The Hegemony guard, of course, could not know he was dealing with a man who'd love to tear off his head and eat it.

"Hand it over now, or you can just hop back on your transport and get the hell off my planet."

"Last I checked, you Terrats only paid the rent here. This is still a *Lyran* planet, bud!"

With an angry snarl, Daelun spun away from Simon. "Franks! What seems to be the problem here?"

Nostrils flaring, "Franks" didn't take his eyes off Kirkpatrick for a second. "I got a read on this one's carry-off, Captain."

"That so? And what's your name, mate?"

Kirkpatrick's gaze remained cool and hostile at the same time. His voice was cold enough to freeze even the Hesperan air. "Don't 'mate' me, *Scheißkerl*! The name's Easton, and I don't take kindly to your mongrel here trying to get into my personal business."

"I'd watch my tongue a little better if I were you, Mister Easton. You happen to be on *Hegemony* property, not Lyran soil, and we don't take kindly to foreigners coming in with weapons they should know enough to leave under lock and key."

"I know full well whose soil this is, Terrie. And the way I see it, a man's gotta protect himself when your kind is around."

"That so?"

Simon swallowed back another belch of stomach acid as he watched Daelun strut forward, bringing himself nose to nose with the enraged operative. Kirkpatrick was Simon's height but noticeably paler in complexion and only slightly sleeker in build. The size difference between him and Daelun made the confrontation almost comical, except for those penetrating, hateful black eyes he now fixed on the guard captain. Only half an act, the expression of murderous intent was so ingrained in the man's face that Simon suspected no amount of "reconstruction" could ever truly mask it—though Daelun seemed oblivious.

Kirkpatrick's stance was that of a panther about to strike. Inwardly, Simon braced for the first swing.

A dull *thud* shook the ground before another word was uttered. Instinctively, Simon glanced at the dusty security trucks, half expecting to see one of them roaring to life, only to realize the drivers were among the detail searching his men.

Thump.

No, not the trucks.

The distant sound rumbled from across the tarmac. Correcting his gaze, Simon saw the moving silhouette far to the south, a shadow dwarfed only by the hulls of several cargo ships in the foreground. Broad, ungainly, but vaguely humanoid in shape, the shadow stomped again. The deep *thump* took a full second to reach him.

Simon swallowed dryly.

> "I know what you're thinking, Simon. That look in your eyes is the same one I saw in the mirror the first time mother showed me those vids. There's no denying that this is the Pandora's Box of our time."
>
> "Highness, I don't think 'Pandora's Box' quite describes this kind of technology. The Hegemony has already blunted five separate incursions into their territory with these machines, these BattleMechs. They're unstoppable."
>
> "Nothing is entirely unstoppable, Colonel. You should know that."
>
> "Well, close enough, sir. The Hegemony's holo-footage may be propaganda, but our own intelligence files agree on the key details. These aren't armed WorkMechs we're talking about. Their armor is far superior to any tank in the field, even at the joints. And they have the weapons to match. Their mobility and flexibility puts any vehicle on the ground to shame, and they can cover just about any terrain. Tanks, fighters, artillery, infantry— nothing can match these things for flexibility, and nothing short of a nuke can hope to touch them in combat without serious punishment."
>
> "Exactly right, Colonel. And as we speak, the Camerons have them. And every other Great House in

the Sphere has spent the last fifteen years trying to get them. So, tell me, Simon: would you prefer to see these weapons in the hands of Lord Kurita first, or the Captain-General?"

The body that slammed into Simon and sent him sprawling to the hot-as-coals tarmac suddenly snapped him back into the moment. A sharp gasp escaped as his hands burned for a fraction of a second. The Terran guard who had fallen against him uttered a muffled curse in a language Simon did not immediately identify before rolling off and regaining his footing.

Alarmed shouts from the other guards and several drawn weapons told the rest of the story, especially with no less than three Waltham L-90 service lasers already zeroing in on Kirkpatrick. What Simon still could not figure out, however, was how Daelun had managed to get ahold of the man's duffel.

The agent must have made it easy.

"Give that back, *now*!" Kirkpatrick demanded.

"Everyone stay calm," Daelun snapped back, his voice cold and level. He hefted the weight of the dingy canvas sack in one hand, and his Waltham in the other. "If this proves to be nothing more than a child's plaything, you'll all be cleared to go about your business—"

"Filthy Terrie—!"

"If not, however..." Daelun's eyes met Kirkpatrick's in another heroic demonstration of willpower. "Well, if not, you gents are all gonna have your buddy here to thank for getting your asses thrown into quarantine for at least a few days."

With that, Daelun cautiously set down the duffel and pulled the zipper open.

Simon felt the other guards around him tense as Daelun reached in, instinctively matching Kirkpatrick's shift while also keeping an armed eye on each of the other "miners" in their midst. Belatedly, Simon worked his way back to a kneeling position, holding his hands apart, fingers splayed.

Sweat trickled down his brow, ran across his lips, and pooled into his collar as the seconds ticked by. He breathed deeply and exhaled slowly, focusing again.

The guards were standing too close, their eyes darting about too quickly. Only one or two of them was calm, he realized. It would be so easy for him and his men to take them all down, even now.

But that was not part of the plan.

Daelun's expression blanked as his unseen hand found the offending object. When he withdrew it from the sack, the look on the Hegemony officer's face ran a quick gamut from surprise to admiration, and finally settled on contempt. Lifting the snub-nosed Kawasaki Shuriken-12 auto-pistol, he quickly checked the magazine—discovering the full fifteen-round magazine that Simon already knew sported the telltale blue-tipped noses of armor piercing "cop killer" slugs.

Emerald eyes fixed Kirkpatrick with an icy stare. "Unless I'm mistaken," he said, "these are contraband even on Commonwealth soil, Mister Easton."

MARIA'S ELEGY SPACEPORT
TERRAN HEGEMONY COMPLEX
HESPERUS II
LYRAN COMMONWEALTH
1 FEBRUARY 2455
1152 HOURS TST

The tiny hold in the back of the cargo truck was a simple metal bay that stank of methanol fumes and human sweat. It featured hard, flat benches welded to its reinforced frame, and was painted in a simple black primer. Devoid of ventilation (unless—as Simon doubted—that sealed portal to the driver's cabin happened to lack the same mesh-reinforced bulletproof glass that let minimal light in through the vehicle's back doors), the bay contained the Hesperan heat nicely.

And amplified it with the combined body heat of twelve men and women the Terrans had seen fit to pack inside at gunpoint.

Squeezed between Johann's wiry frame and McCabe's larger (and far more aromatic) one, Simon did his best to maintain the look of indignation expected of a miner whose new assignment had just been derailed by a colleague's stupidity. Fixing his glare on Kirkpatrick, it was a surprisingly easy task.

Kirkpatrick, for his part, met the colonel's gaze with a twisted grin, as if oblivious to the fact that his last, desperate struggle to stay out of the paddy wagon had left a three-centimeter gash across one cheek and a welt over the other eye from any one of the four Hegemony guards who felt a need to "persuade" him further.

"Smooth moves, Easton," Johann finally said over the rumble of engine.

Kirkpatrick scoffed at the use of his assumed name. "Please, Johnny! I could've taken the lot of them any time I wanted to. We're still on-plan here."

Simon narrowed his eyes on Kirkpatrick, recapturing the man's dark pools and receiving a look of equal contempt for his troubles.

"Don't bother with the lecture, Colonel," he shot back at the unspoken warning. "They don't wire their trucks, and nobody up there can hear us through the engine noise. Worry about bugs when we're brought in for 'debriefing.'"

"All the same, *Easton*, this is *my* show, and we're all in this together. For the sake of the team, you follow the protocols here, got me?"

"Oh, *jawohl, mein herr!*" Kirkpatrick sneered. "You know, for a man whose 'show' this is supposed to be, I can't help but wonder how you managed to zone out when I was busy making the scene for our arrest."

Noticed that, did you?

"You did just fine by yourself, from what I saw, Agent," Johann challenged, leaving Simon's own reply stillborn.

Simon jammed an elbow into Johann's side.

"It got us here, didn't it?" Kirkpatrick answered. "Now, they'll run our names, see we're legit, and put us in quarantine for safekeeping while our CMC buddies work out a deal. Till then, we're guests of the finest in Hegemony Spaceport Security, just as we planned. So relax, Johnny."

"And our ship?" McCabe asked, filling the cabin with his deep baritone even though he was straining to keep his voice to a low grumble. "Something far less obvious would have done the job better, and you wouldn't have had to fend off the billy-club brigade on your way to the paddy wagon."

"Yeah," added Leutnant Shandra. Small of frame and with dark skin and hair, she practically vanished among the shadows that collected at the back of the truck, her voice all but disembodied. "You picked a rather exquisite piece of Snake hardware to get their attention, Agent. Likely they'll be wondering whether we're smuggling more of them."

"And risk a diplomatic incident with one of their best trading partners?" Kirkpatrick shook his head in disdain. "Lyran ships remain Lyran soil, even when they sit on Terrie launch pads."

"Unless there's probable cause for a search and seizure."

Kirkpatrick smirked in her general direction. "Another thing for CMC to worry about, *ja*?"

Simon bit back another remark, reducing it to a heavy sigh instead. The Commonwealth Mining Corporation's contacts would surely back his people's claims, thanks to the Archon's influence and the one other Lyran Intelligence Corps operative who had been allowed to play a role in this mission. But their influence would only provide the minimal support of a legitimate front behind which the commandos could slip on-planet. Though usurped by the national need at the higher management levels, those who would fight hardest for the "miners"—and the sanctity of their transport as private property—were actually middle management. *They* would ultimately have to make the case for both in the face of Hegemony security concerns, concerns backed up by the Hegemony's own influence as the big moneymakers on Hesperus II.

Knowing that, Simon realized full well that all it would take to scramble the deal—and to force his men to have to fight their way out when the time came—was the one CMC middle manager with the initiative to place company profits and the need to keep a customer happy above all directives from the corporate office.

Just one concession, in the name of good consumer relations, and the whole mission could become a bloodbath.

A possibility Simon knew Kirkpatrick was just as aware of—and quite probably even hoped for.

"Enough," he snapped finally. "All of you. We're here, and practice time's over. Stay in character, starting now. And you, *Easton*, had better start showing some more restraint. You're still under my command here. Malf this up for us, and I'll kill you myself. Clear?"

A sudden lurch and a break in the grinding rumble of the engine punctuated the words. As the truck idled—*undoubtedly at its checkpoint,* Simon figured—Kirkpatrick glared back at him.

Agents of chaos, indeed, Simon reminded himself.

Another jolt broke the colonel's concentration as the entire truck shook without warning. For an instant, the shaking reminded him of artillery fire—shells landing too close to a position no sane foot-slogger would ever take in a front-line battle. Then came the second jolt, followed by a third, and a fourth, taking on a rhythm his mind could finally identify, sight unseen.

Sounds like it's right on top of us!

The truck lurched and the thumping amazingly drowned in the noise as the engine rumbled to life once more. But the reprieve lasted only for a few seconds, as they drove into the security compound—a few seconds to prepare for the sight of the monster, up close and personal.

Suddenly, Simon realized his hands were shaking. He clasped them together in his lap, but not before seeing the look in Kirkpatrick's eyes, a look far more dangerous than his barely masked contempt and lethal hostility.

Recognition.

Harsh light exploded inside the bay once more as the spaceport guards threw open the doors and covered their new charges with half a dozen laser muzzles. Blinking away the stars, Simon nudged McCabe away when Daelun's voice ordered the "detainees" to come out.

"C'mon, mates," Daelun barked over the din of engine noise and stomping feet. "We haven't got all day."

Joints creaking despite the short trip, Simon avoided contact with Kirkpatrick on his way out, and his feet struck hard pavement before the scene of a spaceport-turned-military camp. Small, desert-camouflaged VTOLs lingered on the tarmac nearby, sporting security logos and Hegemony insignia. Armed, dusty blue jeeps drove a lazy circuit around a perimeter defined by chain-linked fences six meters high and topped with electrified razor wire. A few guard towers were even visible from their vantage point, their gunners already taking a keen interest in the new arrivals who once again baked beneath the harsh rays of the Hesperan sun. Arrivals who—now liberated from the ovens of the claustrophobic truck bays—paradoxically reveled in the almost nonexistent breeze.

And, towering above all but the larger structures of the spaceport hangars themselves, marched a monster of armor and weapons, a bulbous, bipedal construct that Simon had only seen before in grainy flatpics and amateurish holovids. With each halting, lumbering step, the machine—colored in a semi-flat desert camo scheme and proudly displaying the solar system insignia of the Terran Hegemony on its right "shoulder" weapon blister—shook the ground with explosive force, even though it could not have been marching closer than two hundred meters away.

> "All right, you roaches. Eyes front, mouths shut, and listen up! The Archon, in his infinite wisdom, selected us all for this mission because he has some kind of misplaced faith in our abilities, so I'm not gonna waste my breath with the usual pep talk about how you're the best of the best of whatever. What I am gonna do is direct your collective attention to the vid, where you will find our objective. I'm sure you all recognize them by now. Hades knows that the Terries let us know they got 'em often enough."
>
> "You've got to be kidding us, sir!"
>
> "Rest assured, Hauptmann Daschale, I am not. You are looking at a BattleMech, the Terran Hegemony's ultimate weapon for the last fifteen years. The model shown here is their MSK-6S *Mackie* design. Weighs in at a hundred tons and has been clocked at a land speed of about fifty-five kilometers per hour. It's as deadly as it is ugly, and we've all seen what those weapons

it carries can do to a tank company. Since they first appeared in combat, Mackies *have accounted for over half the Hegemony's battlefield victories against all the Great House armies combined. Only five have ever fallen in combat, and of them, none has been captured for study—by anyone."*

"So the Archon expects us to accomplish what entire regiments have failed to do?"

"In a manner of speaking, yes."

"Impressive, isn't it, *jefe*?" Kirkpatrick's voice hissed in Simon's ear, adding special emphasis to the last word in parody of his Spanish accent.

Blinking, Simon faced him, but his eyes could not manage to focus right. The Corps agent sneered back.

"That's one of the newer ones, I'd say," Kirkpatrick added, his voice still low. "Baby of the litter."

Simon nodded numbly, his mind recalling the statistics. The "baby" did not even have an official name yet, so far as anyone knew, but reports estimated its weight at around 60 tons—maybe 70—making it the smallest of three distinct models now in the Hegemony arsenal. It was slimmer, but no less ugly than the *Mackie*, with a cockpit module that rose above its torso like a bubble of black ferroglass and was flanked by thick blast shields that sprouted up from the shoulders and somehow reminded Simon of the blinders riders often put on Terrestrial horses.

Its right-arm blister resembled nothing so much as a twin-barreled turret, which intelligence reports believed contained high-powered lasers, each easily capable of coring away the thick armor of a main battle tank. Its left arm seemed to house a multi-tube missile-launch system, contained in a simple barrel-shaped housing. With a top speed—according to observations of its Hegemony trials—somewhere just over sixty kilometers per hour, Simon suspected this one was intended to act as more of a scout or interceptor, able to run down even mechanized infantry and light tanks over the most hellish terrain imaginable.

None had been seen in combat yet, but in simply looking at it, Simon could already guess at its power.

"Make no mistake about this, ladies! The BattleMech is nothing like the WorkMech you see behind me. It stands taller, walks on two legs rather than riding on tracks, and uses a far more complex series of advanced myomers than even the top-of-the-line Constructors we have today. But even more significant is the neurological interface system they use to control them, rather than the wheels-and-joysticks approach of a common LoaderMech. Combined with the humanoid configuration, this system effectively allows just one crewman to operate the machine and its heavy arsenal with the same ease as a well-equipped soldier in the field—and all with just about the same speed and coherence of action as raw human reflex will allow.

"It's like turning a man into a giant.

"An armored, heavily armed giant. One capable of withstanding all manner of small arms, and even the best conventional heavy weapons on the market today. Even the joints are well protected; entire Drac tank companies have massed their fire just to saw off a leg of one of these beasts. And we will not be bringing that kind of firepower with us to the objective site."

"In short, under no circumstances are we to attempt to engage a BattleMech in combat, is that it?"

"Exactly, Shandra. If anything, we are even more vulnerable to BattleMechs than armored vehicles. Last year, some Feddie grunts tried to climb one of these things in the middle of a firefight, presumably to plant some kind of charges on the legs or joints. The Terrie didn't exactly oblige them. Rumor has it the Hegemony technicians had to spend little more than half an hour cleaning the blood and gore out of the knee joints for all that effort. Simply put, there are no infantry tactics that have been proven to combat these machines in a straight fight."

"Unless you want to end your career as an ugly red smear, that is."

"Precisely, Agent Kirkpatrick."

"Move it already, people!" snarled an angry voice as Simon felt the insistent nudge of a rifle butt at his back. Raising his hands slightly to show compliance, he marched forward at last, forcing his eyes away from the "baby."

Rolling his tongue around, he tried to swallow some of the dryness out of his mouth, and returned his gaze to his men. Twenty-five of them in all, counting himself, all being herded toward the nearby barracks of dust-covered aluminum, escorted by a dozen well-armed Terran security troopers.

And in the middle of that crowd, a cold, dark pair of eyes glared back, knowing and contemptuous.

It seemed so real at the time...

Rounding the corner on "three," Simon took the high ground, bringing the Mauser & Gray SP-7 submachine gun up to eye level and peering down the sights at another empty corridor. To his right, Leutnant Federico Satori ducked low and did the same from the opposite side of the passage. Simon turned just enough to catch his peripheral vision despite the goggles and issued his commands with a simple nod. *All clear. Move out!*

With absolute precision and utter silence, Satori moved down the corridor, clinging to the wall and matching Simon's movements pace for pace. Ducking low under office-door windows—with barely a moment's hesitation to be sure no one stood just inside—they followed the corridor to a branch, where a pair of thick double-doors stood, closed and magnetically locked in case of fire.

Reaching up to his earpiece, Simon tapped the device twice, sending two barely audible clicks over the team frequency, and was rewarded in less than a second by a series of alternating tones, a chorus of all-clear signals.

So far, so good.

The primary plan had maintained that the offices would be evacuated for a minimum of forty-five minutes as the distraction outside tied up security and disaster-control resources. The eggheads in the factory's tech department—all too close to the "crash" at ground zero—would have to be cleared out for the rest of the night, just in case things got worse. That would assure that the brains behind the construction of the worst weapons seen since the H-bomb could survive to build more of their metal monstrosities tomorrow.

Of course, in their haste to save their own skins, they would have to leave their computers behind and relatively unguarded.

But only for a little while.

The "wreck" that served as their diversion, naturally, had also cut power and communication lines to this sector. Even though emergency generators kicked in to provide some illumination, other key functions—including video surveillance—were down throughout the offices. The intrusion, assuming all went according to plan, would thus go unnoticed.

As long as they did not encounter the handful of guards still expected to be around, that is. After all, to protect a secret of this nature, *someone* would have to stay behind, patrolling for possible intruders or workaholic employees too distracted to have run for shelter—no matter how dangerous the situation outside.

Satori slung his SP-7 back and drew his security codebreaker from a thigh pocket, unraveling the interface cable belt with a subtle flick of the wrist. Inserting the card interface into the door's key-card slot, he strung together the cables in a flurry of motion. Seconds later, red LEDs flashed on the handheld device as the smaller, olive-skinned commando deftly worked the knobs, dialing until all five lights burned green. A soft *click* from the door itself signaled the alarm-free disengagement of the magnetic clamps that held it securely closed.

Simon waited for Satori to stow the codebreaker and unsling his submachine gun before giving a nod and nudging the door open with his knee. Once more, three splayed fingers counted off the seconds before both men swung around to cover the now-open hallway, this time with Simon taking the "low road," while Satori's weapon covered the high ground.

Once more, a dimly lit and very empty hallway revealed no hostiles.

According to the signs, the section Simon and Satori now entered was a data-storage wing for classified projects, one of only two known to exist in this part of the complex, and the one intelligence believed most likely to contain the information the commandos were after. Somewhere down this hall, then, lay the computer stations that could contain the objective information, and to retrieve it, every other operative carried a portable power-supply unit and a package of storage discs on which to copy the data—encryption and all. Code breaking would not be required, as one package could "snapshot" the entire contents of a standard hard drive without bothering with the fine points of password protections and retinal scans—all in less than two minutes.

Luckily, the Terries had not searched the *Firebringer* closely enough to find all these toys.

Unfortunately, the team had only twenty minutes left to reach the computers suspected of containing the data and make the downloads—a process that could not be rushed if secrecy and subtlety were to be preserved.

Satori found the door to the primary station a fraction of a second before Simon noticed the sign, and peered cautiously through the tiny window. Shaking his head, he stepped silently to one side, leaving Simon to cover the other, and on one more count of three, Simon grabbed the handle and shoved it back. Unlocked, the door slid to one side, exposing a room full of personal workstations that the colonel reckoned to be just about half the size of a starship's bridge. As he and Satori covered it, his eyes darted among the red-tinged shadows cast by the emergency lighting, finding nothing.

With a nod, Simon sent Satori into the room and his hand once more reached for his earpiece, when an urgent wail issued forth, nearly piercing his eardrums.

Damn it!

Satori ducked down reflexively, and Simon rolled back behind a mainframe, keeping eye contact with his partner as he clicked his earpiece feverishly, trying to ignore the alarms.

Three short, low tones prefaced the reply, identifying Hauptmann Daschale's team—the one he'd assigned Kirkpatrick to partner with. Daschale reported the situation in a clipped pattern of long and short tones while Simon's heart sank.

"*Hostile contact. B Sector. Hostiles engaged.*"

Damn it! Damn it! Damn it!

A dozen patrolling guards in total, randomly spread across three buildings, and Kirkpatrick's team *again* finds it impossible to avoid a run-in!

With an angry gesture, Simon sent Satori to work anyway, going through the motions of salvaging the operation before it became a total bust, but after seven such simulations, he knew better already. In his mind, he was already replaying the post-exercise debriefing, already seeing that cocky grin on the face of an LIC agent who seemed to take this whole mission as a kind of game with the Hegemony. How many "hostiles" would he claim kill credit for *this* time? And how many of the infiltration team would get "killed" on the way to the dust-off sites?

Then came the sudden lurch, like a grenade blast just beyond the office door, making the computer stations rattle and sending a shower of dust and broken ceiling tiles cascading into the room. Rolling forward, Simon covered his head and felt a tile bounce off his backpack.

What the hell—?

Another lurch, and this time, he felt the floor shake as well. The noise almost drowned out the blaring intruder alarms and brought Simon to his feet. Back in the open, he looked toward the rear of the office, toward the computer node where Satori—

Where *was* Satori?

A third lurch, and the east wall collapsed inward, sending sheetrock panels and metal supports inward, crushing computer stations—chairs, desks, monitors, and all. Rolling away from the collapse, Simon's mind reeled.

This isn't part of the exercise!

"Satori!" he shouted, but his voice echoed strangely.

The east wall came away, filling the room with harsh, blinding light.

The final lurch was deafening, as Simon's eyes finally registered a monstrous silhouette beyond the missing wall. A mammoth metal claw—easily twice his size—ripped into the room, reaching for him with lightning speed...

**HEGEMONY SPACEPORT QUARANTINE CENTER
HESPERUS II
LYRAN COMMONWEALTH
2 FEBRUARY 2455
0300 HOURS TST**

A man's scream—his own?—heralded the sudden return of darkness as Simon Kelswa sat bolt upright on his hard cot.

His clothes were drenched in sweat. The air was hot, stale, and musty. There was no office here. No Satori. No monstrous, metal claws. His hands flexed, finding no weapon in their grip. There were no screaming alarms.

But the thumping remained, hard and pounding, receding into the distance, allowing his racing heart to fill the silence.

Where am I?

The universe refocused again, slowly. Hesperus II. Spaceport quarantine. The exercises were over. The thumping was real, though. Another one of those monsters. A BattleMech.

Simon swallowed dryly, eyes casting about in the darkness. Three other bunks in his cell, all occupied. Bodies stirring only slightly in the shadows, their fitful dreams disturbed by the passing patrol as well. But they did not awaken the same way. They did not hear the scream. Only he did.

Or so he hoped.

Simon forced himself to swallow again, working salty saliva back into his throat. He breathed in another lungful of stale air. The stomping continued to recede. The monster was leaving.

No, not a monster. A BattleMech. A weapon. A tool of warfare. A machine. An objective. *The* objective.

His hands flexed again as his breathing slowed. His heart continued to race, however, its pounding making up for the departure of the unseen machine. A soft tapping, coming from the hall outside, revealed another soul awake in this quarantine center. A night guard, making his rounds.

We're right where we need to be, Simon remembered at last, thoughts finally coalescing again. *Hesperus II Spaceport Quarantine. The exercises are over. Phase One complete. I'm in control. Everything is proceeding on-plan.*

I'm in control.

"Sir...?" asked a weary yet very alert whisper from the bunk beside him. In the darkness, it took him a few moments to identify Johann among the shadows and lumps cast by his coarse bed sheets.

"It's okay, *amigo*," Simon whispered back. "Just a little insomnia."

**HEGEMONY SPACEPORT QUARANTINE CENTER
HESPERUS II
LYRAN COMMONWEALTH
7 FEBRUARY 2455
0945 HOURS TST**

It took Commonwealth Mining Corporation's bureaucratic machine all of six days to argue about the disposition of the twenty-five miners who the Terran government "wrongly imprisoned" at their Maria's Elegy Spaceport. For six days, Colonel Simon Kelswa and his men maintained their roughneck charade by simply being themselves, giving their "guardians" a hard time that consisted of crude innuendo, inappropriate catcalls and wolf whistles (as gender and sexual preferences permitted), and the occasional threat or shoving match during meal times.

For six days, the commandos hidden beneath that callous veneer waited, tensely, for the signal to action, eating the bland selection of protein bars and mystery-meat stews, and drinking metallic, filtered water to prevent dehydration. Idly wondering all the while whether their cover would be blown.

For six days, they watched and waited, while the thunderous stomp of massive, metal-shod feet resounded outside, more powerful than any bass rhythm Simon had ever experienced (even counting the liberty he'd once taken in New Glasgow's downtown ghettos).

After six days, it almost surprised him that the crushing beat of those armored legs still kept him awake at night, reviving the nightmares and recollections of the Drac and FedSuns foot troops crushed beneath the armored giants.

As expected, the Hegemony security apparatus had taken no chances. The appearance of a loaded handgun known by experts to be a favored sidearm of the Draconis Combine's elite commando forces—however its current wielder came by it—was a red flag the nearby factory administrators simply could not ignore. Though the miners' backgrounds had checked out, thanks to the CMC's cooperation and—Simon was sure—some added effort on the Archon's part, the specter of doubt was enough to make the Terries worried.

Worried enough to insist that the miners be transferred away.

CMC's customer-service suits, of course, were only too eager to accommodate the request. After all, it was only twenty-five miners to be moved around like checkers on the interstellar corporate chessboard. The paperwork would be a pain, but the company had more than enough white collars for that as well. At worst, the offending miners would be looking at a month's worth of docked pay for their gun-collecting colleague's indiscretion.

Phrased in the appropriate mixture of wounded corporate pride and obsequious requests for forgiveness (from both the Hegemony officials and their own inconvenienced "employees"), the CMC communiqué was legitimate as far as Simon could tell. Its code phrase, hidden throughout the text in two- and three-letter snippets, quickly assembled in his mind as he applied the memorized key:

"*Prometheus Unbound. Good hunting.*"

As he read the message three times more to be certain, Simon swallowed back the stale aftertaste of Hesperan lizard stew. His heart began to race again.

Looking up, he found, with some relief, that the guard who delivered it had long since departed. Sweeping his gaze across the small, paved, sun-worn courtyard that the Terrans permitted for their detainees' exercise, he immediately caught the eyes of the man who had not stopped watching him for six days. Despite the chaos of an improvised rugby game raging between them, he gave a subtle nod to Kirkpatrick, knowing the Corps operative would catch it.

Phase Two is a go…

TERRAN HEGEMONY BATTLEMECH COMPLEX
HESPERUS II
LYRAN COMMONWEALTH
7 FEBRUARY 2455
1825 HOURS TST

Smack in the middle of a compound full of plain-looking offices and towers, surrounded by a halo of fire and smoke, the first thought that struck Kelswa as he emerged from the *Firebringer*'s hold was a cliché:

Any landing you can walk away from, and all that…

Attempting a confident stride on legs of rubber, Colonel Simon Kelswa swallowed back another acidic belch, trying to extinguish the rancid taste of bile with the half-chewed remains of the protein bar that had miraculously survived repeated mashings from his crash harness. At the moment, even the hot, dry air of Hesperus II felt amazingly cool, and a chill ran along his spine as the sheen of sweat covering his entire body soaked into his coal-black fatigues or dried in place.

Around him swirled a gray haze of smoke, carrying the chokingly noxious fumes of scorched metals and molten polymers. It obscured everything but the remains of fencework and other unidentifiable objects now defined only as halos of flickering firelight. Meanwhile, his ears still rang, robbing sound from the crackling flames, but only muffling the insistent blare of emergency alarms echoing all around him.

Even as a small part of his mind still insisted that he had not survived the wreck that continued to spew flames and dark clouds into the night sky, Simon hefted his SP-7 and proceeded at a hunchbacked jog, waving the rest of his team to follow. Behind him, he sensed twenty of his men plunging into the shadows in three tight groups. Two of them melted immediately into the night, one to his left, and another to the right.

Ahead, half-shrouded by low-hanging clouds of smoke, lay the now-emptied and completely darkened offices of the Hegemony factory complex.

Sparing a moment's time to glance back at his own team, Simon assured himself that all six were alive and mobile, their fatigues, face paint, and gear packs transforming them into low-slung demons of pitch blackness against a flickering, light-gray twilight. Now void of faces and distinguishing marks, only the difference in one gait—a clumsy, stumbling shuffle that betrayed crash-course training in hot-drop missions—revealed which of the demonic shadows belonged to Agent Brian Kirkpatrick.

Leutnant Harrison Johann and four others remained behind, to guard the *Firebringer* and keep her ready for liftoff when the teams returned. Her crash had been but one diversion; her departure again would be quite another, providing chaff for the departing teams when the time came.

Until then, Johann and his team were to make the ship look as dead as possible, keeping the fires burning, the smoke pouring, the local power junctures disabled—and the curious away.

Only twenty-five minutes ago, Simon and his team had been aboard the 1,000-ton shuttlecraft as it rose from the Maria's Elegy spaceport tarmac on columns of white-hot plasma, a mere kilometer away from where they now skulked. Cleared at last to leave, to take its cargo of security-risk miners away to a CMC outpost on the planet's far side, the *Firebringer* had launched seemingly without incident. Then, exactly twelve minutes and four seconds later, with a bright, orange light and a tremendous rumble that no living being in a thirty-kilometer radius could *possibly* have slept through, specially shaped charges concealed along the aft-port hull erupted in a combined blast measuring—Simon guessed—at least a tenth of a kiloton in raw force.

Over the next forty-two seconds, Johann, acting as the shuttle's commander, struggled to keep the ship aloft and moved to return to the spaceport pads, when a secondary explosion, followed by a gout of flame a hundred meters long, heralded the loss of the third primary engine and half the maneuvering jets. As panicked ground-control operators tried to feed instructions to the doomed ship, Johann set the *Firebringer* on a gradual but believably out of control course toward the Hegemony factory complex—begging for help all the way down and "heroically" firing what remained of the ship's retros in an effort to slow the descent.

The plunge took less than ten minutes, but it proved a far wilder ride than any parachute HALO or combat drop Simon had ever taken in his twenty-two-year career—real or simulated. By the time Johann finally fired the full brace of the ship's landing thrusters, in fact, easily one third of the entire platoon—accomplished veterans all—had either passed out from the stress, or emptied the full contents of their stomachs on one another.

Getting out of a drop shuttle's iron womb had never felt so desperate to Simon as it had at that moment. The stench of vomit added a new level of urgency to his fevered effort to retrieve his concealed weapons and tech gear from the ship's hidden floor compartments, to affix the silencer and flash suppressor to his SP-7—all the while fighting back the wave of bile that built up in the back of his own throat.

That they were lucky to have survived the crash at all was something Simon did not intend to dwell on.

Now, as he led his team to their assigned offices, the dry heat of the smoke-tainted Hesperan air felt as refreshing as a cool ocean breeze.

Coming to the door of his team's target, he instinctively hugged the wall to one side, waiting for Satori to take his position opposite. SP-7s at the ready, he signaled off three seconds and nodded. Satori kicked and they both swept the entryway with weapons and low-light goggles.

Nothing but the muted glow of red emergency spotlights filled the corridors. The vid cams, as expected, were dormant.

All clear.

Stepping inside first, Simon shuddered slightly at the rush of cool, freshly conditioned air. Gesturing the others to follow, he walked slowly, silently, eyes darting about for any signs of motion. His weapon muzzle followed his gaze. The hollow, electronic whine of evacuation alarms echoed throughout the empty halls, which extended forward a dozen meters before branching off in two directions.

That the layout did not match the offices they had practiced on hardly surprised Simon. Intelligence—Kirkpatrick in particular—had never actually penetrated the Hesperus factory offices themselves, nor had they succeeded in doing so at any of the suspected Hegemony BattleMech construction sites in the Inner Sphere, despite fifteen years of trying. The arrangement of these R&D offices thus was wide open to speculation and guesswork.

But just how different could a white-collar cubicle hive be?

Simon forced his lips apart for the first time since walking away from the *Firebringer*'s plummet and let out a dry, heavy sigh. Glancing back quickly, he tapped a quick code into his earpiece, transmitting news of their successful entry to the other teams. With most channels intermittently scrambled by radiation pulses from their crashed vessel, the pops and chirps of their pseudo-Morse codes would go unnoticed to all but those trained to expect them, while any patrolling Hegemony guards would be hard-pressed to maintain a conversation outside of a line of sight.

To further reduce the chance of detection, only three men in each seven-man team even possessed communicators, a fact that also left the rest of the teams open to act as computer hackers and a more alert set of unencumbered ears.

Almost instantly, a series of pops and clicks came back to Simon, breaking through the dull ringing that still lingered in his ears. The news was good: all entries successful; no hostiles encountered.

So far, so good...

"Satori, Manikov, Shandra, Jacobi," Simon rasped, "take the left. Faisel, Kirkpatrick, with me on the right. Let's get hunting."

**TERRAN HEGEMONY BATTLEMECH COMPLEX
HESPERUS II
LYRAN COMMONWEALTH
7 FEBRUARY 2455
1836 HOURS TST**

The hunt had been on for only five minutes, and already Simon's jaw ached from how tightly he kept it clamped shut. Agent Kirkpatrick, Leutnant Faisel, and he had already swept through a full computer lab without incident, only to find that its databanks contained personnel records for factory employees. Though some signs had indicated they were near a restricted-access wing, already a promising branch and the ticking clock in the back of his mind had forced Simon to order Faisel down another corridor.

Leaving him alone with Agent Kirkpatrick for the first time since the end of the training exercises on far away Tharkad.

Tapping quickly at his earpiece, Simon sent his fifth sitrep request along to Johann, keeping a mental eye on the crowd that even now reportedly converged on the site of the shuttle's "crash." Flames and smoke still kept them at bay for now, but as rescue vehicles drew near, it was only a matter of minutes, he figured, before the braver among them would dare to pass the barrier of burning debris and look for possible survivors.

As if sensing his thoughts, Kirkpatrick glanced up from his work—scanning another hard drive in what appeared to be an executive office. Though doubt had long since set in that any of these offices would have access to the restricted data, Simon found it safer to keep the Corps agent's mind focused on the job rather than deal with his expectant stare.

Or worse, his conversation.

"They'll be on the ship any minute," Kirkpatrick said, his voice so low and tense that Simon almost had to strain to hear him over Johann's answering clicks. "Has anyone keyed in?"

"Let me worry about that," Simon snapped back.

His eyes hidden beneath low-light goggles, Kirkpatrick's squint was betrayed only by an increased wrinkling around the temples. He had been silent for a few minutes after they entered the building, no doubt still recovering from the savage, gut-wrenching nausea that had so disabled him after the landing—perhaps the only sign of weakness Simon had ever noticed in the man. Now, he gripped his computer and his sidearm much more confidently, and the intensity of his stare—even through unseen eyes—had returned.

"As we're all in this together," he said, "you wouldn't mind if I shared your concern, would you?"

Simon ignored the remark and listened. Johann's news was as expected. Rescue vehicles were working their way through the maze of buildings, but had yet to get too close because of the flames kept burning through his subtle and judicious use of chemical charges. To keep the truly curious at bay, the pilot had added in a few more explosions, erratically setting off small incendiary charges to mimic the pyrotechnic effects of whatever secondary blasts one might expect from a burning shuttlecraft.

For now, it was working.

Kirkpatrick's angry snort punctuated the silence as he removed his datapad from the workstation. An irritated shake of the head announced another fruitless search for anything of value and prompted Simon to check the hall again before moving on to the next room.

"We're behind schedule," Kirkpatrick muttered as he came up behind him. "If I were the Terries, I'd have put another platoon of security in these offices by now, just in case."

"Bet you'd like that, Agent," Simon muttered back, gesturing to another door farther down the hall. "Another chance to add a Terrie Waltham to your collection, huh?"

Though he nodded and followed, Kirkpatrick continued as though he had not heard. "Matter of fact, I'm surprised they haven't scrambled a *Mackie* or two by now. Between their armor and sinks, they can certainly weather a little fire, I'd say. Might consider the secondary dust-off, Kelswa. Scrap the first and get Johann out of there."

Simon narrowed his eyes. That had to be the third time since the quarantine that Kirkpatrick had raised his discomfort about the primary dust-off, the *Firebringer* itself. Of course, assigning Kirkpatrick to his own team at the last minute had probably added to the urgency, reminding the Corps agent just how vulnerable the ship would be once the extraction began. Odds laid even money that the shuttle would escape Hesperus intact, of course, but deep down, Simon knew it was the best way to ensure the Terries were looking the wrong way when the real data got out.

And Kirkpatrick did not much care for being on board the bait.

Well, well, Simon thought. *Looks like there is a limit to that bravado, after all!*

At that moment, a faint sound—a footstep?—somewhere behind them sent Simon spinning on his heel, weapon raised to an intersection down the hall while his raised fist signaled Kirkpatrick to hunch down. Instead, the agent whirled about as well, silenced SP-7 muzzle instantly pointed toward the unseen source of Simon's worry, finger tense on the trigger.

But there was nothing there.

Kirkpatrick waited a few seconds more, then Simon saw his head turn slightly, cocked to one side as if to ask a question.

"All clear," Simon grumbled, lowering his weapon. "Move out."

Kirkpatrick turned fully, his face a dark scowl as met the commando's goggled gaze again. For half a heartbeat, both men froze like that, before it registered in Simon's mind.

Kirkpatrick expected an answer.

"We stick with the plan as is, Agent," Simon growled. "My call."

Kirkpatrick squinted again, hesitated, and turned toward the next office, quickly but silently heading to the workstation there. Once more, the room proved to be little more than an executive's suite; only one computer to hack into and scan. Kirkpatrick plugged in his reader to the external port, briefly supplying enough power from a secondary cell to make its hard drive run. His datapad immediately went to work, scanning folders, checking file sizes, correlating any diagrams, specifications, or keywords, and returning a simple likelihood of success.

Simon stayed by the door, SP-7 at the ready, just in case the sound had *not* been in his head.

"Now is no time to lose focus, Colonel," Kirkpatrick blurted out, giving the display only half of his attention this time. "I've seen how you react to them. I know what you're afraid of."

Simon's eyes widened not so much at the man's ability to identify the source of his unease, but at his audacity in calling attention to it. The words hung like a threat in the air. There was no need to ask what "them" Kirkpatrick was referring to. Already, in his mind's eye, the veteran commando could imagine the thundering march, each footfall an explosion of power and death. Surely the Hegemony's monsters were on their way, just as the agent predicted. Surely they would be here soon, and each second he and his men lingered brought them a second closer to those metal giants.

Giants they could not defeat. Giants no sane man would not fear.

Simon's mouth was bone dry, and he half expected to spit out sand as he opened it. But he would be damned if would let a remark like that slide.

"Now, look, Mister—"

An insistent series of tones sounded in his earpiece, killing the rest of Simon's retort. Kirkpatrick paused for a moment, then let out a snort and turned his attention back to his datapad.

Charlie Team—McCabe's group—was reporting in now. Signaling another successful entry. No hostiles encountered. But with a few extra clicks, Simon found himself releasing a heavy sigh of relief that recaptured Kirkpatrick's attention.

Spark located, McCabe's message said. *Lighting torch.*

Pay dirt!

"They got it?" Kirkpatrick's voice betrayed his disappointment.

Simon gave a sharp nod and held up his hand as he began to tap at his earpiece, first requesting McCabe's location, then forwarding that to all teams. They would need to regroup, to download copies into each team's noteputers. Other computers nearby could be searched as well, giving them all one last chance to mine any more data of value as long as they dared risk. Then they would finally disperse—hopefully as quietly as they came—with two teams making their way to the secondary dust-off site while the third—Simon's—bypassed the gathering crowds and took the *Firebringer*.

The shuttle, of course, would become a target the instant it rose above the factory again, a diversion that would focus the Terries' attention completely away from the real getaway.

It was a risk Simon knew he could not allow any of his men to take alone, one he had forced Kirkpatrick to share with him, to assure the others made it out without incident. Their fate would be decided once more by Johann's superb piloting skills. Given the surprise factor, odds were an even bet that they would get shot down by Terrie batteries or an aerospace patrol during the escape. And above, a JumpShip of Rim Worlds Republic registry—a final touch meant to further throw the Hegemony off the trail—would await them. *If* they survived.

Still, taking the risk aboard an armored shuttle to meet up with a bogus pirate ship beat getting stomped into a greasy red paste beneath metal feet any day of the week. Kirkpatrick—of course—had not thought to complain about *that* part of the plan until after he had been assigned to Simon's team, an act that put him on the *Firebringer*.

McCabe's and Daschale's teams would meanwhile depart far less conspicuously, stowing themselves aboard other unsuspecting daily transports out of Maria's Elegy the following morning. Their escape would guarantee that at least one copy of the data made its way back to Tharkad.

From there, of course, the universe would change...

Kirkpatrick suddenly broke his connection to the computer, but as he did Simon discovered a new manner in the Corps agent's movements now. There was more hesitation in his actions, an almost distracted drift in the way he hefted his SP-7 and waited for the colonel to lead on.

There was a familiar shape to his expression now. It was one Simon knew well, face paint and goggles notwithstanding.

The Archon's words flooded back to him, unbidden: "*I know what you're thinking, Simon. That look in your eyes is the same one I saw in the mirror the first time mother showed me those vids...*"

Fear!

Simon blinked as something clicked inside his head, and a grim smile came to his face. *Suddenly we have something in common, Kirkpatrick!*

Kirkpatrick's expression betrayed a moment's confusion, and Simon nodded his own understanding. Melting into the corridor, they darted back down the halls silently, gathering up Leutnant Faisel, working their way toward the exit.

We're all just choosing our deaths here, aren't we? The thoughts echoed as they slinked through the shadows. *I fear those Hegemony monsters, and you fear burning up on a plunging shuttlecraft. No way to fight back. No way to take the bastards with you. You know my fear, Agent? Well, now I know yours, too!*

Simon focused on the moment as he led his men around another bend and spied movement in his lowlight goggles. Instinctively, he brought his SP-7 up and felt Kirkpatrick and Faisel do the same. At the far end of the hall, two more commandos in black fatigues, face paint, and goggles mirrored their action.

Leutnant Satori grinned back over the muzzle of his weapon, his teeth flashing white-green in Simon's lowlight vision. Weapons lowered as Satori waved his partner to follow.

Two more corners from the exit, and Simon's entire team had fully regrouped.

Less than ten seconds later, all seven men emerged from the cool, red-lit darkness of the building, and plunged headlong into the oppressive, dry heat of the Hesperan night, and the flaming complex around them.

So far, so good...

Simon motioned the team ahead, directing them toward McCabe's building, when an urgent clicking in his earpiece sounded over a distant—and all too familiar—thumping. The first clicks identified Johann immediately.

Contact!

The clicking suddenly became a high-pitched squeal as suddenly night became day, and the ground shook in time with an explosion that sent the entire team scrambling for cover behind the walls of the nearest buildings.

Simon felt hands seizing him, tossing him toward a low barrier behind a parked security truck, a fraction of a second before the shockwave hit.

What in the bloody hell—?!

The rumble subsided quickly enough, but Simon could not see a thing as a superheated wave of hurled dust and debris overcame him.

Coughing up sand and soot, and wincing at a numbing pain now running all along his right arm, he became aware of a second body beside him, even though a thick cloud of smoke enveloped them both.

Johann? Where's Johann?

He tapped his earpiece with numb fingers, but could hear nothing.

Dazed, he struggled to stand, but found his head spinning.

What happened? What went wrong?

He blinked again, still seeing nothing.

He tore away his goggles, and a surreal scene of devastation sprang to life around him. Fire licked at the wreckage of an overturned security van now fifteen meters to his left, blown somehow over him from the other side. The entire façade of the office building beside him—the very same one his team had just evacuated—was now a warped steel grid laced with cracked and shattered windows, half of which glowed from internal fires. He was lying in a street filled with shadows, debris, and smoke, while a secondary office building ahead and to his right burned along its far right side.

All that had spared him from the blast was a black-scorched ferro-concrete barrier lining the side of a parking area, and the man who now assumed a crouching position beside him, his cold, dark eyes taking stock of the colonel's condition.

Kirkpatrick.

"What happened?" Simon shouted.

"The *Firebringer* exploded," Kirkpatrick said, his voice deadly calm.

"Impossible!"

"I assure you, Colonel. Someone must have gotten too close."

"Too close?"

"We have to get to the secondary dust-off site!" Kirkpatrick snapped. "The fires will force the Terries to scatter their people all over. We'll be discovered if we stay too long!"

"No!" Simon yelled, shrugging away Kirkpatrick's hand in the middle of the other man's effort to drag him up. His eyes darted around, looking for his SP-7, suddenly aware the weapon no longer lay in his hand.

Did I black out?

Simon struggled to push himself up on his own, pulling his legs beneath him and shaking off a wave of nausea, assessing a possible concussion from the blast. "What are you saying, Agent?" he breathed out. "What do you mean someone got too close?"

"Damn it, Colonel," Kirkpatrick roared over the sound of a secondary blast, "there's no time to explain—"

Realization struck Simon like another blast wave, even as his vision swam from the heat and concussion of the first. Rage suddenly took over, blocking out all pain and all sound. He scrambled to his feet, fighting back a new surge of nausea, and hurled himself at the agent standing so smugly before him.

"*You—!*"

Kirkpatrick's instincts, honed as sharply as his own, kicked in instantly—unfettered by either shock or concussion. A savage swing of his arm smashed the butt of his SP-7 across the side of Simon's face, followed almost immediately by a hammer blow to the stomach as his knee came up.

Vision turned bloody, Simon doubled over, and he coughed up a mass of half-digested energy bar. He stumbled back a step but did not fall.

"You sabotaged our ship?" he heard himself say. "Our men were on board!"

"I *told* you we should have gotten Johann out of there!" Kirkpatrick yelled back. "The charges were set to explode only if someone without authorization managed to penetrate the hull. Some Terrie guard or SAR trooper must have gotten under Johann's radar."

Simon stepped back again, felt the world spinning around him. His vision was blood red and blurred. Three Kirkpatricks stood before him now, black, demonic shadows against a backdrop of smoke and flames. A ticking noise sounded in Simon's ear that he only half heard, Satori—or someone else—requesting his location, a sitrep.

They could wait.

"Gutless terrorist *chupaverga*!" Simon shouted, each word punctuated by a throbbing pain in his temples. He moved drunkenly to the side, watching the shadows of Kirkpatrick follow, getting his bearings, trying to focus again. "Those were *our* people on board! I knew you were afraid of going back, but to do *this*?!"

"It was your idea to use the *Firebringer* as a diversion, Kelswa! It was you who thought taking the same ship in and out again was a smart idea! You can be as noble as you want about it all, but in the end, it's *you* who put our men in danger! *You did this*!"

The three Kirkpatricks were coalescing into one, but Simon was done waiting already. Once more, he lunged at him, this time aiming for the man's gun arm. Five months of training exercises had revealed which one the Corps operative favored. Five months had taught Simon the man's preferred hand-to-hand style. A true animal, Kirkpatrick would try to deliver his most devastating blow short of firing the SP-7.

At least so long as he considered Simon a minimal threat, anyway.

As Kirkpatrick swung his weapon around again, Simon seized his arm, wrenching it back and down. Balance thrown off, Kirkpatrick stumbled a step backward, and the SP-7 fired. Silenced bullets belched out in a strobe of muted yellow-white licks. Sparks flew from where the bullets bounced off the street, but already Simon was swinging a fist up to crack across Kirkpatrick's face.

The SP-7 clattered to the ground.

Stunned, Kirkpatrick stumbled back another step.

"*Schweinehund*!" he snarled. One hand reached for his web belt.

Simon lunged forward and swatted the hand back with a wide kick, intercepting Kirkpatrick's combat knife before the agent could bring it to bear. The blackened blade vanished in the darkness and smoke, clattering distantly on the pavement.

"Murdering bastard!" Simon roared.

His open-handed blow snapped the agent's head around. Stunned for the moment, Kirkpatrick stumbled back a step, one arm instinctively reaching out to find support from the same flame-scorched barrier that originally protected them both from the *Firebringer*'s explosion.

Pressing his advantage, Simon leaped forward, knocking Kirkpatrick back over the barrier. Needles of pain shot through his knees as both men slammed into the pavement, but the agent's body bore the brunt of the fall. All the wind escaped his lungs in a short, barking cough.

Hissing an unintelligible curse, Kirkpatrick whipped his head upward before Simon could draw his back. Simon took the blow on his chin; stars swam across his field of vision, and the coppery taste of blood in his mouth made his wounded tongue recoil. A new wave of nausea followed as a cloud of smoke and fumes washed over them, once more inspiring a rebellion in Simon's stomach.

Kirkpatrick heaved, finally tossing him to one side with a feral growl.

"Damn it, Colonel!" he croaked, coughing as he forced air back into his lungs and rolled away to find his legs again. "Would you rather have had a firefight at the dust-off site? Have the whole mission blown by some Terrie rent-a-cop too nosy for his own good? Are you so soft and stupid that you honestly think you could do what everyone's been trying to do for fifteen *years* and not take a few lives along the way?"

Simon fought the urge to groan as he quickly drew back and forced himself to rise again. The ground was spinning, shaking. His legs felt unsteady, as though he had just stepped away from the shuttle's crash-landing again. He spat out blood and bile, drew in a fresh lungful of contaminated air, and continued to ignore the ticking in his ears.

A new cut just above Kirkpatrick's left temple dribbled a thin line of blood from hairline to his jaw. His breathing was heavy, and he held his right arm close to his side, fingers flexing. He took a cautious step back, matching Simon's moves as they now circled each other.

"This was *my* show! LIC had its chance—"

"This isn't about the Corps, Colonel," Kirkpatrick shot back. "We're out of second chances here! The Archon spelled it out enough for even a self-important, holier-than-thou jarhead like *you* to figure out! Botch this, and the Commonwealth faces a threat on *three* fronts, not just two!"

"The Archon would never have authorized—"

"*Think again,* Arschloch!"

Simon narrowed his eyes, trying to regain focus. The ground kept shaking, but at least there was only one Kirkpatrick now.

"The *Firebringer* was a direct link to the Commonwealth, no matter how well your plan worked out," Kirkpatrick barreled on. "Do you really think the Archon would have wanted you to risk a third front against the Hegemony for the sake of one more diversion and a glorious death? You're good, Colonel, but don't tell me you're *that* naïve!"

The shaking was getting worse, like turbulence in a storm. Simon struggled to stay standing, to reclaim some semblance of control.

"The Archon wanted no bloodshed!"

Kirkpatrick glanced up, angry eyes searching the skies for a moment before returning to his. "If he wanted no bloodshed, would he have given soldiers a job for Intelligence? Would he have sent *me* along for the ride?"

The clicking in Simon's ears returned yet again, and a dull rumble penetrated his awareness at last, punctuating each shake of the earth. There was a rhythm to it all, and a sensation of growing urgency he could not quite place.

"Colonel!" Kirkpatrick snarled. "We're out of time, and we're in a hostile combat zone! You plan to argue about this further, or will you act like a soldier and lead your troops to the secondary dust-off as planned?"

The clicking in Simon's ears finally resolved into codes his brain could understand, echoing in his thoughts alongside Kirkpatrick's challenges.

It was Hauptmann McCabe, requesting a sitrep from all surviving team leaders.

Satori was answering.

Kirkpatrick was MIA.

Simon was MIA.

His men were leaderless; he had ignored them for too long, and they thought he was gone!

And—something else...

The rumble accompanied the last, an ominous metallic thumping that made the message redundant.

A monster was coming.

No, not just *one* monster; the pounding was too quick, like the thunderous rumble of an oncoming stampede of steel-footed cattle.

One was louder than the rest, closer than he ever felt before.

Thuh-whump!

As if in a trance, Simon turned toward the sound, and everything else seemed to vanish around him...

>   *"...I know what you're thinking, Simon. That look in your eyes is the same one I saw in the mirror the first time mother showed me those vids..."*
>
>   *"...Highness, I don't think 'Pandora's Box' quite describes this technology..."*
>
>   *"...You are looking at a BattleMech, the Terran Hegemony's ultimate weapon for the last fifteen years..."*
>
>   *"...Under no circumstances are we to engage a BattleMech in combat, is that it...?"*
>
>   *"...Unless you want to end your career as an ugly red smear, that is..."*
>
>   *"...'Pandora's Box,' the Archon calls this, Johann. But there's another expression that fits it better, one that some ancient Terran scientists first uttered when they tested the atomic bomb for the first time. The kind of thing they must've longed to make reality ever since, or we wouldn't be facing these things now.*
>
>   *"'I am become Death, destroyer of worlds.'*

"That's the phrase. And now, just one of these machines, Johann, can turn any soldier into Death itself, can turn any man into an unstoppable world-killer..."

Thuh-whump! Thuh-whump!

Each footfall of the lead monster shook the earth, raising a cloud of dust from the ground all around him. Larger bits of debris danced to the rhythm. The sound reverberated across the manmade canyon of office buildings, stopping Simon's heart with every world-crushing impact. Over the din, he was dimly aware of someone shouting at him, calling out his name in angry, urgent tones.

But it was too late.

The monsters were upon them.

Thuh-whump!

With one more bone-rattling footfall, the first monstrosity of metal, its desert-mottled hide harshly outlined in orange light, finally rounded the corner. Backlit by licking flames and flickering streetlamps, with its legs and lower torso wreathed in a low-hanging cloud of gray-black smoke, it looked for all the world like a titanic wind devil, emerging from the Inferno itself.

Simon's eyes, dry and stinging, bulged at the sight. Of their own volition, his lungs drew in another gulp of searing Hesperan air through clenched teeth, mindless of the choking taste of scorched metals and ozone.

The monster's shoulders brushed past three-story office buildings and warehouses as casually as a man strolling through a crowded parking lot. Its head, a bulb of metal atop a mountain of armor, presented a round portal of infinite ferroglass blackness for a face, an eye that swept across the grounds as it turned.

That eye of gleaming darkness, seeking prey, froze Simon in place like a Tharkan gazelle in the headlamps of an oncoming hovercruiser.

It sees me!

The titan paused for a moment, lord of all it surveyed. Its boxy torso swiveled slightly, correcting its balance to maneuver within the tight confines of the rubble-strewn street.

Then, with another soul-smashing crash, it began to move again, straight toward the terror-stricken commando standing just fifteen meters away.

One last time, the expressionless voice yelled out to him, even as the great, metal-shod foot—easily the size of a truck and trailing flakes of pulverized concrete—swung forward in slow motion.

The last thing Simon remembered was a dark shape flashing before his eyes before he was sailing through the superheated Hesperan air.

And then, with a thunderous crash as 100 tons of metal slammed into the ground, the blackness took him at last...

MCQUISTON-CLASS CARGO SHUTTLE *PYGMALION*
OUTBOUND TRAJECTORY, HESPERUS II
LYRAN COMMONWEALTH
9 FEBRUARY 2455
0916 HOURS TST

"Welcome back to the land of the living, Colonel."

The low voice, barely audible above the rumble of the shuttle's drives that even now banished the memory of his fitful dreams and nightmares, contained no warmth or camaraderie. Simon did not even have to open his eyes to know to whom it belonged, but the pain resounding within his head—and the cargo harness apparently thrown across him to keep him in place through the launch—forced him to remain still, rather than lunge for the man's throat.

Instead, he simply tried to take in his surroundings.

He was lying inside a shuttle's cargo hold. A dank one, filled with shadows. As per the plan, the men must have stowed themselves aboard one or more of the outbound ships from Hesperus, like hoboes on an interstellar freight train. Though the air was stale, tinged with the scent of metals and exotic lubricants, Simon could not help but notice its chill.

They had left Hesperus II behind.

And looming over him sat the shadow of Agent Brian Kirkpatrick.

"What've you done?" he slurred, closing his eyes again.

"As if you need another explanation," Kirkpatrick's voice tore at him. "I saved your ass from becoming another red stain on a Terrie BattleMech. You're welcome, by the way."

Simon opened his eyes again, tried to spear the Corps operative's silhouette with his glare.

"My men?"

"Yours and Satori's team are safe and sound aboard this lovely rattrap CMC calls a ship, and this little closet is your room, since you've been under the weather. We linked up right after your little episode. Hauptmanns Daschale and McCabe managed to stow away on two other ships."

"*Episode*?" Simon hissed. "You knocked me out and dragged me here! How can I even trust you now?"

"You're alive, aren't you?" Kirkpatrick asked without a shred of sympathy. Simon could feel the man's eyes boring into him now. His hands—which he realized were *not* bound—longed to reach out and seize the agent's throat, but they had no strength.

"I could've killed you at any time, Colonel," Kirkpatrick went on, answering the unspoken question without missing a beat. "Hell, I still can. And back there, I could have simply allowed you to die, and the Terries would have *still* been none the wiser. That *Mackie* pilot probably never even suspected you were there, the way you stood still and waited for him to stomp you into the ground."

The memory flashed before his eyes anew. The thunderous stomping. The whirling clouds of smoke. A titan of metal, its face an unreadable void of nothingness. The looming, final footfall. Kirkpatrick, leaping forward…

"Then, why?" he finally asked.

Kirkpatrick's shadow approximated a shrug. "You were mission leader, even if you didn't act like one when push came to shove. And—contrary to your opinion—I am neither heartless nor a coward."

"You killed four men—"

"You missed the hundreds of Terrie bystanders, Colonel. All necessary. All casualties of war. Don't even pretend that you can't understand that, in your line of work."

His vision adjusted to the dim lighting, Simon suddenly found that he could see Kirkpatrick's intense stare once more. In those eyes, there was no apology. No request for forgiveness. Merely an acknowledgment of a wanton act of murder deemed necessary for operational security.

"I'll see you hang for this—"

Kirkpatrick's short laugh rang loud in the small hold. The harsh sound, so totally alien to Simon's ears, made him twitch, and drove shooting pains into his temples.

"I doubt that very much, Colonel," the LIC operative said coldly. "In fact, I imagine that once this is all over, your dear Archon will sing praises to both of us, for doing our bit for king and country.

"Because, in the end, we both managed to save the realm. You managed to bring back the plans to the worst weapons ever devised, and I managed to survive your plans to make penance for it."

With that, Kirkpatrick finally moved, crawling to his feet, heading for the bay door just beyond Simon's field of vision.

THE TRIAD
THARKAD CITY, THARKAD
LYRAN COMMONWEALTH
26 MARCH 2455

"…I had lost consciousness by then, Highness, but from what I'm told, Agent Kirkpatrick—" the name fairly hissed through Simon's clenched teeth, "—managed to drag me along until Hauptmann Daschale found us. The platoon then hiked the rest of the way to the spaceport, using cover of night to infiltrate the landing pads and stow us away aboard the outbound shuttles."

Archon Alistair Marsden Steiner sat behind a rich, stained-oak desk that would have dwarfed a smaller man. He wore a simple blue-twill jacket of military styling, adorned only with gold braid and a silver chain from which hung a medallion engraved with the defiant fist that served as his family crest, the same defiant fist that only recently replaced the three-stringed lyre of the old days. The uniform made him seem more like a fellow soldier than the ruler of a mercantile alliance.

Only Steiner's eyes—ice-blue and ever inquisitive—betrayed the Nordic ancestry that had made his mother such an icon of beauty and poise. The rest of his features and manner were his father's, including the square set to his iron jaw, and the brutally close cut of his dark auburn hair. Large, strong hands—the hands of an experienced fighter—folded across one another on the dark blue blotter before him. Beneath them lay a sealed folder, simply labeled STRENG GEHEIM—TOP SECRET.

For a moment, the man who ruled an interstellar empire of billions said nothing at all. For his part, Simon felt another shiver crawl along his back, still unused to the frigid temperatures of the Tharkan winter that even seemed to penetrate the controlled environment of the Archon's inner sanctum. The scent of freshly brewed chamomile—a Donegal blend thoughtfully provided by eager palace servants—wafted past, making the colonel's mouth water just slightly.

One of millions of sensations he'd never thought to feel again since Hesperus.

"There is more you want to say, Simon," the Archon finally said.

The words came with no trace of hostility. No accusation. Merely a statement of fact. Simon suddenly realized his gaze had fallen almost to his shoes, like a frightened child expecting his father to scold him for some grievous offense.

Squaring his shoulders anew, he looked up again, once more meeting the eyes of his commander-in-chief.

"The rest is in my report, Highness," he said. "Although he was not officially part of my command, I found Agent Kirkpatrick's conduct reckless at best and treasonous at worst. Four of my—our men died needlessly in that blast, along with over a hundred Hegemony innocents. Were it not for the classified nature of our mission, I would recommend charges be filed and that he stand before an official tribunal."

The Archon nodded sagely, his mouth a grim line. He had read the report, of course; he simply wanted to hear Simon's words in his own voice, the voice of a commander whose mission nearly failed.

"You know, of course, that no such charges will be filed, Colonel?"

Simon blinked. "Highness, with respect—"

Alistair raised his hand. "Simon," he said, "I have the utmost respect for your judgment, but on this I'm not going to budge."

"May I ask why, Highness?"

"You already know, Colonel. You probably knew it, deep down, even when the *Firebringer* exploded. Once you landed in that ship, you knew there was no way you could lift off in it again, not without compromising the illusion, and leaving the Hegemony to believe that the entire affair was the accident the newsvids claim it was. The 'Rim Worlds JumpShip' we parked in orbit to pick you up would not have held up to any scrutiny once it was linked to a Commonwealth shuttle, but it may muddy the waters a little more being there on its lonesome."

"I took a calculated risk, sir."

"Risk is part of the job, Colonel. I won't fault you for that. But the LIC—and in particular, the likes of the Counter-Terror Division—love to contain risk through the harshest means possible."

Simon blinked again, and felt his pulse racing. "Highness, are you telling me you condone—"

Alistair's expression darkened, but he did not rise or raise his voice.

"Don't be foolish," he said coldly. "Of course I don't condone it, but I *understand* it, and I acknowledge that, in the final analysis, it served the Commonwealth better than the original plan. Hegemony search-and-rescue teams would have been far more suspicious if they found an empty shell than the charred remains of Lyran citizens within. For now, the deaths of those men will seal the secret, long enough for our scientists to get to work on the data you retrieved."

Simon shook his head slightly, discovering once more that his gaze had drooped again.

"Simon," Alistair went on, "I know it's no consolation now, but you and I have both been there. We've both done our service for the Commonwealth, and we've both lost good men in the bargain. Yours—like mine—knew the risks going in. They gave their lives for the Commonwealth."

The chill that ran along Simon's spine felt as though it had begun to seep into his very veins as he met the Archon's gaze one more time.

"Highness," he said slowly, "I can understand that, from the Commonwealth's point of view, but Johann, Gilespie, Armheidt, and Schmidtt deserved better."

With a heavy sigh, Alistair nodded.

Drawing a deep breath of his own, Simon closed his eyes for a second. *It's now or never*, he thought. *Best to get it over with.*

"With all due respect, sir," he said at last, "I would like, at this time, to resign my commission and stand down."

Now it was Alistair's turn to blink. "What?"

"The loss of four men—good soldiers, all—notwithstanding, I submit that I panicked under fire, sir. The presence of the Hegemony BattleMechs repeatedly caused me to lose focus at several critical junctures during the mission, even though I should have been prepared—"

Alistair rose at last, coming to his feet at just a centimeter or two shorter than Simon. His arms, no longer anchored to the desk, crossed now in front of him, and his face became a mask of almost paternal disappointment. Simon fought another urge to inspect his shoes again.

"You refer to the shock of seeing the BattleMechs up close, Colonel? Do you really think anyone else would have behaved differently?"

Kirkpatrick did, didn't he? was the reply that first leaped to mind.

"I was the mission commander, Highness. I lost focus."

"Regardless, the mission succeeded. You—together with all of your men—will be handsomely rewarded for the effort—though no ceremonies will be held, as you can well understand. However, I will *not* accept your resignation on top of all that.

"I still need you, Colonel. Indeed, the Commonwealth still needs you."

"Highness, begging your pardon, with those…monsters… you won't need an old warhorse like me."

"Oh? I beg to differ, Simon. You see, regardless of your fears—fears no sane man would not feel with a twelve-meter-tall, hundred-ton machine stomping over him—you are still among the best spec-ops troopers we have in the LCAF, and I say that counting myself in the ranks."

"Highness—"

"I'm not finished, soldier," Alistair said sternly. He had begun to pace now, coming around his desk to stand before his officer. The fatherly quality in his tone, despite their similar ages, still made Simon want to avert his stare, but this time, he maintained his bearing.

"I am talking about finding the weaknesses in these BattleMechs, these monsters as you call them. For that task, I am assigning you, as the man who extracted their design for the Commonwealth. You will be assigned to assist the teams who will use that data. You will get an inside look of the development and construction of these machines, and will learn their strengths and weaknesses inside and out. You will demystify these demons, show us how they can be defeated, and teach us how to make ours better.

"Nothing is truly unstoppable, Colonel. And if anyone can find the weakness in BattleMech technology, I have every confidence that you are that person. Would you really leave this task to the likes of anyone else?"

Simon stared back at the Archon, feeling numb all over. His mouth felt frozen shut, even though he could still feel his heart racing.

"It's time for those nightmares of yours to end, Colonel," Alistair Steiner said after a while, extending a hand toward the colonel. "And it is time for the Commonwealth to command its own destiny again. Will you help us?"

In a dreamlike trance, Simon extended his own hand, felt Alistair seize it in a grip both strong and surprisingly warm.

"Highness," he said finally, "I accept."

NOTHING VENTURED

CHRISTOFFER TROSSEN

NEW AVALON
FEDERATED SUNS
17 OCTOBER 2455

"Highness, we've made great progress in just the last few weeks. This latest acquisition has given us an incredible jump—"

"Where are you with stability and integration?"

Simon Davion cut right to the heart of it. Having grown up within the fratricidal Davion household, and after almost four decades as First Prince, breaking up conspiracies and destroying his every political enemy, spotting a scientist trying to cover up the truth was child's play.

"We...we're still working on that." The man's face grew ashen. "We believe that the combination of Bravo-Three and Lieutenant Terell will allow us to—"

"So you're no closer to a solution than you were a month ago?"

Beads of sweat formed on the scientist's forehead. "No, Highness."

The Prince, from his vantage point in the quiet, climate-controlled conference room overlooking the sprawling work center, surveyed the activity below. Dozens of white-clad figures scurried between tables covered with unidentifiable electronic and mechanical parts, along with what must have been kilometers of polymer rope bundles. He could almost taste the metallic tang of the air below, ozone combined with spilled coolant and hydraulic fluid.

One quarter of the room was devoted to two fusion power plants and half a dozen large-scale weapons—two autocannons and four beam weapons of some sort, the kind you'd see in a tank armory or fighter-maintenance ship. Numerous oddly shaped metal and ceramic armor plates, as well as a massive armored leg easily four meters tall, lined the white EMP-resistant walls.

The center of activity, however, was a vaguely humanoid-looking, bulbous machine in the middle of the hangar-cum-laboratory. Standing twelve meters tall, it dwarfed the engineers climbing all over it. Thick weapons barrels made up its arms, while two laser tubes jutted out from its lower torso—the source of a dozen different off-color nicknames for the beast. A cockpit screen dominated the contraption's head like a massive eye, while a sensor bundle hung off the head's right side like an ear. It was a study in dichotomy; were it painted red and white, one could easily think of it as a Cyclopean death clown.

The Prince motioned to the machine, code-named Bravo-Three. "Do you have any idea how much it cost us to acquire that machine?" The scientist opened his mouth to answer, but just as quickly closed it as Prince Simon Davion continued. "How many lives we wasted just to get that machine and its pilot away from the Hegemony?" The Prince was building to a crescendo, moving around the conference table and toward the scientist as he did so. "How much political capital we spent transporting it all the way here? And how much effort it was to keep the whole operation secret?"

A drop of sweat rolled down the scientist's face. His legs quivered, and he unconsciously wiped the palms of his hands on his lab coat.

The Prince turned back to face the scientist. "And just how much divisiveness it is causing within my High Command?" He moved closer to the scientist. "Half of my advisors are telling me that we should be training soldiers how to pilot this thing and the other half are telling me that we should be conducting live-fire trials on it so we can figure out how to destroy them better. But no, I listened to you, Dr. Carino."

To his credit, Carino stood fast under the verbal assault, though the shake in his legs worsened.

"I listened to your advisory committee, Doctor. And I have nothing to show for it. Less than nothing! I've wasted hundreds of millions and the efforts of both the Ministry of Intelligence and the Foreign Ministry in getting you three of these BattleMechs!"

The Prince moved to the window, turning his attention back to the bustle in the laboratory and giving the scientist a brief respite from his rage. "Tell me, Doctor, why should I give you any more time and funding?"

Simon Davion half-expected the doctor to stammer out an incoherent answer, or not even answer at all. Instead, the Prince watched Carino's reflection in the window wipe his hands on his lab coat again and pull himself up straight.

"Highn…" His voice faltered, caught in his dry throat. He swallowed and tried again. "Highness. You've read our reports and you've heard our briefings. It took the Terran Hegemony *years* to design and integrate all of the *Mackie*'s subsystems. *Decades*. We've had little more than a year since receiving Bravo-One, and that was just pieces salvaged from the battlefield. Bravo-Two at least was mostly intact, but we've still only had that for six months. Reverse-engineering something as complex as this takes time. A lot of time. Perhaps years."

The Prince turned back around and gave Carino his iciest of stares, draining what little color had returned to the scientist's face. "Understand this, Doctor. We're not talking about just any research project, here. We're talking about the survival of the Federated Suns. And time is a commodity in *very short supply*."

Carino stood there, weathering the same fury that had broken generals and heads of state. Shaken but still standing fast, he replied, "Understood, Highness."

Flanked by two security guards, and with his personal aide a pace behind and to his left, Simon Davion marched briskly down the warmly lit corridor. This was his favorite place in the whole palace. The floor was Avalonian granite shot through with fiery veins of yellow and orange, buffed to a high sheen. Columns of pure white marble held up a lofting frescoed ceiling. Within alcoves created by the columns were statues and paintings of the leaders of the great House Davion, and by extension the entire Federated Suns.

Occupying a pie-slice of the Inner Sphere and surrounded by dangers unlike any mankind had ever faced in its millennia of recorded history, the Federated Suns was a nation constantly poised on the brink of war, its Prince forced to balance the weight of the world on his shoulders like Atlas as he juggled the day-to-day problems of his nation.

The Terran Hegemony, situated to the "north" of the FedSuns on most maps and occupying the middle of the Inner Sphere, was currently the greatest threat to the Davion state. Centered on the birthplace of humanity, it was the richest, strongest, and most advanced of the major powers.

Worse still, it alone possessed the most destructive piece of battlefield machinery ever developed—the BattleMech.

Yet that wasn't the worst-case scenario. No, that would be the Draconis Combine, which occupied the pie slice on the "right" of the Federated Suns, and the Capellan Confederation on the "left," both getting their hands on that technology. If that happened, no number of soldiers and tanks and fighters could stop those other nations from gutting the Federated Suns before fighting each for what was left. And the Prince wasn't about to let that happen.

That's why he loved this corridor so much. Yes, he found comfort in the memories of his progenitors. But more importantly, it reminded him of his responsibility. Responsibility to his family, to his nation and to his vassals. The frescoes on the ceiling depicted the history of the Davion family and its Federated Suns, including their victories and their defeats.

Simon Davion still wore the calf-high black boots of a military officer, which he personally polished each evening.

Despite his seventy-seven years of age, he kept a standard quick-time pace. The footfalls of the four pairs of boots, all in step, echoed down the corridor, announcing his arrival to the guards lining the hallway, who crisply snapped to attention as he passed.

Ahead, the prime minister emerged from his own office, falling into step with the group. "How did the meeting with Dr. Carino go?"

That brought the Prince out of the past and back to the present. "Better than I expected. He got the message, though I think he was a little distracted. I thought I sensed a little fear in there."

"It must have been your unique charm."

The Prince responded with a mock look of astonishment. "Why, Duke Garth, what are you trying to say?"

"Well, sir." A wide smile played across the man's face. "You did shoot your cousin, the *President* of the Federated Suns, dead. In front of the entire High Council."

Garth was one of a very few people in the universe Simon Davion could joke with about such serious subjects. "Yes, but in fairness, I did have myself appointed First Prince before getting rid of all of my enemies. Besides, he needed it." The Prince's mirth darkened. "And I think I've got a piece of paper around here somewhere that says I'm 'not guilty.'"

Despite the outwardly light attitude, Duke William Garth knew that, even four decades later, his old friend still felt some guilt over the incidents that had left him the very first Prince of the Federated Suns. He mentally berated himself for bringing it up, especially before this meeting, and quickly changed the subject. "Is Carino's team getting anywhere?"

"It'll take time, yet. They'll be burning the midnight oil for the next few months, if the look on his face is any indication," the Prince said.

"Well, I think I might have some news that will help us along."

Simon Davion's curiosity was piqued as Duke Garth led him to the Security and Intelligence Committee room. The occupants stood as one as the doors opened and the Prince's aide announced his entrance.

The Prince took his seat at the head of the massive conference holotable. Garth sat beside the Prince. He motioned for the ministers, generals, and advisors to take their seats as well. A handful of aides and computer techs took positions behind their own consoles. Displays lined the walls of the darkened room, providing a wealth of information about the Federated Suns and the rest of the Inner Sphere.

A pall of smoke hung over the room. The committee had apparently been there for hours—otherwise the air purifiers would already have removed the mixed smells of pipe and cigar tobacco.

The doors closed behind the Prince, a red light above indicating the room was locked and secured against electronic observation.

The Prince's question was simple. "What do we have?"

Duke Delton Felsner, deputy foreign minister, stood up and moved to the podium at the end of the table. "Highness," he said, "we have independent confirmation from three sources that the Lyran Commonwealth has acquired the technical data necessary to successfully construct their own BattleMechs."

That got the Prince's attention. He instinctively looked at the map of the Inner Sphere. The Lyran Commonwealth occupied a pie-slice directly on the opposite side of the Terran Hegemony from the Federated Suns. The two nations also shared borders with the Draconis Combine, a fact that had long ago made them allies of convenience, if nothing more.

"Our reports from agents within the Commonwealth's government and military industry indicate the Lyrans pulled off a commando assault on the Hegemony's Hesperus II BattleMech production facility," Felsner continued. "They stole the plans for the *Mackie* as well as detailed information on its subsystems, and have returned to Tharkad with them. Reports indicate minor damage to the Hesperus factory."

"Do the Terrans know?" Davion asked.

"We're not sure yet, Highness," continued Felsner, "though they have heightened security along the borders, and especially at facilities involved in producing BattleMech components. They may not know the Lyrans got their hands on the information, but at the very least, they suspect the Lyrans were behind the incident."

"Bureaucracy at its worst. The Hegemony awarded a *Mackie* contract to a factory on a Lyran-controlled world." That was one of the generals.

"To be fair," the Prince responded, "Hesperus is a world jointly held by the Hegemony and Commonwealth. But still, it did take our Steiner friends ten years to break in and steal the jewels."

Prince Davion's tone was less than complimentary, which brought a few chuckles from the group.

"I don't think there's any question," said Duchess Willemina Groth. "If we know they pulled it off, then the Terrans know. And their incompetence cost us more than we can afford!" Her anger was justified. In the wake of the Lyran raid, her Ministry of Intelligence had lost two clandestine ops teams and more than a score of other agents both inside the Terran Hegemony and out.

"Easy, Willemina." Prime Minister Garth wasn't about to let the meeting turn into an anti-Lyran bitch-fest. "The Lyran raid closed some doors for us, but it also closed those same doors for the Combine and the Confederation. Do you really want to think about what would happen if they got their hands on the *Mackie's* plans before we did?"

"So where does that leave us?" The Prince's direct question ended any further digression. "A raid on the Lyrans? Or are you proposing that we play defense to prevent proliferation to anyone else?"

Duke Garth responded. "No, sir. We were thinking about something a little less drastic."

"Such as?"

Garth continued. "It's been a while since we sent a special envoy to the Steiners, and there's a few new economic issues that need to be discussed. Maybe we can kill two birds with one diplomat."

"Do you really think they'll even acknowledge they have the BattleMech, let alone put it on the table?"

"I think if we send the right ambassador, we might be surprised with the results. Especially if we give him the right tools for the job."

Garth's mischievous grin intrigued the Prince, who never ceased to be amazed by his old friend's capacity for cloak and dagger. "I take it you've had a discussion or two about this before I got here?" Greeted by nods and thin smiles from around the table, the Prince could only say, "Tell me about it."

"Lord Felsner will be our chief negotiator. Delton, why don't you tell the Prince about Operation Venture."

Felsner, still at the podium, slid into his presentation, displaying the confidence of someone who had spent his entire life within the royal court, an attribute that belied his true origins.

"Thank you, Duke Garth. Highness, Operation Venture will secure the information and technology the Federated Suns requires to construct its own BattleMechs. It will be executed as follows…"

THARKAD
LYRAN COMMONWEALTH
22 MARCH 2456

Ambassadorial perks were often anything but. As the Federated Suns' ambassador and special envoy to the Lyran Commonwealth—not to mention deputy foreign minister—Lord Delton Felsner occupied spacious quarters on the DropShip *Donovan* in comparison to the other berthing compartments on the ship. He was also assigned two bodyguards and two personal aides to assist him as he prepared for his mission during the five-month journey from New Avalon to Tharkad. Befitting his station, Felsner and his small team were the first allowed to debark the DropShip.

Yet instead of walking down into even a special arrivals waiting area, he and his team left by an emergency exit. They quickly moved down the stairs to the tarmac, the biting Tharkan wind whipping at their jackets and sending a shiver through his entire body. Seeking asylum from the frigid assault, his team darted into a maintenance door that led down another stairwell, this time into the bowels of the spaceport terminal.

Five individuals awaited them in the maintenance corridor at the foot of the stairs, where the study in contrasts couldn't have been greater. Amidst the hothouse labyrinth of leaking pipes that reeked of stale water and lubricants stood this group, all clad in well-tailored suits. Four were, despite their civilian suits, obviously bodyguards. The fifth, wearing a small sun-and-sword pin on his lapel, was too dapper, too rakish to be anything but a political appointee.

The weakling approached Felsner, who stood at the center of a diamond formation of his own travel team. "Ambassador Felsner!" he started, shouting over the rumble of a departing DropShip as he presented his credentials to the aide who stood ahead of Felsner. "Hadrian Voork, deputy protocol officer. Ambassador Deir instructed me to meet you and escort you to the embassy."

Felsner's gaze darted around, surveying the scene as his aide confirmed Voork's identity. His own guards were tensed, ready to pull their weapons and throw themselves in front of their ambassador. Eyes were constantly moving, looking for any sign of danger.

For his part, Voork stood still, betraying neither emotion nor intent as he looked directly at Felsner. He was well trained, at the very least. By whomever he worked for.

The aide turned back toward Felsner and nodded. The credentials were either legitimate, or such good forgeries that they fooled a diplomatic corps intelligence expert. And if a forgery, Felsner and his people would probably be dead no matter what they did. The inherent danger in interstellar diplomacy.

Felsner's aide handed the identification back to Voork, who slid the case into an interior pocket of his suit jacket before continuing. "Gilreth and Nomi here will assist you with your luggage and cargo." He motioned to two of his own guards. "Ambassador, if you'd like to follow me to the vehicles?"

Felsner's other aide followed Gilreth and Nomi back up the stairs, and Felsner motioned for Voork to lead. Voork's two guards took point while Felsner's two trailed the group, which wound its way through a long series of service tunnels before emerging onto an underground loading dock. The humidity of the tunnels at once gave way to the cool, fresh air from outside and the whine of almost a dozen running hovervehicles.

Four hover limousines, six hover sedans, and a hovertruck sat there, adding to the cacophony of the already noisy spaceport. Two dozen more security guards stood post around the area, scanning the empty underground garage for potential threats. But Felsner's eyes were immediately drawn to a group of four individuals with noteputers in hand. Secretaries.

Specifically, to a blond with a conservative hairdo and even more conservative, almost frumpy, and ill-fitting outfit.

What's she doing here?

That wasn't her hair and those clothes certainly weren't *her*. Nor were the eyes; even twenty meters away, he could see the color was wrong. In fact, the whole look—the demure hang of her head, the slumped shoulders, the frizzy bun of dark blonde hair... When she put on an act, she put on an *act*.

Though embroiled in a conversation, she glanced up, locking eyes with him briefly before returning to her discussion.

That sent a brief spasm up his neck as he fought the impulse for a double take. He quickly refocused on the rest of the scene, mentally chiding himself for that lack of control. *She must be here for a reason, and likely deep undercover.*

One thing was certain, though: he wasn't walking into a trap. At least, not one set by Voork.

Voork led the group to one of the hover limousines, waving the secretaries over. "A communiqué to Ambassador Deir requested a schedule and security briefing on the way to the embassy. Miss Dempsey here—" he motioned to *her*,"— can cover that with you. Though if I may, I would rather brief you on some important Lyran matters that have come up in the past few days and will impact your schedule."

If someone had arranged this, she must have something important to say, and chances were it had nothing to do with the schedule. Or protocol. And he wasn't about to wait.

"No, I will take the schedule briefing first."

That surprised Voork. "Are...are you sure, Ambassador? The schedule will most likely change—"

"Voork, I'm not about to argue with you or explain my methods. If the schedule changes, then so be it. And if something has happened that will impact our trade negotiations, I'm sure Ambassador Deir will brief me personally."

This guy is about as clueless as his boss.

His tone of voice gave Voork no wiggle room. Knowing he had no other possible response, the other man bowed slightly. "Of course, Ambassador."

The aide opened the hover limousine door as one of Felsner's bodyguards took the limo's front passenger seat and the other took position in a nearby hover sedan. Felsner motioned the blond woman in first and climbed in after. His aide entered last, closing the door behind them, which deadened the whine of the hover vehicles and the rumble of the spaceport to almost nothing.

Felsner and the woman both took the rear seats while the aide took the forward seat, facing the two of them. "Miss Dempsey" removed an electronic device from her briefcase, but waited for Felsner's nod before activating it and placing it in a cup holder. A white-noise generator, it would ensure that no one would be able to monitor or record their conversation.

Felsner tapped a button, signaling the driver that they were ready to depart. A few moments later, the hover limo rose off the ground and sped away.

He couldn't contain himself any longer. "What the hell are you doing here, Tess? Last I heard you were off in the Hegemony somewhere. You weren't on the embassy personnel list."

Teresa Premit, undercover agent of the Federated Suns Ministry of Intelligence, let a wide smile play across her face. "Good to see you too, *Lord* Felsner."

Her emphasis of the word "lord" made Felsner's aide obviously uncomfortable, but he held his tongue when the Deputy Foreign Minister laughed at her retort.

"Sorry, Tess. It's just been so long, and to see you here of all places." He glanced at his aide, who was looking back and forth between the woman and Lord Felsner, obviously still trying to comprehend what was going on. Though the younger man had been a part of Felsner's staff for several years, he'd never seen anyone speak to the deputy minister that way, much less a mere secretary.

Felsner decided to end any further confusion, at least for the short term. "Tess, this is my senior ambassadorial aide, Meldrach Suisso. Meldrach, this is Miss, uh, *Dempsey*. She's an old colleague." He'd briefly considered telling Suisso her real name, but thought better of it; the less people who knew her true identity, the better. And by using her assumed name, Felsner told the man not to dig, lest he accidentally blow her cover. "She works for the Ministry of Intelligence, though what she's doing here on Tharkad, I'm not quite sure yet."

"I heard you were coming here, and just figured you'd naturally need some backup." Her tone was simultaneously sweet and sarcastic, causing Suisso to squirm just a little more in his seat. Or perhaps it was the hover limo accelerating out of the underground structure.

Tess's tone turned serious. "The embassy had some personnel turnover. Two ops agents were compromised, and shortly thereafter the chief of station accepted a better offer. With the Lyrans."

Felsner nearly exploded with that revelation. "What?! Is the entire embassy compromised?"

"Don't know yet. I've only been here a couple of weeks, but I don't think so. The new chief of station came over from New Earth. You know him, I think. Harlan Vnuck." Felsner nodded. "Director Groth moved him here as soon as she heard, but we're still playing catch-up. We have eight of us in Intel at the embassy, and right now only Vnuck knows who we are. We have some background information on the Lyran negotiators, but nothing we can use against them. And our other intel assets on-world have gone underground for the time being."

Around anyone else, Felsner would have guarded his thoughts and emotions. In the privacy of the hover limo, however, with two trusted associates, he could let his temper rage. "Is Deir running an embassy here or a goddamn circus? Dammit! Why haven't I…" He threw a glass—the first thing he could grab—across the compartment, shattering it on the far bulkhead. "Is there any good news in there?"

Both of the cabin's other passengers remained silent, Suisso carefully plucking bits of shattered glass from his suit jacket. Tess continued a few moments later, once Felsner regained his cool. "It's not quite as bad as it sounds. Ambassador Deir still doesn't know the precise nature of the negotiations you will be conducting, and the details of the operation hadn't reached Tharkad by the time the embassy fell apart. Based on everything we've learned, including from a few strenuous *interrogations*, we still have operational security."

Sitting in silence for a minute, he considered the potential risks and weighed them against what needed to be done. Of course, it wasn't much of a decision—the Prince was depending on him. "Okay, for now we go. How much time do we have to prepare?"

Premit didn't miss a beat. "You have at least two weeks before presenting your credentials to the Archon, and at a minimum another two before negotiations can begin. We've got time to at least develop briefing packets on the principal negotiators."

"Okay, then let's get to it. And Meldrach, remind me when this is all over and done with that it's time for the *good* Ambassador Deir to retire."

**THARKAD
LYRAN COMMONWEALTH
7 MAY 2456**

"Ambassador Bernstorff, on behalf of the Federated Suns, I would again like to express our gratitude to the Lyran Commonwealth for agreeing to these talks, and for generously providing these extraordinary facilities."

Felsner hated this part of the negotiations the most. Nevertheless, it was part of the job. "I hope that our progress thus far will lead to a mutually beneficial treaty that will not only further our two great nations, but also prove to the entire Inner Sphere that there can truly be peace and friendship between two Great Houses."

The real negotiations were where a true master of speech and debate could shine. But this…this was nothing but verbal excrement. A self-congratulatory exercise where the winner was the one who'd made himself out to be better than his counterpart on the other side of the table without making it actually sound like he'd done so.

It was the Lyran ambassador's turn to prattle on, but Felsner wasn't listening. He was going over the strategy for the day's negotiations, something he'd—unfortunately—have plenty of time to do.

These platitudes would go on for fifteen minutes at least, followed by a recap of negotiations to date—likely to take another half-hour. They'd break for light refreshments, then conduct an hour of actual negotiations before they took lunch (all two-and-a-half hours of it—if they were lucky!). Afterward, they might get in one more hour of negotiations before a half hour summary and the closing "ceremonies," where the two ambassadors would once more pat each other as well as themselves on the back.

It wouldn't be so bad if this hadn't been the *fourth* time they'd met for discussions, twice the week before and twice this week, including today. By the end of the day, they probably wouldn't have even clocked a total of eight hours of actual negotiating.

Worst of all, he'd had to actually negotiate with the Lyrans to get two days per week instead of one.

Felsner laughed to himself. *And people wonder why nothing ever gets done in government!*

Well, it could have been worse. He was in the palace of the Lyran Archon, sitting on centuries-old furniture in a room decorated with murals depicting the history of Archon Alistair Steiner's ruling family. He had eaten the best fare the decadent Steiners could prepare served on fine china rumored to have once served Terran leaders in the twentieth century. He could have been eating bugs in a cold, wet ditch with a rucksack and rifle on his back instead...

Lyran Ambassador Karl Bernstorff had prattled on for several minutes—long enough that Felsner needed to wet his throat with a few sips of water—and was only now showing any signs of ending. *He really does like the sound of his own voice.* Once done, he and Felsner both leaned across the table for a handshake and a look to the holo-photographers who'd already taken dozens of similar pictures in the past three meetings.

A person's handshake can reveal a great deal about him. In the case of the Lyran ambassador, Felsner had guessed quite a bit long before their first handshake, which only confirmed his suppositions.

Bernstorff's well-manicured fingers were long and supple, and his skin was smooth and soft, with just the hint of calluses. He'd obviously never done a hard day's work in his life, though he probably played some sport like golf, tennis, or koba. He'd squeezed a little harder than was comfortable for him, probably in an attempt to seem stronger than he really was. Only today, his handshake wasn't quite that hardy.

Out late last night, hmm?

The slight redness in Bernstorff's eyes confirmed that observation. As did the daily intel briefing he'd gotten an hour earlier. Good. A tired negotiator, especially one that had a tendency to drink a little too much at lunch, was a sloppy negotiator.

The two ambassadors, along with their negotiation teams, sat down, but they were far from ready to begin talking. Fine. That would give Felsner the time to appraise the opposition before brass tacks time.

First, the senior deputies offered their own self-congratulatory platitudes. Then came the forty-three minutes of recap: after three meetings, the two sides had agreed to a continuation of their free-trade policies, had agreed in principle to a free exchange of certain technologies (even though both sides already had access to those very technologies, it would at least open up the potential for more critical tech concessions later on in the negotiation process), and had agreed that their two nations were close allies with a long history of friendly relations. It took a whole day to come to the final agreement, one that meant absolutely nothing.

The summary was followed by another thirty-eight minutes of diplomatic small talk over coffee and pastries in the adjoining antechamber. Felsner and his Lyran counterpart both sat in facing overstuffed chairs that smelled of cigar smoke, politely talking about nothing while their respective staffs worked the room. The cacophony was almost melodic as it echoed in the high-ceilinged chamber.

"Fascinating, isn't it?" Ambassador Bernstorff's question came out of the blue.

Felsner was momentarily confused. His own conversation had taken a sharp turn from something about the coat of arms and crossed swords on the wall next to them to…this. He wondered for an instant if he'd missed something while he watched the activity around him.

"The interplay. The sycophantic ballet. They think they're so important." If Felsner hadn't known otherwise, he would have thought the Lyran ambassador was drunk. But he was stone cold sober. "You and I, we know the truth. The conclusion is not in question. We know how this will all end. And the process is nothing but a prolonged ceremony. It isn't even the game it used to be."

Felsner looked at his counterpart curiously. He'd never expected such honesty from the man. Bernstorff was a career diplomat with a taste for hedonism, as his file indicated, probably bored with his professional life. But here…either he was being absolutely honest, or he was a far better actor than the Federated Suns ambassador had thought.

In any case, Felsner was willing to play along. "Interesting thought. But not entirely true."

"Oh, yes, we'll surprise each other a couple of times in the coming weeks, and we'll come to an agreement on a few things that will make our lives slightly better. They may think otherwise, but we know that we will never really change anything. Pity."

Now *that* was interesting. It almost sounded like…*regret? Maybe it's time to ratchet this up a notch?* Felsner replied in the most noncommittal manner he could. "Well, far be it from us to stand in the way of tradition. Shall we continue this inside?"

The rest of the day proved equally enlightening and even a bit productive. By the beginning of the afternoon session, Felsner was sure that his impression of Bernstorff was accurate. So he made his first attempt at the prize. Besides, he was deathly tired of talking about agriculture.

"So, in the spirit of cooperation and friendship we have built today, perhaps we might change topics slightly?"

That got a reaction from the Lyran negotiation team. The deputies and assistants had studied their agriculture and agro-tech briefings and still wanted to show off their knowledge. On the other hand, Bernstorff, who'd been having trouble concealing his boredom especially after what must have been a six-drink lunch, perked up immediately.

"We would be pleased to redirect the discussions to any topic our close friends from the Federated Suns would like." A few in Bernstorff's negotiation team looked as if they were about to say something to their ambassador, but swallowed their words. They knew their place.

"I cannot help but think that, after talking so much about the exchange of information relating to agriculture, perhaps we can talk about a broader topic." He had to be careful, here. Touch on the important subject, just to get it out there. "Our two nations have long been the closest of allies. We share a love for personal freedom, and our peoples consequently enjoy a prosperity greater than any other."

He was carting out the greatest hits and getting just the response he expected. Some of the Lyran negotiation team members smiled or nodded while most guarded their responses, unsure where the Federated Suns ambassador was going.

"At the same time, we share common enemies in the form of the Terran Hegemony and the Draconis Combine, the two greatest threats to peace and prosperity in the Inner Sphere."

That prompted a response from the Lyran side of the table. Bernstorff's military advisor hung on Felsner's every word while the rest of the Lyran team scrambled to pull up the appropriate information on their noteputers.

"Perhaps, then, we can share the information and technologies that will not only help us feed and clothe our people, but also help us both to contain these opponents, and ensure our continued prosperity and advancement?"

That was a mouthful! But Bernstorff now sat up straight and leaned a bit forward in his chair. *He might just take the bait.* The other man's military advisor, on the other hand, was tensing up. Felsner noted a bit of a flush in his cheeks, an ever-so-slight twitch in his right eye. *He sees where I'm going with this.*

"What I'm talking about is the free exchange of information. Troop deployments, force assessments, leadership profiles, and the like. Or, if we'd like to be so bold, even information regarding the identity and location of known foreign operatives.

"But that's not all I'm talking about. I'm also talking about the exchange of technologies that we will need to contain our opponents. Who knows? Perhaps we could even work together to jointly better our military capabilities."

The hook was baited. *Now all you need to do is nibble.*

The surprise on Bernstorff's face shone bright. With luck, he was just as excited by the prospects of where such exchanges might lead. Or at least with the possibility to play the diplomatic game he seemingly loved so much.

"Ambassador Felsner, what you propose is bold. Certainly more audacious than many of us expected." Several on Bernstorff's team were visibly agitated. "But it is intriguing. And absolutely worthy of discussion."

Stop playing hard to get. Take the bait, dammit! At least the Lyran ambassador was holding the door open, even if his own staff looked ready to stand up from the table and rush out.

"I am pleased that you see the value in these discussions." The only problem with diplomacy was you could never get right to the point. But as frustrating as the process was and as much as he often hated it, Felsner not only accepted it, he excelled at it. "The sharing of intelligence information has long been a delicate matter, as it would be for any government. But I think we can overcome centuries of obstinacy—" *there was a good word,* "—and learn to share what we know. It will certainly take some time and discussion, but as a show of good faith, by our next meeting I can present you with a sample of what we can provide."

Didn't take the first bite? Well, just have to cast again.

That definitely piqued the Lyran ambassador's interest. And surprised the hell out of the Lyran delegation. "My dear friend, what you propose is as unanticipated and extraordinary as it is audacious. And it surely will set the tone for those negotiations."

He's getting close...

"And in that same spirit, in an effort to aid our own soldiers and citizens in understanding who our closest allies are, perhaps we can also discuss joint military training, or even the joint development of weapon systems?"

Come on, it's dangling here for you....

Most of the Lyran delegation was sitting silently, either dumbfounded or frantically glancing through talking points on their noteputers. Except for Bernstorff. And his military advisor. The Lyran's military advisor saw exactly what Felsner was up to. Fortunately he was sitting two chairs away from his own ambassador (they weren't scheduled to talk specifically about military topics for weeks yet!), and wasn't in position to immediately get his ambassador's attention, at least not without breaking protocol.

Bernstorff was interested and engaged. He was obviously willing to go along for the ride. This must have been the most diplomatic excitement he'd had in decades. "Ambassador Felsner, I would be pleased to discuss any such military matters with you."

Here it comes!

"Then perhaps we can even be so bold as to discuss a technological alliance that can only benefit our two great nations while at the same time preventing the Terrans from gaining hegemony over the entire Inner Sphere."

"You pick a most delicate subject, as I'm sure you know well…" The Lyran was stalling, looking for the right words. Perhaps he just needed a nudge.

"I do. But these are trying times, and perhaps bluntness is what the process needs." Felsner was talking serious and straightforward. "I believe our two nations' recent successes can benefit us both."

"We certainly have heard rumors."

"As have we." Felsner needed to keep him talking.

"These rumors."

"Your Archon's plan was bold and audacious! As I hope our agreements here can be."

Bernstorff nodded. "Our acquisition of the BattleMech will herald…"

Gotcha!

"That is…"

The Lyran ambassador realized he shouldn't have said that, as did his military advisor who quickly jumped in. "Of course, any ongoing research efforts we might have related to those technologies would be strictly classified and certainly out of our direct knowledge." He looked at Bernstorff. "Ambassador, perhaps any further discussions on these subjects should be continued after consulting with the appropriate offices?"

Spin it however you want. It's on the table. That's all I need right now.

"Yes, yes, of course." The Lyran ambassador was a little deflated, but quickly recovered. "You obviously have an ambitious platform in mind. I believe this would be an opportune time to take a break from negotiations so that we can revisit the schedule."

Felsner smiled. "That would be just fine."

**THARKAD
LYRAN COMMONWEALTH
3 JULY 2456**

"Let me get something straight."

Lord Delton Felsner sat across the table from Teresa Premit, cheerfully answering the many questions she had about the entire diplomatic process. As a covert agent, the nature of diplomacy and negotiation had to be anathema to her.

"The goal of these negotiations is to secure the—" She stopped herself abruptly. While they were in a private room and had a white-noise generator operating, they were nevertheless in a public restaurant, one frequented by many high-ranking Lyran bureaucrats and government officials. In fact, a Lyran minister was there dining with his family and their dozen bodyguards. "To come to an agreement on this one topic."

"Yes." Felsner smiled as he took another bite of his schnitzel. Moist and tender, battered and perfectly pan-fried in butter, it was the best he'd had in a *long* time. The aromas of meat and savory spices emanating from the entire restaurant had made his stomach rumble in anticipation.

"Then why the hell aren't you talking about it?" Tess seemed hopelessly confused. Or, more appropriately, hopelessly frustrated. She undoubtedly understood the principles of diplomacy—in some respects, it closely resembled the process of interrogation. It was probably the execution that made no sense to her.

Meldrach Suisso held in a laugh. He was sitting at table with the two, along with Dana Nikitos, Diplomatic Corps Security agent, having a casual dinner. To anyone who saw them enter the restaurant, the foursome, along with the quartet of obvious bodyguards that stood sentry in front of the private dining room, appeared to be celebrating some minor diplomatic accomplishment.

In actuality, Felsner needed to get away from the embassy and the sycophants who inhabited it. And, well, he loved a good schnitzel.

The ambassador raised his flagon of beer. "That's just not how it's done," he said before tipping it back for a swig of the heady and somewhat bitter dark liquid.

"Okay!" Tess dropped her fork onto her plate in frustration. "I'm not unintelligent. I have a degree in criminal justice. I made it through the academy. I was an honor candidate at field-training school. Do you know how many fail that course? Eighty-six percent of the applicants! That's almost nine hundred per class. And it's not like any slouches make it that far."

Felsner wore a wide grin. "What are you trying to say, Tess?"

"It doesn't make any goddamned sense!" She nearly screamed it.

"Yes."

"And you *like* this shit?"

"It's not as bad as it sounds. The benefits are good, and I don't get shot at on a regular basis."

Tess popped a piece of roast pork into her mouth and chewed it in silence before answering. "You're crazy."

"Yes."

That brought a smile even to Agent Nikitos's face. Meldrach, who had lightened up considerably since first meeting Tess more than three months earlier, shook his head and laughed.

Felsner wasn't the typical ambassador.

He took another bite of his schnitzel and washed it down with a gulp from the flagon of weiss beer in front of him. "Well, if you're going to have any future as an ambassadorial scheduling secretary, then perhaps we need to give you a lesson in interstellar diplomacy."

Tess choked back what would certainly have been a rude comment. Instead she batted her eyes and said sweetly, "Please, Mr. Ambassador, give me the benefit of your very many years of experience."

"Okay, but I'm going to finish my food before it gets cold. Mr. Suisso, why don't you start?"

Meldrach placed a steaming forkful of stew into his mouth.

"I suppose we should start with the basics," he said after swallowing the spicy mixture of potato and venison. He kept the fork in his hand, using it like a teacher wielding a pointer. "What are we trying to do? We want to get the other side to agree to give us what we want while giving them as little as possible."

She nodded. "Okay."

"Now they want the same thing. They want to get more than they give. So that's where the negotiations come in. Probably the best way to think of it is as a card game."

"Only in this card game," the ambassador interjected, "everyone has a few aces up their sleeves, and no one really has as much money as they have chips in front of them."

Tess paused for a second. "So basically, it's all about bluffing."

Suisso answered, "Mostly. The ante starts out small, but gets bigger and bigger the further we get in the negotiations."

She shook her head. "Okay, I get that you gotta beat around the bush on the little stuff. But what was the deal with…" She stopped herself short again. "With getting them to admit to having *it*?"

"And now the master's course." Felsner, having just finished the spätzle in the dish beside his plate, took another swig of beer before continuing the lesson. The buttery aftertaste of the noodles reacted with the beer in a way he'd long ago learned to love. "This is where it gets interesting."

"Somehow I doubt it," she said under her breath. The dig must have been too much to resist. "Sorry. Go on."

The ambassador didn't miss a beat. "Okay, so before we get to the table, both sides have to agree on each day's agenda: what the guys in the room have to talk about. But sometimes the talking leads to strange and unexpected places. And when it goes there, you have to play it by ear."

"You're still nowhere near a point, are you?" She looked frustrated again.

"Patience, Miss Dempsey, patience." Felsner had given up his condescending tone, and was actually trying to impart some wisdom now. "I know they taught you that back at the academy. Just bear with me."

"Okay. I'm sitting here, silent, awaiting a point to be reached."

Tess could be simultaneously charming and sarcastic, but as impatient as she might act, Felsner knew she was also a professional. Her eyes were always on the move, reacting to the sound of someone walking past the door to their dining room or to a tray of glasses being dropped off in the kitchen. Just like the five other security agents in the room.

And, for that matter, himself as well.

"We'll just pretend that was an apology and move on." Felsner, upending the flagon, finished his beer and continued. "What you have to understand is that negotiations can't stray from the topics on the agenda *unless* both sides agree to it. Then we're only limited by ourselves."

"You know, this is really making my head hurt. So what was the point of tricking him into saying what he said? I mean, if he doesn't want it to come up, then it can't come up, right?"

"Ahh, but that's the thing. He screwed up. *He* let it slip that they had something they didn't want anyone else to know about. And now it's out there. It's on the table."

"So you can talk about it because he slipped up?"

"Correct!" Felsner beamed like a proud father. "So now the Lyran leadership will start discussing the pros and cons of giving that to us. Which will get them into the right frame of mind when we *convince* their ambassador to agree to it." He paused for a second to give more weight to what he would say next. "And that's where the Ministry of Intelligence comes in."

"Well, we'll see what we can—"

She broke off as Agent Nikitos sat up stiffly, whispering excitedly into the microphone concealed in her cuff that kept her in touch with the outside security detail.

Something was wrong.

Meldrach noticed it last, but not by much. Felsner had trained him how to intuitively read body language, after all. He grasped at the sudden tension, looking for the threat.

Dana Nikitos leapt up, grabbing Felsner by the arm. "Bomb! We've got to move!"

She pushed him ahead of her as they bolted toward the private room's rear exit. Tess likewise grabbed Suisso by the scruff of the neck and bolted for the door. The four other bodyguards closed in around their ambassador and, guns drawn, burst through the door to the kitchen.

Throwing cooks and busboys out of the way, they made their way at top speed through the kitchen's heat to the restaurant's service entrance. Looking back, Felsner saw that

Tess and Meldrach followed close behind. Though she didn't have a weapon exposed, Felsner knew Tess had her free hand on one, ready to pull it and kill whoever stood in their path.

Another guard, this one a Lyran, stood post inside the back door. He freed his weapon at the sounds of the approaching commotion, leveling it at the oncoming wall of bodies. Nikitos screamed "*Bomb*!" at the man, whose eyes went wide.

It took him a fraction of a second to process what he was seeing and what he'd heard. He sprinted past the group, heading forward toward the dining rooms, likewise yelling "Bomb!" into his sleeve.

The group burst into the alleyway as the sounds of panic erupted in the restaurant behind them. Felsner yelled at the top of his lungs, "Vehicles!"

Nikitos shook his head. "Too far away! We gotta find cover now!"

They were running down the alleyway when the shockwave from the blast picked all eight of them up and slammed them into the ground.

UNKNOWN LOCATION AND DATE

"Ambassador! Sir, can you tell me your name?"

He barely heard the words through the ringing in his ears. He opened his eyes, but saw only a blur. A dark blur.

He was scarcely aware of the motion around him. The cacophony of alarms and panicked voices. The smell of smoke. But his head hurt. It was like his skull had been split in two by an axe.

He couldn't move. Anything.

He tried to speak, but no recognizable words came out. And he tasted blood on his tongue. Then the dark blur turned just dark. He knew he needed to stay awake...but maybe after a short nap...

"He's crashing!"

He was moving. Only he wasn't the one doing the moving. It was a rhythmic movement, like he was swaying in a hammock. He loved lying in his hammock, letting the warm sun play over him while the children ran around the yard, screaming and having a jolly old time. But he gave that life up, didn't he? Twice, in fact.

Maybe he'd finally come to his senses. He had been getting sick of the tedium of government service, and now perhaps he could be the grandfather that he'd always wanted to be but for some reason wasn't already.

...*Something*...

He wasn't swaying side to side. It was more like he was floating on air. And he felt so warm. So content. He was among others—he could hear them talking off in the distance. And there were electronic sounds.

Floating in the pool on an air mattress. Yes. That was it. And the grandchildren were playing their games around the pool.

...*something wrong*...

He was thirsty. His mouth was dry. His throat scratched when he tried to swallow. He reached over for the cold drink—the one that had to be there. But he couldn't move.

What's going on?

It was also dark. Oh, but that's because his eyes were closed. He opened his eyes. This time he saw nothing but a bright white blur. The sun was really bright today, and he wondered why he wasn't wearing sunglasses. He closed his eyes again to float back off to another peaceful nap.

The sounds of the children's games increased in tempo, as did their banter. That was comforting as he slid once again off into the warm embrace of sleep.

He sensed someone. Or something. A presence. Comforting, in some way. There was no danger, no worries here. He was safe and secure, warm and comfortable, wanting for nothing. His sleep was over, so now it was time to open his eyes and get on with the day.

It was bright, brighter than any place he'd seen. Pure white. It took him a few moments to adjust to the light, but everything was a bit fuzzy. Just out of focus. Not that there was much to see. All white. Normally, that would have caused him no end of consternation; after all, he was a man of action, someone who wasn't satisfied until he had control of everything around him. But not here and now. He was happy, and he had that presence to keep him safe. He knew he was in capable hands.

Then she came into view. The most beautiful thing he'd ever seen. No matter he couldn't quite focus on her. Dressed head to toe in resplendent white, except for her hair, which fell from her head in long locks of heavenly gold. This must be her: his guardian angel. He hadn't thought about such things for...for a long, long time.

He didn't consider himself a religious man; he hadn't prayed for many years and only attended church services when politically expedient. In fact, he and his God had what he considered a falling out after his wife and children were killed in a freak accident. But somewhere deep down, he still held on to something of his beliefs. He must have, for there she was, his guardian angel. Proof positive of the Almighty.

But he was suddenly frightened. If he was seeing her now then...then something had happened. Something terrible. He tried to think back, to recall that awful thing that caused his...

He barely managed to croak out a question. "Where am I?"

The pure white form took his hand. Her touch soothed his fears. "Someplace safe." The sound of her voice was like that of an angelic choir.

"Wha...what happens now?" Never once in his adult life had he been in an unknown situation. He always had at least an idea of where he was going. But not here. And though her touch comforted his fears, he was nevertheless curious about what lay ahead.

She placed her hand on his forehead and moved it down over his face, closing his eyes. "Rest now. You will have all the answers you need soon enough."

As he faded away, she leaned in close and whispered, "Don't worry. I will be here with you."

Once more, he allowed himself to fall into the blackness of sleep.

"Ambassador? Ambassador Felsner?"

This time, instead of warmth and comfort, he felt spears of pain shooting up and down his body. And instead of the melodic tones of a heavenly figure, the words were the nasal tones of a man he despised.

He opened one eye tentatively, closing it quickly against the bright glare. He squinted, blinking a few times to get used to the light. That only brought spears of pain to his head. The pain subsided after a few moments, and he opened his eyes to see a number of figures surrounding his bed.

I must be in Hell.

"Ambassador, we couldn't be happier that you are better!" The nasal voice again, belonging to Ignatius Deir, the Federated Suns ambassador to the Lyran Commonwealth.

Felsner groaned, which, while more than he really wanted to say to the man, he hoped would prompt Deir to leave and take all these other people with him.

Deir didn't take the hint. "We were quite worried about you. But I just knew you would pull through. After all, it takes more than a mere bomb to put down an envoy from the Prince."

A bomb! Yes! Still groggy, his faculties were beginning to come back to him. His entire body hurt and...his brain tingled. As did every other part of him. He just hadn't sensed it immediately behind the pain. Some sort of medication. That would limit him.

Then again, so would the pain.

The group assembled around his bed stood silently. Some shifted uncomfortably. Others stood firm. Felsner recognized a number of faces, but wasn't yet sure from where. A couple of figures in lab coats—those must be doctors and nurses. He noticed the multitude of humming and beeping electronic devices surrounding him, including one that let out a loud and annoying *BING!* every few seconds. A hospital room.

But most of the people in the room wore tailored business suits of some sort. Expensive. And there were a few different styles. Some very New Avalonish and a couple very Lyran in cut. And a few very plain, with strange bulges in odd places on hips or under arms.

Bodyguards.

Ambassador Deir was uncomfortable with the silence. In the long moments that Felsner lay there, still getting his bearings, Deir twice opened his mouth as if to say something, but quickly closed it again. Felsner wondered if it was because the man couldn't think of anything appropriate to say, or because he realized there wasn't anything appropriate to say.

"How are you feeling?" Stupid question. Definitely the first reason.

"Wa...thir...thirsty." That was all Felsner could say, and even then he barely whispered it.

A nurse leaned over and placed a straw in his mouth. He took a couple of tentative sips before taking a longer draft. It wasn't water, but it was cool and seemed to hit the spot. He couldn't quite place the flavor. Likely some sort of electrolyte drink. It reminded him of something he liked back in his younger days.

The first gulp went down hard, his raw esophagus stinging from the liquid. But the next few were easier, and he felt his throat soften. Much better.

"Thank you," he said to the nurse. His voice was recovering, though he still didn't have much strength behind it. "Can I sit up?"

The nurse put a small control in his hand and pushed one of the buttons with his thumb. That raised the head of the bed so he could see the whole room. He thanked her again before turning back to the assembled group.

"What happened?" He really wanted to know. He didn't remember.

Ambassador Deir stepped forward beside his bed. The man probably thought a familiar face would comfort Felsner. "The restaurant you were eating at was bombed. Your security detail saw a known Kuritan operative leave a suspicious package behind and got you out in time, but you all were still very close when the bomb went off, and it was a very powerful explosion. You were hit by falling debris. You've been unconscious for eleven days. The doctors say it was touch and go for a while there, but you should recover fully. Your doctor was particularly impressed with your strong constitution."

Just shut up and give me the facts! Felsner didn't think much of his ambassador to the Lyran Commonwealth. Deir was weak and prissy, which was probably why the Lyrans liked him so much. And had a voice that made you want to rip his throat out.

"What about the others?"

Deir looked down at that question. That wasn't good. "The bomb and the resulting collapse of the structure killed ninety-seven, including the Lyran Minister of Education."

A few of the individuals in the room reflexively looked downward. All were wearing suits of a Lyran cut.

"But...that's not all. Mr. Suisso died at the scene. He lost a lot of blood."

Felsner's gut dropped.

"And Miss Dempsey succumbed to her wounds as well. Apparently Mr. Suisso was trying to protect her from the falling debris, but...I'm sorry. I know Suisso was a close associate of yours."

The universe fell out beneath him. *Tess? Dead?*

"This tragedy has struck us both, and shall not soon be forgotten or forgiven."

That was a new voice. Stronger, more guttural than Deir's. Felsner looked up at the figure that moved forward. He'd looked familiar, but it was the voice that placed the man as Ambassador Karl Bernstorff.

"Thanks to information provided by your embassy security detail, we were able to find not only the perpetrator of this tragedy, but also those who aided him in this terrorist attack."

Felsner looked up at the man, whose words he'd barely heard. Still trying to come to terms with Tess's death. She was untouchable, unflappable, and absolutely unkillable. She'd served in the Ministry of Intelligence for more than a decade, traveled to dozens of worlds, and survived covert wars that had killed those supposedly better and brighter. And to die because of a damn terrorist bomb?

"Those Kuritan scum will pay for their crimes with their lives," Bernstorff went on. "Their ambassador has, of course, denounced the bombing as the act of isolated degenerates, but that won't save them. We've also used the information you've graciously provided us to round up more than a hundred foreign operatives here on Tharkad. We will not allow them to poison our friendship. That I guarantee."

Felsner tried to push his feelings out of the way, but couldn't manage it. He found himself losing control, something he could not afford to have happen in front of any of *these* people.

"Thank you. I need some time..." He was barely spitting the words out as he choked down his own emotions. He temporarily got hold of himself, though. Enough to say, "Could you excuse me? The painkillers are wearing off, and I...I just need some time to absorb all of this."

Bernstorff nodded his head. "Of course. And we can postpone our negotiations for however long you need to recover."

With that, the majority of the group turned to leave. Deir hovered at Felsner's bedside as if he had something else to say, but the nurse shooed him out of the room. "My patient needs his rest. I'll let you know when you can come back in."

Deir tried to stay, but the rest of the medical staff escorted him out, closing the door behind them. That left Felsner alone with his nurse.

Her patient was still trying to hold back his emotions, though, and didn't want *anyone* in the room. "Listen, the painkillers are just fine. Just go away, please."

"Well, I know when I'm not wanted."

Huh? Felsner looked at the woman, who pulled a white-noise generator out of the pocket of her lab coat and activated it. That's when he first looked up at her, right into the face of his guardian angel.

"Hey, babe."

"Tess?"

**THARKAD
LYRAN COMMONWEALTH
22 AUGUST 2456**

Almost seven weeks since the restaurant bombing, and Felsner still struggled to catch up. He'd lost a month of time recuperating; the pain, and especially the pain medications, had prevented him from getting much headway.

That his hospital room was actually in the Federated Suns embassy hadn't helped. In fact, the frequent visits from Ambassador Deir and his staff frustrated Felsner more than being bedridden.

Once his doctors released him, he jumped right back into the diplomatic process. He hoped to use the Lyrans' denunciation of the terrorist attack and their willingness to support joint operations against the Kuritans to get them to agree to share BattleMech technology with the Federated Suns.

Unfortunately, while Ambassador Bernstorff was more than willing to give Felsner a number of concessions, he was steadfast in his unwillingness to give even a centimeter in discussions for the BattleMech.

All I need is some damn leverage!

Then again, the Lyrans did expel the entire Kurita diplomatic contingent from their homeworld, and had imprisoned several dozen known and suspected Combine operatives.

Leave it to the Kuritans to screw themselves. Then again, if one of my guys hadn't seen the bomber by sheer coincidence, I'd be done with.

Apparently the nature of his negotiations had gotten out to the Federated Suns' enemies. Felsner had known his job would be painfully difficult. He just hadn't expected that to be so literally the truth.

It was the day after the fourth session since Felsner returned to the negotiation table, and he met with his negotiation team within his own embassy. With the death of Meldrach Suisso, they were short by one valuable member.

"We're behind schedule and running out of time. Tell me we have something."

Negotiations ended next month. He could get an extension from the Lyrans without much difficulty, but he and his team had been on Tharkad for almost five months and they were still nowhere close to an agreement.

And neither were they any closer to having enough dirt on anyone in the Lyran government to actually tip matters in their favor.

That was what frustrated him the most. He'd come to Tharkad behind an intelligence team that had been tasked to either find something they could use or to manufacture something. That team had arrived to an embassy embroiled in chaos and a broken intelligence network.

"We think we do," said Rendar Urani, Felsner's domestic advisor and protocol officer. The stress in his voice was palpable. In the wake of Suisso's death, he was buried under additional workload, even with the addition of a knowledgeable and competent intelligence and military advisor to the team.

That was the other problem. Tess was a field agent and a damn good one, not a bureaucrat. But that didn't stop the Federated Suns' Deputy Foreign Minister from appointing her to his negotiation and advisory team.

Of course, they had to come up with a new identity for her. She had survived the bomb blast with a concussion and a few bruised ribs, along with a couple of hairline fractures. She was lucky. Meldrach had indeed protected her with his own body and paid the price for it.

She'd remained conscious long enough at the scene to see that Felsner was still alive and that his three surviving bodyguards had summoned both medical attention as well as additional security assistance. Then she'd passed out. She woke up the next day in a local safe house. Undercover Federated Suns agents had rescued her from the hospital, faking the death of Miss Dempsey lest she let some classified information slip while in a drug-induced haze.

The nurse disguise kept her in proximity to him while he was convalescing. It wouldn't do when it came back to negotiation time, though.

So, unbeknownst to her, Felsner had a new identity created, one she would have strenuously objected to (and had almost constantly since assuming that role). As Leftenant Colonel Angela Conrad, she was rushed from a station within the Federated Suns' Terran March to Tharkad. Or at least that's what her orders said, as confirmed by her diplomatic passport.

In fact, Felsner was having a little fun with her, payback for all the shit she'd given him over the years. While she could finally give up the oversized clothes, mussed-up hair, and slouch of Miss Dempsey, now she had to cut her hair short and dye it bright red—a style that was all the rage within the Terran March.

Tess sat silently at the table with the rest of the negotiation team. It wasn't as if she was uncomfortable with the people at the table. In fact, several of them had come from the Ministry of Intelligence.

No, she felt like she was in over her head, and the setting didn't inspire confidence. Within their own embassy's private dining room, the group sat at a long table surrounded by finely woven tapestries and huge paintings depicting the various leaders of the Federated Suns and their exploits. In each corner of the room were busts of the greatest leaders—Robert Davion, Lucien Davion, Reynard Davion, and of course, the current First Prince, Simon Davion—watching over the proceedings as if to nod their approval or frown in displeasure.

The room was designed to put foreign visitors at a disadvantage, but it worked its magic almost as well upon natives of the Federated Suns, too.

"Okay, so what do we know?" Felsner demanded, his voice resonating in the massive room.

Urani started. "We'll start with the background. Ambassador Karl Erwin Tomas Bernstorff Graf von Eschenberg von Wormstadt von Ludendorf. Personal aide to the Archon on foreign affairs and chairman of the Committee on Defense Appropriations."

"Married, with four children," continued Andrea Suel, one of the intel agents pressed into service for Felsner. "Wife is Elisabeth Ophelia, née Romer, daughter of Graf von Sevren, who is CEO of Sevren Steelworks and has further holdings in more than a dozen major corps. The two have been married for twenty-six years, but she has lived on Eschenberg for the last twelve while he's been here on Tharkad."

"This is information we already know. So what's new?" Felsner's patience was running thin.

Urani took over. "He likes younger men, much like the rest of the men in his social stratum." That in and of itself wasn't unusual. Extramarital affairs on Tharkad were the norm among the Lyran nobility. "According to our files, he's got several on the side. Let's see... Okay, he's currently got three different boyfriends on the side, and a couple of others he's had in the past few years. And it looks like he's also got a girlfriend to boot."

Felsner asked the next logical question. "What do we know about the boyfriends?"

Suel had that information ready and picked up without hesitation. "All three are early to mid-twenties. Two are junior assistants in the Lyran bureaucracy. Both are in casual relationships with several other men at the deputy minister level or higher. Neither is a security risk. Both have been approached by other governments and organizations, but nothing. It looks like they are well taken care of: good apartments, plenty of money, and nice lifestyle. Oh, and easy jobs."

Felsner summed it up concisely. "So what we have is a couple of pampered professional boyfriends?"

She continued after a second. "Correct. Nothing there. As for boyfriend three, he's quiet, professional, a friend of the family. Nothing there either. In the ex-boyfriend category, only one of interest. He also had a bunch of benefactors, only he liked to talk about it, and the press had some fun with it a couple of years ago. The boyfriend found himself shipped off to the Periphery, and the Lyran public affairs people spent six months spinning the story."

"All right," Felsner concluded. "Just another minister who needs a certain amount of...release. How about the girlfriend? What do we have there?"

"Okay, this is where it gets interesting." Premit took a second to collect her thoughts before continuing. She felt Simon Davion's eyes boring into the back of her head while

Lucien Davion scowled in contempt at her. "Thirty-five, single, from Eschenberg. Apparently another family friend. She's a banker right here on Tharkad, mainly personal finance. For the last decade, she's made between two and three trips back to Eschenberg each year, in and of itself not unusual, though her trips are usually within a week or two after Bernstorff's own trips home.

"They've got a regular appointment with each other. Every two weeks, they meet for dinner, then to a hotel for the rest of the evening. The restaurant rotates between about five or six of his favorites, but it's always the same hotel: the Eidelweiss Grand. Nice place, off the beaten path."

"What are you saying?"

Felsner's question reminded Tess of something he'd told her a few days earlier. "*You're not in intel-gathering, you're in intel-analysis. It's your job to give a quick snapshot and then your assessment. Convince me one way or the other without overloading me with irrelevant facts.*"

"Okay, here's the thing. This girl is his only standing date. With few exceptions, the only time he sees her is on their standard Sunday-evening liaison. Now what's strange is that he absolutely does *not* have a standing date with any of his boyfriends. When he needs a release, he calls one up, and they typically meet at the boyfriend's apartment. They *never* go to a hotel.

"And here's the other thing. The *only* times he and his girlfriend have met outside of their scheduled dates has been after he's concluded a major negotiation. He doesn't take her to parties. In fact, it looks like they actually make sure they're not at the same place at the same time, except for their dates. He doesn't do this with anyone else. His other relationships are an open secret. But this one: it's different."

Felsner asked, "So what do you *think*?"

She sat silently for a few seconds, running every possible scenario through her mind. "I don't know what they're into, but I think Ms. Eva Sorken may just be what we've been looking for."

Robert Davion looked at her with a smile on his face.

**THARKAD
LYRAN COMMONWEALTH
30 AUGUST 2456**

Sometimes undercover work could be routine and mind-numbingly boring. One might have to get oneself a "regular" job and spend weeks or months trying to build a cover, looking and acting just like any other person who has to drag themself out of bed every day to go to a hated workplace with coworkers only slightly less detestable than child molesters.

And then there were times when the anticipation, nervousness, and adrenaline rush merged to create an incomparable high.

Tonight was one of the latter times. And for the first time since arriving on Tharkad, Teresa Premit was completely in her element.

Friday night, and Eva Sorken was going out for an evening of dinner, drinks, and dancing with her girlfriends. They thought she'd been cooped up in her apartment for far too long. That was just fine by Tess.

She and her team of undercover agents were going to kidnap Eva.

A bunch of rich city girls looking to unwind and maybe to get a little action to boot. Well, there's one girl who'll get more than she wanted!

Tess and her team followed Eva as one of her friends picked her up from the upscale—and very secure—apartment she owned in Rivvenfeldt. Meeting up at a little bistro, the six women ate and drank and laughed for an hour and a half before leaving.

By the time Eva and her five friends reached the Scorpion Pit, a trendy nightspot as popular for its massive dance floor as it was for the illicit substances dealt there, they were loud and unruly, dancing and flirting their way into the club—obviously feeling the drinks they'd had at dinner.

As soon as the women were inside, Tess signaled her team to go. She made a beeline for the front door from the Dachen coupe she'd driven to the club. In her peripheral vision, she could see her two other "inside men"—Julius and Damon—get out of their own vehicle and wander toward the club. And as they did that, she knew her two last operatives took their own positions—one to cover the front door and one to cover the rear, both on the lookout in case their target slipped out of the club, also ready to make a quick getaway.

As Tess approached the door, her heart pumped hard, almost in time with the rapid thumping beat of the music from inside. No matter how many ops she participated in, the anticipation always got to her. She was on edge, which was just the way she wanted to be.

Complacency is how you get killed. Keep alert, kiddo!

That was her mantra, and she wasn't about to compromise her own safety or that of her teammates to get the job done. If there was a single problem, she wouldn't hesitate to call off the op.

She walked up to the doorman and handed over a twenty-kroner bill. The cover charge was pretty steep, but hey, it was a trendy place.

He was a big guy, wearing a tight black T-shirt that showed off his well-muscled torso and arms, and black leather pants over black leather boots. His long hair covered his ears and the back of his neck—what there was of it—and he wore the obligatory sunglasses in the dead of the night.

It's a statement.

He looked her up and down before accepting the bill. She looked shit-hot and knew it—and so did everyone else: a short green dress that left her midriff and back bare and very little else to the imagination, complemented by green heels, a matching clutch purse, and topped off by a wild multihued hairdo. She'd left her entire team in awe when she walked out of the bedroom of their safehouse with that outfit on, but what the hell. She didn't often get to show off.

Besides, the idea was to get people to notice everything *but* her face. Before "picking up" Eva at her apartment, she'd put on facial appliqués to make her look like her target. She didn't want anyone to recognize her.

The doorman motioned her into the club, concentrating more on her other attributes than her bulging purse. She walked through and down a small corridor before turning the corner and stepping into the Scorpion Pit.

Damn!

It was like all nine rings of hell wrapped up in one. Hundreds of bodies partially obscured by an almost-permanent cloud of fog writhed in time to the deafening beat blaring out of the club's speakers while red spotlights played over the entire scene. Then the smell hit her...a combination of sweat, bile, and the smoke from hundreds of different burning substances, some legal and some not.

God, I hate places like this!

From her position on the entry balcony she moved down to the tier right below her, a raised level filled with tables that surrounded the massive, and filled, dance floor. Its red glow only added to the club's hellish image. The place was dark otherwise, with strobe lights and laser beams flashing on and off in synchronicity to nothing, momentarily illuminating pitch-black corners where people were doing things she didn't want to think about.

She had but one thing on her mind: Eva.

There.

Tess picked her target out, sitting at a table with her friends.

Premit snatched a half-full champagne glass from a nearby table, its occupants too enthralled with each other to even notice. She tapped her ring against the glass twice and twice again, wirelessly transmitting clicks that told her cohorts that she'd spotted their prey.

Both inside men clicked their acknowledgment. All five of them wore earpieces that picked up the signals and could also transmit voice; not, of course, that they'd be able to understand much within the thump of the club. But at least the brief keying of the transmit button, hidden within otherwise decorative rings worn by each of them, could be heard without much difficulty.

Tess looked back toward the entry and after a few seconds spotted her two cohorts. Julius had secured a seat at one of the club's many bars, this one on a third level overlooking the whole place, while Tess and Deven moved toward each other. They met in the middle and took over a table fifteen meters away from Eva.

Their subject and her friends sat at their table, ordering drink after drink for an hour before four of them, including Eva, stood up and went down to the dance floor. Tess and Deven watched the group work off their frenetic energy for a few more minutes before they headed down to the dance floor together. Drink in hand, like so many others, Tess began to move in time to the beat.

Their bodies shifted and contorted in unison, moving slowly from the edge of the mass of humanity toward and circling around Eva and her friends. One of them always kept their eyes locked on their target even as both scanned the crowd for potential dangers. Above them, their third comrade maintained an overwatch, likewise paying close attention for any obstacles that might present themselves.

After ten more minutes, the two closed in on their target. They came within a meter of Eva, closely studying the way she moved, the way she whipped around, and especially the way her eyes and head worked the crowd. She was on the lookout, but not for danger. Her gaze played briefly over Deven, moving to Tess with a flare of jealousy before continuing to scan the rest of the throng. That brought a smile to Tess's lips. Just a bit of satisfaction at making another woman jealous, if only for a moment. It also told the undercover operative that Eva was indeed on the lookout for action. And that might make her job much easier. Unless, of course, she hooked up with someone before Tess and her team were ready.

No sense in waiting.

Champagne glass still in hand, raised above her as if a torch to light their way, Tess tapped the signal that let everyone know they were going to make the attempt right now. Tess and Deven moved away, melding back into the crowd briefly while they prepared.

There wasn't much to do in preparation, really. Julius got up from his seat and, drink in hand, worked his way down toward the dance floor as Tess and Deven moved once again closer to Eva. When Julius was in place, standing on a small stair by the edge of the dance floor and right next to the corridor that led to a set of restrooms as well as a back exit, she made her move.

The plan was simple. Tess would transfer the glass from her right hand to her left, "accidentally" bumping Eva and in the process spilling the drink on the woman, profusely apologizing in the process and demanding to help her clean up.

But then Murphy and his laws made their debut for the evening.

The throbbing beat changed tempo, and the throng turned temporarily from a writhing mass to a thrashing mob. Arms that were either in the air or wrapped around partners suddenly thrashed about like a mass of tentacles. A woman close to Tess knocked the glass right from her hand without even noticing it, splashing the liquid over half a dozen individuals—none of them Eva—and sending the glass to the floor, where it smashed to bits.

Shit!

Worse still, not only did Eva not get splashed, she and her friends were leaving the dance floor. They must not have liked the change in music.

Using the metal clasp on her purse, Tess quickly tapped out on her ring the "miss" code, alerting Julius to the failed attempt. But when she noticed the group of women moving toward Julius, she just as quickly tapped the code for him to make his own attempt.

Riskier, but worth a shot.

It took the women some time to make their way out of the unruly crowd, giving Julius the time he needed. Just as they reached the edge of the dance floor, Julius swung into action, grabbing Eva by the hand and pulling her back into the mass. Julius was tall with chiseled good looks and a build that showed easily through his ruffled white shirt and snug black trousers. The women simply stood in astonishment as the stranger and their friend began moving to the beat. Their gaping mouths quickly turned to smiles, though; they turned and went to their table.

Eva was dancing with this man she'd never met before and having the time of her life. She whipped her head back and laughed as Julius led her through a series of wild moves.

Tess and Deven moved to the crowd's periphery. Tess took up the position on the stairs where Julius had been standing while Deven disappeared down the black corridor. From her vantage point, she studied her target, mentally ticking off the seconds before the drugs from the medpatch Julius slapped on Eva's hand took effect.

Yeah, you're starting to feel it now. Your heart pounding, everything seeming to speed up. Oh, but you're still looped from the drinks you had back at the restaurant. Or maybe you're getting high from whatever's in the air.

Now you're spinning. No, wait, the entire world is spinning. You're beginning to lose focus. Pretty soon the nausea will hit. And there it is. You need to get off of the dance floor, and now. If you're lucky, all you'll need to do is splash some water on your face.

But tonight your luck runs out.

Julius led her off the dance floor and down the darkened hallway to the restrooms, where Tess waited for them, her bulging clutch bag in hand. She followed behind by a few beats, plucking the wig from her own head and rushing forward to plop it onto Eva's lolling head as soon as they all disappeared into the blackness of the corridor.

Tess wrapped her own arm around the woman, who was rapidly losing consciousness, as they moved past the restrooms. The stench of years of vomit, urine, and who knows what else absorbed into the walls nearly caused the veteran agent to gag.

They turned a few corners. Julius picked Eva up in his arms to climb a flight of stairs. Deven stood at the top, black mass in hand and holding open the emergency exit whose alarm he'd rushed ahead to disable. He tossed the mass to Tess and took Eva from Julius.

"Deven, hold on!" Tess commanded.

"What? We've got to get out of here!"

"Just wait a sec!" Tess slipped the shoes from Eva's feet and stepped out of her own, dropping them onto the woman's limp form. "Go!"

Deven disappeared into the alleyway with the woman. With luck, they'd be away in a minute or two.

Tess and Julius turned around and rushed to the bottom of the stairs. As they made their way back through the vile corridor, Tess ripped a brown wig from her purse and pulled it down over her own still-short red crop of hair. She entered the women's restroom, Julius taking up position outside. Multicolored neon lights lit up the room, especially its hanging cloud of smoke. Women touched up their makeup and hair, or smoked, or injected themselves with who knows what. No one even batted an eye at Tess, who ducked into a stall.

Okay, places like this have their uses.

She didn't have much time. She stripped off her own dress before slipping into the black dress Deven had passed to her, one that had taken a woman on the team more than two hours to find a copy of—nearly the entire time it took Eva to get from her front door and to the club.

It wasn't a perfect match, and the heels were at least a size too small, but it could have been worse. This was the part that Tess had worried about.

She carefully stuffed her green dress into her purse and adjusted her brunette wig using a tiny makeup mirror that she likewise shoved into the purse. Tess emerged from the stall and looked herself over in the restroom's mirror one last time. She knew she'd never pass as Eva close up to anyone that knew her, but at a distance…at a distance, especially in this club, no one would ever know the difference. Not even Eva's friends.

She hoped.

Tess left the restroom and slipped her arm around Julius's waist. They returned to the dance floor moving and swaying to the beat, immediately making their way to the closest bar. Tess looked over to where Eva's friends were seated and, making eye contact, waved, letting them know she was just fine. They waved back, but didn't move from their seats.

Yeah, that's right, I'm just fine. Now don't bother me…

Tess and Julius both sat at the bar and ordered drinks, leaning in close toward each other. Tess placed her hand on Julius's forearm while he teased her thigh with his other hand. She laughed and tossed her hair back. To anyone else, they'd look like two people totally infatuated with each other.

A moment later, they both heard the two-two-two clicks that told them Eva was safely away. But Tess wasn't satisfied.

She wanted to be sure, so she brought her hand up to her mouth like she was laughing, keyed her mic and said, "Verify," hoping she'd be heard over the music.

A second later, they both heard again the two-two-two clicks.

Okay. It's done. Now we gotta get out of here.

Julius must have been thinking the same thing, asking, "So what's the plan?"

Tess thought a moment before answering. "Let's finish our drinks and have one last dance."

"And then right out the front door?"

"Absolutely." She looked towards Eva's friends, who were giggling and pointing in her general direction.

That's right. We're going to go home together tonight. And then I'll call in sick tomorrow. And the day after. And the day after that. And maybe in a few days I'll send you a message from off-world. "We hit it off so well we decided to take a trip...."

She turned back to her companion, whose hand continued to creep up her thigh. "By the way Julius, if you move that hand any farther, you'll get to feel firsthand just how sharp carbon fiber–reinforced nails are."

Her hand moving up his own thigh, he squirmed and answered, "Yes, ma'am."

**UNKNOWN LOCATION
THARKAD
LYRAN COMMONWEALTH
31 AUGUST 2456**

Eva opened her eyes to total blackness.

She blinked a few times, but still nothing. Tried to lift her hand to rub her eyes, but she couldn't move. Her arms, her legs, even her head. What was going on!?

Her heart pounded like a jackhammer. Beads of sweat ran down her face and under her chin. She struggled against the invisible binds that immobilized her, but she couldn't get her breath. She couldn't breathe! She felt the walls closing in.

"Help! Help! Get me out of here!"

Her screams echoed around what could only be a small room, but all she heard were her own staccato heartbeats.

She pulled. She struggled. She thrashed about. Nothing helped.

Her hands! Yes! Her hands worked. And so did her feet. She couldn't move her arms or legs, but she could at least move *something*. Maybe she could feel what was keeping her from moving!

Nothing! She couldn't touch anything. Feel anything.

She screamed again. "Help! Please help me!"

Nothing. But someone had to be there, right? Someone had to be able to help!

Then the room lit up brighter than a supernova.

She clamped her eyes shut. The light. It was too bright, hurt too much. But she couldn't block it out!

Once more she screamed, fright overcoming her.

The smell hit her a few seconds later. It was a strong, pungent odor. Urine. But it took her a while longer to realize where it had suddenly come from, that she was sitting in a puddle of her own waste. Combined with the funk of her sweat, it was overpowering. Her stomach heaved. If she'd had anything in it, she'd have vomited it all over herself.

She was weak. Dizzy. Her head pounded in pain with every accelerated beat of her heart. And now was hoarse from her screams.

But at least she was beginning to adjust to the blinding lights.

Eva tentatively opened her eyes, squinting and blinking rapidly. She sat there, naked, reclined and tied down to some sort of exam bed, tubes and wires attached all over her body.

Why would anyone want to do this to her?

"Help me. Oh please, oh please, oh please..." Her whimpers barely made it past her lips.

A noise. A door opening? Someone walking toward her! She still couldn't see anything past the overpowering lights, but she heard and felt the movement nearby. Her heart continued to race.

A female leaned over the frightened woman and spoke. "Hello, Eva."

Eva looked up into a face she recognized, a voice hauntingly familiar.

"You...you're me... Who are you?"

The other woman smiled.

"Eva Sorken."

In the next room, Delton Felsner observed the interrogation through the wall of medical monitors, computer displays, and tri-vid images. The three other individuals in the room with him monitored Eva's medical and psychological condition, and could adjust the flow of drugs and other intravenous fluids to make her more susceptible to the questions asked. Or to strengthen her so she could remain conscious.

One of the agents, of course, was a trained medical specialist who could step in if Eva's vitals went south. Deven and Julius were the other two, and concentrated on their own monitors.

"You...you're me... Who are you?"

"Eva Sorken."

Tess had been practicing Eva's voice for the last twelve hours, and while Felsner knew she wouldn't be able to fool Eva's friends or family with her impression, he figured it would be good enough for someone as confused, frightened, and incoherent—and drugged—as Eva was.

Eva continued to whimper, "No, no, no, no..."

Then she began to cry.

Good. That'll blur her vision even more. Tess's makeup isn't perfect, but it'll work.

"Why am I here?"

Amidst Eva's sobs, Felsner could barely make out the words. A technician worked the controls, amplifying the woman's frightened whispers. Of course, they expected that question sooner or later, it just wasn't the one they wanted to hear yet. Eva was vulnerable, to be sure, but there was no telling if she had dissociated yet. Well, only one way to find out.

He nodded, and had another man pass word to Tess to begin.

Moving behind the bed and out of the woman's sight, Tess signaled the tri-vid camera in front of them that the agents should increase the flow of drugs into Eva's system. Reappearing on the woman's other side and leaning in close, she answered Eva's question, whispering into her ear.

"We're here because of our crimes. We're criminals, and we deserve to be punished."

"No…no, that's not…"

Tess slapped the bed next to the woman's head, nearly screaming her reply.

"Yes it is! And we know it!"

Eva would be having trouble concentrating. Her gaze roamed wildly around the room, unable to focus on even Tess, whose face was less than a meter away. "No…we didn't do… nothing wrong."

Tess signaled the other room again, this time to decrease the drug flow. She waited a few moments before continuing, walking back around to the woman's left side.

She leaned in close again, her voice low and seemingly full of regret.

"Yes, I'm afraid we did. We're criminals… We lied. To our friends and to our family."

She leaned in even farther, barely whispering her final statement into Eva's ear.

"And all because of *him*."

Good, Felsner thought. *Tess is getting her thinking about Bernstorff. Shouldn't be long now.*

The problem was that they didn't know precisely what Bernstorff and Eva were up to. All they had was supposition and circumstantial evidence. They needed something harder. But that didn't stop them from using what little they did have to start the flow of information.

"I… Who? It's…it's not…"

Tess remained close, giving voice to Eva's conscience with a whisper.

"Yes, we do. He talked us into it, but we're just as guilty as he is."

Tess watched Eva carefully, and Felsner did the same as he hovered over the monitor. She was back to whimpering, but anyone could see that there was something there, that maybe Eva was just about ready to spill everything. He watched as Tess went out on a limb, making an educated guess.

"Why do you think we sit in that apartment all alone? Because we like it?"

She came around the bed again, almost mouthing this into Eva's right ear.

"It's time to confess."

Felsner watched the medical monitors closely. Heart rate and blood pressure had dropped considerably from the sky-high readings of just a few minutes ago. The drugs had helped that, but mostly it was Tess, psychologically moving Eva from fear to guilt. Now all the Federated Suns operative had to do was keep nudging Eva closer and closer to that mental precipice and let her fall over herself. Then everything would come pouring out.

These were unusual methods of diplomacy, to be sure, but they were necessary. What he did in the negotiation room wasn't all that dissimilar, only there he didn't have the opportunity to pump his opponent full of drugs. And if this interrogation were to uncover information that could be used to get the Steiners to sell the BattleMech to the Federated Suns, and without any further loss of life, then so much the better.

Deven looked back at his ambassador, pointing to the neural readouts in front of him. "She's thinking about something and not liking it too much. Right-side activity is down, and left is up. She's not rationalizing anymore."

"Good," Felsner responded. "Then maybe we won't have to be here all night. Tell her."

Deven leaned forward and repeated what he'd said into the microphone in front of him. Looking up at the tri-vid image, both men watched Tess drop her head as she listened to Deven through her earpiece and then nod.

Felsner knew what those readings meant. Eva wasn't trying to cover herself with lies. Logic was commingling with exhaustion. She was feeling guilt.

But Eva wasn't quite there yet. She was still crying softly, the weight of her emotions colliding with mental exhaustion. She needed just another small nudge.

Tess leaned directly over Eva, their faces mere centimeters apart, and looked right into the woman's eyes. She spoke softly and with as much compassion as she could muster.

"It's time we gave up the guilt. It's killing us."

"Oh…okay."

Tess smiled down at Eva, hoping it wasn't the look of smug satisfaction she felt in her gut.

**THARKAD
LYRAN COMMONWEALTH
5 SEPTEMBER 2456**

"I believe this would be an opportune time for a break, if I might suggest. With your approval, of course, Ambassador?"

Lord Delton Felsner looked back at Ambassador Karl Bernstorff and smiled. "I believe that is an excellent suggestion."

They'd been talking for the past several hours, and everyone needed to stretch their legs. "Then shall we reconvene in, say, fifteen minutes?"

With a nod Felsner stood up, as did Bernstorff. Both leaned over the table and shook hands.

Felsner didn't let Bernstorff get too far away from the table before getting his attention. "Ambassador, perhaps I could have a moment with you *in camera*?"

The request was a little odd, but then again, the entire negotiation process had broken or seriously fractured almost every convention and unwritten rule in the book—much to the enjoyment of the Lyran minister, who seemed like he hadn't had this much fun in his three decades of service to his nation.

"I trust you will not use this opportunity to bring up subjects that have been tabled?" Bernstorff was obviously getting tired of the issue of the BattleMech, something he simply wasn't budging on.

"No, Ambassador, on my honor I will not bring up that subject." *Though* you *might.* "No, this is something I think you will agree is best discussed in private."

The Lyran nodded and, arm held out to direct Felsner toward the door to a private sitting room, replied, "Then how can I refuse you?"

The two walked toward the room with Tess, in her guise as Leftenant Colonel Angela Conrad, falling in behind them, noteputer in hand. Bernstorff gave Felsner a quizzical look, obviously wondering why this aide was following them.

Felsner addressed the ambassador's unspoken question, speaking low so no one else in the rapidly clearing negotiation room could hear. "We've come across some more, uh, *sensitive* information. And it involves someone in your delegation. The colonel here is most familiar with it, if that isn't a problem?"

Bernstorff stopped for a moment to think about what he'd just heard. "*Nein*. Of course not."

The implication that someone on his staff was involved in something untoward was enough for him to quickly wave off the two aides that were moving across the room to join them. "We will be just a few moments." That stopped them in their tracks.

Felsner and Tess both continued into the room while Bernstorff followed them, closing the door behind them.

This was the kind of nice, cozy room that Felsner loved. Darkly stained wood paneling and floor, fireplace, a couple of windows looking out over the perpetually snow-covered landscape, and a few paintings of some obscure historical figures. Two overstuffed chairs were placed at an angle so they half faced each other and half faced the fireplace, with a small table on which sat a pitcher of water and two glasses between them. Two small couches faced each other with a rug between, the chairs on one side and the fireplace on the other.

Best of all was the smell, the warm aroma of a good hardwood burning in the fireplace. Not gas, not a hologram, a real honest-to-goodness fire. They probably had someone come in to keep it stoked just for instances like this.

It was an intimate room designed to make its occupants feel comfortable, a welcome change from the massive and off-putting negotiation chamber.

Normally this would be the kind of room the home team could use to put their opponents off-balance, to woo them into letting their guard down before launching another diplomatic attack. Sure, everyone knew the tricks, but they still worked.

Only this time it would be the opponent that had the advantage.

Felsner took position in front of one of the overstuffed chairs, while Tess stood next to him in front of one sofa. Both sat as soon as Bernstorff moved in front of his own chair and motioned for them to sit.

The Lyran minister started. "So, what information do you have that is so sensitive that we need privacy?"

"Ambassador, if I may?" Usually an aide did not speak before her superior in this sort of environment, and Tess played the part with all the deference and humility she could muster. She pulled a white-noise generator from her pocket and held it up for the men to see.

Felsner continued on Tess's behalf. "You may, of course, do what you will with this information, but I think you'll agree that we should take no chances with it before then."

This piqued Bernstorff's interest. They had broken off in private only once before, when Felsner and the poor, departed Meldrach Suisso had presented Bernstorff with detailed information concerning foreign agents operating on Tharkad, but even then they hadn't requested such security precautions.

"If you feel it is necessary, then by all means."

Tess activated the device and handed it to Felsner, who placed it on the table between him and the Lyran.

"So, what is it that you have there?" Bernstorff's curiosity was getting the best of him.

Felsner began. "First, let me say that we are providing this information in the spirit of our agreement to share critical intelligence." This was an official meeting, whether on the record or not, and there were some protocols that had to be followed. Even if it would take a radical turn momentarily.

Bernstorff nodded in agreement, adding, "Thank you. The information you previously provided was very valuable."

"What we have here is even more critical," Felsner continued. "We only just came into possession of this. The identity of a high-ranking member of your government is engaged in treason."

That got a start.

"Well. That is unheard of!" He was acting indignant, but it wasn't very convincing. "Every minister, deputy, and advisor is required to swear an oath of loyalty to the Archon and to the Commonwealth. No one has ever broken that oath!"

Of course not. Just like you didn't steal the BattleMech from the Terrans.

"Greed is a powerful motivator, Mr. Ambassador. What we have here is proof that a minister in your government has been using his influence and power to line his own pockets."

Bernstorff blanched.

Hitting a little too close to home?

"We...well, that sounds like corruption, not treason. Surely not treason!" The Lyran minister faltered briefly, but quickly recovered. "Allow me to let you in on a little secret. Bribery and kickbacks are a way of life to a nation of merchants. As wasteful and detestable as it is, it is an unfortunate fact."

Hmm...trying a little distraction, are you? Not going to work!

The air was a little dry in the room, and Felsner took a drink of water before continuing. "This is more than just pedestrian corruption we're talking about." He shook his head in reinforcement. "No, this is far worse. Hundreds of millions of kroner diverted each year to line the pockets of the minister and his friends. Millions that, I'm sure you'll agree, could have been better put to use. And these friends? Captains of industry who have become only richer by defrauding the Lyran people of this money by foisting overpriced boondoggles on them."

Bernstorff was trying hard to keep control, gripping the chair's arm tightly lest he give anything away with his arm or hand movements. But he didn't quite succeed. His face was still drained of color, and he was blinking rapidly with every accusation, licking his lips every few seconds with a tongue likely dry and rough as sandpaper.

"Colonel Conrad has the rest." Felsner pointed to Tess, who tapped her noteputer to bring up the salient file.

"Through various sources, we were led to this woman, Eva Sorken." Tess turned her noteputer so the Lyran ambassador could see the picture of Eva she had displayed on the screen.

Bernstorff lost even more color from his face. Any composure he was trying to maintain melted away, his mouth agape.

Tess didn't even stop for effect. "As it turns out, she handles all the money for this minister. An old family friend, we're told. So what happens is the minister uses his influence to get major military contracts awarded to corporations owned and run by his friends, many of them members of his wife's family. They're never the low bidder, but they spread around enough bribe money to make that not a factor. And then, you know what happens? They jack up the costs and get their minister friend to authorize it, calling it normal cost overruns. Then they split the money and laugh all the way to the bank!"

Felsner stared at the Lyran the whole time, watching him rub the sweat from his palms, lick his lips, seeing his chest rise and fall rapidly. Then the eye movement as Tess finished what she had to say, rapidly jumping back and forth across the room.

Looking for a way out? Maybe something you can say or do?

All three were silent for a long minute. That Bernstorff was panicked was blatantly clear; his foot tapped a rapid rhythm, and he shuddered with every crackle and pop of the burning fire. The high-pitched hum of the white-noise generator only added to the tension he must have been feeling.

Felsner sat back, enjoying the warmth of the fire and the comfort of the chair while Tess leaned forward staring intently at the Lyran, a satisfied smirk on her face.

Finally, the despondent Bernstorff looked over, regaining his composure before he spoke. "What do you want?"

Felsner's answer was absolutely unambiguous. "You know what we want."

Bernstorff sighed. "The BattleMech."

See? I told you I wouldn't bring it up.

"Yes."

"You understand that is the one thing I was instructed not to agree to. The one thing I *cannot* agree to. Even if I did, the Archon would just invalidate the treaty. I can't—"

"Yes, you can." Felsner's voice exuded nothing but strength and confidence. "If you put your mind to it, you can convince the Archon of the logic of it."

"What logic?"

"Well, sooner or later we will gain the technology, so why shouldn't it be on your terms? The time to cash in is now."

That calmed the Lyran down some. Set his mind to thinking.

Felsner continued. "Think of it this way. We're going to give you huge sums of money so that you can build us some of these wonderful machines. Then we're going to give you more, to buy the parts from you so we can build them ourselves. And then we're going to give you *even more* so that you can give us the plans to do it all ourselves.

"And all the while, we're going to send you our best technical minds to help you build better factories and design better BattleMechs. Oh, and by the way, as foreign minister and chairman of the Appropriations Committee," Felsner said with a smile. "*You* will be the one who chooses precisely which corporations will be on the receiving end of all of this."

"The military will object." Bernstorff was thinking on his feet now. Wrapping his brain around the new problems. "They won't want to give *anyone* the BattleMech."

He's coming around.

"They'll just have to get over it. And they'll see the benefits soon enough. The Hegemony and the Combine will have us on both sides to deal with. We'll sign a mutual nonaggression treaty. And we'll do some joint training, just to keep the Camerons and Kuritas guessing." Felsner wasn't done, though. Not by a long shot. "And how can your generals even think about speaking out against the treaty that the hero of the Lyran Commonwealth negotiated?"

"What do you mean?" Bernstorff's frown was back. Suspicion flared in his eyes.

Good. Here it comes.

"Why, Ambassador Bernstorff, you will have brought the mighty Federated Suns to its knees, begging you for its very life, because its massive military wasn't enough to protect it from the Hegemonists. No, *they* had to come to *you*. And in this time of danger, you drained their coffers so that your nation could pay for its own massive arming projects without costing your citizens one kroner extra."

The Lyran dropped his head in resignation. "And what happens to those files in your hand?"

Tess handed the noteputer over to him, replying, "We believe that you are the best judge as to what agency should receive this information."

"And Eva?"

Felsner answered that. "As it turns out, she just accepted a job offer on New Avalon. Though I think she'll be back in a few years . Say, once the final technology transfers are complete." The Federated Suns ambassador stood up and extended his right hand. "We have a deal?"

Bernstorff likewise stood and, mustering all the dignity he could, took the proffered hand.

"*Ja.* You have your deal."

NEW AVALON
FEDERATED SUNS
19 JANUARY 2457

"Ambassador Bernstorff, on behalf of the people of the Federated Suns, I would like to personally thank you for your part in these historic negotiations. You have saved us from the enemies that seek to destroy us both!"

First Prince Simon Davion's words were sincere, without even the hint of being mere bureaucratic lip service.

With a bow, Duke Karl Bernstorff replied, "Highness, it has been my honor and pleasure to work with Lord Felsner to bring this treaty to fruition."

It may not have been the truth, but there was a time and place for that. And both had long ago passed.

The two had just signed the treaty that would see the Federated Suns gain the technical know-how to build their own BattleMechs. And he had confirmed his treasonous colors—he had sold out the nation he'd sworn an oath to. No, strike that! He was a traitor *and* a thief. But unlike the Kuritas, he didn't believe in the nobility of suicide. He liked life too much, enjoyed its pleasures more than he hated his own life.

So there he was, alone, on the homeworld of those that had found out his darkest secret and used it against him. Despite the presence of members of his own nation's delegation to New Avalon, he felt like the loneliest soul in the universe.

Of course, the setting didn't help. The Prince's throne room was massive, large enough to fit more than a thousand nobles, dignitaries, and bureaucrats, along with two companies of elite bodyguards. There were but a handful of individuals in the room today, their voices and the sound of their footfalls on the polished marble floor echoing throughout the chamber.

At least he could take comfort in the fact that the treaty would benefit his nation. And his own personal fortunes. Not that money was the point anymore.

The Prince turned to Felsner, who stood next to the Lyran ambassador. "And Duke Felsner, your entire nation thanks you and your delegation for your service. You are a shining example of what it means to be a citizen of the Federated Suns!"

"Thank you, Highness. You are too kind."

Felsner's words just about made Bernstorff sick to his stomach, but the ceremony was nearly over. Because of the nature of the treaty, it was secret—after all, neither side wanted the Hegemony or any of the other Successor States knowing about it until both could construct sizeable BattleMech armies. That meant no press and no hordes of low-level functionaries with whom he'd have to spend hours more before his four-month return trip to Tharkad.

At least this time he wouldn't have to spend it with the architect of his treason.

It only took a few more minutes for the ceremony to conclude. Two assistants took the requisite tri-vid photos, there was a toast, numerous handshakes, and then the group was dismissed. There would be a state dinner that evening to honor his visit to New Avalon "in the name of friendship." And that would be it. He could finally get off New Avalon and forget about this whole debacle.

In fact, when he returned, he would start giving generously to charities throughout the Commonwealth. The military budget for building the Lyran 'Mech corps would force cutbacks in domestic programs, so perhaps he could ease that problem and even convince other wealthy businessmen and nobles to do the same.

It wouldn't make up for his treason, but it would be a start.

"*Herr* Bernstorff, a word?"

He stopped, cringing. He'd hoped he would never have to hear Felsner's smooth and self-confident voice again. All he wanted to do was get out of this palace and off this world.

Felsner came up alongside the Lyran, motioning him to continue walking. "Ambassador, please. I know this hasn't been easy for you, and I'm sure you want to return home?"

"*Ja*. The trip has been long, and I have not seen my family for some time. I would like to get back to them."

"I understand. All we ask is that you wait a few days before leaving."

Bernstorff's eyes went wide, his face rapidly losing color. "Wh...why?"

Felsner slapped him on the shoulder like an old friend as they passed out of the throne room. "*Herr* Ambassador, your imagination is playing havoc with you. Our intelligence agencies are preparing reports on foreign agents known to be operating in your Lyran Commonwealth for you, and I'm sure that you would like to bring at least some of the money we've promised your government back to your Archon?"

The Lyran sighed in relief. "*Ja*. Yes, that would be appreciated. Thank you."

Ahead, a blond woman turned the corner from a side corridor and approached them. Bernstorff stopped again when he caught sight of her, his arms and legs noticeably shaking. Tess, wearing a conservative business suit, joined the two of them.

"Besides," Felsner continued, "I'm sure it'll take you a few days to arrange credentials for your new aide, here. And we still have to discuss how else the Lyran Commonwealth can aid the Federated Suns in the future."

FALL DOWN SEVEN TIMES, GET UP EIGHT

RANDALL N. BILLS

ROLIN FIELDS, TANADA PROVINCE
OSHIKA, OSHIKA PREFECTURE
GALEDON MILITARY DISTRICT
DRACONIS COMBINE
17 DECEMBER 2415

"But why? Why do you have to go, Ito?!" Takeda tried. He did. But he still sounded like Iza and he knew it; baby sisters were even more annoying than older brothers.

I'm not a child!

He stamped several times, trying to find warmth. Trying to find an answer as they headed towards the *goji* pens in the total darkness. Only his brother's flashlight, almost smothered in the midnight and heavy falling snow, lit their way.

Usually the wide open, near-treeless plains of Rolin Fields seemed to bring Takeda his only source of joy. A blank slate for the harsh fingerpaints of a desperate imagination. Whether the dog days of summer and the brutal heat, or the dead of winter's cold, the fields became any number of alien planets. Fedrats aplenty swarming the borders. Takeda ready and willing to defend the homeland with a laser rifle in hand. But now, the snow and darkness covered the fields, leaving Takeda with the impression of standing on an island where nothing else existed. He shivered. Blamed it on the cold.

"Because, little brother. I have to."

Takeda shook his head, anger leaping at his older brother's words. "I'm not little."

"You're only twelve."

"Almost thirteen!"

"Right, almost thirteen."

Takeda stopped and growled at his brother's tone, ready for a fight. But Ito didn't give him the satisfaction and kept walking. Takeda stamped harder in the snow, banging thick, well-worn wool mittens together for warmth; forgot to tell Mom they needed mending, again. It seemed as though the little warmth he'd started with in the short walk from the house had left along with the light.

Looking around, the darkness closed in with the departing flashlight, and that sense of nothingness abruptly smothered him. He began to pant. Takeda ran forward, catching up to Ito as they came to the small barn and its enclosed pens. His teeth started to chatter.

"Just gonna leave me to freeze in the snow? Like you're gonna leave the farm?"

Ito didn't turn, but slipped the flashlight under an arm. He heaved against the door to raise it up slightly out of the hole in the ground. Sidling forward and slipping into the barn, he looked like some gnome, breath steaming in the night, coming to steal a *goji* or two. At least that's what Ito used to tell him. But he knew it was a lie now.

All a lie.

"Brother," Ito finally responded without turning, "I left you there because you're being slow. You know with the power out we've got to get the generator going, or the *goji* will die."

"Yeah, I'm not *stupid*." Takeda stomped through the slight opening, then stood with arms crossed over his well-patched coat as Ito heaved the door closed. If possible, the barn was even darker. The skittering sounds of the knee-high insectoids always made his skin crawl, but he'd never let on. Never.

They walked through the rapidly cooling air towards the back room, wending in and out of the alien *goji*. Never mind that only poor people would eat such meat. It's what their family had raised for years and years.

His father's words came back to him: "If Granddad was good enough to raise *goji*, then so am I. And so are you."

Well, screw you, Dad. And you too, Ito. I don't want to be poor anymore. And I hate goji*. And you're leaving me here to rot and do all the work by myself since Dad's fall.*

Ito entered the room first, twisting the flashlight into a knothole in the wooden blank separating the main pens from the generator shed. He strode to the front of the ancient piece of junk and began manually priming the engine.

Takeda stamped into the room, ignoring the *goji* crap caked on his boots. Ignoring the horrible smell that could kill a dog at a hundred meters. Pushed his back against the wall as though to support the whole barn. *You do all the work. Stupid Ito. Stupid barn. Stupid farm!*

Long minutes passed. The soft sucking sound of the primer couldn't cover the clicking of multiple legs on exoskeletons. Takeda wanted to tear off his ears.

Ito finally stopped and glanced up, face mostly in long shadows. "Brother. What's going on?"

"Nothing."

"Of course not. That's why you're moping in the corner."

"I'm not moping."

"Yes, yes, you are."

He thought about swearing, or a hundred other things. But that wouldn't do anything. His big brother always won. Always. And now he would win again. "You won't answer my question," he said, and spit on the ground. There.

Ito's shoulders slumped, as though an added weight were abruptly on his back. "Takeda. I did, and you won't listen. You won't believe. I've got to go. This winter's the worst yet. Ma says it's only going to get worse, not better. She can feel it. And I'm just one more mouth to feed. I need to go, Taki."

"Don't call me that. That's a kid's name."

Ito straightened, his face falling completely into shadows, before moving toward him slowly, crouching down until they were face to face. Despite the fall of light behind his head, Takeda made out his brother's face: the close-cut black hair, small mouth and nose, but slightly wide-spaced, brown eyes. Always serious, Ito's expression made Takeda's eyes itch, which made him even *more* angry. *Not going to cry. You're not going to make me. I'm not a kid!*

"There's nothing I can do here but watch us all starve to death. But I can do this. Someday you'll understand, Taki... Takeda." He finished with a nod, as though for once accepting that Takeda might be growing up. "You can be mad all you want. Just don't be mad at Mom and Dad. Not their fault. Nobody's fault. Just have to make do with what we have."

I won't cry! But the itchy feeling wouldn't let go, and Takeda blinked rapidly. His brother turned away slightly. *Was that a tear? Was that a—*

"Takeda, promise me one thing."

He didn't want to promise his brother a thing. But on this stinking farm, in this horrible hole of a barn—a barn he would be tending for years now—his brother finally treated him like something more than little Taki. For that, he'd answer. "What?"

"Whatever happens, don't forget about family."

He looked up into his brother's eyes as Ito turned back. For just a moment, despite the darkness, it seemed he could see a huge pool of sadness. *"Don't forget about me,"* it seemed to say. Takeda breathed deeply, pulling in the stench and the cold and the anger of being deserted, and finally nodded.

Ito nodded back and returned to bang and prod the machine.

I won't forget.

But despite what they just shared, he didn't know what it was he wouldn't forget: the friendship that seemed to flow between them for a moment, or the feeling of a long, long cold road stretching into the distance. A road he would walk alone. *But not always, Ito! I'll make something of myself. I'll leave too. You wait and see!*

He jumped at the guttural roar of the engine as it sputtered to life.

D FOREST
NEW SAMARKAND, NEW SAMARKAND PREFECTURE
GALEDON MILITARY DISTRICT
DRACONIS COMBINE
2 JULY 2426

The horror swept through the darkened forest, fast and furious: a growl of bass rumble vibrating the inner ear until you just… must…scream. Razor sharp teeth flashing like chips of white bone bared in black clay; pink tongue quivering, a suckerworm blindly groping for fresh blood. Glowing, crimson eyes hypnotic in their preternatural rage; dark pelt almost invisible, only a hint of mammoth muscles stretching a skeleton to the breaking point in its driving, programmed need…

Ito Tesuo struggled to keep his heart from beating so loudly he'd miss a nuance that might save his life, but the primal terrors of beasts in the dark beat about his head like vulture's wings already tasting imminent and terribly violent death.

He cocked his head. He had never known that death wore such savage clothing.

Despite the terrible, awful fear squeezing his chest in a grip promising death, Ito managed to find the entire experience interesting. His breath rattled in his throat. He coughed till stars exploded in front of his eyes, and he bent over, helpless to the nameless thing coming to steal away the victory he'd fought so hard the last five years to grasp. Blood throbbed in his neck, until it must burst from the pressure of a heart beating frantically under an onslaught of adrenaline. Sweat-slicked hands grasped the knotted wood, the rough-cut whorls rasping flesh in promised slivers and blood. Finally giving up, he gulped air loudly, drawing oxygen to a brain starved of input…

…the lessons hammered by the *sensei* with brutal efficiency surged to the fore. He dropped into a light trance, blotting out onrushing death, the cool of the night jungle, the rasping of leaves as a cool, light wind wafted, causing crazy chiaroscuros to undulate, as the moon's light dappled the darkness in further shadows and scant highlights.

Succeed.

The word thrummed with power. Ito hunkered down, breathing falling into a slow, steady pattern as he mastered fear, and the word, limned in power, came surging again to the fore from his sensei:

Succeed!

Despite honor, despite duty, despite anything, there is only one thing that must drive each of you. Succeed. Failure is not an option. Not because it is demanded of you, but because you *demand it.*

Five years of relentless training in college, and it all came down to a fight in the dark with a horror rumored to have been imported from another world? Just didn't seem to make sense. What did hand-to-hand combat with a simian beast have to do with insurgency work and counter-terrorism and infiltration and all the other skills honed to allow him to graduate where so many others failed?

But either he lived through this moment, or he didn't.

Succeed.

So be it.

A snarling ball of fury exploded into the small clearing, a roar shattering the night until he just knew eardrums must shatter. Fear tried to batter its way from its prison as the thing rose up on all-too-humanlike back legs and towered until it seemed to fill his eyes, the sky, the universe. His hands seemed to lose their grip on the spear, palms slick.

It lunged.

Ito screamed.

SUN TZU SCHOOL OF COMBAT
KAZNEJOV, KAZNEJOV PREFECTURE
GALEDON MILITARY DISTRICT
DRACONIS COMBINE
27 FEBRUARY 2428

"Takeda?!" Justin rushed into the barracks.

Takeda Tesuo turned toward the overly loud call, a smile gracing beefy lips, a smile that grew as he noticed several dark looks among those getting ready for the ceremony. *Ah, Justin, how you irk them.* "Calm down. Calm down. Deep breaths. What's up?"

The other student, red bushel of hair, broad face and too many teeth behind too-small lips, stumbled down the center aisle of bunks and skidded to an abrupt halt behind him. He tried to speak, but it only came out in heavy panting, and he ended up bent over.

Takeda slapped the younger man on the shoulders, his large, thick-fingered hand almost sending the boy into the concrete floor. "I said, deep breaths. You know, you wouldn't have this problem if you'd run with me in the mornings."

"I'm gonna be an aerospace pilot," Justin finally got out, straightening. "Not some mudslinger that needs to run everywhere."

Takeda glanced around and smiled more openly—stretching his broad neck mockingly—at the additional looks directed at such a comment. They all turned away. "Justin, we prefer 'grunts.' And since I'm not going to be here much longer, I'd advise you to keep your feelings about us 'mudslingers' to yourself. Some of these 'slingers don't take to you as well as I do."

The younger cadet abruptly glanced around, skin tone vanishing beyond its already pale countenance into corpse-like territory. Takeda bellowed laughter, then turned around, dismissing the lot of them. Glancing in the mirror, he adjusted the high orange collar on his white tunic, then glanced down to make sure the belt woven into the tunic rightly displayed the clasp—fashioned in the Kurita Dragon crest—at center. His barrel-like chest often made that task difficult. A quick stomp settled the black pants and feet firmly into red boots. Smart, dangerous, chocolate-brown eyes under an almost sheared-off forehead and crew-cut black hair met a will of steel in the metal reflection.

Today is my day. I have done this. First in my class.

He nodded at himself once, then closed the locker door and swept out of the room, knowing Justin would tag along like a lost puppy.

"Takeda."

"What?" He kept walking, passing the barracks. Headed down the main thoroughfare to the stadium and the area where the cadets would assemble for the graduation ceremony. Several jeeps, the whine of their electric engines crawling up his neck in feathery brushes, swung by, carrying everything from other cadets to military police, family members to the press, and even the quick glimpse of heavy brass now and then.

"The reason I came. Jules, you know, the mail girl?"

Nothing could dampen his spirits today, and another smile tweaked lips. "Of course I know the mail girl." Everybody *knew* the mail girl. Justin just seemed too innocent to figure it out yet. *Ah, to be a first year again...*

"Well, okay. Yeah, the mail girl. She was running behind, what with all the graduation gifts and mail and having to run that extra detail 'cause James got hurt on the range, and so—"

"Justin," Takeda cut him off. The boy could run at the mouth enough, you'd think he'd be able to hit the obstacle courses better. Then again, he was a flyboy. They were soft.

"Right. Sorry. Just excited. You never talked about your family. Had no idea."

Takeda stopped so quickly Justin almost ran into him and danced back. "What?" Takeda asked in a calm voice, thick hands stiff, planed for combat.

Too many teeth flashed. "Your family. I've got a letter for you from your parents. Jules told me to give it to you right away. Couldn't resist *that* favor, right? Anyways, I thought you said your parents were dead?" Innocent, open-faced Justin extended the letter.

Takeda looked away from clear eyes—only the boy's innocence kept teeth intact—and took in the letter as though it were a viper, nestled in the tall grass and ready to strike.

"I mean, I could've been wrong, you know," Justin fired on. "But I thought for sure after I ran into you and you about busted my arm, you told me you didn't have any family. But this is great. A letter. And on graduation day! My parents really couldn't care less where I'm at, as long as I'm not in their house, so this is nice. Must be nice. Mind if I read over your shoulder? It..."

Justin's inane, thousand-kilometer-an-hour mouth continued spewing, as long-suppressed memories of cold and stink and endless alien chittering rose from the depths. The bright day darkened, eyes flattened and muscles tensed, as though enemies were closing, and a desire to kill rose. With lightning speed, he snatched the letter from Justin's hand, slipped it under his tunic and turned away, fleeing—no! Not fleeing, *continuing* towards the assembly area.

"Hey! Takeda. What's up? You're not going to read it? Come on. You've got a family?! Brother? Let me guess. Brother and a sister, right?!"

Takeda swiveled around, coming nose to nose with Justin, flat eyes projecting death. The young cadet withered as though left to dry on a sun-baked plain.

"I said I have no family."

He swiveled back away, marching on as though to war, leaving a shocked and hurt Justin tilting in the wind.

This is my day. No one else. My day. Mine! Top of the class. I've won blades! I will be a samurai. A soldier for the Draconis Combine.

That is all *I am!*

ISF HEADQUARTERS
NEW SAMARKAND, NEW SAMARKAND PREFECTURE
GALEDON MILITARY DISTRICT
DRACONIS COMBINE
9 OCTOBER 2435

"Ahhhhhh."

The yawn came hard and strong, and Ito leaned back in the ancient chair, arms stretching until his spine popped deliciously. Shaking the incessant demands of sleep from his eyes, he stood up and swung his arms around, careful not to reach too far in any direction, or he'd smack the cubicle walls.

The single light source from his cramped desk tried vainly to keep the dark of the large office room at bay; the mammoth, four-kilometer-on-a-side ferrocrete bunker of the Internal

Security Force headquarters loomed all around as though it was a small planetoid, ready to crush him with its gravity well.

He scratched unceremoniously at the scars on his chest and discarded the errant thought, along with the fluttering wings of horrors in the night.

"Ito. Do you ever sleep?"

Ito jerked around as a woman's face loomed out of the darkness, materializing into the blunt-nose, square-jawed Illena. "Jesus. You want to kill me, woman?!" He breathed in the musty air of the lowest levels of the facility, trying to calm a racing heart.

"Jesus?" She cocked her head, humor dancing in green eyes. "Don't you mean 'Buddha?'"

He glanced around, suddenly all too aware of dark corners and shadowed alcoves. "Right."

"After all," she began, voice falling into the clipped, short tones of their supervisor, "'we have to uphold the ideals of House Kurita, even if the current ruler would wash away our Japanese heritage.'"

Ito leaned against the old partitions and broke into a smile. "Yeah, but it's not like Parker Kurita was all fired on all things Japanese, or his brother ahead of him, even before Nihongi took the throne."

She leaned across the same partition slightly to his left, face a scant half-meter from his. "True. But our current most beloved Dragon does seem to be going out of his way to make us despise the Combine's origins."

He shrugged. "I'm just a poor farmer's son, Illena. What do such warrior traditions have to do with me? I'm more worried about the economic havoc denuding our power. How many mercantile families have been put to death now?"

She returned the shrug. "I've lost count."

"Exactly. How long can this be kept up?"

There was no answer to that question. Nihongi Von Rohrs was the ruler of the Combine, and his word was law. And despite the extreme early morning hour and the absolute knowledge they were the only two working in this section of the lower levels, they both glanced around, abruptly aware at how their talk would be taken if it carried to the wrong ears.

Nihongi's purges of Draconis society were starting to be felt within these very walls.

An uncomfortable silence heightened the sense of helplessness over the current state of affairs, and abruptly the feeling of the looming bunker once more pressed against the base of Ito's neck; he unconsciously scratched at his scars again.

Illena finally broke the silence. "What are you working on?"

"Endless reports." He turned back, painfully aware of the hundreds of data discs stacked like detritus awash on the forgotten shores of his desk. "Got enough here to pull down a Nadrin Vapor-Whale. They've got me studying kroner reports."

"Uh?"

"The latest Lyran reform attempt out of Archon Katherine. A unified currency."

"The Lyrans are becoming a danger."

"Yup. Their Commonwealth Scout Corps is nothing but a means to try forging a new military. I don't buy this 'exploration' crap."

"Of course."

He looked back at the tone in her voice, then shook his head sheepishly. "I know. I know. We're just grunts. Info finders. And our Lord Dragon is already slicing away at the Lyran flanks, seizing worlds. Of *course* our superiors know all about this."

"Exactly."

He sighed heavily and tried not to fall into the yawn it spawned. "I'm just meant for great things, that's all. I can feel it."

"Aren't we all?"

Searching for sarcasm, Ito met her frank stare for a moment before nodding, refusing to be drawn into *that* conversation again.

"Anything *actually* interesting?" she asked in a conciliatory tone.

He nodded, accepting. Of all places, here you had to know who your friends were…and pay them back. Often.

"Maybe."

"What?" She stepped closer and paused at the edge of the cubicle.

He slipped carefully back into the chair—didn't want it breaking again—and waved her into his personal space. "I've gotten some weird stuff coming out of the Hegemony."

"We're always getting weird stuff out of the Hegemony."

"I know. I know. But we're so concentrated on the Lyrans and Davions right now. What with the war against the Lyrans and the Archon's stunning moves these last years to centralize power and unify her realm—"

"And keeping an eye on the Davions so they don't stab us in the back while we're not looking..."

"Exactly. All of that is making news out of the Hegemony, when they've been so quiet on our border of late."

"Well, they've got their own issues. Lord Jacob—" she dropped her tone, "—is about as loved as our own lord, and his offensive against the Federated Suns and Capellan Confederation only hurt him more."

"Too true. The Battle of Tybalt was a paltry victory for what they paid in men and armor."

"Exactly."

"So they're focused elsewhere, and so are we, and I'm telling you, I'm getting some weird stuff out of the Hegemony."

"What exactly?"

"Hesperus." While Ito talked, he pushed through the stacks until he found the right disc, then slipped it into the computer and pulled up several smuggled shipment manifests. "Look at this. I've run modeling on Hesperus back almost ten years, and they've been slowly ramping up the importation of a wide range of raw materials, as well as specific-made parts. And you know this can't be the whole picture."

"Parts. You're worried about parts?"

He glanced up, exasperated. "Come on, Illena. Give me a little more credit than that. I've run serious numbers. Been working on this for over a year now."

Illena leaned over his shoulder, resting her hand on the back of his neck. Out of the corner of his eye, he took in the line of her jaw and found it pleasing; a soft sniff brought a hint of jasmine, underscored with the light touch of sweat and skin too long from a shower.

Buried under work, like all of us.

"These look like WorkMech parts. At least, some of them. No idea what these are here, or this." She turned to find his eyes on hers, and they shared a smile. "But it's just parts. So they're ready to open a new WorkMech production line. So?"

"No, no. It's more than that. Damn hard to track it effectively with the Terran Hegemony Complex on a Lyran world. We thought it ludicrous for so long, but while the rent must be hell, the bureaucracy surrounding the place is a better defense than a regiment of armor. Makes infiltration exceptionally difficult, having to pass through two sets of safeguards. Regardless, I think they might be trying to arm WorkMechs."

She rolled her eyes, despite their friendship and possibly something more. "Please, Ito. Everyone's been trying to arm WorkMechs. Shiro-age armor is still better than one of those jury-rigged monstrosities."

"I know. But I think they're making something completely new. Not a jury-rigged machine. But one designed from the ground up."

"Just like everyone else, including us. To dismal failure. And there doesn't seem to be enough here for you to really make that conclusion."

He leaned back in his chair, worrying at his lip. "I know."

"And our wondrous supervisor?"

He shook his head, crestfallen and slightly angry.

"Exactly."

"But I *know* something's here."

"Okay. I think you've got great instinct, Ito. So run with it."

He glanced up at such supportive words to meet slightly peppery breath and a stroke of satin lips to his.

"And be careful with that photo," she said softly, before she strode away, leaving him thunderstruck.

He slowly stood, looking into the shadows that already swallowed her as though Illena ceased to exist, except for the slight warmth tingling his skin. *If the supervisor finds out*...he glanced back around to let his eyes rest on a worn and faded photo of his family tacked to the wall, a photo he only brought out at this time of night. After all, when you're a shadow, you can't have connection to anyone, right?

So dangerous, that photo. And so dangerous, that kiss.

A smile blossomed, pushing against the dark. *But there's something there. And I'm going to find it. The Terran Complex. Illena. Find both.*

Seventeen straight hours in the chair, and the lingering malaise sloughed off as though unused skin as Ito dove back in.

**NEAR NEW BOUNTIFUL
ST. JOHN, DEMILITARIZED PREFECTURE
RASALHAGUE MILITARY DISTRICT
DRACONIS COMBINE
6 JULY 2439**

"Demilitarized. Right." Takeda laughed.

The thirteen men left in his company chuckled as well, as the last rays of sunlight painted the rolling fields of spina-wheat into a deep ocher.

"How many times they gonna try to take St. John back?" *Chu-i* Jack Tolnik commented around a stalk of wheat. In his tan-and-brown fatigues, face paint, and heavy weaponry, the sloppy grin and wheat stalk seemed all the more incongruous. But he was as steady a soldier as any Takeda had commanded.

"I believe this makes four."

"Best move yet. You've got to give the merchants that. Sucker most of our troops in the region to Lovinac with a decoy fleet, and then pounce on us here." He shrugged as he eased back into the wheat towering almost four meters into the air.

"Almost. But almost isn't good enough."

"Good enough to cut our regiment to ribbons."

Cold blue eyes speared Tolnik, who somehow still managed to shrug it away when men twice as experienced and ten times as powerful quailed under the burning gaze. But Tolnik nodded, and lapsed into silence.

The wind rustled the wheat like a rainstorm across 10,000 kilometers of some of the richest soil in the dozen worlds of the entire, newly forming prefecture. Takeda eased back into position, carefully moving the last shield of foliage out of the way. Beyond, a subtle removal of wheat just below the crown of the hill they occupied allowed an unobstructed view for long kilometers. Binoculars brought the distant armor column into sharp focus. He counted almost thirty-seven tanks and twice that many infantry carriers, slowly bulldozing their way through the wheat fields.

Looks liked they finally learned to not follow the roads. A cruel smile stretched fleshy lips almost taut. *Time for another lesson.*

"Sula."

"Yes, sir."

"We ready to go?"

"Yes, sir."

He paused, knowing they'd have to begin moving again. But he wanted to savor the plan a little more. And give his men another few breaths of peace after the last four months of guerrilla work that had worn them down to their current paltry numbers. But enough.

The cruel smile moved to something more.

Enough.

Finally, the sun dipped fully behind the mountains, casting shadows across the entire landscape. As the column ran at its closest point to their current position, only ten kilometers distant, he held up his hand and clenched it into a fist.

Through the binoculars, Takeda made out half-a-hundred columns of light, spewing up into the darkening sky in a massive perimeter around the entire Lyran line of march. Almost like fireworks on New Year's.

Stupid merchants. You always think in terms of money and the bottom line. And never in victory. Of course we've taken so many worlds from you. As we'll continue to do until you're no more.

The burning napalm flares set the dry wheat on fire in a conflagration that lit the night in ghastly oranges and sickly reds and yellows. He nodded in appreciation of the Lyran acumen as the armor column quickly moved to break out from the circular inferno already racing toward and away from their position. Reluctantly, he lowered the binoculars and stood as he turned around. The merchants had a lot more on their plate than worrying about spotting a single soldier buried in the wheat on a hill ten kilometers away.

"Ladies and gentlemen. Lunch break is over and the main entertainment has begun. But we're not invited, and if they catch us, they might be a tad upset."

"Not to mention the fire," Tolnik spouted as he spit out his stalk, stripped a new one, and mashed the end between brown-stained teeth. "Even with the prevailing wind running against the fire, it'll be marching our way fast."

"Right you are. And damn spina-wheat burns hot as hell. They should've learned that lesson last month. Armor's no good if the crew is boiled alive or your diesel fuel blows."

"No way for a soldier to die," Brian said softly.

Chocolate-brown eyes found Brian's blues, and this time Takeda tasted the satisfaction of a flinch and turned away. "But they're not soldiers, *Kashira*. Don't forget that. All they think about is money and the bottom line. We know victory is more important."

"Command may not be happy about you destroying all this food," Tolnik joined in Brian's defense.

"I believe I'm the only one here who should worry about Command." The words slapped his remaining troops fully awake and to attention, even Tolnik. "We're soldiers of the Combine. If I must burn this entire continent, or this entire world, that's what I'll do. Our Coordinator has demanded victory, and that's what we'll give him."

The distant *thump* of an explosion heralded the first detonation. Hard to tell at this distance, but it sounded more like ammo cooking off than diesel (either way, it would tear the tank in half). He smiled and nodded.

Exactly.

He began a ground-eating trot, his men filing in behind him as they disappeared into the night.

**EDINBURGH
SKYE, ISLE OF SKYE
FEDERATION OF SKYE
LYRAN COMMONWEALTH
9 OCTOBER 2449**

"Damn it." Ito ground his teeth until he thought enamel flakes would coat his tongue.

Hurrying away from the café—casually, of course, to try avoiding undue attention—he wiped sweaty palms on the front of his one-suit, fingers brushing the multi-headed arrow logo of the corporation that had supposedly paid his wages for the last seven years. He did his best to ignore the missive burning a hole in his pocket.

Leave it to Shipil to screw up a shipment to one of their *own* facilities.

The unseasonably warm Skye autumn day brought a sheen of sweat to his brow quicker than he could wipe it clean—not nerves, not that at all. He crossed Johanson Street over to Fourth, and then proceeded past a veritable cornucopia of quaint window shops, tourist traps as far as the eye could see. But Ito saw another vista and moved with alacrity, wending in and out of the constant stream of people (outworlders and locals), before finding his current flophouse.

A quick jangle of an ancient key let him past the rusted iron gate and into the shoulder-width alley crammed between a clock and a doll shop. Refuse clogged the narrow lane with almost sedimentary determination, and he stepped carefully to avoid a reprimand for slicking the hem of his one-suit with garbage. Never mind that he never saw a single customer at Shipil, and left every day covered with the grease and grime of refurbishing ancient drop shuttles. Ito wasn't allowed on the production line of the newest vessels coming out of Shipil Company's production yards. Oh, no. Not even three years would get him that privilege yet. Such thoughts burst and faded like fireworks against the growing frustration.

How long can I be at this?

Reaching the back of the alley, he scrabbled up steps threatening to toss him down at each footfall before reaching the decrepit apartment over the doll store. But at only fifty kroner a month, he wasn't going to complain. After all, a dirt-poor farmer from Alkaid didn't have the know-how or money to get more than a stinking, rat-infested flophouse above the "quaint" part of Edinburgh (meaning much too expensive for what you got, and if you scratched and sniffed, you wouldn't like what you found...or what you found wouldn't like you).

Before moving through the door, he checked the almost invisible thread licked and slicked into place over the door jamb. Nothing wrong. Sidling through, he paused and breathed deeply with closed eyes. Others developed astute hearing, but smell worked well for Ito, and he'd gotten out of more than one dicey situation in the back alleys of Edinburgh through his overactive nose and the smarts to take its advice immediately.

After almost a minute, he moved into the room, ignoring the alarming creak of ancient wood and slid into the single chair at the edge of the stained and moldering card table. Trying to avoid gnawing on his tongue, Ito pulled out the missive, smoothing out the crumpled paper.

Betty's marmalade won't be delivered for another three months due to an early frost on the harvest.

The paper rasped against dried skin, and he lurched out of the seat, frustration radiating from every pore. Three years. He'd been the one to discover the existence of the Hegemony's BattleMech, and for his success his supervisor had assigned him to a low-level infiltration cell on the Lyran world of Skye.

Because you couldn't directly infiltrate the Terran Complex on Hesperus II, or even the system, without raising too many flags. So you circled it, like a vulture creeping up for the kill. A creeping that took years. Years of subtle bribes and moving individuals around from world to world and company to company, like *go* stones on a game-board tablet. Years of failures, and yet you kept going. And his was just a small part of the network. A web cast by the Internal Security Force to snare the ultimate prize.

He stalked to the fridge, yanked it open, and ignored the fetid smell of despised sauerkraut fermenting in the back (would the woman ever get the hint he couldn't stand the stuff, or her advances?!), pulled out a beer, closed the door, and popped the top. He gulped it down as if to quench some fire burning within. He began to pace, while the paper on the table mocked his failures.

I finally track down enough Nostia gems to satisfy the bloated pig so he'll pass along my transfer orders to a roving cargo handler, and Shipil ships it to god knows where?! And now, the second part of the interim plan was in jeopardy. He'd have to cut his losses. Move again. Perhaps even leave Shipil.

A lopsided smile pushed and prodded against stiff muscles, until he flopped back into the chair and swore as it creaked, threatening to dump him to the floor. But he could see the article, buried on page twenty-four, below the fold of *Edinburgh Now!*

Jason Torgil, resident of the lower east side and a mechanic for Shipil Company, was found dead yesterday. Apparently a robbery gone astray, Mr. Torgil was killed by a shotgun blast to the face and chest. The sobbing girlfriend, a Mrs. Klark, who owns the doll shop over which Mr. Torgil resides, says she found his body when she brought up a fresh batch of sauerkraut and smelled something funny.

The final tension left as he laughed and laughed. *Ah, Illena. We wanted this. And yet here I am, stranded on this horrible Lyran world, without enough resources to do my job effectively with the ongoing purges, and where are you?* Melancholy settled resolute, but he managed to keep a smile. *Just have to make do, right?* He glanced towards the well-worn photo on the wall.

And where are you, little brother? Where are you? Are you in a hellhole as well? He shrugged aside such maudlin thoughts and began making preparations for moving on.

Succeed. He silently flogged the word, trying to find the power it once held, and ignored the slight echo, as though the room within was mostly bare.

Or entirely empty.

LOCATION UNKNOWN
KAZNEJOV, KAZNEJOV PREFECTURE
GALEDON MILITARY DISTRICT
DRACONIS COMBINE
27 FEBRUARY 2457

"Who are you?" The disembodied voice cracked the silence.

Takeda Tesuo lay on his side. Head canted back, he sucked air shallowly, careful to not breathe too deeply. The flagstone's deathly cold leached away life quicker than the trickles of blood.

"Who are you?"

He was long past the point of trying to guess the reaction to any response. At times speaking would evoke pain, while other times silence did the same. He had tried every trick in his book, and they had all failed. But in the end it didn't matter. None of it did. Survival mattered, and to do that, he had to let go. Let go of the anger and the killing urge. Because he'd tried that angle too. And while the man's blood felt good pumping its last rhythm across scabrous fingers, the punishment had been almost more than he could bear. And all the more galling as it took him unaware. He knew the one sure way to crack him would be to stake him in a pen with *goji*. But they didn't know that, and he'd die before he let that slip. But when they buried him to his chin in the cave and he couldn't move beyond craning his neck and the darkness took him for so long...that was a torture. Exquisite in its simple finesse, in that they did nothing but allow his own mind to feast on itself.

He'd have to remember that one.

"Who are you?"

The smell of his own feces- and urine-soaked rags obscured any olfactory hint of who the person (or persons, as that happened now and then) might be. And despite his best efforts, the muscles in beaten thighs and along his chest began to tighten. He sank teeth into a tongue savaged from such abuse to keep from reacting to broken ribs.

"Who are you?"

Someone that will kill you when this is done. That brought a sickly smile of satisfaction and a slight gush. He relished the coppery tang partly quenching his thirst as blood dribbled onto the inside of his right cheek, and his tongue tasted the sweetness before he swallowed.

"Who are you?"

I'm one who will survive this. I'm one who will not be beaten. Everyone has tried my whole life to beat me, and I've survived. Just one more thing to survive. One more test.

"Who are you?"

They'd tried this tactic as well. So many times. A calm, incessant questioning that came as a balm after the fury of beatings and the spewed hatred. But in the end it could drive you as insane as anything else. One more thing to survive.

"Who are you?"

"*Samurai,*" he finally breathed between clenched teeth. Despite resolve, he winced as muscles tensed for a blow.

"Who are you?"

Despite the beatings and the silence and the erratic behavior of his torturers, he'd yet to find the answers they sought. *What do they want? I am samurai. I will pass this, and be stronger than ever.*

I was chosen.

But why?

Because I'm the best. I've succeeded across half a hundred battlefields. I've lived and claimed victory when so many others have fallen. How many merchant worlds bear the Dragon banner because of me? How many Fedrat worlds?!

The two sides within jostled questions fast and furious, up and down the scale of reason, trying to spot the clue that might unlock the darkness.

The Dragon. *I* am *samurai.*

But am I? I've moved beyond samurai. I'm becoming something new. A new type of soldier the likes of which the Dragon has never known. The likes of which the Inner Sphere has never known. A super killing machine to strike in the dark. As the ninjas of old, so have I become. Just one final key.

The Dragon. The ninjas. Invisible. Secret. Nothing.

"Who are you?"

"Nothing." The words slipped from red-smeared and swollen lips. But they hung, rang with power.

A minute light blossomed, shielded in the corner. Yet it still stabbed painfully into eyes long accustomed to darkness. He flinched as his whole body reacted to the pain of testing.

"Takeda Tesuo?" the voice said with real compassion.

He opened lips to respond, almost falling into the last trap. Despite the rigidity of muscles and coming pain, he firmly shook his head. "I am nothing."

A grunt of satisfaction, and the light increased to the point his sensei's face came into focus. He blinked rapidly, while two brutes moved back from the edge of violence and stepped away. The man extended a right hand, which Takeda ignored. He gritted his teeth and gingerly moved into a sitting position.

Another grunt of approval. "Takeda. Welcome to Draconis Elite Strike Team One."

GALILEO INSTRUMENTS, SATELLITE OFFICE
MOORE, ALGEDI PREFECTURE
BENJAMIN MILITARY DISTRICT
DRACONIS COMBINE
1 DECEMBER 2459

Ito unlocked the front office door and allowed the slim man to slip in, bringing a gust of wind and the scent of pine trees following him like an obedient pet, before closing and relocking the shuttered door. Without saying a word, he walked back through the reception area, past the single restroom, and down a short hallway to his office. Easing into the room, he sidled around his desk to take up position behind it as he eased into the tilting seat.

Utterly insignificant. *But by such actions do we find the steel to face the future.* Though he managed to keep it silent, he chuckled grimly. *I'm almost fifty. Fifty. And what have I got to show for it? A career predicated on the death of endless superiors to land me in this unenviable position.* He tried not to sigh, but the other man's eyes noticed everything. Everything.

Ito decided on a frontal assault. "This could not be handled through a standard courier and missive?"

The other man, likely half Ito's age, blinked slowly, a cat watching prey and waiting for the fatal mistake. "*Iie.*"

Ito raised an eyebrow, and the other man shrugged and glanced around in answer. Despite the situation, Ito's ears warmed at the implied rebuke. *Of course these offices are clean. But you still shouldn't be stupid enough to speak Japanese here!*

The man finally spoke. "No, this could not be entrusted to a courier."

While Ito tried to focus on him, the man seemed to simply blend into the wall. Bland features and eyes and hair and clothing. Only mildly Asian-looking. The perfect spy. *But how perfect would you be stuck in this hellhole, against an impregnable target?*

"How long have you been working on cracking the Terran Complex?" the bland man asked.

Ito glanced around the room, at the knickknacks and bric-a-brac that almost half a decade in this office had brought. Statues and scrolls and fake flowers and plaques: the life of a real Galileo Instruments office chief.

Eyes paused on an ancient, faded photo before continuing.

The life of a man diligently working to move Galileo beyond New Oslo. A man trying, for business reasons (of course!), to widen the trade barrier into Lyran space his efforts cracked with Shipil. *After all, they build drop shuttles and we build control equipment for spacecraft. A match made in heaven, right? A match that should've allowed me to expand the seeds I planted in Shipil all those years ago, and yet for almost twenty years lay barren as an asteroid behind me, and nothing to show for it.*

His eyes narrowed as he brought them back to the ISF man (no name, never that) and showed grim teeth. "I believe you know that better than I?"

The other man nodded, still standing in the doorway, as though he found the reek of the place too much. Too mercantile. Too Lyran, despite its Kuritan soil.

Isn't that what you needed from me?! The internal shout fell away, echoing.

"Despite your continual advancements, you have shown no success."

Only his already-gritted teeth kept him from shouting back: *Of course I haven't! Not when our Dragon has eviscerated us!* Despite the hollowness within, he maintained enough self-preservation to keep lips sealed.

"The Lyrans succeeded where you failed."

Because they have more money than god, and they shower their operatives with it.

"As best we can tell, four years ago. Four years ago they stole the plans."

An educated guess my staff generated.

"We received word more than two years ago that they were building a 'Mech based on stolen plans on the world of Coventry."

Information I netted and provided.

"And three years ago your cell on Tharkad was eliminated."

A cell compromised after another purge.

"And now the battle of Loric. A single company of these BattleMechs annihilated the Bloodthirsty Giant's entire armored regiment. Captain-General Marik dead, his forces decimated, and their decades of success thrown into disarray. How soon until a 'Mech army comes calling to the Dragon's doorstep?"

It already has, pig! Or is our Dragon working under revisionist history, and the fight on Styx never happened? All too soon, a real army would come marching, in place of the token show of force in '43. All too soon.

"And it may not be just the merchants. Rumors persist that the Davions have acquired 'Mech plans from the Lyrans."

Not rumors, pig! My network acquired proof after the debacle on Tharkad. You simply refuse to believe it, as our precious Dragon Von Rohrs would have all our heads if he was aware all the enemies at our doorstep now have access to 'Mech technology.

"And you sit here, the highest-ranking field agent deployed, and you have utterly failed."

Failed to understand why I keep this charade up.

"You should have succeeded long ago."

Succeed. The word from a different life would've pounded within, straightening spine, sharpening focus to the accomplishment of any goal. Now it fell away into nothingness, without even a flick of an eyelid.

"You are being recalled."

Of course.

It didn't hurt as much as he thought it might. Twenty years of his life flushed away on an impossible task. The fact that the Lyrans had stolen the plans (regardless of such salt on a gaping wound) made it ten times as difficult, as the Terrans fortified their complex on Hesperus until all the Combine regiments might not crack it. But all was hollow within. The only bright spot was the small look of surprise that suffused the other man's features at his total lack of response.

You wanted me crushed by a lifetime thrown away. But I've long been crushed, pig. Long crushed.

He stood without a word and slowly came around the desk as the other man turned away and headed back down the hall.

With casual ease, Ito pulled the old photo from the wall, tucking it into the pocket of his slacks, before shutting the door tightly, leaving a false life behind as easily as casting aside a used food wrapper.

Garbage.

**DEST TACTICAL COMMAND CENTER
PESHT, KAGOSHIMA PREFECTURE
PESHT MILITARY DISTRICT
DRACONIS COMBINE
24 JULY 2460**

Takeda paced like a caged animal within the confines of the back courtyard. One hundred forty paces up the side of Barracks A. Four hundred twenty-two paces along the first of four primary complex centers. One hundred forty paces back down the side of Barracks B, and six hundred and forty-two paces across the open field next to the razor-wire tipped, five-meter-tall fence and the dense forest beyond. The brilliant afternoon sky, with white smudges like a child's fingers brushing against blue paper leaving a trail of clouds low on the horizon, brought little enjoyment.

Still alive. He almost faltered in his steady, ground-eating pace. *My brother is still alive.*

A roar in the distance cracked the air, but Takeda hardly blinked, long used to the primal roars. He stomped on. After one more circuit, his feet began to ache, and he abruptly stopped, fury exploding like a supernova. From one breath to the next, darkness and chittering and falling snow occluded sight before he bit into his tongue until blood threatened. The killing urge rose, until the day ceased to exist.

"Takeda."

The word floated on the air like pollen, hesitant and unsure of a reception on such hostile ground.

I am not a child.

Ungritting his teeth, Takeda slowly turned and found a wave of emotions sweeping him away as a stranger, yet not. He moved close and stopped several meters away. Both men stood staring, eyes drinking.

The white, balding hair, slight paunch, and wrinkled skin spoke of a soft life. A failed life. The anger at his stomping like a child abruptly vanished, as this apparition of failure stood stoically. And so it came to this.

"You're old," he finally spoke, voice harsh as the synthetic sand saturating the entire region surrounding the DEST Tactical Command Center; a sand to eat through rubber, flesh, and even armor with equal voraciousness.

Ito nodded once.

"Not just your body. Your eyes. You're old."

Another nod.

Another roar sounded in the distance, and Ito visibly winced as he glanced sideways toward the perimeter and the simian creatures beyond.

Revulsion coursed through him until it threatened to kick in a gag reflex. *Old. Weak. Failure. Everything they say about you is true.* "You're a failure." *As I am not. Look what I have done with my life. Commander of DEST One!*

"In ways you cannot imagine."

"Then why have you come?"

Ito cocked his head as a tired smile pulled at his lips and humor peeked through weary eyes. "Um, little brother, you brought me here. I assumed after my recall that I'd either be fishing, or with the fishes."

Despite all Takeda's effort, anger stitched blotted lines across his skin, and his fleshy lips wrenched into a harsh frown as he sealed back words that rose. *I have no need to speak those words now. Not after all this time. Not after my accomplishments.*

Déjà vu swept him as sadness enveloped Ito's countenance. The situation brought too strong a memory, and Takeda turned away to stare off over the distance of the giant structures of the command center and the numerous anti-aircraft weaponry dotting roofs like semi-sentient and horribly violent gargoyles.

"I'm sorry, Takeda."

"Sorry for being a failure?!" he snapped back, refusing to meet his brother's gaze. "It is the Combine and the Von Rohrs you have let down. Not me."

"I'm not sorry for that failure. Of all my failures, that is the least of my sorrows. I'm sorry to have left you. You. And Mom and Dad."

Anger at Ito's words swam like a balm of hot tea to chilled limbs, and he pushed aside any feelings the latter words evoked. He turned to face his brother straight on, head back, thick torso thrust forward as though facing a gale, brown eyes snapping with righteous indignation. "You fail the Von Rohrs, and you're not sorry?! You should be careful of the words you speak, *brother.*" He almost spit.

"I'm long past caring about the words I speak, Takeda. If death comes, I'm ready for it. I've learned that, at least, in my own service to the Dragon. I serve as I've always served. But there comes a time when service must mean something. When a servant can expect the master to make his contributions meaningful."

"We serve. What does it matter how the master acts? He is lord."

"Yes, but lord of what? Of us. And we serve faithfully in the knowledge such contributions will be used wisely. Not cast aside, out of hand."

The aged look slowly melted away from Ito as the conversation continued and he warmed up to the debate. Takeda's anger only solidified at the apparent enjoyment his brother took in such words.

"It's not our place. We serve."

"Damn it, Takeda. Listen to yourself. Because you sure as hell aren't listening to me. I *know* we serve. But we have a right to expect our lord to provide us the support to accomplish his commands. Not to have him standing at our back, randomly slitting the throats of subordinates and superiors alike, leaving you wondering when for no reason other than the cast of bones you'll find a wet ribbon slicking your own throat."

Anger pulsed until his vision began to flee. He panted with the intensity of it, hands almost tailor-made for killing clenching into powerful, thick fists. "You speak treason." He growled it out as though pulling a blade along the breastbone of an enemy, attempting to wrench it free. "What they say about you is true."

"Treason? Listen to you. Have any of us seen our *Dragon*? He's our lord, but not god. Why does he hide? We don't even know his name? Kozo? We think. It's not Nihongi. But they hide behind the walls of Shiro City, and they suck the carcass of the Combine dry from the inside."

"Treason." Tendons popped on rigid fingers, skin taut and bones aching with the desire to kill.

"What? You going to kill me here, little brother? *Please*. If so, be done with it. But I've no fear of the eyes of the Dragon. I *am* the Internal Security Force. I've done my share of wet work. I've done what needs doing for twenty long years, while my lord tied my hands at every step. I would gladly follow the Dragon anywhere…

"…if he were *worthy* of following."

Nostrils flared, and a light hint of gunpowder from the afternoon practice range wafted by, raising the desire to kill to an unbearable level. "You shame me."

Ito laughed, bitterly, eyes hot with self-recrimination. "I shame myself. But for reasons you'll never understand."

Takeda ignored the words. "But you're no longer a part of my life. I long ago renounced my blood in service to the Coordinator. Perhaps if you'd done the same, you would not be standing here clothed in failure."

Ito opened his mouth to speak, then slowly sealed his lips before moving a little closer, eyes intent as though to strip away the layers of protection Takeda had woven around himself long ago.

Finally stopping just out of reach, he spoke. "So that's what all this is. You think I'm a failure, and you brought me here to rub your success in my face. Ah, Takeda, you disappoint me. You're alive. You've done well for yourself. That's all I care about now."

Takeda's nose wrinkled, and the gag reflex did kick in. He spit on the ground between them. "And that is why you failed. Family means nothing. The Dragon is everything. I brought you here to see if you were truly as tainted as the rumors said. I wasn't wrong, older brother. You should feel free to take a stroll beyond the gates in the jungle. Your life will end as messily as it has obviously been lived."

Ito shook his head, the sadness once more etched into his face like fissures in the broken façade of an ancient stone statue, weathered by weepy streaks of dirt and disuse.

"Will I see you again?"

All of a sudden, the bottled anger jetted out as though through a release valve, and the harsh sarcasm of a lifetime erupted as Takeda laughed. "Will you see me again? That's what you want to know, brother? I'd just as soon see you dead. But I won't have that on my hands."

"So that's a no?"

"No. Which is too bad. Because you'll miss the chance to congratulate me when I succeed where you failed."

"Uh?"

Takeda laughed until tears started. "Ah, *brother*. Where you have failed, the Dragon will send his new soldiers. Where twenty years of fumbling in the filth of civilian clothing failed, we will take in one swift stroke."

Confusion turned to alarm and for once anger. "You can't!"

Laughter continued to bubble at the ridiculous emotions tweaking Ito's face this way and that. "I most certainly can. And I will."

"No, you can't do that."

"And why, oh-so-successful Ito, should I listen to a word you have to say?"

Ito stepped within arm's reach, face mottled with his own fury, and some of Takeda's enjoyment eased into a new feeling as he changed stance slightly and prepared for another eventually. *I don't want to kill you, brother...*

"Takeda. Listen to me. Call me a failure. I don't care. If that makes you feel better, then etch it on my forehead and run around yelling it. But for god's sake, listen to me. I've spent twenty years studying the Terran Complex. Yes, I've done my studying on your new troops, and before the Lyran stunt, I would say you could easily pull it off. But the security since the merchant's smash-and-grab has increased a hundredfold. Nothing outside of ten regiments will breach that security. I'm telling you, super soldiers or not, you *will* fail."

Takeda grunted, as though his stomach had been punched, and stood on the verge of violence before curbing desire. "I have *never* failed in my life, brother. And I won't fail now. Just because your life's in ruins, do not paint your failures onto me."

"Takeda!" Ito practically shouted, anger and some emotion he couldn't pin warring with equal intensity across his brother's face. "This is not about me. This is about stupidity. There's a reason we've failed for twenty years. And now it's only worse. And he's sending you. If you go to Hesperus, you'll die!"

Shaking with the desire to kill, Takeda's vision receded again for several terrible moments, until he mastered himself once more. "I'm *not* a failure. I'll succeed. Before a year has passed, I'll show you a success you never achieved."

He turned and stormed away.

YAMASHIRO (SHIRO CITY)
NEW SAMARKAND, NEW SAMARKAND PREFECTURE
GALEDON MILITARY DISTRICT
DRACONIS COMBINE
20 OCTOBER 2460

Tapping his breast pocket to feel the assurance of the photo within, Ito jaywalked to the accompaniment of the angry horn of a passing hover transport, and plunged into the sidewalk milling with people heading home from work in the late afternoon. The somber purple hat worn by his target kept vanishing, forcing him to crane his neck and try to speed up without giving his position away.

The wash of civilians along the streets of the ancient capital of Yamashiro on New Samarkand assaulted his senses, but years of training overcame his body's slow decline and he managed, just, to keep up without compromising the tail. After all, it only took three weeks to establish enough of her movement patterns to finally know when would be the best time for contact. *Not bad for an old fart.*

Fifteen minutes of brisk walking later, and Ito slowed, suddenly faltering in his resolve as he neared the café. *What will she think? She just might turn me in.* He paused on the other side of the street, drinking in her features, and tapped the photo one more time for strength.

I've got to do something to try stopping you, Takeda. Something. And if I can't stop you, maybe, just maybe salvage something from this mess. From this life. He scuffed his shoe several times against the curb, swallowing the petrol fumes coating his tongue from the New Samarkand Metals plant at this edge of the city, then crossed the road—this time with the light—and stepped up to the table. Without preamble, he seated himself.

Without looking up from reading her newssheet, she spoke. "I prefer to be alone, thank you."

He smiled, as her voice—a voice he'd dreamed of for so many long years—soothed any worries. Even if she turned him in, to see her one last time, to hear that voice, even if it might never whisper in his ear again...all worth it. "I'm sure you would, Illena, but I'd prefer to sit with you."

She glanced over the newssheet, green eyes now haloed in wrinkles and the perturbed line marring her forehead melted away under an incredulous, stunned look.

He waited for her to respond, but after the waiter came and went, depositing a coaster and a glass of water and she still sat as though poleaxed, he finally broke the tableau. "You actually going to speak with me? Or did you somehow manage to lose your voice after all these years?"

She slowly leaned forward, placing the newssheet on the table, then reached out a hand to poke him. Roughly. "You're real. You're here."

"Of course I'm real. And here."

"Could you be more stupid?"

"What?" Emotions seethed at the anger in her voice.

"They're hunting for you. You vanish off Pesht, and then just show up here? Here!"

"Please," he said, glancing around surreptitiously, "not so loud."

"Not so loud?" Green eyes went from shock into anger. "Not so loud. What are you talking about? You're within spitting distance of our headquarters. And *you* tell *me* not to be loud? More importantly, I'm assistant lead to the counter-terrorism section. Good god, Ito. I've got to turn you in, and you come to me?! And you tell me to keep my voice down?!"

He fiddled with the paper napkin on the table, began pulling it apart. "Because you're the only one I could turn to for help."

"What are you talking about?"

"I've got a plan."

"Well, I would hope so, because right now you're looking pretty crazy."

"Can we go someplace else?"

"I've got to turn you in," she said, pain etching harsh lines into the crow's-feet around her eyes.

"I know, I know. But just hear me out. I've got a plan. Hear me out, and if you still think I'm crazy, then you can turn me in. I won't run. Not from you."

She slowly smiled as anger gave way to some other emotion he was too afraid to pin down. Afraid his years of longing and hope, despite all his service, would not be returned.

"I know a place."

**TRADER-CLASS JUMPSHIP *STAR OF THE NORTH*
UNSETTLED SYSTEM, VIRGINIA SHIRE
FEDERATION OF SKYE
LYRAN COMMONWEALTH
3 JULY 2461**

"And that's the plan, ladies and gentlemen," Takeda said, smiling broadly. Sitting around the conference table on Deck C of the *Star of the North* JumpShip, DEST One had met one final time to review the battle plan. "When do we jump?"

"Twenty-one hundred hours," *Chu-i* Sul spoke from the opposite side of the table.

He nodded. "Any final questions?"

Tai-i Staverson spoke up, voice thick with a Rasalhagian district accent, the man's sheer acumen and dedication overcoming any doubts about his loyalty, considering his region of upbringing. "In place of the fuel-air explosive, why not simply use a tactical nuke? The idea is to demolish Maria's Elegy Spaceport and pull off as many forces as possible from the Complex for our HALO insertion, right? Not to mention minimizing their ability to respond to our liftoff. Then why not ensure that goal? Fuel-air ordnance might not be enough."

Takeda nodded, visions of a mushroom cloud vaporizing an enemy city like candy canes dancing in a child's mind before Christmas. "I made the same argument. However, I've been handed my orders. It's believed the Ares Conventions bind us too tightly. Despite the anonymity of our assault, a nuclear device might force the hand of the Terrans. Might force them to spend undue time and resources trying to find the culprits. Some deaths and stolen plans are one thing. Death on the scale of a nuclear device would be something completely different. Would likely bring in the Lyrans as well. And while

I'm not worried about that, it brings unneeded complications and risks."

Staverson nodded in return. "And if the Terrans found out we used the device, they would likely stop at nothing coming after us."

"Exactly. Lord Cameron would have no choice but to respond. The Archon as well. And they both have years ahead of us on development of the BattleMech and arming their militaries. We go with the plan as is. Any other questions?"

None. He met each trooper's stare with hot, audacious eyes, promising success. Each nodded in return, confident of their abilities and of the skills of their leader.

Me. I've done this. The smile grew as they unlocked themselves from their chairs and began to expertly shoot down corridors to their stations in preparations for the final jump.

TRADER*-CLASS JUMPSHIP *IMPERIOUS
UNSETTLED SYSTEM, COVENTRY PROVINCE
PROTECTORATE OF DONEGAL
LYRAN COMMONWEALTH
3 JULY 2461

"How did you talk me into this?" Illena said, snuggling closer in the zero gravity, skin touching along most of their entwined bodies.

"Because you can't resist me," Ito responded.

She playfully punched him, sending them rotating, the sheet—her attempt at a modicum of decency—slipped away, revealing wrinkled skin, brown spots, and sagging breasts. She caught him staring down the length of her body and turned away to bury her face in his chest.

"Don't," he said softly, reaching to her chin and gently forcing her eyes back to his, scant centimeters apart.

"I'm old," she whispered, face revealing the shame of him seeing her like this.

"And I'm not?!"

"No one has seen me like this in…in a long time."

"Except for yesterday. And the day before, and the—"

She cut him off with another quick thrust of knuckles to ribs.

"Not too old to bruise me but good."

"Exactly."

"So you came along for the sex, then?" This time he managed to block the punch.

"I came along because you're too stupid and pigheaded to do this alone."

"Ah, so you agree with me."

"I didn't say that."

"But you always told me my instinct—"

"Has run dry after so many years. Why else would you be doing this?"

"Um, I hate to bring this up, but I wouldn't be here without you. I burned every bridge and every connection I've got. I'll be lucky to not be cut down as soon as I cross back over the border. I couldn't have done it without your connections as well."

"And they'll cut me down before you. I've burned even more bridges."

They lapsed into companionable silence, luxuriating in the feel of a long-lost body held close, the release of spent sex, and of finally doing something. Something that actually might help the Combine.

Even if that help meant defying the Dragon himself.

The intercom buzzed, startling them both out of a light doze. Reaching out a languid hand, he tapped the control. "Ito."

"Ito. *Tai-sa* Coller. The meeting begins in fifteen."

"*Domo.*"

"*Arigato gozaimasu.*"

He clicked off. "Meeting. Right. What a great euphemism. More like a firing squad." He looked away from the speaker to find Illena smiling broadly and already moving away toward her waiting clothing.

"What?"

"You may have said it informally, but you spoke Japanese."

He paused, before shaking his head and reaching for his own clothing in the small, Spartan berth. "Hanging around these troopers is getting to me."

"And being in the ISF never did?"

He shrugged as he pulled on a T-shirt, slid into underwear, and snatched his floating pants. "I've been among Lyrans for so long. *Gaijin.*" He shrugged. "My father tried to raise us with some of his heritage, but wasn't a huge stickler for it. Too poor, too much time to spend on raising *gojis* and feeding the family than to teach us to read and speak Japanese, much less all the traditions to go with it. And during my time in training?" He shrugged again. "Always seemed more of a pain than a blessing. If our fearless leader feels our traditions are worthless, who am I to disagree and follow such outdated traditions?"

"You've been gone so long," she countered, voice muffled for a moment as she pulled on her own shirt. "I keep forgetting. While you've felt the purges more than anyone, you've not been on the inside. Not felt a subtle rhythm growing within the halls of headquarters. The slow, true embrace of our Japanese heritage. Where once it was a joke, or a way of distinguishing ourselves from civilians and Unproductives, it's becoming a culture of passion. Something to believe in."

"When we cannot believe in the Dragon?"

Green eyes met brown, and they nodded as one. Finished dressing, they entered the passageway, grasped handrails, and maneuvered down the corridor. Without any real zero-gravity training, they looked ridiculous, and soon found laughter to hold off mounting anxiety as they poked fun at one another until reaching the large berth commandeered to act as the briefing room.

The tension in the berth slicked the walls as they entered and spotted *Tai-sa* Coller, along with *Tai-i* Madula, Jips, and Hondus. All four heads swiveled their way. Cool and reproaching eyes found theirs, then held as everyone settled into chairs and locked themselves into position.

While the joy of reunion, even after nine months, still roiled within, nerves finally worked to the fore, and a tic started pulsing in his arm. *Not the friendliest reception I've gotten.* He pulled on years of negotiating among enemies and began.

"I first would like to offer my most humble apologies. I deceived you. And for that you've every right to throw me in the brig, or worse."

Four cool sets of eyes, four blank façades. He could always read a Lyran. Terrans less so, but he could still do it. But his own countrymen? Especially this new type of soldier? It's not only that they were hard to read. He was slightly terrified of what he'd find if he scratched the surface too hard. *Like my brother?* He jittered away from that thought as though leaping away from a leper. He swallowed, setting such disturbing ideas aside, and pulled on the reserves of his skill and the calming balm of Illena at his side.

"However, in my deceit, I still serve the Draconis Combine," he continued, knowing how fine a line he walked. Knowing his brother would see right past that line, but hoping these men would miss it. Needed them to miss, or all was for naught. *I couldn't stop you, Takeda. I could only do the next best thing.*

"Though I misled you to this point, nothing in my reports was misleading. Everything I told you is the truth, as far as I've been able to ascertain with the extensive network I put in place."

Their continued silence and unblinking eyes unnerved him, and he continued after tapping callused fingertips several times across the hard plastic tabletop.

"And when you confronted me with the truth of my deceit, I've presented you with nothing but the truth in return. Every scrap of information I've gleaned in twenty years. There's no one outside of the Hegemony more intimately familiar with the workings of the Terran Complex on Hesperus."

He swallowed, trying to work moisture into his mouth and glanced aside momentarily to find Illena staring hard at the four DEST officers, as though waiting for their inherent violence to overcome any sensibilities and reason. He turned back just as *Tai-sa* Coller finally responded.

"*Hai.* You lied."

Ito waited, as though expecting more and then realized the part he would play in this. The accused. Been down that road so many times. He bowed deeply, despite the long years, falling back into the familiarity of Japanese customs, like old clothing pulled from mothballs.

"And for that, we will exact our recompense when the time is appropriate."

Another bow, this one held longer.

"However, I have consulted with the entire team. Since our departure from Pandora, we have pored over your information, trying to find error or additional duplicity."

Such a calm delivery. *The man might as well be talking about a tea ceremony with the next-door neighbor instead of my life. Illena's. The possible future of the Combine!* Ito tried to suppress a shiver. Failed.

"Despite our best efforts, there is only one answer. Your conclusions are correct. There is at least an eighty percent chance of failure on DEST One's assault of the Terran Complex, while your own plans provide an almost seventy percent chance of success."

Ito remembered to breathe.

"But one question. Why not take this to your superiors?"

Ito laughed bitterly before cutting off the sentiment as Illena tapped his foot with her own in recrimination. "In the eyes of my superiors, I'm a failure. Do you really believe they would lend any credence to my words? My reports? Would you and DEST Two have given any time to poring over the information if you were not already stuck en route to my target?"

Silence once more shrouded the confrontation, as four sets of eyes pounded into his. For just a moment, the ridiculous thought spun up that they were conversing through some type of ESP, which is why they never once turned toward one another or even blinked; all their energy devoted to a mind meld that allowed them to better present a united front. A façade that would not falter or blink from flogging him for his lies.

He swallowed past the nervousness and anxiety and, as before, decided on the frontal assault. "Look. I lied. I already told you that. I used every trick in my bag to grease the wheels and get you and a JumpShip moving toward a target. I appropriated you with lies. I seduced you with lies. And there's a trail of lies and deceit leading back almost nine months as I worked to try salvaging something from the lunacy of the coming assault on Hesperus. I told you I'll pay your price, and I will. But if you feel the plan might actually succeed, then be done with this judge-and-jury bit. We're a jump away, and we'll need every last bit of time to fine-tune my plan, now that you're fully on board." *And I can't go with you. Not my type of fight. And I'm old.* The last bit galled.

Finally, *Tai-sa* Coller glanced at his junior officers, receiving a nod from each. The last, Hondus, stared out from deep-set eyes under a rocky overhang of a brow and a nose the envy of any raptor. His eyes seemed to pierce Ito's more fiercely than even the *tai-sa*'s, poking and prodding, before finally nodding as well.

"We serve the Dragon as well, Ito," Coller said. "And while you must pay for your crimes, we admire and understand desperate times often call for desperate measures. Provided we achieve success, which will help to mitigate your due for such deceit."

Ito nodded and leaned back in his chair, as though he'd just run a marathon. He knew what his brother would say. Knew he would consider it an attack on his successes. Would consider it a move to one-up his little brother. But it wasn't that. Not that at all. He'd finally come to grips with the fact he could neither change his brother's mind nor halt the ludicrous assault on Hesperus. But what he could do was try to pull some small victory out of defeat.

He ran hands over a stubbled face, scrubbing and rubbing deeply at sore and tired eyes. He'd spent almost twenty years working in, around, and among Lyrans and, by association, Terrans. Why strike at the impenetrable Terran Complex, when the Lyrans were building 'Mechs on Coventry? Safe in the heart of Lyran territory, no one could possibly come to fight on Coventry, much less steal BattleMech plans. Right?

But the Lyrans didn't think along the lines of stopping a theft of *their* BattleMech plans. Why would they? They already had it. and were quickly moving toward an army of BattleMechs as fast as their endless coffers could disgorge money.

A lazy smile crossed Ito's lips for the first time in too many years. *Time to show them the error of their ways.*

TERRAN HEGEMONY BATTLEMECH COMPLEX
HESPERUS, RAHNESHIRE
FEDERATION OF SKYE
LYRAN COMMONWEALTH
23 JULY 2461

Damn. Damn. Damn.

The words ran as a metronome to the steady *thud* of the approaching BattleMech while the constant personal-weapons fire pinned them in place. Half his team dead. The other half as wounded as Takeda. Fury surged and waned and surged in an ever-widening gulf of rage threatening to split into madness and swallow him whole. It kept him lucid and awake despite the loss of blood from the sucking chest wound made by the heavy-caliber bullet that had penetrated his armor.

This cannot be happening. I must succeed. I must. *So close.*

Fingers subconsciously found the rhythm as well, tapping on the satchel and the more-precious-than-gold contents within.

The ground shook with the detonation of another grenade. Pinned between the inner and outer complex walls, the chunks of concrete—blasted by their own ordnance for shelter—provided little enough cover. Enough to keep from being slaughtered outright, but not enough to keep the death toll from slowly rising. And while they managed to keep the three separate teams of troops gunning for them from overrunning their position, time was up.

I've succeeded my whole life. Every step of the way. Me. I did it.

A soft voice rejoined that he did *this* as well, but he managed to ignore it among a new furious round of gunfire. He leaned out from behind his current rocky shield and fired off a short burst from his machine gun, the muzzle flash overloading his night goggles, gun vibrating and hot in hand. He leaned back for cover as a spattering of bullets tore through the space his body had just occupied.

He glanced toward his remaining soldiers, their plain black clothing, nondescript weapons and gear making them almost invisible in the night. And more importantly, making their affiliation invisible. *In that final act, I'll succeed.* Despite losing half the command and the coming knowledge of the demise of the rest, he smiled savagely at the stoic resolve and ruthless efficiency with which they dispatched any Terran or Lyran unlucky enough to pop up a head.

He convulsively gripped the satchel as a new wave of pain radiated out from the bullet lodged along a rib, and a new torrent further soaked his sneak suit. Who would've believed such defenses? Again, the smile lurched into a crazed grin. And despite it all, they'd *still* almost succeeded. They had the plans and they'd almost got away. Almost!

The fire stopped abruptly, as though they had entered the heart of a furious hurricane. Takeda breathed shallowly to keep the stench of sulfur, gunpowder, and burned meat from his lungs and listened intently. A tap on his shoulder and he glanced back to find Staverson pointing not down, but up. Back behind them, and up and up.

With a fear he only equated with *goji* and the night and frigid winters, his bowels turned to water, and his jaw dropped open as the twelve-meter-tall metal giant finally cleared the southeast corner of the inner complex with a rumble that shook the ground violently, and raised its weapons.

With his defenses shattered for the first time in his entire life by a nightmare made reality, words he'd refused to ever contemplate bobbed to the surface.

You were right, brother. You were right.

The words didn't hurt nearly as bad as he feared.

The night and reality vaporized in a ball of horrific energy.

YAMASHIRO (SHIRO CITY)
NEW SAMARKAND, NEW SAMARKAND PREFECTURE
GALEDON MILITARY DISTRICT
DRACONIS COMBINE
11 NOVEMBER 2461

In the darkened room, Ito wept openly, tears splashing onto a worn and ancient photograph. The paper, already curling and cracked, began to de-adhere under the salty liquid assault, and the captured image grew fuzzy, then incoherent, and then passed into a mulch of soggy chemicals and paper. A testament to its age.

"You have left me in a bad way, Ito Tesuo."

The soft, hypnotic voice spoke for the first time in long minutes since delivering the news. News the brain knew would come, but the spirit tried to ignore. News that shattered.

"You see, not only did you steal DEST Two, but then you had the audacity to return victorious when DEST One failed. Who would have thought five operatives could simply sneak in and out without a single person the wiser? Perhaps we should've tried that on the Terran Complex instead of the more direct approach, eh? But that's neither here nor there. You still leave me in a bad place. Do you see?"

Robbed of speech for long minutes, Ito swallowed convulsively several times, tasting the almost claustrophobic mustiness of the room—as though fresh air never touched this place—and the salty tears of a loss with which he could not cope. Despite the years. Despite his own fear of what his brother had become. Despite everything, it had been family that supported him through the long decades. Family was everything.

Oh, Takeda. I failed you.

"Do you see?" the voice prodded again, the soft syllables almost snakelike in their delivery.

He'd given up trying to penetrate the thick gloom and discern the individual talking to him from the depths of the alcove, and so tried for a response with eyes still sealed tightly shut. "No, I don't see."

"*Tsk, tsk.* Are you what the Internal Security Force creates? I was right to cleanse your numbers. If we are not to be devoured by our enemies, we must have brains and insight beyond your obvious capacity."

The matter-of-fact delivery slid under skin with the ease of a shiv, and anger sparked and died, smothered under sorrow. *Think what you want. But it's over now. Nothing you can do will hurt me further.*

"Must I spell it out for you, Ito?" the voice continued in tones drenched in condescension. "I *am* the Dragon. I cannot do wrong. I cannot *be* wrong. And yet DEST One failed. *My* plan failed. And yet you, a disgraced ISF agent pulled from the field, not only managed to steal my DEST Two, but then you had the audacity to succeed."

He tried to blot out the words, back throbbing and knees numb from hours of kneeling on the teakwood, but they slipped and slithered like vipers through the tears and harrowing sadness, finally prickling to life a lifetime of skills. A spark of worry ignited.

"Now, DEST One left no evidence. The Hegemony will never be able to trace it back to me. Much less the silly merchants. In fact, from what we can discern, despite their security, your brother came exceptionally close to success. Will the Terrans want to broadcast that a handful of agents almost breached their most secure facility? I do not think so. They will blame it on a drop shuttle accident or some other convenient excuse and sweep it under the carpet as quickly as possible. As any ruler, we write history and can ignore that which does not suit us.

"But while I rule, the Warlords of the military districts can be...troublesome. And such a catastrophe as this can only cause some to think above their station. To think thoughts that can only end in the parting of necks. And that is so messy. No. This cannot be laid at my feet. My plan obviously was the right plan. My plan obviously was perfect. It's the execution that must be flawed."

The spark turned into a conflagration, galvanizing sorrow into desperate rage. "You cannot do that." Ito snapped erect from his slouched position, on the verge of rising to stand.

Shadows moved, as though Von Rohrs had raised a hand. "Ito," the vague outline spoke calmly, "I would advise you not to leave your knees. My guards can be a little protective of my health, and I'm afraid you will not die instantly, but you will be stopped. And then you *will* wish you'd been killed in my presence."

Ito clenched down on muscles threatening to mutiny despite the danger—a danger all the more real for the calm certainty of its delivery. "You can't do this."

"Can't? That is not a word I know." The dry chuckle came as though a joke only the Coordinator might understand.

"You'll place the blame on Takeda. You'll destroy his memory. His life!"

"Of course. Where else could the blame be placed?"

The fury became a torrent of vile hatred for this despoiler of all that made the Combine great. Of what had destroyed his life and now threatened to destroy his brother's as well. *You are no leader. You're filth, deserving of the death to which you consigned my brother.*

His mind stuttered and spun as the frustration burned and flared at the situation. "You send him to his death and then will destroy all his achievements as well?!" He could hardly speak, his tongue so slicked with revulsion.

"But he failed. There can be no atonement for failure."

The crushing weight of those words sent him over the edge; he almost surged to his feet in a desperate bid to meet a scrawny neck with hands ready to kill. His mind still spun, racing to find an answer. Finally, as muscles threatened to tear out of his will's grip, an idea effervesced. Words Illena spoke. Long-term plans. His whole life had been about the long-term plan. And now it might be so in death as well.

Succeed. For the first time in too long, the word rose with a hint of its previous power, illuminating the darkness within and shedding light on the path he was already moving down. *Yes.*

No, hai. A calm flowed across inner wounds, raw and bleeding, bringing a surety of knowledge. *I serve. I serve the* Combine.

"Von Rohrs," he began (*I'll never call you Coordinator!*), "there is another path." *But would he bite? Would this son, as the father before him, accept such a solution, when they've tried so long to destroy our heritage?*

"And what could that be?"

"In this place, on these grounds hallowed by generations of Coordinators back to Shiro Kurita himself, I would take upon myself my brother's failure and absolve him, and you, of shame."

Silence descended, until long minutes stretched and the tension built until it dug a dull blade along his stomach. He shivered at the premonition, wondering how he could so embrace that which meant so little to him for so long. His mind teetered as the silence became oppressive and he wondered if Von Rohrs even occupied the alcove any more.

For the Combine I serve. For family. For the brother I failed.

"You would choose this path?"

"If it means Takeda's legacy remains whole, yes. *Hai.*"

"Mmm…" the sound vibrated between lips, as though a tuneless ditty. "My plan is absolved in a way the Warlords cannot dispute, as it would call their own devotion to the samurai path into question, leading to problems from *their* subordinates. And you are no longer a part of the picture, and your victory is mine? You cease to exist and Takeda is victorious, albeit in death. Is there a downside?"

Ito held his breath, knowing the question remained absolutely rhetorical.

With an abrupt move, the shadow surged into partial view, causing Ito to lurch back in fear.

Instantly four guards appeared from hidden doors, striding to Ito, one slipping a blade out. *He will kill me and be done with it. And Takeda's life will be destroyed!*

But the guard halted and dropped the blade to the wooden floor, the sound a gunshot in the gloom-filled room. The bare blade actually managed to gleam in the near darkness, pulling eyes like iron filings to a lodestone, before Ito raised them to find a still shadowed outline looming near.

"I accept your offer, Ito Tesuo. But I know you well, Ito. And the irony of this is not lost. For you to embrace what you've taken so lightly is most amusing. It will make good dinner conversation."

Ito allowed the words to skim off the surface of his calm and began stripping out of his top. No appropriate clothing or tea ceremony for the ritual. Instead a devil's bargain in the dark. A life lived in the dark, as ever. "Then you agree?"

"Oh, yes. Oh, wait, *hai*. Right? Of course I agree. The solution, while surprising, is exquisitely perfect. I get everything I want, and you die. Of course I accept. Your brother's memory will be left alone."

Ito nodded, hesitated just a moment as the remembrance of Illena's soft lips and laughing smile illuminated inner darkness, then reached for the blade. She would understand. *We have given our lives in service.*

And this is the long haul, Von Rohrs. I lived my life planning across decades to reap what I sow. And now I give my life to further plant that seed. You despoil the Combine. And by taking my own life in this way, it will remind those who come after of the roots to which we must return.

The sword felt light as a feather as he settled back into a casual crouch. A quick flick of the blade split a strip of cloth from his shirt, and he wound it around, giving his hands a place of purchase. The ring of another sword leaving its scabbard behind announced a guard ready and prepared.

Someone will come along and remove your line. A true Kurita will sit on the throne once more. Perhaps not in your lifetime. But a day will come when we remember who we are.

I serve the Combine.

The blade bit deep and hard, pain radiating out like a supernova, but he managed both strokes before the guard's blade took his head.

A DISH SERVED COLD

CHRIS HARTFORD AND JASON M. HARDY

**ANTIPODES CONTINENT
LORIC
LYRAN COMMONWEALTH
9 APRIL 2459**

False thunder hammered the ground. The floor trembled, and fresh cracks shot through one of the bunker's concrete walls. Lights flickered and dust showered down on the plotting board, sparkling like rain as it fell through the holographic projection.

The blast hit Captain-General Geralk Marik like a heavy mallet against his chest. He grimaced and gripped the table edge tightly, his attention focused on the blue lines plotting out enemy positions. Lines which, until this morning, had been isolated from his position by a broad swathe of purple. Now they looked like arrows shooting toward his command post.

The Lyrans had pushed through some of his most hardened troops.

"Their artillery has us bracketed, sir." The young commtech split his attention equally between his lord and his sensitive communications gear. "That was a direct hit on the western logistics park."

Geralk grunted. Ammo and food supplies gone. Problematic, but far from fatal.

He leaned over the table. His purple uniform was creased, dust-covered, and smeared with a crust of dried blood from earlier fighting. Slouched over the table, he felt a weight far beyond his thirty-nine years.

"What about our counter-battery fire?" he asked.

"Inconclusive, sir. Captain Mathews says they're off on the eastern edge of the Lean Massif, on the far limit of our range."

"Damn it. Where are the fighters? We need that battery silenced!" He scarcely heard the reply as another massive projectile slammed into the ground, and the trembling started again. This time the flash of the explosion was clearly visible through the bunker's window, and Geralk could smell the acrid smoke of burning plastics and flesh. "And their pushes?"

"The western assault is being held at the Djansky crossing, but our losses are mounting. The northern one is crawling along the Kohlan Road—we've slowed them enough for the 471st Armor to roll into position. They should hold."

"At least the Elsies can't come across the massif any easier than we can," Geralk said. "But damn their artillery." As if on cue the earth trembled, lights flickered, and more dust rained down.

"And find that spotter!" Geralk snarled.

More flames were visible though the thin slits of the bunker's windows, and the explosions of ammunition mixed with the cracking of flames, shouts from the camp, and the regular *thump-thump* of the Marik artillery's counter-battery fire.

"Galaine! What's the status of the eastern perimeter?" Geralk asked the commtech.

"No reports, sir."

"Then get me a sitrep."

Galaine made a series of attempts over the comm, becoming increasingly agitated with each failure. "No answer, sir."

Geralk stared at him, unbelieving, then threw his baton onto the map table. The image wavered and collapsed. Turning, he dashed to the doorway and leaned out, twisting to look east at the massif. High on the ridge near the security post were flashes of light: tracers and explosions. Though easily half a kilometer away, he could see several large figures through the smoke of the burning stockpiles. Very large figures, from his point of view, but they were likely just people casting large shadows through the setting sun and mist. Nothing on the field would be *that* large.

"I think we found our spotters," he said grimly. "Send the security company to the eastern perimeter." *And let's hope they hold.*

Galaine waved to him urgently. "Captain-General, message traffic for you, sir."

Damn amateurs. The slightest hiccup and everyone wants to speak to the Captain-General to make sure their 'Vital Report' gets through. He sighed. "Which position?"

Galaine paled. "None, sir. It's the Lyrans."

Geralk snatched the headset. "This is Captain-General Geralk Marik. Who's this?"

"Captain-General, I am General Marcus Andrews of the LCAF. I'm here to tell you you're done." The voice was clear and precise, slightly colored by a guttural accent.

"What?"

"You're pinned. You're undermanned. Yet I'm still willing to offer you the honors of war—something you generally neglect to offer us." The bitterness in the general's voice came through clearly.

"Pinned?" Geralk scoffed. "You've pushed through a few infiltrators. I hardly think I need to surrender." He was calm and collected as he spoke, but put enough ice in his voice to chill the entire planet. "I think you overestimate your position."

"And I think you underestimate the threat facing you. But you'll see soon enough. *Ihr Begräbnis,* Metzger."

A wall of fire rained down on the camp from the hillside; lasers, missiles, and cannon shells washed over the camp like an Olympian storm. The concussion knocked Geralk flat, and he could smell singed hair—his own.

The figures on the hill moved, striding down the slope as their weapons struck at the weak Marik defenses; not illusions at all, but fully as tall as their shadows had made them appear. Like angels of death, they descended toward the camp, swatting away temporary buildings and immolating defensive positions. Armored vehicles in the Free Worlds camp began to fire back, but they were few and far between.

Struggling to his feet, Geralk snatched the singed purple beret from his head and threw it into a corner of the damaged bunker, then grabbed a padded armor vest and a worn helmet and put them on.

"Pull everyone back across the Sumire River," he said as he donned the gear. "Hold there if you can. If not, pull back to the DropShips."

Galaine relayed the orders, then turned to his commander. "And you, sir?"

"'I'm going to buy the breathing room you need." Pulling on the gloves he wore tucked into his belt, he strode outside and toward his tank parked adjacent to the command post. The massive vehicle bucked as it fired shell after shell at the metal predators stalking into the fringes of the camp.

Geralk reached up and triggered the mike on his helmet. "Michael, I'm mounting up."

The firing stopped and the Captain-General hauled himself toward the turret hatch. Sitting in the entry, he turned back to Galaine, who stared up at him. "Get out of here now. That's an order."

"But, sir, *you* must evacuate, too. "

"Turn tail and leave the troops? Never. I'll be the last one back to the rally point." He grinned. "Didn't they tell you, Galaine? Mariks are invincible."

Galaine smiled weakly. He saluted his commander, who dropped into the tank and pulled the hatch shut.

Within moments, the turret-mounted cannon resumed its volleying at the approaching giants, its revving engine adding acrid fumes to the already-bitter air. Edging forward, the vehicle's body swung in line with the massive main gun. He saw his targets more clearly now as they strode forward on heavy metal feet, their huge limbs bristling with every possible deadly weapon. They were like nothing Geralk had ever seen, and he found himself almost dazed by their aura of power.

He snapped out of it, churning tracks into the temporary roadway as he sped alone toward the approaching walkers, a lone mortal charging a pack of titans.

**ATREUS CITY, ATREUS
MARIK COMMONWEALTH
FREE WORLDS LEAGUE
11 MAY 2459**

Dark spots appeared on the dusty cap she clutched as tears fell from Simone's eyes, her angular cheeks streaked with the remains of her makeup. It was undignified, but no one commented on the young woman's display of grief.

She sat alone—tall, thin, scarcely nineteen years old—on the throne in Parliament's chamber, and wept as the weight of the realm settled onto her shoulders.

The reports coming back from Loric were sketchy, but still contained enough information to be devastating.

"How?" Her voice was scarcely more than a whisper.

"He fought valiantly, Lady Marik, buying time for others to withdraw." General Mattias Ivanevksy spoke, heading the delegation. His normally florid face was drained of color, his mouth drooping into his white beard. "The Lyran machines—these 'BattleMechs'—were unstoppable."

"I know he led the rearguard." She sniffed. "How did he die?"

The general looked uncomfortable, glancing at his assembled colleagues and at the empty parliamentary benches. "He died…with honor."

"Dammit!" Simone smashed her fist on the arm of the marble throne. The blow made a feeble *thud* rather than the echoing crash she would've liked. "Just tell me, Ivan. He was my *father*."

"As you command, Captain-General." Technically the title wasn't hers yet, but as the sole eligible Marik—her brother was only eleven—she would succeed Geralk unless she refused the post. "His tank was disabled, but he refused to surrender. He kept shooting at the BattleMechs—and by all accounts crippled one—but eventually they overran his position. They—" he hesitated, "—crushed the Captain-General's tank."

Simone Marik struggled to keep her composure during the brief report. She wiped away her tears, leaving a puffy and streaked face with red-rimmed eyes, but her spine stayed stiff, and she projected resolve in the midst of her grief. "And the rest of our forces? What happened to them?"

"The command staff complied with your father's orders, pulling back to the river line and holding it into the next day. But the Lyrans moved in and surrounded several elements, crushing them or forcing them into surrender. The last transports containing survivors left Loric on the twelfth. We're anticipating some form of diplomatic approach in the next few weeks to discuss repatriation."

"And the dead?" Her voice shook but was stronger than moments earlier.

"They have been interred on Loric. We were unable to recover your father's body, but we believe it lies with the others."

"He would have liked that. The troops were as much his family as Carlos and I."

Ivanevsky nodded, pausing to give the new Captain-General time to cry again if she felt it necessary.

She didn't. Her bearing stayed strong, and her voice hardened into ice. "And the other worlds?"

"Holding. It appears the Lyrans have only a handful of these BattleMechs. They can achieve local superiority, and we should expect a pasting where they bring these machines, but they don't have enough to support strategic operations." He paused. "Knowing the Lyran industry, however, it's only a matter of time before they field these machines in much greater numbers."

"So we need our own BattleMechs." It was not a question. She beckoned to a small, dark-suited man who was lurking behind the FWLM officers. He was tanned with dark hair, looking like a holovid star shrunk down to three-quarters size. "Something for the National Intelligence Agency, I think. Director Sanders, do you have appropriate assets?"

The wispy, quiet figure thought for a moment. Jervais Sanders's memory for minutiae was legendary in governmental sectors. Then he nodded. "There are a couple of operatives I can set to work on it. Alarion gives us the best chance, I think."

"And the timeframe?" The streaks on her face were now the only evidence of Simone's recent grieving.

"I can issue appropriate directives as soon as the operation is approved—"

"—which I will do immediately after the confirmation hearing tomorrow," she interrupted.

Sanders nodded. "We will likely need twelve to twenty-four months communication and operation time."

Simone leaned back and faced the generals once more. "Can we hold that long?"

"Provided our assessment on the quantity of the walkers is accurate…"

"It is," said Sanders, his whispery voice sliding through the room's echoes.

"Then we can hold," Ivanevsky said. "We'll have some short-term losses—more worlds may fall while their BattleMechs are on the move. I've issued precautionary orders limiting our vulnerability to the machines, but that won't stop them from coming. However, I believe I can prevent our losses from blunting our overall strength. For a year or two."

Simone thought for a moment, then placed her bony hands on the hard armrests of the throne, her pale eyes seeming to pull in strength from the rest of the room, filling her gaze with determination and even ferocity. "Then I pray our enemies become overconfident, and don't see the hammer blow of our vengeance falling upon them."

**ALAR HEAVY INDUSTRIES
ALARION CITY, ALARION III
LYRAN COMMONWEALTH
16 DECEMBER 2461**

"So what happened, Mr. Rive?" The speaker's diction was clear, precise, and cold, matching the atmosphere in the room. The voice had an edge that could cut glass. "Tell me. Please."

Desmond Manvers, CEO of AlarCorp, sat in a room that seemed designed just for him. He was at the head of a table whose top was centimeters-thick glass; the walls around him were stone polished to a reflective gleam. The only non-reflective surface in the room was the AlarCorp logo etched into the table's surface. The effect of all the shiny surfaces was disorienting to many visitors to the room, especially when they saw the CEO surrounded by a seemingly infinite number of ghostly mirror images. Manvers had two assistants flanking him, but they seemed almost as insubstantial as his reflections.

Manvers' shoulder-length gray hair brushed the top of his elegant blue suit. The tall, dark back of his chair loomed over his head, in contrast to the small, barely padded chairs around the rest of the table.

A king must have his throne, Chief Engineer Gunther Rive thought, self-consciously rubbing his close-cropped blond hair while noticing how awkwardly large his off-the-rack gray suit suddenly felt. The seats in which he and his two companions sat felt like they were made of stone.

"Well, Chief Rive?" Somehow, Manvers's voice seemed to have become even colder.

"It appears we...have a leak," Rive said. He'd never been arrested, but he couldn't imagine the experience would be much worse than this. His stomach felt like it had been braided, and the room seemed to be spinning and tilting dangerously to Rive's right. He almost leaned to his left to compensate, but he had enough self-possession to realize how that would look to Manvers. "On Project Ymir. Some details of the TTS have appeared in the *Alarion Technical Review*. None of them are directly attributable to Ymir, but their specs are too close for comfort."

"And you identified this similarity?"

"No. Elias did." He gestured to Elias Singh, the project's chief electronics engineer, sitting on his right. Older than Rive, Singh wore a trademark orange turban that was the one point of color in the otherwise sterile room.

"And you reported it right away after Mr. Singh informed you?"

"No. We weren't sure at first, and wanted to compare specifications."

"You weren't sure? Aren't you intimately familiar with the project? Isn't that your role?" Manvers's jaw clenched and unclenched, and the grinding of his teeth was almost audible. Other than that and the occasional curt, authoritative hand gesture, he sat still. To his right, one of the assistants keyed a running log of the conversation, while to his left the other kept up a flow of facts and figures, displayed on the liquid-crystal display beneath the desktop. The screen showed stock prices, up-to-the-second news, equations for calculating profit and loss on various transactions, and—Rive presumed—details of the present meeting and its attendees.

"We wanted to examine the matter in more detail before issuing a wider alert. Calling in security right away might have been counterproductive, had it been revealed to be just a superficial similarity."

"And was it?"

"It didn't appear to be."

"Mr. Singh, did you agree with the decision not to involve security right away?"

Singh leaned forward to address the figure at the head of the table. His voice was soft and trembled slightly. "As Gunther said, we wanted to avoid overreacting."

"It was a simple question. Did you agree with the decision?"

"It was—"

"Yes or no will suffice."

Singh took a deep breath. "Yes."

Manvers focused his attention on the third member of the team, sitting on Rive's left. "Mr. Connor, did you likewise concur? Did you think not involving trained security was a good idea?"

Daniel Connor tried briefly to match Manvers's cold gaze, but failed miserably. The young man's eyes darted away quickly, scanning through many of Manvers's ghosts around the room, before finally settling on a spot somewhere over Manvers's left shoulder. "We could have talked to security sooner, though it wasn't our fault."

"So you don't concur."

Rive shot the younger man a worried look, and suddenly wished he hadn't. Manvers would be alert for any signs of discord between the three of them.

As if on cue, Manvers turned his attention back to Rive. "Mr. Rive. Do you have a problem with Connor's assessment?"

"Not a problem, no. We discussed the matter, and agreed that the best way to proceed was how we did."

"I'm sure you're familiar with the security procedures, yes?"

All three nodded. The assistant made notes.

"Well, let's leave that for a moment. What was your assessment of the situation? How did it come about?"

"We concluded that the details in *ATR* were from the Ymir schematics, at which point we contacted security."

More notes. "And how did the leak take place? Who had access to the information?"

"Security and ourselves determined that eight people had access to the leaked information: the three of us, yourself, and four members of the production team. Assuming, that is, no electronic infiltration of the systems."

"And your assessment as to the origin of the leak?" Manvers sounded increasingly impatient. Clearly, he knew what conclusion he wanted to reach—he just needed the conversation to get there.

Rive leaned forward, resting his palms face down on the work surface. "I'm sure none of my team was responsible. We follow procedures rigorously, and have a high regard for security matters."

"That's as may be, but you still have a leak. An unexplained leak on a project vital to the corporation." Manvers steepled his fingers. "Pending a security review, I am placing you all on administrative leave until January twelfth. Your pay and benefits will continue, but your security clearance and facilities access are suspended until then."

The room seemed to tilt so hard that Rive nearly fell off his chair. This had all the qualities of a bad dream, except he was fully clothed. He almost had to ask Manvers to repeat himself, to make sure this was really happening, but he didn't think the boss would appreciate that.

He tried to compose himself by reviewing his options. He could fight the prohibition—workers' rights in the Commonwealth were strong—but that would label him a troublemaker. Better to work with the system and save the big guns for later, in case Manvers wanted to take it further. He hated accepting the decision—it felt like capitulation—but as the MechWarriors who relied on their product knew, sometimes a tactical withdrawal was in order if the war was to be won.

Hearing no objection or comment from the three condemned men, Manvers rose to his feet. "I will see you all in a month's time. Security will liaise with you in the meantime." He strode toward the glass double doors, assistants in tow, and pushed his way through without offering his hand to the employees, as if their very touch had become poisonous.

"Well, that's us screwed. The old man had made up his mind before we got there." Connor was fuming.

Rive motioned him to silence with a chopping motion of his right hand, pointing at the control panel of the elevator. It was well within the bounds of possibility that Manvers had the executive lift bugged. Almost a certainty, in fact. Guards had escorted them from the boardroom to the elevator shaft, and the controls were—Rive assumed—security locked so only their programmed destination would work.

They rode in silence the rest of the way down to the main lobby—the sixty-second ride feeling more like an hour—and stepped out into the cool atrium. The trees and plants gave the place a feeling of life that contrasted with the austereness of the office where they had just received their spanking.

"So what now?" Connor was the first to speak, as ever. Getting out of Manvers's oppressive presence was like ripping a gag from his mouth. "Will security lock us up? Can we beat the rap? Are we—"

"Dan, give it a rest." Rive was in no mood to indulge the younger man. "We just have to see what security wants, and deal with things as they arise. At least we're being paid—that's more than I expected from the old ghoul." He felt his temper rising, finally making him angry now that the actual conflict was over.

"As fate wills," was Elias's only comment. He was lost in thought.

"But what do we do? Should we get lawyers?" Connor asked, a panicked look in his eyes.

"Probably. I don't know. Look, go home, sleep on it, and we can talk more tomorrow. I have other plans."

The trio split, each heading their own way: Singh to his family, Connor to somewhere that probably served too much sugar and had lots of game machines, and Rive to the Brunswick Tavern in downtown Alarion City.

He was on his second beer, hunched over the bar with his tie undone and hanging loose around his neck when slender arms slipped around his waist just after he caught the scent of roses.

A tall, slim brunette leaned close and kissed his cheek, a strand of loose hair brushing his neck. Rive leaned back into her, his left hand lifting up to caress her cheek and neck, then pulling her closer for a more deliberate kiss.

"God, I'm glad to see you, Sandi."

The elegant young woman dropped onto the seat next to him, depositing her black briefcase alongside his brown one on the floor, her green tailored skirt hitching up as she crossed her legs. Rive, beaten down by the day, didn't bother to hide the fact that he was staring at her, particularly her thighs. He gestured to the barman for a refill as well as a drink for his companion.

"Well, I gathered from Lanai what had gone down today." Lanai was Elias's wife, Sandi's colleague in the contracts department. It was through Lanai that he'd managed to hook up with a high-flying lawyer like Sandrine Miller. At first he thought she was slumming—a bored corporate lawyer looking for a bit of excitement. He wasn't, of course, going to object to being exploited by someone like her, and somehow after eighteen months they were still together. The thought of something more permanent—kids and marriage—had crossed Rive's mind on more than one occasion, but he didn't dare broach the subject, fearing those would be the accursed words that would make her vanish into thin air.

The barman deposited the beers, and immediately Rive took a pull from his, grasping the glass in his left hand while the fingers of his right held tight to Sandi. "Suspended on full pay 'pending an official investigation.' Someone has to take the fall over this, and I think you're looking at him."

She squeezed his hand, massaging it with her thumb. "I know firsthand how much of a bastard Manvers can be, Gun. Most of us in contracts have fallen afoul of him. The good news for you is, he hates to squander resources." She took a sip of her beer. "I think your job is safe." The faint traces of her Skye accent seemed out of place here on Alarion. Foreign. Alien. Alluring.

"Well that's nice to know. He won't let me go, but that doesn't rule out the other million or so punishments he has to offer."

"He knows what you're worth. I know what you're worth. It seems the only person who doesn't is you." She looked him straight in the eye, and as usual her piercing green gaze stilled him. "Have some trust in yourself. Yes, you might get a slapped wrist, but unless you outright gave away trade secrets, that's as far as it will go. Trust me."

"I do, but it annoys me that the others and I will probably be punished for something we didn't do."

"Unless they find who *did* leak the material."

"Right. Unless they do. Of course, there's as much chance of Security doing that as there is of a single power uniting humanity. They stop people getting in or out, but they're not much for investigating. Finesse to them means dealing with the perps while leaving corporate assets intact." He almost spat the last.

"Shh." Her free hand came up and caressed his cheek. "Give them a chance. You never know." Her fingers trailed down his jaw line and onto his lips. He kissed her fingertips. "Home time, I think."

**ALARION CITY, ALARION III
LYRAN COMMONWEALTH
12 JANUARY 2462**

Sunlight, filtered through the leaves of the tall, narrow trees outside the apartment, dappled the breakfast table, . The late summer sun had been above the horizon for some time despite the early hour, but the long run into winter was beginning. It would be another two or three months before the ski runs on Mount Halloran—one of the few non-restricted mountain peaks near Alarion City—opened, but the peak of warmth had already passed.

Rive sipped his orange juice—an expensive luxury—and then bit into his toast. His glass clinked as he set it down on the stone tabletop. His attention was not on the meal, and he scarcely noticed as Sandrine, immaculately dressed in a charcoal trouser suit, set her plate down opposite him and slipped into the wooden chair.

"Only toast, Gun? You'll waste away." The smell of eggs and black pudding, the breakfast staples of distant Skye, wafted across the table. Normally Rive would have found it appetizing, but not today.

"I'm not sure my stomach can handle anything more. We're due at the big man's office in an hour. Judgment day."

Sandi reached across the table and patted his shoulder comfortingly. "Believe in yourself. You'll be fine."

He sighed and nodded, then continued to look forlornly at his breakfast. The moment he finally turned away from it, Sandi smoothly snatched a piece of his toast and popped it in her mouth.

"Well, if you're not hungry…" She laughed, and he grinned back. His smile was weak, but it was something.

"Ten thousand kroner." Daniel said for the millionth time as the three technicians rode the metro back toward their offices. "I'll never pay that back." His older colleagues stood there in quiet contemplation, the shock of the judgment yet to fully sink in.

Contributory negligence, Manvers had said. *Poor security protocols and practices that allowed* persons unknown *to gain access to AlarCorp's proprietary information.* That there was no direct proof that the leak had come from the team mattered little—security had ruled out any other possibilities.

"I think you're an awkward individual, Mr. Rive," Manvers had said. " And I don't like it when people disrupt our harmonious working environment. But you are good at your job—all of you are—so I'll hold off on firing you. For now at least." *Because you want something to look forward to, don't you, you vindictive swine?* "Instead, per clause 6.23.7b of your employment contract, each of you will be subject to a financial penalty to cover the costs of the investigation, to be collected through wage deductions or paid in full as you see fit." The three men had been dismissed to return to jobs that suddenly paid quite poorly.

"Lanai and I have deposit money for our own house," Elias interjected mournfully. "Had a deposit, I should say."

"We are so screwed," Daniel whined. He paced anxiously as the train rattled along. A sharp turn almost threw him off balance, but he caught a handhold. "I know, we should appeal. They can't punish us for something we didn't do."

"We pay up or he fires us. Or worse. That's the story." Rive dangled from a strap as the train decelerated sharply, pulling into their station. The trio moved out. "Manvers has hung us out to dry. Yes, we could appeal—we'll check with Sandrine and Lanai—" Elias nodded, "—though it's a little out of their area of specialty."

Part of the mass moving out of the station, they were swept toward the gate. At the barrier, Rive reached out his CredCard and swept it past the reader to open the gate. It made a rude noise. To his sides, he heard similar rejections. His eyes met Elias's, and the two men sighed.

Extricating themselves from the station proved to be an exercise in diplomacy—convincing the staff that there must be an administrative hiccup with their AlarCorp-issued CredCards and then paying for the tickets with the card from his personal account.

At first Rive thought it was some glitch associated with their predicament and the fine, but later in the day, as he tried to go about his normal business, it quickly became apparent that the difficulties ran much deeper.

"You're not cleared to enter here, sir," the guard stated at the entrance to the archive, his posture rigid and his hand hovering near his pistol.

"I need the power coupler schematics for the integration routines," Rive said, surprised by the guard's obstinacy.

"That may be, sir, but I can't allow you through." He was polite and menacing at the same time.

"I have Red Two clearance." He held out the ID card again, touching it to the reader.

"That clearance is insufficient for this area, Mr. Rive."

"Since when? I've always gotten my own archive material." Since the Hesperus raid, he inferred. "What level do I need?"

"I can't tell you that, sir, but I can say that the status change took place in mid-December. If you wish to access the facility, you will need to consult your line manager for a security upgrade, or else arrange for an authorized person to enter the archive." It was obvious from his manner than the guard did not expect the former to happen any time soon, not while the specter of treachery hung over Rive's team.

Rive walked away shaking his head. Manvers had locked them out of the technical archive, hampering their ability to work. What else were they to be denied? Was Manvers pushing to get a response, seeing if they would knuckle down or buckle under the pressure? Or was he just angry, and lashing out at Rive and his people however he could?

The rest of the morning didn't go much better, and Rive was seething when he met Sandrine for lunch at the AlarCorp canteen, finding her in the vast swarm of identical beige tables.

"You didn't call," she said. "I wanted to see how things went."

"Phone block," Rive responded sullenly, taking a bite out of a sandwich. Distracted, he hardly tasted it and dropped it onto the plate. "I have to get all out-of-wing phone numbers approved."

Sandrine looked up from lasagna and snorted. "Well, talk about bolting the stable door after the horse has escaped." A chunk of the pasta and sauce disappeared into her mouth.

He glared at her. "What's that supposed to mean?"

She shrugged casually—she hadn't caught the tone in his voice yet, since most of her attention was still centered on her food. "The info went out, and the phone block isn't going to make it come back, that's all."

"The leak didn't happen because my phone was unblocked!" Rive said too loudly. Several nearby coworkers glanced at him, then turned away, straining not to stare.

Sandrine finally looked directly at him. "No, no, shhhhh. That's not what I'm saying. Of course that's not what I'm saying. That's the main reason you shouldn't have your phone block, naturally—you had nothing to do with the leak. I'm just saying that, even if you had, a phone block would be a meaningless gesture at this point."

Rive was somewhat mollified, and he lowered his voice. "It's not meaningless. It's there to piss me off. Manvers either wants me to stay here and work through this stream of little humiliations he's throwing out, or he wants me to quit. I'm not sure which choice would make him happier."

"Why would you care what makes him happy?"

"So I can do the opposite," he muttered.

Sandrine smiled sadly. "Poor Gun. I wish I had something useful to offer, but I'm afraid there's little to be done at the moment."

"What about the appeals process?"

Sandrine chewed thoughtfully. "I'll need to check specifics when I get back to the office, but I think the war statutes get in the way. Under LCAF directives, AlarCorp can take any measures it deems fit to ensure security. It's stretching it in this case, but knowing Manvers, he wouldn't hesitate to justify it in that way."

Rive swore. "Tightfisted swine." His fist slammed down on the table. Again, the rest of the employees resisted the urge to gape.

Sandrine reached across and rested her hand on his fist. "We'll work something out, I'm sure of it. Just give it a little time." She smiled at him. "Right now, however, I need to get back before they decide I'm shirking. We'll talk more when I'm home, though I'll be late. It's gym tonight." She stood up, leaned across the table and gave him a peck on the cheek.

Rive, glowering, barely noticed.

The recruiter held a small plastic box, no more than five centimeters per side, near his stomach. He pressed a small button on the right side, and it cycled through pictures of three men. He stared at them, memorizing their faces, while the blue glow from the screen lit up the underside of his face.

"The entire personnel files, naturally, are in there, as well," the man across the table said. Sunlight pierced through a fast-moving break in the clouds, and the small coffee shop, with its white latticework chairs and round glass tables, looked absurdly cozy. Steam lazily drifted up from their cups.

"What kind of recruitment are we looking at here? Straight or transitory?"

"Transitory," the contact said, his face swallowed by the large mirrored lenses of his sunglasses.

"Really?"

"Really."

"They're ready for that?"

The contact shrugged. "Getting there. One of them is pretty much our man already, though of course he has no idea. The other two will come around."

"What's the timeframe?"

"Immediate. Make your first contact whenever you see fit."

The recruiter scanned through the faces again. "It'll take some time. Laying the groundwork. You know, developing the right approach."

"Of course. We trust you to do what is necessary, and will compensate you for your time."

The recruiter smiled. "Of course you will."

ALARION CITY, ALARION III
LYRAN COMMONWEALTH
18 JANUARY 2462

Lanai Singh pressed her nose against the glass and stared at the dress, a sleek and elegant dark silk ball gown, bias cut with a lattice back. A month ago—a week ago, even—she would have bought it without question. Now she had to watch every penny. It was a hard transition for someone as used to luxury as she was. She sighed.

Sandrine's hand came to rest on her shoulder. "Come on, Lan, best not to think about it." Hooking her pale arm through Lanai's much darker one, Sandrine guided her friend away from the window. "Damn Manvers for a cold bastard," she muttered, pitched so only Lanai could here her. "Still, it would've looked good at Jen's do."

"Jennifer Searle is having a party? I hadn't heard." Lanai frowned.

"Oh. Yes. I think Sasha mentioned it in passing. Jen didn't say anything to me directly, so, you know, I can't be sure." Sandrine spoke quickly, awkwardly. She was all too obviously trying to preserve Lanai's feelings.

Lanai took one more longing look at the dress until Sandrine tugged her arm, forcing her away.

"Witch," Lanai mumbled, meaning Jen. "You may have your blasted party without me. I'm getting used to it—there's a lot of that going on."

"There is," Sandi replied. "We're suddenly personae non grata. Guilty by association, thanks to the CEO's little stunt. It'll blow over." She squeezed Lanai's arm. "I hope."

"Just fix it."

The folder thumped onto Rive's desk. He tried to glare a hole in the manager's back as the officious little prick strode away, wishing for an instant that the anger he felt would transform into a PPC bolt and vaporize the bastard. *Hell of a lot of nerve.*

Before the leak, Rive's team had been treated with a modicum of respect. Now, even though the leak had not been directly attributed to anyone, the fine made people assume they were guilty—careless at best, spies at worst. It had become *de rigueur* to dump thankless tasks on them. Refusing was hardly an option; their stock was that low.

He opened the dossier and gazed briefly at the contents before pushing it back across the desk. He stood and angrily marched out of his office, stomping down the short hall to the kitchenette. He poured a glass of water from the cooler and sipped it slowly while peering through the armored window into the technical bay. Elias was up to his elbows in the drive train of a light 'Mech that had been mangled by a rookie pilot, while young Daniel was hanging from a hoist, straining against the weight of the component Elias was working on. A far cry from Connor's usual computers. Since returning to work, their former high-level tasks had been replaced with mundane servicing and grunt work. The skills they had spent years to acquire had seen little use.

Just like that piece of crap, Rive thought, looking at the crippled war machine. *King of the battlefield now, pushing the damn Mariks back from world to world. Now it's little more than scrap metal unless we can coax some life out of it again. Hell, my damn* career *is scrap metal—but I don't have anyone coming to fix it.*

He swallowed the last of his water and dropped the paper cup into the recycling bin. For a moment he stood in contemplation, then pulled on his overalls and keyed through the security door into the bay. At least he could do *that* without asking for permission. Of course, his entry into the secure space was logged, and the bay cameras were watching his every move, so it was not as if he could feel like he had been given a lot of trust.

He grabbed the hoist and indicated that Connor could take a break. The young man slowly released his grip on the cabling, making sure Rive had control of the bulky device. Myomers held the main weight, but manual pressure provided fine control. Connor slipped the remote into Rive's top pocket.

"Fizz?" Connor asked.

Head lost in the mechanisms, Singh grunted. Rive shook his head, and the youth headed off for sugar and caffeine.

"How's it look, Elias?"

"I'm surprised he was able to limp back to base. It's a full-replace, I think—grease-monkey job."

"Right." Rive scowled. "I'd rather be back doing R&D and analysis than this. And we have two more lined up, by the way—DiMaggore just dropped them off."

Singh swore. Gunther didn't understand the language, but the meaning was clear, probably aspersions on the execs' parentage. "Gods, will they ever give us a break?"

"I doubt it," Rive replied. "Manvers seems to want us trampled."

Singh threw up his hands. "Is the man such a child? What does he expect to gain from this? Does he think maybe one of us is harboring a guilty conscience and will step forward after enough mistreatment? Then one of us should *confess* already and end this misery."

Rive stepped forward, anger moving him without thought. "Are you accusing us? I'm not confessing anything! I'm innocent, dammit!"

Singh's eyes widened, and his jaw opened and shut before he could say anything. "No. Gods no, Gunther, that's not what I meant. Of course I don't think you had anything to do with the leak. It's just the frustration talking—I want this to be over."

Rive slumped, the anger leaving as quickly as it came. "I know, I know. I'm sorry, Elias. I overreacted. Come on, let's forget it and get back to work."

Singh nodded, and the two men continued on the menial tasks that now dominated their days.

29 JANUARY 2462

"This is getting beyond a joke," Rive muttered, each word an effort. It was approaching midnight and he lay on his back, head in Sandrine's lap and the pages of a technical report held before him. Sandrine looked down from her own sheaf of financial documents, then brushed back his hair. "A full day's work, and then they dump these reports on us."

"It goes with the management territory." She sighed, removing her reading glasses and resting them atop her head like a barrette. "Particularly when the boss is pissed."

"Or a sadist."

"Same thing." She smiled, but it was forced.

"I need to check my contract to see what it says about working hours. Manvers can't expect a full day in the shop and then all this time on paperwork."

"I believe the wording requires 'all the hours required to carry out the duties of employment,' or words to that effect. I'll need to check the specifics, but that's pretty much standard for AlarCorp."

"So technically it's all above board." He swore and threw the report across the room. It bounced off the bookcase and fell to the floor. "Bastard lawyers."

Sandrine set her documents down gently on the arm of the sofa then, almost casually, cuffed him on the head.

"Ow! Present company excepted, of course." She shifted her weight slightly, and Rive sat up and turned, a dark expression on his face. Sandrine returned his gaze impassively. "Sorry."

"We 'bastard lawyers' are used to it."

"Does saying 'beautiful bastard lawyers' make it better?" Rive said deadpan, leaning forward to peck her on the cheek. She pulled away, feigning affront, but a smile tugged at her lips. "Sorry," he repeated. "It's my own fault for not knowing what I signed my name to."

"If I had a kroner for every time someone didn't read an employment contract properly, I wouldn't need to work here. There's a reason companies employ smart—"

"—and pretty," he interjected.

She grinned. "—and pretty people like myself." She reached out and grasped his hands in hers, then leaned forward, resting her forehead against his. "To be honest, it's not even the small print that gets most people. People read into things what they want—and sometimes suppose things are there that aren't."

"You lost me. Such as?"

"The number of days of annual leave, their sick-day entitlement, the length of their notice period, that sort of thing. Can you tell me what your contract says about those?"

Rive blinked and sat back. "I get twenty days leave, seven holidays, am allowed about a week off sick, and have a notice period of a month."

"You're certain?"

"Near as I recall. I don't recall all the specifics."

"Most people can't, which is my point to some degree. You'll be glad to know you got the holidays right, at least."

He blinked. "And the rest?"

"The standard AlarCorp contract makes no provision regarding sick days and so the Commonwealth statutory minimums apply, which is ten working days per annum, though no more than three days at a time self-certified."

"Fascinating," he said, deadpan.

"Most people are ignorant of their entitlements and tend to drag themselves into work, saving the company a significant amount of sick pay. People's ignorance used against them." She disengaged her hands and reached down for the wine glass on the side table, taking a long sip.

Rive slumped back against the opposite arm of the sofa. "Ah, the joys of corporate life."

"Yes. A lot of corporations are, at heart, greedy sociopaths, but AlarCorp sometimes seems particularly bad."

"Didn't use to be," Rive said.

"Didn't use to be *for you*," Sandrine corrected. "You don't notice how bad a sociopath is as long as you're on their good side."

"Sociopaths have a good side?"

"Everyone has a good side," she said, and kissed his right cheek. "This is yours."

"Flattery will get you almost anywhere," he said, but then his face fell again. "Ah, damn it, sometimes I wish I could just leave the whole corp behind."

"Then look around. You're highly skilled, I imagine any number of companies would be happy to have you."

"Right. Except I've got a non-compete clause in my contract, meaning I have to stay out of my field for a year after leaving AlarCorp—see, I read at least that part—and I'm pretty much completely broke after the fine Manvers leveled. Not to mention the fact that pretty much every supervisor I have at the moment would offer a toxic recommendation to anyone who asked. I'm as good as unemployable."

"I probably shouldn't mention the strategic occupations clause of your contract."

"Strategic occupations?"

"Strategic occupations. Even if you tried to quit, Manvers could call on his government contacts and claim you were a key asset of the corporation."

"Like that shows," he interrupted sarcastically.

"Well, he can jerk your chain as much as he wants, knowing there's little you can do about it.

"So I'm screwed. We're screwed—Singh and Connor with me."

"Don't give up," Sandrine said. "You never know—something could happen that turns the whole situation around."

Rive noticed, though, that she didn't offer any suggestions about what that "something" might be.

ALARION CITY, ALARION III
LYRAN COMMONWEALTH
12 FEBRUARY 2462

It was a Sunday, and Rive had a few hours in the afternoon where he didn't have to think about work. Sandrine was off with friends, leaving him an afternoon of solitude. He'd been looking forward to this all week. He'd selected the perfect spot for lunch, a place that had warm sandwiches, cold beer, and every sport in the galaxy on holovid. The décor was subtle and understated, wood paneling and some football memorabilia, allowing the holovid action to stand out that much more.

He got a table, ordered enough fried appetizers to cause cardiac arrest in an entire platoon, and happily watched the action all around him. He would have felt completely content, except he knew this was only a brief window in his otherwise oppressive daily life.

He was halfway through his appetizers and already working on his second beer when a tall man in a dark raincoat ambled toward his table. Rive watched him suspiciously, disliking the man on sight. His black hair was too slick, his young face too chiseled, his bearing too confident. He looked like all the up-and-coming managers who had been treating him like nuclear waste for the past month or two. Yet for some reason, he was walking toward Rive's table.

"Hey, buddy," the tall man said. "Place is pretty crowded today. Mind if I take a seat here?"

Rive looked around to confirm that most every table was, in fact, full. He shrugged, hoping the noncommittal gesture would discourage the man. It didn't.

"Thanks, pal. Which game are you watching?"

"All of them," Rive grunted.

The man laughed. "Okay. Let me see if I can keep up."

He kept his eyes moving from screen to screen, occasionally asking about action from earlier in each game. Rive provided him with curt answers.

"Well, I gotta hand it to you, Gunther," the man finally said. "Your mind doesn't miss a step. Can't say I'm surprised, though."

Rive dropped the hunk of fried cheese he'd been gnawing on. He purposefully hadn't mentioned his name to the man, yet the stranger was talking like he was quite familiar with him. *Crap*, he thought. *Even my relaxation time gets screwed up.*

He eyed the stranger suspiciously. "Do I know you?"

"No. For the time being, though, you can call me Johnny."

"Johnny, huh? Clever alias."

The man tilted his head. "It'll serve its purpose. What you have to understand is, I can't be talking to you. So it's better that you don't know my name, because then, as far as you know, you've never spoken to me."

"Uh-huh," Rive said. He would have been convinced the man was a crackpot, except he'd known his name. Part of him felt like taking a quick walk out of the restaurant, but he had a huge hoagie coming to his table in a matter of minutes. And the man, though possibly crazy, seemed fairly harmless.

"Now, there's something else I should tell you about the conversation we're about to have," Johnny said. "In the course of it, I will not make you any offers. I will not offer any guarantees. I will only offer some advice that I firmly believe you should follow. That's it."

"Okay," Rive said, thoroughly bemused.

"Let me tell you first that I know what's happened to you at AlarCorp. I also know you're extremely talented and your abilities are being wasted. I think that's a shame."

"Yeah, you and me both."

"I know each and every clause in your contract that's making it difficult for you to end your misery by seeking employment elsewhere."

"How do you—"

"Standard AlarCorp contract—I've seen a million of them," Johnny interrupted. "Since I know what's in your contract, I also know what you need. You need someone who knows your situation, knows your abilities, knows just what you need to get out, and has the resources to provide it."

"And you're that person?"

Johnny smiled. "No, no, no. I'm just a guy in a restaurant giving you some friendly advice."

"Which is?"

"You're in a growth field. There will be more and more jobs in your area in the future. Some of them will be—some of them *are*—on Alarion. I realize you have a non-compete clause in your contract. Twelve months, right? So do something else for twelve months. Find another job. If I were a betting man—and, in fact, I am—I would wager that by the end of the twelve months, you'd have a fine offer waiting for you."

The beer dulled Rive's senses a little, but not so much that he didn't get the gist of what Johnny was saying. Given his current situation, a new offer—*any* offer—had appeal. But, of course, strangers were generally not to be trusted.

"And what happens during those twelve months?" Rive asked, playing along for a little while longer. "I'm not employable in my actual area of expertise, and I come with baggage and a whole sheaf of negative references. Who's going to pay my way for that year?"

Johnny smiled. "An excellent question. Naturally, I can't answer it directly. All I can do is…"

"...give me advice, I know. Go ahead."

Johnny reached into his coat and pulled out a news flimsy. A large ad had been circled several times in red. The headline read "*Business and Engineering Job Fair.*"

"Go there," Johnny said.

"A job fair? What am I, a graduate student?"

"Look, you don't know me. You don't trust me, which is good, because I'm just a guy who walked up to your table in a restaurant. But all I'm doing is giving you advice. Go to the job fair. You want to know if you can trust me? Go to the job fair. Find out."

Johnny stood, leaving the flimsy on the table. "Keep it. Oh, and you should show it to your friends, Singh and Connor. Nice meeting you, Gunther." He walked away.

Rive didn't bother watching him go. *Stark raving nutters*, he thought. *One for the record books.*

But when he left two hours later, he took the flimsy with him.

13 FEBRUARY 2462

Elias Singh slumped forward, elbows resting on the table and fingers massaging his temple. It appeared that he might remain in that position indefinitely, as he didn't move when Rive deposited three cold, wet bottles on the worn table.

McNeil's, a pub one or two precarious steps above a dive, wasn't their usual venue, but that was the point. It was away from AlarCorp, a place where they usually weren't seen, and noisy enough that they wouldn't be overheard.

"Another triumphant day of work, eh, boys?" Rive said.

Singh snorted. "I'm starting to believe we're a day or two away from being asked to scrub toilets."

Connor looked more energetic than Singh, but his expression was just as dour. "Scrubbing toilets would be a relief. At least we'd have a clear sense of purpose, and we'd be doing a job we knew was *useful*. I've done mundane—I worked in fast food when I was at college—but this is different. It's malicious. Deliberate." The youngster looked atypically serious. "Hell, there are moments I wish we *had* leaked the info. Then we'd at least have gotten some sort of reward for this, rather than simply being persecuted because someone wants a scapegoat."

"There's an old phrase: 'may as well be hung for a sheep as a lamb.'" Elias agreed. "There are moments I feel the same."

Rive looked at them warily. "That could be construed as treason against the Commonwealth. Or breach of contract against AlarCorp, if nothing else."

"Well, pardon my Kuritan, but screw AlarCorp, and screw the Commonwealth if this is how honest, hardworking people are treated!" Elias was more animated than Rive had ever seen him.

"Right," Rive said. "Okay. This is why I wanted to talk to you about my lunch yesterday."

Singh and Connor exchanged dubious glances, but their frowns eased somewhat and their brows de-furrowed as Rive told them about his meeting with Johnny.

"It sounds like this guy Johnny's been watching too many spy holovids, with this cloak-and-dagger act," Connor said. "I wouldn't give him a single kroner of credibility."

"But he knew my name. That has to mean something—I don't know what, but it's something."

"I do not think it means we have to trust him." Singh said.

"No. I don't think so, either." Rive pulled out the flimsy Johnny had left him. "But there's this. A quick and easy way to look into Johnny's advice. The way I see it is, there's a very slim chance that he actually knows what he's talking about. And if he does—well, it could be our ticket out. I think, for that chance, I'll go ahead and stick my head in a job fair."

Singh nodded slowly, but Connor still did not appear convinced. "I don't know," he said. "Could be a trap."

"Who would want to trap us? Why?"

Connor thought long and hard and came up with nothing. He just shrugged.

"All right. This is what I wanted to tell you—I'm going to this. For the hell of it. You can come with me if you want."

Neither Connor nor Singh was ready to say they'd be there, but the fair was only five days away, and Rive thought a few more workdays would help make up their minds.

CONVENTION CENTER
ALARION CITY, ALARION III
LYRAN COMMONWEALTH
17 FEBRUARY 2462

Rive felt quite old. Connor, by contrast, seemed to fit right in, and had started conversations with a significant number of attractive young ladies as the three men wandered the floor.

Interactive kiosks and wide holovid screens filled the entire large room with flashing lights and blaring noise. The ordinary people beneath these displays were almost invisible in the glare of the lights.

While Connor seemed to be enjoying himself, Singh and Rive had spent most of their time in the middle of the convention floor wondering what they were supposed to be doing.

"Are we supposed to find someone?" Singh asked.

"I don't know."

"Is someone supposed to find us?"

"I don't know."

They stood around for another ten minutes. Nothing happened.

"Perhaps we should walk around," Singh suggested.

"Okay," Rive said. "We can't do much worse. I'll separate Connor from that brunette."

Once Connor was free, they made a slow circuit around the floor, talking to the occasional recruiter just in case someone on the floor had something to tell them. After an hour, they'd found no reason for them to be at the fair at all.

"Any job can pay you," a speaker at a small booth was saying as the three men approached. "Many jobs can be rewarding. There are only a few jobs, though, that allow you to earn a living while strengthening your country."

About eight people surrounded the speaker, and most of them nodded in agreement. The speaker had his hooks in.

"When you work for Stanislaw Consultants, you work for our men and women on the front lines. We consult on every matter critical to their livelihood—transporting food, ammunition, and other supplies, managing shipping lines, dealing with personnel issues—if it's relevant to today's military, we work on it. If you are lucky enough to be one of us, you will become a vital part of the war effort, working hand in hand with our brave military."

Rive smiled. It was a pretty good sales pitch—all the man was offering was a desk job that most likely involved reviewing endless invoices and supply lists, but he was making it sound like the next best thing to piloting a 'Mech on the front lines.

He jerked his head, telling the other two it was time to move on. Unfortunately, Singh and Connor had already been pinned by another Stanislaw recruiter. Connor shifted restlessly, left foot to right and back again, while Singh managed to hide his impatience a little better. Rive walked over to see if he could rescue him.

"I think you gentlemen will find we have openings for people with a wide variety of skills and experience. Our company's operations are as broad as the war effort itself."

"Yes, yes, I'm sure it is," Singh said. "Unfortunately we are somewhat pressed for time at the moment. If you could, perhaps, leave us a brochure…"

The recruiter beamed. "Certainly! Certainly, gentlemen. One for both of you." He handed a small brochure with an impressive holographic version of the Stanislaw logo, a DropShip passing in front of a misshapen moon, on the cover. "And one for your friend," the recruiter said as Rive approached, handing him another brochure.

"Thanks," Rive said, and pulled the other two away.

One hundred meters past the Stanislaw booth, they passed a trashcan. Connor dropped his brochure inside.

Three steps later, Rive stopped dead in his tracks. "Connor. Go back. Get your brochure."

"From the trash? You want me to dig through the trash?"

"*Get* it!"

Connor shrugged and retrieved the brochure.

"Open it," Rive said.

Connor did as he was told, and his eyes widened. Singh did the same.

"Do you all have the same note?" Rive asked.

They compared brochures. They all had a note in small, tight handwriting written on the bottom. Rive's brochure had his name at the top of the note—the other two had their own names. Below that, there was a brief job description: *"Goodwill Ambassador. Twelve-month contract. No experience required. Duties at the discretion of the employee."* Rive figured that was business-speak for "you can do whatever you want."

Below that were two figures, one for annual salary, one for a signing bonus. Both were implausibly handsome.

The final line had contact information for someone named Emile Morton, with a note saying, *"Tell him Johnny sent you."*

19 FEBRUARY 2462

"When something seems too good to be true, there tends to be a perfectly good reason for it," Lanai Singh said. "Going down that road is just asking for trouble. I would have nothing more to do with it."

"Part of me agrees with Lanai," Sandrine said. "But there could be reasons for a legitimate company to behave this way."

They had gathered for a conference of war in Rive's apartment—Rive, Connor, Singh, Lanai, and Sandrine. From the beginning, Rive was inclined to write off the whole incident as some underhanded scheme that was likely to do him more harm than good, but he couldn't just dismiss it on his own. He was hoping his friends and coworkers would reinforce his instincts and encourage him to do what he should do—forget the whole thing.

So far, except for Lanai, it wasn't working that way.

"We should call," Connor said. He was the only one standing, and he wasn't still for more than five seconds at a time. He had circled Rive's living room at least a dozen times. "What's the harm in calling? These guys know something about us, and they want us. Why not find out what's going on?"

"And Stanislaw is a legitimate organization," Sandrine said. "Pretty good track record, long-standing contract with the military, unblemished reputation."

"But why would they want to pay a bunch of engineers to do whatever we wanted?"

"That's a good question," Sandrine said. "But I may have an answer. Stanislaw has some pretty strong ties to Coventry Defense Conglomerate. I've actually found a number of people who have moved back and forth between the two companies. It could be that Stanislaw is recruiting you to employ you until your non-compete clause is up, then they'll pass you along to CDC, and you'll be back to doing the jobs you're trained for."

She tapped her finger on the side of her empty glass, becoming more animated. "In fact, as I think about it, that makes more sense. If you try to go anywhere, AlarCorp might invoke the strategic occupations clause in the contract. But then Stanislaw comes back and shows that you're vital to the war effort if you're working for them, too. Either way, you're crucial. So AlarCorp loses its leverage."

"So CDC is behind this?" Singh said the corporation's initials with near-reverence. Technically, they were already CDC employees—AlarCorp was a CDC subsidiary—but the two operations had completely different sets of management, and often operated more like competitors than cousins.

"Could be," Sandrine said. "That would explain the subterfuge. The companies have a strict agreement about tampering with each other's employees. Manvers would not be happy if he discovered CDC was poaching his engineers, and we all know what an unhappy Manvers is like."

The three men nodded vigorously.

"The trouble is," Rive said, "we can't *prove* what's happening. What Sandrine says sounds credible, but I could design at least a half-dozen equally credible scenarios that end up with us getting royally screwed by this Johnny guy. And I don't know how to prove what's actually happening."

"You don't have to prove anything," Lanai said. "As long as there's such a large chance that this entire offer is not on the level, you should have nothing to do with it. You should not consider it any longer." She folded her arms tightly, doing her best to demonstrate that she thought the matter was closed.

Sandrine's brow was creased in thought, though—she may not have registered anything Lanai said. "You know, I've dealt with CDC before. I know some people over there. Of course, no one will say anything for certain, but...well, I think I could get a decent idea of whether this is on the level."

Lanai looked around frantically, for the first time understanding that she might not win this debate. "No. No! It shouldn't go any further! No inquiries! This is a crazy risk!"

But the three men had seen the figures written in their brochures. And they'd all imagined what this Stanislaw Consultants job might be like compared to what they were doing now.

They all turned to Sandrine.

STANISLAW CONSULTANTS HEADQUARTERS
ALARION CITY, ALARION III
LYRAN COMMONWEALTH
8 JUNE 2462

It was a wonderful job. Hell, it wasn't a job—it was a wonderful paid vacation. Rive reported to no one. He watched sports on his terminal more often than he did anything that could be called work. He even had a comfortable office chair.

Connor was having as much fun as he was, perhaps more. He had become a feared competitor in several virtual gaming arenas, and his index fingers and thumbs often twitched when he was away from his terminal. Only Singh seemed restless in the new job, impatient for actual work instead of a full year of filling a meaningless title.

Rive was more patient. He'd used his learning and knowledge to the best of his ability for several years at AlarCorp, and it had landed him, for a time at least, at the bottom of the corporate junk heap. He was ready for a break.

He came home each night with a bounce in his step. Sandrine had jokingly complained about it once.

"I think you're just rubbing it in," she had said. "You know I'm still working under Manvers's whip, and you just like to rub it in that you're living free and easy."

"It's your own fault," he had told her. "I was ready to let this whole offer fall by the wayside. You were the one who convinced us it might be on the level. Without you, we probably wouldn't have gone ahead at all."

Sandrine had grimaced. "Don't remind me."

In truth, Rive could tell Sandrine was happy with his job change. In his last few months at AlarCorp, he was fairly certain he'd been a complete bastard to live with. Sulky, churlish, barely able to go for ten minutes without complaining about work in some way or another. Now he didn't talk about work at all, which was quite easy, considering he almost never did any actual work.

It was a good life. It would get old, he was sure—he didn't believe he could spend the rest of his life without performing some useful function or another—but for now it was extremely pleasant. If Sandrine really knew what she was talking about, in a little less than a year he should be getting an exciting new offer right in his field. And to this point, all her guesses had been right on the money.

MECHANICAL ENGINEERING DIVISION
COVENTRY DEFENSE CONGLOMERATE
14 MAY 2463

"I'll be honest, we went back and forth about whether to keep the three of you together," Winthrop said as he led Rive down the clean white corridors of Coventry Defense Conglomerate's Alarion facility. He walked with an awkward bounce in his step. "We think you have a lot to teach us, and some of us thought it might be better to spread your knowledge across various teams. In the end, though, we couldn't get away from the success you three had working as a unit. In my experience, when you find a group like that, you don't break it up. So, as long as it's acceptable to you, we'll reunite you with your old team."

Rive grinned like a child on Christmas. "That's perfectly acceptable."

Winthrop fumbled with a doorknob, then successfully turned it and led Rive into a large office filled with state-of-the-art workstations, 'Mech models, three desks, and anything else his heart might desire. A long window looked over the vast production floor, where sparks flew, joints were coupled, gears were greased, and the multi-pronged business of CDC went forward.

Connor and Singh were already there. Both smiled broadly and walked toward Rive, hands extended. He was having none of that—he brushed their hands aside and grabbed each man in a hug.

They hadn't seen much of each other for most of their time at Stanislaw. Their individual interests had pushed them apart, and with no joint projects to work on, they ran into each other less and less. Rive had actually started feeling guilty whenever he saw Singh, as his coworker's palpable hunger for real labor reminded Rive of his own indolence. Now, though, they were all together, all on the job, and there was no reason to feel awkward about anything.

"There's one more person I'd like you to meet," Winthrop was saying, pushing his thin voice above the din of the happy reunion. "Mr. Russell Schwieger from Human Resources will be helping you get oriented and acclimated to the way we work here."

As if on cue, a tall figure appeared at the door to the office. His dark hair was slicked back, his grin was blindingly white, and even though Rive had only met him once in his life for a few brief minutes, he would never forget the man's face. He stepped forward, extended his hand, and almost called the man "Johnny."

"Mr. Schwieger?" he said instead.

"Yes. You must be Gunther Rive." Schwieger grabbed his hand, his smile wide, his eyes knowing, but his voice not betraying a hint that he'd ever met Rive before in his life. "I can't tell you how happy we are to have you working with us."

As the first week at CDC wound down, Rive hadn't found anything to dampen his enthusiasm for his new job. His immediate supervisor, Herman Winthrop, had made it clear that he thought too much hands-on leadership interfered with creativity and progress. Naturally, he'd like Rive to keep him apprised of what the team was working on and what kind of progress they were making, but a quick note written at the end of each week would be sufficient.

That left Rive, Singh, and Connor to play with the considerable stack of toys they had inherited. Other teams seemed almost absurdly eager to share their ideas and plans with Rive's team, and in one week he felt he'd made more progress than he had during the entire last six months of his time at AlarCorp. Each evening, he came home bubbling to Sandrine about his latest ideas.

"You understand that only about a tenth of what you're saying makes any sense to me, don't you?" Sandrine said one night. "You can tell me that you put legs on a 'Mech to make it walk, but anything more technical than that, and I'm lost."

Rive smiled apologetically. "I'm sorry. I'm sure I've been difficult to put up with recently. It's just that... God! Compared to what we're doing now, AlarCorp seems like it's some relic from the Stone Age! Of course I knew the power of the things we were working on—I knew they'd dominate any field they were dropped into—but I never realized the *future* these things have in front of them. The *possibilities*! What they'll be able to do someday..." He could only shake his head in wonder. "It'll make what we have now look like scrap metal."

"Well, you've hit the big time," Sandrine said, at least half-sincerely. "All I ask is that as you continue your glorious march through technological history, you remember that you wouldn't be there if I hadn't talked you into it."

He pulled her to his side. "I owe everything I have to you," he said, and kissed her firmly on the cheek. "Everything."

**PRISON FACILITY
ALARION CITY, ALARION III
LYRAN COMMONWEALTH
24 NOVEMBER 2463**

He never knew there could be so many shades of gray. The metal counter in front of him was a dark, steely gray. The chair he sat in was lighter, the gray of clouds that could only muster a drizzle. The window in front of him, shot through with strands and fibers to make it unbreakable, was almost white but not quite, so it put a grayish cast on all objects seen through it. His jumpsuit was the bland gray of metal primer. And the receiver in his hand was two shades darker than his suit, one shade lighter than the counter.

The only color Rive saw was Sandrine, sitting on the other side of the glass, wearing dark green and burgundy, blue eyes wide, her hand clutching a receiver as gray as Rive's. He tried to picture how she looked on happier days—like any from the past half year. Until everything had fallen apart. Until yesterday.

"You need someone better than me," she was saying.

"There's no one better."

She shook her head fiercely. "No. I know contracts law. What you're into now…I don't have any experience. At all. I don't even know anybody who does this."

"Could you ask around?" Rive unsuccessfully tried to keep the desperation out of his voice. "Someone must know someone who can help me."

"Of course. Of course." There was a pause. Sandrine's lips trembled, her eyes moistened.

"Sandi. Don't. Please don't."

"Sorry. I'm sorry. It's just… *God*, Gun, what's going on?"

"I don't know. I wish I did."

"Treason, Gun. They're talking about charges of *treason*. They're making Manvers look like an absolute pussycat!"

"Look, Manvers would have done the same if he could have proved anything. He just couldn't."

"Are you saying Coventry can?" Sandi said. "Do they have proof?"

Rive leaped to his feet. "No!" he yelled. "Of course not! There *is* no proof! I didn't do anything!"

"*Rive*!" yelled a guard from the end of the room. "Settle down!"

Rive took a deep breath and sat back down.

Sandrine was crying freely now. "Sorry, Gun, sorry, I know, I know..."

"No, no, I'm sorry. I shouldn't have yelled. You've done everything for me, I know you wouldn't accuse me of anything. It's just..." He ran his hands over the stubble where, until this morning, his hair had been. "How could this happen? How could this happen again?"

"I don't know. But I'll find someone, Gun. I'll find someone. We'll work it out. Hang in there, okay? I need you to hang in there until I figure out how I can help you."

"Okay. Okay, Sandi. I will."

They hung up their receivers, and the guard came to escort Rive out, leading him to the five completely different shades of gray that made up his cramped prison cell, a barren room where all he could to was think about how his life had turned into a repeating nightmare that was worse the second time around.

26 NOVEMBER 2463

Two days later, his new lawyer came by and was able to meet Rive in a private room. The walls were painted beige—just that fact alone, that the lawyer had been able to expose him to some color, made Rive trust her. She wore a brown pinstriped suit, dark hair coiled in a tight bun at the top of her neck. She had the long, gaunt face of an endurance runner, or a greyhound.

"Mr. Rive, I'm Claudia Thorne. I'd say I'm glad to meet you, but such words tend to ring hollow in these circumstances."

"Yeah," Rive said.

"I hope you'll forgive me if I forego small talk and get right to business."

"Of course. I insist on it."

"Fine. Naturally, the first matter of business is getting you out of here. You'll be arraigned tomorrow, and I believe I should be able to get an affordable bail. You have no record, you have ties to the area—you haven't been off-planet for decades, correct?"

Rive nodded.

"And the affair at AlarCorp won't come up. Thankfully, it is not a matter of public record, and the executives are eager to keep it private. I doubt it will be discussed in this case, and even if the prosecution tried, I would argue it is irrelevant, since there was no finding of any actual guilt on your part."

"Okay. So that means…"

"That means, assuming all goes as I believe it will, you'll be back at home tomorrow afternoon."

Rive exhaled, letting out more air than he realized he had been holding. "Okay. Good."

"Fine. Next matter of business—getting you a separate trial."

"Excuse me?"

"You do not want to be tried jointly with Mr. Singh and Mr. Connor. You should ask for a separate trial."

"Why? We're a team. We stand together."

"Your loyalty is admirable," Thorne said, though the tight frown running across her lips indicated that she felt otherwise. "However, I'd like you to remember the facts. You were on a team with those two men at AlarCorp, and there was a leak. Then you formed a new team with them at CDC—and there was a leak. A leak far more damaging than the first had been."

"What are you saying?"

Thorne sighed. "Mr. Rive, I believe it's time you started giving serious consideration to the possibility that one of your colleagues may be guilty."

"No!" Rive hit the table so hard that pain shot through his arm. "I'll never consider that! Dan and Eli are like family to me! How could I suspect one of them?"

"Just look around, Mr. Rive. Look at where your 'family' has put you, first at AlarCorp, then here. All I ask is that you consider it."

Rive fumed. He remained angry through the rest of the conversation with Thorne, barely hearing most of what she said as she reviewed the preliminary case against him. He continued fuming as he was led down the sterile hallway into his drab cell.

Then he had a long, quiet night to think it over.

8 DECEMBER 2463

The pounding at his door had been going on for five minutes. Rive had almost reached over to turn off the lights, but then remembered that would be a sure sign that someone was home.

"Gunther!" *Knock knock knock knock.* "*Gunther*! Look, I know you're in there. I *saw* you walk in. I just want to talk, okay? Just open the door."

Rive looked helplessly at Sandrine. She shrugged. He was hunched by the couch, pushing an end table against the wall as he tried to stay out the view of any windows. She had hidden behind a potted forsythia that, in truth, provided little coverage.

"*GUNTHER* !" *Knock knock knock knock knock knock knock knock knock.*

Rive sighed, stood, and walked to the door. He didn't open it, though.

"All right, Dan," he said. "All right. I'm here. What do you want?"

"Open the door, Gunther," Connor said.

"Not at the moment. Tell me what you want."

"I want to *talk*. About what you *did*. You have your own lawyer? A separate trial? And we haven't heard from you for weeks. What are you doing?"

"I'm lining up my defense, Dan. That's all."

"The hell! Getting a separate trial isn't just 'lining up your defense.' It's the first step to trying to pin the blame on one of us, isn't it? You're going to try to make one of us take the fall for you!"

"No, Dan, of course not."

"Then why won't you *open your door*!" Connor renewed his pounding.

Rive took a deep breath. "Look, Dan, this isn't the kind of conversation we should be having without our lawyers!" he yelled so Dan could hear him above the pounding.

The noise abruptly stopped. "Lawyers, Gun? We have to talk through lawyers now?"

"No, no, of course not, Dan. It's just...when we're talking about this whole leak thing, about our trials, yeah, we should have the lawyers involved. But we can talk about anything else together. If you want to come in, that's fine, we can talk about whatever you want. Just not the trial."

Connor didn't respond. Rive peered through the peephole and saw Connor's back as his friend strode quickly away.

He turned, head hanging. He wished he had adequate answers for Dan. He wished he knew what was going on, what had happened, so he could make some decisions that he knew were right and fair. But he didn't know anything. So he was left to take advice from Thorne, who seemed like she knew what she was talking about. And now he was on the verge of losing Eli and Dan as friends; after all, they'd gone through together. He was helpless, buffeted and pushed by forces far bigger, far stronger, and far more mysterious than anything he understood.

He pulled himself out of his sorrowful reverie long enough to see Sandrine still crouched behind the bush, peering around the leaves, wondering what was going to happen next.

He smiled, but there was no happiness in it. "You can come out now."

KELLY, LANGSTON, AND THORNE LAW FIRM
21 DECEMBER 2463

Claudia Thorne had called half an hour ago and asked Rive to come to her office as soon as possible. He had asked if later that afternoon was okay, and she had paused briefly, then repeated that she'd like to see him *as soon as possible*. He left for her office immediately.

The law firm of Kelly, Langston, and Thorne took up a quarter of one floor of an old warehouse. The brick walls were worn, but the wooden floors were polished and new, the doors were thick glass, and both the artwork and the receptionist looked very expensive indeed.

"I'm here to see Claudia Thorne," he told the receptionist. "I'm Gunther Rive."

"Of course, Mr. Rive," the receptionist said, his voice like cool velvet. "Please proceed back and to your left."

Thorne was waiting for him, sitting behind her desk, hands clenched and twisting back and forth. She stood and unclenched them to shake Rive's hand, then renewed the twisting.

"The prosecution has sent me some files," she said, as usual dispensing with any non-business talk. "There's trouble."

"What kind of trouble?"

"Take a look." She pushed some printouts in front of him. "CDC likes to keep track of the flow of data within the company. Each time a file is moved or copied, it's given a stamp to show where it's been and where it's going. Naturally, CDC doesn't advertise this feature heavily to its employees, and only a few people within the company know how to access the stamp. Now, these printouts all have the stamp revealed, there in the lower-right corner. The last number in the list indicates the final CDC computer to hold this information."

"Okay," Rive said.

"This is all leaked data that is now in the hands of the authorities. Notice that in each case, the number at the bottom is the same."

Rive nodded.

"Mr. Rive, that number corresponds to the portable computer issued for your use."

Rive's head spun. His legs shook. Sweat broke out on his forehead, but his chest felt ice cold. The world beneath him felt like it was trying to throw him off.

Thorne waited while he absorbed the impact, remaining still in her chair. Apparently comforting distressed clients was not one of the services she offered.

When Rive was finally composed, she said, "I'm afraid that's not all. I'd like you to take a look at this letter."

It was on AlarCorp letterhead, and it was signed by Desmond Manvers. Rive was too dizzy to make much sense of it. It seemed to be saying something about *"patriotic duty,"* and *"Doing what's best for the Commonwealth, even though it may not be what's best for AlarCorp."*

"What's this mean?" he gasped.

"It means the prosecution somehow convinced Manvers to testify. He'll talk about the leak from AlarCorp, their investigation into it, and why you were punished."

"I thought you said that was irrelevant!"

"They're arguing it shows your character. The judge seems sympathetic."

"Oh my God," Rive said. He could barely open his mouth—it was so dry, all of its parts were sticking together. "Oh my God."

"I know it looks bad," Thorne said. "And let me be clear— it *is* bad. *Very* bad. Which is why I'd like you to listen to an acquaintance of mine."

Thorne pressed a button on her desk. "Send in Mr. Smith, please."

Rive's head suddenly felt heavy. He lowered it into his hands, closed his eyes, and waited for the world to stop spinning. It seemed to help. Vaguely. After a minute or two, he was able to raise his head.

Standing next to Thorne was Russell Schwieger. Johnny. Looking elegant as ever in a purple silk shirt with a dark blue cravat.

"Mr. Rive, I'd like you to meet Mr. John Smith."

Rive tried to laugh, but only three dry coughs came out. "John Smith? Please."

Smith—Johnny—shrugged. "Names are tools, used when needed. That one will do for now."

Rive looked at Thorne. "You know him? For how long? What do you know about him?"

Thorne pursed her lips. It might have been a smile, but Rive couldn't be sure. He'd never seen her smile before.

"I'm afraid that falls under attorney-client privilege," she said.

"Sorry to hear about what happened," Johnny said. "Bad luck. I had high hopes for you at that job."

"Yeah," Rive wheezed. "I'll bet you did."

"Now, you're in a bad spot," Johnny said. "You're going to be convicted. The press is well on its way to prejudging you and making sure you get an unfriendly jury, and the evidence Ms. Thorne has just showed you is more than enough to make them send you up the river. Or just up a few steps to the hangman. Whichever." Johnny smiled, though Rive didn't find anything he was saying remotely funny.

"So you have a choice," Johnny continued. "Stay here. Continue on the course you're on. Rush toward execution. Or get out. Now."

"Now? Out? Where?"

"You'll come with me. I can get you off-planet and far away. Well out of the reach of any authorities, local, Lyran, or otherwise."

"You'll take me foreign."

"Correct. Consider it a transfer—you've actually been working for my country covertly for quite some time. Now you'll just be doing it openly."

Rive shook his head. "No. No."

"It's that or death."

Rive slumped, defeated. "Death, then."

"Perhaps I should make myself clearer. Death for you. Death for Elias Singh. Death for Daniel Connor."

Rive reared back with sudden life. "They didn't do anything! Your 'evidence' only implicates me, not them! Leave them out of it!"

"Mr. Rive, you forget who I am—Russell Schwieger of CDC Human Resources. I have a large number of resources in the company. If I need evidence linking the two of them to your leak, I'm certain I'll be able to find it."

"Create it, you mean."

Johnny shrugged lightly. "Whatever. And I'm sure Desmond Manvers would be happy to smear all three of you equally with his testimony."

Rive collapsed back into the chair. Lanai had been right. His instincts, so long ago, had been right. *When something sounded too good to be true...*

"Why are you even bothering with me? " he said, voice sagging. "You've got plenty of access already, don't you? You've been in CDC longer than me. Why bother with me? "

"Ah, I have plenty of access to human-resource matters and a few other areas I've managed to poke my way into," Johnny said. "The tech files, though, are a tougher nut to crack. And then there's the interpretation of them. We could read them day and night, but we're having trouble finding people who can *build* the things. And this kind of job is a little too important to trust to rookies."

Well, at least someone values my skills, Rive thought bitterly. It didn't make him feel any better.

"Now, if you're smart enough to take the lifeline I'm offering, you'll do more than just survive," Johnny continued. "You'll prosper. Your own offices. Your own team. A salary beyond your imagination. No more pesky leaks. And similar offers are being extended to Mr. Singh and Mr. Connor—they might even decide to join you."

There was only one thing left to say. "Sandi…"

"The stroke of fairest fortune for you," Johnny said brightly. "I already had the opportunity to talk to your friend Sandrine and discuss the situation with her. She expressed her desire to go wherever you go."

Of course she did, Rive thought. *Of course she did.*

**MERCHANT-CLASS JUMPSHIP *PINNACLE*
ZENITH JUMP POINT, ALARION SYSTEM
LYRAN COMMONWEALTH
21 DECEMBER 2463**

It was still the same day. Rive couldn't really believe it. It was the day that had ended his life. Johnny said there was a new life waiting for him light years away, but he couldn't believe that. He felt dead. But his heart ignorantly beat on.

Alarion was fading behind him. He probably could have found some sort of window—either an actual view or some sort of vid—but he didn't want to. Instead, he sat in a cabin that was only slightly better appointed than his jail cell. There was a flimsy metal end table, a cracked plastic coffee table, and a couch and two chairs whose upholstery felt like burlap.

He was on a merchant vessel of the Federated Suns. He didn't know how he had gotten clearance to be on it. He didn't know how he got past spaceport security. Johnny had done it. Johnny had been planning this day for a long time.

Sandi was supposed to be on the ship somewhere, but in the chaos of his rush on board and the hurried takeoff, he hadn't been able to see her. Now that they were away, though, Johnny had promised he would find her and bring her to Rive.

The door to his cabin opened, and she was there. Her hair was out of place. Her blouse was untucked in the back. But her eyes were calm, while he imagined his were dancing like marbles in an earthquake.

She ran to him, embracing him for a long time. Neither of them spoke. Finally, she pushed back.

"I can't believe this is happening," she said. "I just...I can't believe it. But we'll find a way through."

"Yes, we...yes, I'm sure that..." But Rive couldn't keep up the charade. "Who are you really?"

She blinked rapidly, looking confused. "What?"

"Your name. Is it really Sandrine? Is at least that much true?"

"I don't—"

He slammed his hand on the end table, leaving a fist-shaped dent that buckled the entire piece. The force of the blow surprised even him. "The leaked files came from my computer! You convinced me to take the Stanislaw job, to trust 'Johnny'! You set me up with Claudia Thorne, who happened to know Johnny! I was dumb enough not to see it until now, but I'm certainly not dumb enough to keep pretending. Now what the *hell* is your real name?"

She sighed. "Sandrine... My name really is Sandrine. And I'm really from Skye."

"What planet?"

"Zaniah. It was a League world. Most of my family died when the Commonwealth took it. We still remember."

He took a deep, rattling breath. "Well, you're going to get them back. You're going to get them back plenty, aren't you?"

"Yes," she said, and her voice carried a bitter edge he had never heard before, but an edge, he now knew, that had been pushing her all the years he had known her.

"And me...and us?" It was a meaningless, insignificant question given everything else that was going on. But he had to ask it.

"We were necessary," she said flatly, but then her face softened somewhat. "But I spent a long time with you. I couldn't...go that long without something genuine being there. I suppose."

He had hoped an admission of that sort would do something to the dark hole in the middle of his stomach. It didn't. "But you made this all happen," he said. "You stole the data from my computer. You got me arrested on capital charges. You made it so I had no choice but to defect."

The steel returned to her face. "You're coming. The tide will turn. I did what I had to."

"I could blow my head off on this ship," he said. "Never give your country anything."

"You could," she admitted. "It's up to you. But is this worth your life? Have the Lyrans truly done so much for you? Are they so noble? You're just changing fights between two sides that, honestly, are deeply imperfect. For you, the main difference is that the side you're on now is going to treat you better than the old one—treat you like a hero, pay you well. Is that worth killing yourself over?"

Rive didn't respond. Sandrine waited a long time then finally shrugged. "You'll make your own decision," she said. "Goodbye, Gunther." She turned toward the door.

"Wait," he said. She stopped. "Your last name. What's your real last name?"

She shook her head sadly. "Sorry," she said. "Classified." She turned again and left.

He watched her go. Knowing her last name would have been nice, but it wasn't necessary. Enough about her was burned into his memory. He would never forget.

He wasn't going to kill himself. To be honest, he wasn't sure he had the guts. He'd go to the Free Worlds League. He'd do their work and, most importantly, save the money they paid him. As much as he could as fast as he could. Then he'd find her. It may take years, decades even, but he could wait. That's all that was pushing him along now, all that was giving him the will for life.

Somehow, someday, he would have his revenge.

**NEW MILAN
ALULA AUSTRALIS
FREE WORLDS LEAGUE
3 MARCH 2469**

Tracer fire lanced toward the behemoth, streams of phosphorous mixed with the lead shells. Most went wide, but the Lyran gunner, in an act of suicidal courage, walked the fire across the battered landscape to where it intersected with the bipedal war machine.

The *Icarus* rocked back slightly as the shells slammed into it, but most simply ricocheted off. Like a vengeful demon, the combat machine twisted and extended an arm toward the gun emplacement. Man-made lightning scoured the bunker from the landscape, transforming the dusty scrub into a raging inferno. Men and equipment scorched together into twisted, unrecognizable shapes.

"How do you like it?!" Hector Galaine screamed in his cockpit. "The boot's on the other foot now!"

Did this make up for Loric? The nightmares of the bloody carnage there still haunted him, but his experience against the Lyran BattleMechs and his technical aptitude—he'd been a young commtech back then—made him a natural for the Free Worlds' program. He'd been involved from the outset, in fact, meeting the technical teams on Atreus and then helping with the development program. This first League war machine lacked the refinement he'd seen in reports from the Hegemony, but it was a product of the League, a counterbalance to the program in the Commonwealth and a chance to stem almost a decade of reversals and retreats.

He twisted the torso to the left and snap-fired at a fleeing tank. It disintegrated in a spectacular ball of fire, its ammunition cooking off and showering the surroundings like sparks from an anvil. Another volley, and another fleeing tank died, then another, then another. He was unstoppable, a titan among mortals.

A heavy blow snapped Galaine from his reverie. Of all things, a squad of infantry had caught him with a mass volley of handheld missiles. He scanned the console. No armor breaches, but it didn't pay to be careless. He scoured the infantry's hiding place with his secondary weapons. He felt rather than heard the rotary cannons spin up and spit their hail of death against the unprotected troops. Some of the Lyran grunts ducked into the rubble, escaping the deadly rain, so the League MechWarrior triggered his missile packs. Flames engulfed the hilltop.

For seven years the battle of Alula Australis had raged, commencing with a lightning assault by Commonwealth 'Mechs that had made short work of the FWLM defenses. The LCAF had failed to capitalize on their advantage, however, and the conflict had bogged down into a bloody stalemate as the Lyrans had deployed their scarce war machines elsewhere. Until a week ago, the League had given ground slowly, and the LCAF had little reason to fear the Eagle's talons. Then in less than a week, the FWLM's own BattleMechs had reversed the tide of the campaign, pushing the Lyrans back into a single bastion that would not—unless they received massive reinforcement—withstand the whirlwind unleashed against them.

Galaine's war machine strode through the shattered compound, vigilant against further attack. None came. He scanned the sensors as the machine climbed the steep hillside, but there was no sign of life. A blip on the magres marked Pressfield's approaching machine, a twin to his own, approaching on an intercept course. A moment later, the two

'Mechs crested the ridgeline side by side and looked down on the Lyran bastion.

In the distance, several kilometers away, the egg-shaped transports were clearly visible. As they watched, plumes of smoke erupted from the base of one and it rose into the sky on a plume of brilliant flame, climbing slowly but accelerating toward orbit. Other vessels seemed to be in various stages of launch prep.

"Eagle command, Talon One. Point Epsilon secure. The Elsies look to be bugging out. Tacfeed on channel two." He threw several switches, broadcasting his camera pickup signal to the command post. "Shall we press them?"

"Negative, Talon One. Hold position and observe. Let the rabbits run."

The battle was over. The demons of Loric had returned to the Lyrans in kind. Starting here and spreading to any planet Simone Marik cared to send them, the Marik 'Mechs would take back what was there. After years in cold storage, the Captain-General's revenge was finally heating up.

THE SPIDER DANCES

JASON SCHMETZER

**HAPPEN MILITARY RESERVATION
40 KILOMETERS EAST OF BARTER
XANTHE III
FREE WORLDS LEAGUE
17 MARCH 2466**

Halle Ostend tried not to watch as Esterhazy slipped the guard a twenty-eagle bill to look the other way while he held the solenoid down. The buzzing door covered her quiet, tittering giggle, which was fine. That giggle was not for anyone's ears except Esterhazy's.

She slid her hand into his sweaty palm as the door slid open, and let him pull her through. The guard might have been smiling. She couldn't see past the strap of his helmet, but his cheek rose.

It was a smile or a sneer. Ostend didn't really care which—she knew six silent and at least ten noisy ways to kill Esterhazy before he could turn around. The guard didn't matter.

"We're not supposed to be back here," she whispered after the door closed. Esterhazy was taller than she was—maybe a meter-ninety, almost two meters. He was the wrong side of forty, thicker around the middle than he realized, and his temples had already begun the long, slow retreat toward the back of his head. The back of his neck was red—he was usually red around her.

Most men were.

"Who's going to stop me?" Esterhazy asked. He looked over his shoulder at her, grinning. It made the jowl on his cheek fold over. "I'm senior technician, remember?"

"Fine," Ostend said, pouting. "*I'm* not supposed to be here."

Esterhazy laughed. "*I* say you can be here, baby."

Ostend giggled again. She thought about how easy it would be to grab the back of his head by the hair, slip her other hand around his chin, and twist hard. There would be the *pop*. She shivered.

Esterhazy stopped at a T-intersection. His head went back and forth. Ostend leaned her weight onto his hand, his arm. Her eyes flicked back and forth, noting details. Light fixtures. Whiteboards on doors. Scuffs on the wall.

"This way," Esterhazy said, pulling her to the right.

"Aren't the engineers this way?" she asked. Not that she knew—Ostend had never penetrated this far into the secured area of Happen. But she knew there were engineers back here, and they had to be one direction or the other down the hallways. *And if they're this way, that's good information to have...*

"No, they're the other way," Esterhazy said. He stopped in front of a door, read the code, and tugged her down one more.

Ostend gasped a little, squeezing his hand. "Robert," she breathed, leaning in close.

"Here," he grunted. His fingers clumsily punched the keypad . A shrill tone sounded. He'd entered the wrong code. "Damn it."

"Robert..." she purred, sliding up his arm. She flicked her tongue against the lobe of his ear, carefully keeping the shiver of disgust in check when she felt the hairs in his ear brush against her tongue. "Now..."

"I know—" The shrill tone again.

"Now—" A nip.

"Oh, god..." He slumped against the doorframe. *Beep.*

"Let me," Ostend said. She slid around him, careful to always let part of her body rub against part of his. "What's the code?"

"Delta-six-niner-echo-seven-four-four-two." His breaths came in gasps. His hand—those large, clammy, clumsy hands—played across her body as she keyed the code. A chime sounded and the door opened.

"Oh, god, yes," Esterhazy grunted, and shoved her into the room before him. Her hips hit the edge of a desk, and she let herself drape across it. Her fingers wrapped around the other side. She chewed on her lower lip, eyes flicking around. A desk chair—some stupid print framed on the wall—a glowing calendar—a *console*. Her eyes narrowed. She ignored Esterhazy's porcine squeal of delight as the door slid shut behind him. She ignored his hands grabbing her roughly on the hips.

The glowing hibernation indicator glimmered at her. Ostend smiled, widely. She blew her bangs back off her forehead. Esterhazy was fumbling with her skirt, her zipper. He was giddy with pleasure, high-toned squeaks of urgent pleasure whistling with every breath.

Ostend arched, let her eyes unfocus. Esterhazy wouldn't need her attention for a minute or so—time she spent memorizing the keypad code, memorizing the steps to the doorway, the face of the guard outside. The flash of pleasure that warmed her face had nothing to do with Esterhazy's hot skin, and everything to do with the inner heat that came with her relishing of the Capellan Confederation's salvation.

BARTER
XANTHE III
FREE WORLDS LEAGUE
18 MARCH 2466

Hector Little sat on the low-slung chair and stared at the code on the noteputer's small screen. The flat device sat on the coffee table in front of him, displaying the free mail client and the single open message awash in a sea of spam and come-to-Jesus messages. Little steepled his fingers beneath his chin and stared at the code.

"I've got it too," Nicholas Drake said from across the room. "It's Halle's code."

"Me, too," Sasha Feodoreyva called from the bedroom. "Both accounts."

Little exhaled slowly. "Acquisition."

"Only took her six months to find the right guy," Sasha said, laughing. She walked in from the bedroom, elbow clamping her own noteputer against her side. She was tall, two meters, with long brown hair and black eyes. Her skin was pale—chalk-white pale, so pale Little saw the blue spider webs of her veins when the light was right. Her fingers were long and scarred. Callused.

Little looked at those deadly fingers. Then he tapped the message closed on the screen of his noteputer and erased it. Two new messages for male enhancement had come in while he'd been staring at Ostend's cipher.

In the holovids, this would be where he, the intrepid deep-cover spy in the enemy's lair, would delete the message, close the email account, and then destroy the noteputer in a firepit or basement incinerator. He would then burn the room and walk out, jacket over his shoulder. Little's small mouth twisted in a grin. *In the holovids...*

In the holovids, they didn't talk about the National Intelligence Agency crackers that would follow Ostend's supposed spam message to every account it was deposited in, and would notice if one or two or four accounts all closed within minutes of reading the message. That would be a flagged event—the little software bots would sniff it out right off. People didn't close their account after reading spam. They just deleted it and went about their business.

He tapped the noteputer off and stood.

"What about Danilov's team?" he asked Drake.

"Nothing in a week," Drake said. "The last report had Kane and Tibbett still on flight ops, and Dan said he thought he had a line on a shuttle. The passenger lists on the outbound shuttles are still pretty tight—we could get two, maybe three spots on one bird. Not all of us."

Little sniffed. "Well, if Ostend gets the data, we're going to need to get it off-world. Quickly, if possible."

"Aerospace fighters are fast," Drake pointed out. "Kane could do a long-hop, just bug-out for orbit."

"There are faster fighters than their *Dragonfires*," Feodoreyva observed. "Still, it's not a bad backup plan."

Drake sniffed sharply and stood up. "Let's not get ahead of ourselves. We still have to get the package, and we have to get it from Happen to Barter. We have to get it into the spaceport during what is almost certainly going to be a military lockdown. We have to get ourselves through that same perimeter." He gestured with the slim noteputer in his hand. "One step at a time, children."

Little grinned at him. Drake was the oldest man in the room—the oldest man on the team. He was near fifty, Occidental, with grayed hair streaking toward silver and deeply-lined eyes. So far as NIA knew, he was a surveyor from Lopez here to help lay telecommunications lines between Happen and Barter. The Mary laborers he worked with knew him as a dab hand with a survey laser and someone they could confide in. Drake just had one of those faces that made people want to trust him.

The Maskirovka *loved* recruiting people with those kinds of faces.

"So we tell Halle to get it," Little said. He sat back on the low sofa, putting his right ankle on his left knee. *The picture of a man at repose*. The thought made him smile. "And we tell Dan and the others to start working on active escape routes."

Sasha sat down across from him. She sat with her back erect, her knees together. On Xanthe, Sasha Feodoreyva was a has-been holovid actress from Amity. She carried herself with the sneering entitlement of the aristocracy and never—ever—dropped cover. "And we three?"

"Wait. Watch." Little looked at Drake. "You can push your crew toward Happen?"

Drake smiled. "It's already on the schedule."

Little grinned. "Good."

**HAPPEN MILITARY RESERVATION
40 KILOMETERS EAST OF BARTER
XANTHE III
FREE WORLDS LEAGUE
18 MARCH 2466**

Parsifal Nehru keyed the admittance signal and waited. The corridor behind him was bustling with uniformed activity, and no one paid any more attention to the young-looking man in the lieutenant's uniform than they did the potted rhododendron in the corner. Nehru felt his lips twitch in the ghost of a grin, and silently chastised himself. *If you cannot even fool the door...*

The door slid open, and Nehru stepped through. A corporal was sitting at the desk inside the door, staring at a noteputer on his desktop. He didn't glance up when Nehru stepped through the door.

"The general's out just now," he said. His finger tapped the screen—advancing a page, Nehru guessed—before returning to its former post alongside his lower lip. "If you'd care to come back—"

"I'll wait, thank you," Nehru said. "Corporal...?"

The man looked up. Nehru saw his eyes widen slightly when they saw his collar flashes. He saw the edges of the corporal's mouth flatten. *Biting back an obscenity*, his mind filled in. The blush began as the corporal lurched to his feet. Nehru saw it coming.

Nehru saw everything.

"Sorry, sir," the corporal said. He braced to attention, his eyes lifting off the collar flashes and focusing on the doorway behind him. "I didn't see—"

"Quite all right—" Nehru glanced at the name tape on his breast "—Corporal Platt. The general is out, you said?"

"Yes, sir. He's on a last-minute inspection in the restricted branch, sir."

"Indeed." Nehru glanced around the office. "His aide...?"

"Captain Mallory, sir."

"Yes, Captain Mallory. The captain is with the general?"

"Yes, sir." The corporal frowned. "I'm sorry, sir, but was the general expecting you?"

Nehru smiled. "Personally? I doubt it." He reached into his uniform jacket pocket and withdrew a digital ID card. It read PARSIFAL NEHRU, LIEUTENANT JG across the top. The insignia of the Forty-ninth Xanthe Grenadiers flickered beneath. When he drew his thumb down the right edge, however, the rank and the insignia shimmered and changed.

He set the ID card on the desk and watched for the corporal's reaction. "If he's not a complete moron, however, he's been expecting someone like me."

The corporal looked down. The name had not changed. But where it had said LIEUTENANT, now the card read COLONEL. And the insignia was no longer the wreathed moon of the Grenadiers.

The blood that had fueled the hot flush on the young corporal's face vanished while Nehru watched.

The insignia was now the crossed swords and lightning bolts of the Inspectorate.

The corporal's eyes snapped back up and he braced again, his skin turned pale-white.

Nehru smiled. He'd seen the flash of recognition in the corporal's eyes.

He saw everything.

It was forty-three minutes until the general returned to his office. Nehru spent much of that time in contemplation of the art on the wall behind the desk. He let the corporal sit down after ten minutes; the young man didn't dare return to his novel. He'd been clicking through message reports like a metronome. There was no chance the man was reading them, but it provided something for his finger to be doing while Nehru stood near him.

The door slid open. "—And tell Moorman I'm not taking any more excuses. He has to get the new *Icarus* prototype off the floor and onto the range in two weeks. Or else."

General Vocaine was a large man, with wide shoulders and a waistline that not even his obvious corset was keeping in check. His hair had been red when he was a younger man—now it was high and dry, dirty salt-and-pepper tufts.

His cheeks were florid from the exertion of carrying his bulk around. Nehru didn't let his distaste reach his face.

"Of course, sir," the younger woman in a captain's uniform said as she followed him through. "You have a meeting with the base commander in twenty minutes…" Nehru smiled as Captain Mallory saw him. "Yes, Lieutenant?"

Vocaine flinched. He looked to where Nehru was standing near the wall, obviously seeing him for the first time. His eyes gave Nehru a practiced once-over, took in the young face and JG rank flashes and passed on. He keyed the door to the inner office.

"I am Nehru, Captain," the inspector said. "My business is with the general."

"Then you can talk to me," Mallory said. Her brow furrowed. Nehru watched as her mind went through the obvious perambulations; a junior lieutenant with business with a general? One who isn't obsequiously deferential to the rank in the room? "The general is a busy man."

The door to the general's office slid open. The general stepped through.

"Not too busy to be naming classified military projects as he walks down a public corridor," Nehru said calmly. He might as well have been commenting on the clouds in the sky that morning for all the ire in his tone, but his words had their desired effect.

"Now listen, Lieutenant—" Mallory began, but the general turned back around.

"What did you say?" Vocaine demanded. "I'll handle this, Tasha." He stepped right up to Nehru. He was easily ten or fifteen centimeters taller, and forty kilos heavier. Nehru didn't retreat. He was a small man; he was used to people invading his space. You couldn't grow up in the *favela* on Regulus and be touchy about space. "Listen, *Lieutenant*—"

The desk corporal made a sound. "Sir—"

Vocaine ignored him. "I don't know what you learned at OCS, but you don't damned well barge into my office and tell me how to talk *in my own goddamn section*." He jabbed a thick finger near Nehru's nose. There was grease caught beneath his nails, the same grease the technicians used to lubricate the actuators on the new machines. It smelled differently than any other grease, and there was enough of it there for Nehru to smell.

The corporal tried again. "Sir—!"

Vocaine didn't look away from Nehru. He appeared surprised—appalled, perhaps—that Nehru was meeting his stare evenly. "What!"

"His ID, sir," the corporal said. He held it out. Captain Mallory snatched it from him and looked at it. Her jaw was set firmly. She read the displayed information and hissed involuntarily. Her eyes looked at Nehru—he saw her in his peripheral vision—and then focused on the back of Vocaine's head.

"General..."

"Buddha's balls, woman, out with it!" He spun around. "What?"

Mallory held out Nehru's ID. He knew the swords-and-lightning of the Inspectorate was still displayed. As was his actual rank. Vocaine took it, glared down at it. Nehru saw the muscles bunch in the back of the general's neck. He straightened and turned back around.

"This is real?" he asked, more calmly than he'd spoken yet. Nehru let one of his eyebrows rise a millimeter or so. The general shook his head. "Of course it is." He held it out, then gestured to his office. "May we step inside?"

Nehru slid his ID into his pocket. He nodded and beckoned the general ahead of him. Captain Mallory and Corporal Platt were staring. Platt's mouth was hanging open. Neither of them had ever before seen a general be deferential to a colonel—especially not a colonel in a lieutenant's uniform.

Nehru nodded to each of them and followed the general into his office. Their confusion was something he was used to. He was a colonel. Vocaine was a general. But they were not in each other's chains of command.

And everyone—*everyone*—answered to the Captain-General's Inspectorate.

Vocaine sat behind his desk. The desktop was empty, aside from the tablet noteputer the general set down and a stack of datacards he placed next to it. There was no blotter, no writing utensils. Vocaine worked on his noteputer exclusively, then. *Or there are drawers.*

Nehru stepped in front of the desk and clasped his hands behind his back.

"Sit down?" The general gestured to the wire-frame chair next to Nehru.

Nehru shook his head.

Vocaine lowered his hand into his lap. "So."

"General Vocaine—"

"You're here to relieve me, then?" Vocaine cut him off without looking at him. He'd evidently found something of inestimable value to regard under his fingernails. Grease, perhaps. "Because we're behind schedule?"

Nehru smiled thinly. "No."

Vocaine looked up. His frown displayed his confusion. "Then...?"

"I am not a courier, General," Nehru said. "If you were to be relieved, you'd have gotten orders. I am far too valuable to waste delivering orders." He paused, listening to his own heartbeat. The hum of the air conditioning system reverberated just beneath hearing. He felt it, deep in his chest. "Information is leaking from Happen, General. Information from your project."

"That's impossible." Vocaine's lips pulled back from his frown, showing his teeth. "Our security is airtight, Colonel."

"Not so airtight that you're naming the specific chassis under construction here in the doorway to a public corridor." Nehru held the general's stare. "No one is to know what kinds of BattleMechs we're constructing here, General. No one."

"My people are trustworthy—"

"*No one* is trustworthy," Nehru said simply. His voice was calm, but his tone was steel-tinged. "No one."

Vocaine opened his mouth to retort, then evidently thought better of it. "You said information is leaking. Not that it might—*is*. What information?"

"Both the Lyran Intelligence Corps and the Maskirovka know we are constructing BattleMechs. The Lyrans, of course, already have their own. The Capellans do not." Nehru wetted his lips. "The Maskirovka is on Xanthe right now."

"You know this? For certain?"

"Of course we know it. They have operatives on all our worlds. Just as we have NIA agents on each of theirs."

Vocaine leaned over his desk, interlacing his fingers before him. "Then it's a general threat you're worried about."

"No, it's the team that has almost certainly penetrated this military reservation already that worries me."

"Penetrated? Happen?"

"Yes, General. Do try to keep up." Nehru slid a datacard out of his pocket and proffered it. When the general took it out of his hands he spoke. "I dealt with the normal Mask cell on Xanthe three weeks ago. The Confederation still lacks BattleMech technology. Therefore, there are still operatives here. And Happen is the most vital target on Xanthe."

"I don't—"

"Our 'Mechs grant us parity with the Steiners," Nehru said. "And, of course, the Terrans. But if the Capellan Confederation gains access to the technology before we're able to bring significant numbers of them to bear, we'll be deadlocked there, too."

On the wall behind the general's desk was a framed two-dimensional print of a *Mackie* BattleMech surrounded by burning tanks. The *Mackie* wore the Marik eagle—the tanks had no identifiable markings, nor were they identifiable models. Simply made generic enough to represent the enemies of the Free Worlds League being crushed underfoot.

"And you think the Mask has infiltrated my unit?" Vocaine asked.

"It would idiocy to assume otherwise."

"Then you're here—"

"To stop them," Nehru said. "You will alert your security teams. I have protocols for searches to be run. They are on that datacard. Possible responses to be flagged are also appended. On the Inspectorate's authority, I have warned the governor that I may be halting all traffic to and from Xanthe soon. On that same authority I will shortly visit General

Bangs—" the base commander, "—and tell him the same thing about Happen."

Vocaine looked up at him. "You seem awfully young for a colonel," he observed.

Nehru smiled. "I am very good at what I do, General," he said. "If my appearance helps other people to underestimate me, so much the better. Perhaps you think I should have arrived in the black holovid storm-trooper's outfit, complete with commissariat cap and black-visored goon squad?"

Vocaine shook his head.

"I thought not." Nehru inhaled sharply, audibly. "Now. Shall you introduce me to General Bangs?"

HAPPEN MILITARY RESERVATION
40 KILOMETERS EAST OF BARTER
XANTHE III
FREE WORLDS LEAGUE
19 MARCH 2466

Halle Ostend looked up and smiled politely as Ned Reyes sat down across from her in the staff cafeteria. She was sitting by herself near the end of the line, smiling and giving little waves to people she knew as they passed, but her attention was—so far as the room was concerned, at least—glued to the novel displayed on her noteputer's screen.

"What are you reading?" Reyes asked. He slid his fork beneath the slab of suspicious-looking gray meat and sniffed it carefully. His cap was pushed back high on his head, letting a bit of his brush-cut black hair show. The silver tabs on the shoulders of his gray security uniform mimicked military insignia without actually being them.

"Barrett," she said. "*Twice Met by Moonlight*."

"Is that the one after or before *Starlight Epitaph*?"

"After," she said. Her eyes and her smile said, *"Wow."* Her mind muttered *shit*. "You read Barrett?"

"When I get the chance," Reyes said, continuing the game. Every week or so he sat down in the cafeteria across from her. He always asked what she was reading, and never recognized the title. Anyone watching would see a man with a crap job trying to court a woman two steps above his pay grade. "Are you free tonight, Halle?"

"Sure," she said. "What'd you have in mind?"

"Meet me here, twenty-hundred? Just a cup of coffee, maybe a walk in the courtyard?" He smiled and cut his meat. "Nothing much. I don't get to talk to many people about books."

"Me either," she said. She tapped her book closed and stood up. "I'll see you tonight then, Ned. I've got to get back to work."

Reyes stood and tipped his hat. "Sure. See you then."

Halle deposited her tray on the conveyor and walked into the corridor. It was a four-minute walk back to her desk. She spent every second of those four minutes commanding her heart to slow down, commanding her skin to cool.

Starlight Epitaph meant danger close enough to threaten the mission. Not now.

Not when I'm so close!

If NIA was on to them, there was no sign in the cafeteria. Reyes was waiting for her when she arrived, already holding two cups of good Galisteo coffee and smiling. They sat for a few minutes, talking about Barrett's books.

He was popular on Marik and Atreus—his novels were simple affairs, thrillers who set the fiercely loyal NIA agent Malcolm Rae against the best of the LIC. The Maskirovka, when it appeared in his pages at all, were portrayed as slant-eyed buffoons incapable of discovering the cost of bus fare, much less military secrets. *I wonder what he'll say when he learns the Maskirovka stole the plans for Marik's BattleMechs?*

"Shall we go for a walk?" Reyes finally asked.

"I'd love to," Halle told him. No one appeared to watch when they stood up and walked out the door to the courtyard. There were several other couples sitting apart from each other already, and several more had preceded them out into the two-square-kilometer park. Happen's residents—military and civilian—were forbidden to leave except on the weekends. "Walking" in the courtyard was a popular pastime.

"Is this safe?" she murmured when they were down one of the trails and out of sight of the cafeteria building. A Xanthe grass-shredder *scritched* in the night, calling for a mate. She'd heard them often when she was out at night. Esterhazy liked to come out here in the dark, when she couldn't convince him how much she liked "christening" other peoples' desks.

"As safe as can be," he whispered back. The rustling leaves would give most passive recorders trouble; the trees would block directional microphones. Unless there was a listener hiding in the shrubs—and they both knew how to look for those—they should be safe. "We've got trouble."

"How much trouble?"

"We need to go tomorrow—or else abort."

Halle stopped walking. She slipped her arms around Reyes and leaned in close, as if she were going to nuzzle his neck. His hand came up automatically, pressing against the back of her head.

"Are we burned?" She smelled the coffee on her breath as it was reflected back from his neck. Reyes shivered. They might only be acting, but a woman's breath on a man's neck usually provokes a common reaction.

"The Inspectorate is here."

Halle hissed a curse. "You're sure?"

"Bangs called us all in and told us himself. They suspect."

"Us?"

"Does it matter?"

Halle squeezed his shoulders and leaned back. "Tomorrow, then?"

"Can you be ready?"

"I think... Yes." She considered. Esterhazy had been getting insistent lately. She'd put him off since their last visit—demurely, to be sure—and he was getting anxious. It shouldn't be any trouble to urge him to retrace his steps. She named the corridor junction where she'd seen the guard. "Can you take his place?"

Reyes nodded. He tipped his head down, as if he were going to kiss her. She smelled the coffee on his breath now. "I'll signal," he said. "You have a plan to get out?"

Halle smiled. "I'm going to ride out through the front gate."

Reyes smiled back. "A diversion, then?"

"Tell Quinn we need the big one."

Then she kissed him. Just in case anyone *was* watching.

**XANTHE RESERVE MILITIA AERODROME
BARTER STARPORT
XANTHE III
FREE WORLDS LEAGUE
19 MARCH 2466**

Fyodor Danilov looked at the message displayed on his noteputer and frowned. *Tomorrow?* He cleared the message and stuck his head into the next room. "Edgar. Tomorrow?"

Edgar Tibbetts was reclining on a cot, skimming through the day's news. He set his 'puter down and stared at Danilov. "Tomorrow?"

"That's what it says."

"Shit." Danilov watched the other man think. "No. Day after next. Best we can do."

"Little won't like that," Danilov said.

"Little's not in charge of getting us wings," he said. "There's nothing tomorrow. Military flights. We're not getting on those." He looked down at his 'puter and tapped the screen a few times. "Day after we got three liners and half a dozen shuttles. Easier."

"I'll tell him." Danilov nodded and pulled the door shut as he went. He tapped the message screen open and sent two words: *day after*. Then he closed the messenger and slid the noteputer under his arm.

At the other end of the corridor, he stopped in front of a door with an electronic keypad. The sequence was the same, and the door slid open. Two men in uniforms looked up as he entered.

"Feel better, Dan?" one of them asked.

"Yes, sir," Danilov answered. He went to the third console, the one marked FLIGHT CONTROLLER, and sat down. "Sorry, Captain. Really had to hit the head."

Captain bar-Danan shrugged. "Nature calls, right?"

"Right, sir. Any traffic while I was away?"

The officer shook his head. "Nothing. We had a memo from higher, though. The governor sent a warning order that he might have to close the port sometime next week, though. Just the off-planet stuff—the air-breathing stuff can continue."

Danilov nodded as he slipped his headset back on. "Sounds like easy work for us then," he said.

And next week is just fine, he thought. *We'll be long gone by then.*

HAPPEN MILITARY RESERVATION
40 KILOMETERS EAST OF BARTER
XANTHE III
FREE WORLDS LEAGUE
20 MARCH 2466

Reginald Bangs was a tiny man. He stood a meter-sixty in his dress boots, but Nehru suspected there were several centimeters of lift in those boots. He stood behind a bank of hunched-over men and women who were all intently massaging data from a string of consoles.

Nehru stood near him, eyes mostly unfocused, letting his ears listen and his peripheral vision watch for the telltale jerk of someone finding something unexpected.

"You could have come straight to me," Bangs said quietly. "I've dealt with your office before. You needn't have surprised Vocaine that way."

"General Vocaine needed surprising," Nehru said, not looking at the small general. "He was getting complacent. Complacency breeds mistakes, and the Maskirovka needs only one mistake to succeed."

"It might help if you told us what we're looking for," Bangs said a moment later.

Nehru resisted the urge to sigh. He hated sighs. There was no more useless sound than a sigh—it said, *"I'm disappointed, but not enough to actually speak."*

Instead, he blinked his eyes back into focus and turned to regard General Bangs. "I have given your security analysts a series of checks to make. They will determine if there is more to be done."

"Checks?"

"Facial recognition, mostly."

"You know what these spies look like?"

"No. But I have security recordings of everyone seen near the safehouse we raided to eradicate the long-term Mask team on Xanthe. Right now your computers are comparing those faces to the faces of your staff and soldiers."

Bangs ogled. "But that's—"

"More than six thousand people," Nehru said. "And the cameras caught nine thousand discrete faces."

"That's…"

"A lot of faces," Nehru said. "You might return to your duties, General. I'm more than capable of standing here alone."

"But if one of them pops up—"

"You'll be the third person to know."

Bangs frowned. "Third?"

Nehru blinked, keeping his eyes closed perhaps an instant longer than necessary. "The first person will be the technician sorting the data. I will be the second. You will be the third."

"Oh." Bangs glanced both ways down the rows of analysts poring over screens and noteputers. "Then—"

"Sir?"

Nehru spun. A young woman at the far end was holding up her hand halfway. Her attention was still on the screen in front of her. Nehru strode over to stand behind her. Bangs followed.

"Soldier?" Nehru prompted.

"We've got a match," she said. She toggled the screen out of the waterfall display of searched comparisons and brought up one that was blinking.

A grainy security camera image filled the left side of the screen; on the right was an ID card mug shot. Nehru watched the flickering traceries as the computer illustrated points of congruence—cheekbones, chin, distance between the eyes. It was the same man.

Nehru straightened. "Tell me, General," he said. "Where might I find civilian auxiliary Ned Reyes?"

Esterhazy was slobbering, he was so excited. He followed Halle down the corridor, toward the same armored door as the other evening. She made sure to put a sway into her hips, but moved fast enough that he couldn't get a finger under the seam of her skirt, despite his determined attempts.

It was mid-morning. The first shift would be just about into their coffee break. When she'd first discovered the console, Halle had planned to come back during third shift, when no one but the manufacturing crew was on. The design and testing teams kept a more normal schedule, but production ran around the clock. She was a little concerned that the man whose office they intended to…borrow…would be in it. But Esterhazy said he'd take care of that.

"Senior technician, remember?" he'd boasted.

It had been ridiculously simple to get him to agree. All she'd had to do was wear the herringbone skirt and her hair back. A judicious lean over, a loose button on her blouse, and a lascivious whisper in Esterhazy's ear had been all that was required to bring the large man away from his break-room snack and into the corridor.

"Again," she'd moaned.

"What, now?"

"Now."

Esterhazy had glanced both ways down the corridor. "Where?"

"The same place as before." She'd stepped close to him, close enough that her shoes had touched the edge of his boots; close enough that her breasts had pressed against his stomach. "It was so amazing, Robert. I need it again. Now."

That was all it had taken.

They were getting close. Halle turned the last corner and saw Reyes standing the guard post. He was judiciously ignoring her, but he braced to attention when Esterhazy stumbled after her. She smiled at him from beneath her bangs and spun around, falling backward against the door.

"It's a different guard," she whispered to Esterhazy. "Can we still...?"

Esterhazy grinned. "Of course we can." He ignored Reyes and keyed his code into the keypad. The door slid open. Halle stepped through backward, her left hand clutching the lapel of Esterhazy's coveralls. The technician followed her through, and the door slid shut behind him. He pushed her back farther, against the wall, and pressed himself against her. Then he kissed her. He tasted like two-day-old corned beef.

Halle shuddered. He would think it was excitement. Excitement and revulsion were two heads of the same coin. She twisted away from him and started down the hall. "Now, which room was it...?"

"Eight-Bravo," Esterhazy said. He pointed. "There."

"The door..."

Esterhazy stepped past her and hit the door announce. The sound of the chime carried through the thin extruded plastic. He waited. Halle leaned in behind him and breathed on his neck. He moaned almost inaudibly.

"Knock, knock," she whispered.

He signaled again. No one came to the door. He grunted and keyed a combination into the keypad. The door slid open.

He half turned, grabbed her hand, and twisted, flinging her into the room before him. Her thighs hit the desk hard and she fell across it, just like the other night. She heard the door slide closed behind her, straightened up, and spun around to sit on the edge of the desk. She slid back so the backs of her knees were against the edge of the desk. A blotter and a noteputer shifted beneath her.

Esterhazy was still by the door. He was wringing his hands in front of him, watching her. His eyes flicked from her face to her chest to her knees and back, a half second at each point. As if he couldn't decide what he wanted to look at.

She moved her knees apart and smiled.

Nehru was forced to give the man his due. They'd found Reyes standing his assigned guard post, just outside the restricted section of the east wing. He'd shown only the confusion one would expect from a guard pulled off his shift by a group of armed military police. Nehru hadn't seen any indication that Reyes suspected why they'd picked him up. That either meant there weren't any indications to see, because Reyes was innocent...

...Or it means you're not seeing it.

They'd taken Reyes to a detention room in the military wing. His hands were free, although they'd taken his equipment belt. He was watching his own reflection in the one-way glass. Nehru watched him through it. The noteputer in his hand held Reyes's complete employment history. An analyst was searching the Xanthe net for his records—*all* of his records.

"How long will you make him wait?" General Bangs asked. The base commander had mobilized his MPs in record time—Nehru had no complaints on that—but he'd remained, intent on watching the interrogation. He was standing to the side, as if Reyes could see him through the mirrored ferroglass.

"Not long," Nehru said. Was he *too* calm? Was that what was making the hairs on the back of Nehru's neck rise? "If for no other reason than if he's not who we're looking for, we're wasting time."

Two base MPs stood behind Reyes, hands crossed in front of their belts. They wore helmets and body armor, but their only weapons were batons. Unless Nehru sent them out, they'd remain while he spoke to them. *What if one of them is a Mask spy?*

A rare chuckle escaped his lips. Bangs flinched. He'd been staring at Reyes.

Paranoia is my business. He stepped toward the door, holding the noteputer out to Bangs. The general took it, frowning.

I can't very well suspect everyone.

Esterhazy rushed toward her. Halle held out her arms, encircling his neck as he slammed into her and the desk together. He grunted with the impact, but his hands were already fumbling with his belt. She squeezed his neck tightly, putting her mouth near his ear. She exhaled.

"Oh, god yes," he burbled.

"Robert..."

"Yes..."

"You disgust me." She felt him stiffen and try to pull back. She moved her arms in a certain way, a way she'd been trained in many years ago, and applied the pressure and torque just as she'd been taught.

There was a *crackle*, like a door opened too far on its hinges. Esterhazy collapsed. His feet kicked spastically, and a wet spot appeared on the front of his coveralls.

Halle pushed off the desk and stood over him, looking down. Despite the angle of his shoulder, his face was looking up at her. His mouth opened and closed. His eyes darted frantically back and forth.

She leaned down, again placing her mouth near his ear. "*Xiexie*," she whispered. "The Chancellor thanks you." Then she stood up. His eyes were staring.

She kicked him as hard as she could in the lower back. His head flopped over to face the other direction.

Laughing, she stepped over his corpse and to the console. The datacard from her bra was already in her hand. The software worms knew exactly what files to look for. Halle keyed the card in and looked up at the door. Her mind was already tracing her steps out of the restricted section.

Nehru sat across from Reyes, not speaking. The two men regarded each other. Reyes's face was earnest, innocent. He was sitting upright, not slouching, with his hands clasped in his lap. Nehru sat the same way. They could have been two men waiting for the tram at the stop.

"Do you remember being on Galveston Avenue in Barter several weeks ago?" Nehru finally asked.

Reyes frowned. "I'm on Galveston Avenue a lot, sir. It's on my way home, when I get out of here for the weekend."

"Home?"

"I keep a flat on the west side," Reyes said. He named the address. "It's just a little loft, but I like my own space, you know?" He glanced to the side, not far enough to see the guard behind him, but Nehru knew that was what he was looking for. "Sir? Is something happening in Barter? Is that why you're talking to me?"

"No, Mr. Reyes." Nehru smiled thinly. "Nothing in Barter."

Reyes frowned. "Have I done something wrong?"

"Do you think you have?"

Reyes shrugged. "I don't think so. I mean, I traded Johansson his shift today, but he said he wanted the late shift and—" he smiled, "—well, I've got a date tonight, sir."

"Are you usually assigned to the post you were holding today?"

"No, sir."

"Do you know what's on the other side of that door?"

"Sir?"

Nehru squeezed his hands together, beneath the level of the table. "Do you know what goes on in the restricted section?"

Reyes leaned back. "I'm not cleared to go in, sir," he said. "No, sir. The scuttlebutt—" His eyes widened, and his mouth closed.

"'Scuttlebutt'?"

Reyes swallowed. "Rumor has it it's 'Mechs, sir." He twisted to look at the guard behind him on his left, but the guard might have been made of stone for all the reaction he showed. "It's just a rumor, you know? What the guys talk about in the break room when we're not talking about women?" He laughed—it only sounded half-forced. "Heck, sir—you know how it is. Some days you hear the Captain-General himself is behind the bulkhead."

Nehru smiled thinly and nodded.

"Sir?" Reyes slid his hands up on the table, holding them together. "Can you tell me what this is about?"

Nehru stared at him. He opened his mouth to answer—and then he saw it.

The corner of Reyes's mouth twitched. It might have been a tic—it might have been a trick of the light. But Nehru saw it. And something about the tiniest of movements made his mind go *click*. He knew what the micro-expression he might have seen was.

The tiniest of smirks. As if Reyes knew what he was suspected of. As if he knew there was no way Nehru was going to make him. As if Reyes had *won*.

Nehru spread his palms flat on the table.

"Tell me," he said quietly, "about the Maskirovka."

Reyes was gone.

Halle had the data. She *had* it, on the datacard in her bra. The worms had done their work and downloaded the files they'd been sent for. It was a library of information. The datacard was the size of her thumbnail. No one would see it unless they peeled her out of her lingerie. She giggled. That hadn't turned out so well for Esterhazy.

But Reyes was *gone*.

The armored door out of the restricted section had opened when she was walking toward it. If all had been going to plan she'd have found Reyes waiting outside. He wouldn't have commented on her lack of security pass to be inside. She'd have moved to the next part of the plan, and no one would be the wiser until they found Esterhazy's body.

Instead, she saw the black-armored shoulder of a military policeman. He was standing in Reyes' place, but he didn't appear to be checking IDs. Of course, the mousy-looking man who'd just entered had known the keycode. There'd be no reason to check his security. But a woman who obviously wasn't a scientist coming out? That would be something to pay attention to.

Halle glanced back the way she'd come. She could go back, palm Esterhazy's ID. That wouldn't do her any good if the guard was at all paying attention, and she'd only need it if he were doing so.

The man who'd entered nodded at her and moved in the other direction. The door slid closed.

What to do...

She could trip the diversion. Her finger caressed the slim rectangle of her communicator. Quinn's little surprise would get the whole complex's attention—but if she used it now she wouldn't have any way to get out of the front gate. The entire plan depended on her getting the datacard out of Happen and to Barter. It was Danilov and the others' responsibility to get it off Xanthe.

Shit.

She couldn't trigger the diversion yet. Halle stepped toward the door.

Luck was with her. The door slid open as she walked closer. Another lab-coated scientist was returning from his morning break. Halle stepped more quickly, angling to slide through the door at the same time as the man was trying to come through. He flinched and stepped to the side, gesturing her out before him.

"Thank you," she said, smiling brightly. She reached out and touched the scientist's shoulder briefly before turning and walking down the corridor away from the MP. Her steps were sure and even. She held her shoulders level and put a bit of sway into her stride. If the guard was looking at her, she wanted him looking at her ass and thinking *damn*, not looking at her back and thinking *did she have a badge*?

Every step toward the corner was an ocean of time. Halle's heart thudded in her chest, and she felt her face flush despite her best efforts to remain calm. When her left leg moved forward she felt the strap of her bra pull and the fabric atop the datacard shift micrometrically.

She turned the corner.

She smiled. *Now for the hard part.*

Reyes blinked. "The Maskirovka?"

"How long have you been on Xanthe?"

Reyes stared at Nehru, shaking his head slowly. "I think there's been some kind of mistake," he said. "I'm from Loyalty."

Nehru tapped his index finger against the tabletop, once per half second. When he spoke, he bit the words out at the same rate, as if his fingertip were punctuating. "You are part of a Maskirovka cell. You were on Galveston Avenue because you were coming from, or going to, the safehouse we raided three weeks ago. You have accomplices here in Happen, and likely other operatives in Barter." He leaned forward. "You. Will not. Succeed."

Reyes frowned. He blinked. He shook his head. He looked every centimeter the innocent, confused man accused of a horrible crime he hadn't committed.

Then he *moved*.

The table and the bench Reyes sat on were both stainless steel. Both were bolted to the floor, and both had rounded edges. Reyes's hands were free. He stood up quickly. Nehru jerked back. The two guards behind Reyes lurched into motion like stone gargoyles shedding the day's skin. They weren't fast enough.

Reyes hopped like a man might a jump rope. He pulled his feet up and then slammed them down against the back side of the bench he'd been sitting on. That launched him backward toward the right-side guard like a man-sized rocket. He ducked his head forward, hitting the guard in the chest and slamming him back against the wall. Even with his body armor, Nehru heard the air *whoosh* out of the large man's chest. The two of them collapsed, Reyes atop the paralyzed guard.

Even as he fell, Reyes's arm snapped out, catching the second guard near the collar rim of his body armor. The arm recoiled, using its muscle and the momentum of the two men falling to pull the second guard down atop of him.

Nehru stood, his hands flat on the tabletop. His shoulders and forearms tensed as he prepared to fling himself over the table.

Reyes's arm snaked around the second guard's neck even as that man slammed his hands down to try pushing back. Nehru saw the corded muscles in Reyes's forearm bunch and flex—he heard a *pop*—and the guard flinched and went limp.

Nehru leaped over the table.

It had been maybe three seconds—maybe less—since Reyes had moved.

By the time Nehru's boots struck the floor Reyes had shoved the corpse of the second guard off him and thrust himself back, using his legs and the wall as a fulcrum to shove himself upright. He was grinning like a madman, his eyes wild. Nehru's left foot swept back, looking for balance as he prepared to kick.

Reyes's foot flashed up and then back, driving his boot heel into the diaphragm of the first guard. The man wheezed, a high-pitched sound that didn't sound like it could have come from a man, and retched down the front of his body armor. Reyes chuckled.

He blocked Nehru's kick with his hands, directing the colonel's foot away from his stomach even as Nehru tried to withdraw it. For an instant he thought Reyes would hold on, to try twisting his leg and popping his knee. He set himself to jump and twist, to keep the spy from finding the necessary torque to break the joint, but his foot came back down to the floor beside him.

"Not enough," Reyes said. "Come on, Inspector."

Nehru snarled. The door to the interrogation room burst open and more guards crowded the door.

Reyes looked that way, eyes narrowing. His upper lip curled into the beginnings of a sneer. Nehru sucked in a breath, searching for balance. The first guard shoved through the door, stun baton held high and ready.

Reyes grunted. He brought his hands together in front of his chest. Nehru recognized the move—he was going to sweep the guard's chin with the sharp, hard bones of his elbow. Reyes moved fast enough; he'd get inside the guard's reach before the big man could bring his arm down. And his elbow, with Reyes's obvious muscle behind it, would kill the guard if he struck in the right spot.

Damn it!

Nehru stepped away from the door and away from Reyes. His hand dipped to the small of his back even as Reyes drove his shoulder into the guard's downward-moving arm. The impact deflected the baton's blow away from Reyes's head and down his back. It would hurt—the baton's voltage would hurt no matter where it struck—but it wouldn't drop him. Nehru's fingers closed on the butt of the small hold-out pistol nestled there. He drew it as quickly as he could.

Reyes's arm snapped around, as if he were punching himself in the chest. His elbow took the guard along the side of the neck. There was a wet *crackle* and the guard collapsed, hands grasping at his throat. Reyes stamped his foot down on the guard's knee. A hoarse, choked-off scream whispered through the room.

"Reyes!"

The Maskirovka agent's head snapped around.

Nehru fired.

The bullet entered Reyes's head through his right eye and punched through the thin bone behind it. The caliber was too low and the round too slow for the bullet to exit. Reyes's other eye bulged as the hydrostatic shock increased the pressure inside his head for a moment. Then he collapsed.

"Damn it," Nehru whispered. He lowered the gun. More guards crowded the room. The first pair knelt beside the wounded man in the doorway. His fingers, still clutching at his swollen throat, were growing feebler.

Reyes's body shuddered as its bowels released. The stench of shit and blood filled the small room. It combined with the burned-gunpowder taint to scratch at Nehru's sinuses. He watched the stain of urine spread across the corpse's pants.

I was right. He slid the small gun back into his holster.

They are *here.*

The medic's uniform was hidden where Reyes had said it would be. Halle pulled it on after taking her communicator out of her pocket and setting in on the seat of the ambulance. The keycard was in the front seat, and the engine caught on the first try. Halle left the ambulance in park and picked up her communicator, thumbing through her contact list until she found the one she was looking for.

Emergency.

She entered a series of numbers and pressed send.

Nehru watched as the orderlies lifted Reyes's body onto the gurney. General Bangs stepped past them, one hand covering his nose. He watched the body as he moved, as if afraid it was going to come back to life and attack him. Nehru watched him set his shoulders as he turned to face the Inspectorate officer.

"Are you all right?" Bangs asked.

"We need to get back to the security room," Nehru said. "I need to know everyone Reyes has been in contact with in the last three weeks."

"But—"

"But nothing. He's dead."

Bangs stared. "I know he's dead. You killed him."

Nehru closed his eyes. Despite every effort, his mind showed him the fantasy of actually asking who tied Bangs's shoes for him in the morning. How anyone so inanely *thick* could rise to general's rank—and be put in charge of *this* base, of all of them—Nehru opened his eyes. He reined in his thoughts.

"There will be more than one," he finally said.

"But—"

"But *nothing*! God *damn* it, General—" Nehru stopped. He closed his mouth. His fingertips were tingling. He wondered if that was leftover adrenaline from the fight or new adrenaline from the instant's fantasy he'd just played out in his mind where he shot Bangs, too.

A muffled *thump* echoed through the wall. Nehru felt the floor shake in a minuscule tremor through his boots. Alarms screamed to life. Nehru looked at the ceiling, ordering himself to calm down.

"There's been an explosion!" one of the guards said. He was holding his hand over his earbud. "Near the motor pool—a petrol tank."

"An attack?" Bangs asked. He was watching the ceiling, as if afraid it was going to fall. "But he's dead!"

"More than one," Nehru repeated. Bangs looked at him. Then he twisted around to look at Reyes's body.

"You think—?" Bangs looked back and forth between the gurney and Nehru. Nehru watched him.

Nehru said, "General, perhaps it is best if I continue with General Vocaine. You must see to your base."

"What?" Bangs blinked and focused on him. "Yes, of course. Vocaine can help you with the security feeds."

Nehru nodded and stepped past him. The hallway was crowded with guards and medicos; all of them were standing around, looking at the walls and each other. *This is what passes for emergency response on Xanthe*, Nehru thought. The loiterers spread out of his way like he was a plague-carrier despite their distraction.

More than one, he thought. Then he stopped. *An explosion*. Nehru spun, reaching for the nearest radio on a guard, shouting that the gates be sealed.

They were *here*.

Halle looked in the rear camera screen and watched the Barter-side gates of the Happen military reservation dwindle behind her. The badly burned man in the back of the ambulance moaned, but Halle ignored him. She was feeling good, riding an endorphin high that no drug could match.

She had *done* it.

The privates on gate duty knew they probably should've been more alert than to pass just anyone leaving Happen when there'd just been an explosion. That's why Halle had stopped to find a body before she headed for the gate. When they had planned this extraction, she'd worried it might take her too long to find a suitable diversion.

But Quinn had done his job with the bomb well. There were plenty of bodies lying around.

Halle put her foot down on the accelerator, whistling softly under her breath.

The datacard was still in her bra.

BARTER, XANTHE III
FREE WORLDS LEAGUE
21 MARCH 2466

It was evening before Quinn's message came through. Little was skimming the latest batch of spam in his inbox when it pinged. He opened and scanned the codewords, then keyed the noteputer off. Halle Ostend and Sasha Feodoreyva stepped out of the small kitchenette.

Little looked up at them. "He's coming here."

"He, who?"

"The Inspector."

Sasha muttered a curse. "Quinn's okay?"

Little gestured to the now-dormant noteputer. "He's going to try slowing him down."

Halle hissed. She opened her mouth, but then closed it. A moment later, "Is that wise?"

Little shrugged. "We need every second."

The two women went back into the kitchen. Hector Little stood and went to the small balcony window of the apartment. It was a different one than the suite where they'd first gotten Halle's coded message. He touched his pocket, where a datacard with the stolen data rested against his thigh. They all had a copy. He grinned. There were dozens of copies.

The Maskirovka's commitment to stealing the Mariks' BattleMech technology was total; every agent sent was expendable. No plan was too risky. No tactic was off the board. It was the Confederation's life to get the secrets of the giant walking war machines, just as it had been for the other major polities. The Hegemony opened its lead in technology every day. The Confederation's enemies loomed ever closer on every border, with more and newer BattleMechs. The plans *must* make it back to the Confederation.

The best way was for Little's team to carry them back into the Confederation. To that end, each of the team members in Barter had a copy of the plans. Several copies. One on their person; one in their luggage. One hidden in secret folders on their noteputers. There were ten separate datacards hidden around this safehouse, and Drake was across town dropping others. He had been gone all day.

Even if every member of Little's team was slaughtered by morning, the data would be safely hidden. Buried emails and advertisements broadcast the hides to other Maskirovka agents. Even if they died tomorrow, they had gotten the data out of Happen. The next team would only have to get on-planet and find one of the copies Drake was more or less littering the city with.

That was the worst-case option, of course.

Little rubbed his hands together. The calluses on his trigger finger scratched against the thick ones on his opposite hand.

Tomorrow.

The firing had mostly died down by the time the guards let Nehru up. He stepped away from the ferrocrete wall of the entry alcove. Across the way, the sniper's remains were afire—one of the guards had been carrying a grenade launcher with incendiary grenades—but that didn't stop the others from burning through magazines.

He's already dead. Nehru supposed it was impossible to keep the simple-minded from asserting their manhood. Especially when it was done so impotently.

"Are you all right, sir?" the sergeant of the guard asked.

Nehru nodded. "We need to go."

The sergeant dithered. "There could be more of them—"

"*Now.*"

Nehru stepped around him, or meant to. The shoulder boss of his plate ballistic armor caught the sergeant's shoulder. It was like bouncing off a steel I-beam, for all the sergeant jerked away as soon as the contact was made. Nehru snarled at the unaccustomed weight, but he had to admit that recent events had made it wise.

Bangs's security chief had insisted the inspector wear full body armor when he left the building. He'd been adamant, completely unafraid of Nehru's Inspectorate authority. The man's face had been a study in contradictions; shame that he'd failed his task and allowed the Maskirovka into Happen; and resolve that there would be no further breaches of security. Nehru approved of his paranoia. *Especially now.*

Esterhazy's body had been found barely half an hour after the explosion. It hadn't taken Bangs's security geeks more than ten minutes to confirm the complete schematic and base data file for the BattleMech program had been downloaded.

The man whose office had been penetrated was taken to a security cell.

Bangs had looked like the hangman was behind him when he brought Nehru the news.

"It's out," he'd said. "The cameras were disabled. Reyes, we think."

Nehru had breathed slowly, consciously, through his nose.

"Senior Technician Esterhazy is dead." Bangs's lower lip trembled for a half-instant. "Murdered, it looks like. His neck was broken."

Nehru had nodded.

Bangs swallowed. "What do we do?"

Nehru licked his lips. "We go," he began, as if he were speaking to a mentally retarded house pet, "to Barter. And we find them."

Which had led to this convoy into the city. And a sniper's attack on the security private dressed in the black Inspectorate uniform that had preceded Nehru out of the ferrocrete alcove. He didn't know the private's name. That rankled him—it hurt in his gut, somewhere beneath his stomach. He'd have to learn the boy's name, after. When there was time.

The sergeant opened the door of the armored executive car. "We'll get you into the city, sir," he said. "The escort is spooling up now." He gestured behind him. As the firing finally died down, Nehru heard the first *whop-whop* of a helicopter spinning up its rotors.

Nehru slid into the back seat of the car and looked at the two men already sitting there. One was General Vocaine, who'd been co-opted from his position as head of the 'Mech bureau and assigned to liaise with Nehru and the Barter military. The other was Force Commander Bateson, the Happen base security officer. He was pale, even in the poor light.

"Sir," Bateson said, "I must offer my resignation. To have such a blatant failure—"

"Quiet," Nehru said. He looked to Vocaine. "What news?"

"We know what the link was between Reyes and Esterhazy," Vocaine said. His cheeks were even more flushed than they had been the first time they'd met in Vocaine's office. "A girl from the secretarial pool. Halle Ostend."

Nehru raised an eyebrow in question.

"The date that Reyes mentioned? That was Ostend." Vocaine tapped his noteputer's screen and turned it so Nehru could see. "She was also boffing Esterhazy."

"Arrest her," Nehru said. He tapped the intercom for the driver's compartment. "Let's go. Barter. I'll have an address sent up." He looked at Vocaine. "Send him her address in Barter."

"She's not here," Vocaine said.

Nehru stared at him. He looked at Bateson, who was trying very hard to sink back into the plush leather seats. Back at Vocaine. "Do we know where she is?"

"She drove an ambulance out right after the explosion."

Before I closed the gates. Nehru reached up and wiped his eyes with the back of his left hand. "An ambulance."

Bateson spoke up. "I already spoke to the guard on duty. She had a casualty in the back—still alive. Told him she was headed for the trauma center in Barter."

Nehru looked at Vocaine. He shook his head. "Never arrived. They found the ambulance in an alley. The trooper in the back was dead of his wounds." He licked his lips. "Burns. Very painful."

The urge to throw up his hands nearly overwhelmed Nehru. He looked at Bateson. "Are you a Maskirovka spy, too?" He grimaced. "Never mind."

The car lurched into motion. When Nehru put his hand on the sideboard, he felt both the car's engine's vibrations and the rhythmic thumping of the helicopter. His mind was abuzz with six different tangents at once...

"Call the governor in Barter," he said a moment later. "Remind him the ports should be closed. I don't want anyone getting off this planet."

"All civilian and merchant traffic has already been frozen—"

Nehru cut Bateson off. "No. Everything."

"But we need the military patrols—" Bateson stopped. "You don't trust the garrison in Barter, either?"

Nehru speared him with a glance. "I trusted your people," he said harshly.

Bateson deflated.

Vocaine frowned. "That's not—" he began.

"That is," Nehru said. "Until I have that data back in my possession, no one is above suspicion."

Danilov watched Captain bar-Danan stare at the mouthpiece of his headset telephone. The tower was quiet with all the traffic halted. Most of the civilian liners were empty—it had been hours—but he knew if he tied into a channel showing the starport concourse it'd be overrun with shouting civilians and screaming children. Starports like the one in Barter were small enough that they never appeared that busy, because the steady trickle of people was always moving *through* it. Plug one end of that trickle, and it quickly became a torrent.

"Repeat that last, please," the captain ground out. The edges of his neck burned red with restrained emotion. Danilov touched a key on his console that sent the channel bar-Danan was speaking on to his headset without activating his microphone.

"—All traffic is grounded. That includes the interdiction flights."

Danilov frowned. Bar-Danan closed his eyes.

"How, may I ask, are we to ensure the airspace remains closed with *no fighters in the air to close it*?" bar-Danan asked quietly. His voice was far calmer than Danilov's would have been in the same situation.

"Orders," was the reply.

Bar-Danan glanced at Danilov and shook his head. "Listen. You tell the governor—or whoever—that we've got the port locked down. For whatever reason that he doesn't deign to tell us mere mortals. You further tell him that it will be impossible for us to maintain that security once we've grounded all of our own squadrons. So I—me, personally—will not be held responsible, nor will anyone in my department, when—not if, *when*—whatever the hell is so important escapes into the open, clear skies."

He clicked the line closed. Then he looked at Danilov.

"Was that wise?" Danilov asked.

"I don't care." Bar-Danan pulled the headset off and dropped in onto the counter in front of him. "It needed to be said. Eventually one of the bureaucrats will learn that you can't just say something and make it come true."

Not likely, Danilov didn't say. Instead, he said, "What are they looking for?"

"No idea." Bar-Danan placed his handset back in its cradle and stood to stare out of the ferroglass at the frozen starport tarmac. Shuttles and freighters sat in blast pits. Danilov stood up to watch as the steam vents closed, cutting off the wisps of waste heat that showed a vessel getting ready for launch. Nothing moved on the runway.

"Whatever's going on," bar-Danan said, "I hope they catch them quickly. This idiocy will gut the economy." He glanced at Danilov with a wry grin. "And of course, the HV news is going to *crucify* the governor." He chuckled. "Maybe it'll be over faster than I think."

Danilov grunted. A few minutes later bar-Danan walked out, leaving Danilov alone in the tower.

He sat down and toggled his noteputer live. When the text-message program had loaded he typed in a number and sent one word.

Then he closed the program and triggered another program that would reformat the noteputer back to its factory settings. Six times in a row.

**BARTER
XANTHE III
FREE WORLDS LEAGUE
22 MARCH 2466**

The sound of Sasha Feodoreyva's hand striking the composite countertop was sharp. Had the countertop been glass, it might have broken.

Hector Little ignored it. He stared back at her, carefully not looking at the others through the small alcove in the kitchenette.

"There's no other way," he said.

"There's always another way," Sasha spat back.

"Dan is the only one who's never been here," Little told her. "We've been very careful to make Tibbetts his only contact. There's no way they can tie him to us. We're going to get made, probably by lunchtime. The cameras around town will have caught Halle coming here. They will have caught all of us coming and going. *They have our faces*."

Halle Ostend made a slight sound. "That's a lot of data to sort," she said. "Maybe we can wait—"

"No. We can't."

"Why not?" Sasha demanded.

"Because the Inspectorate will *not* open the port until he catches us." Little stopped speaking and closed his mouth. His right hand touched his trouser pocket, where the little personal communicator was still nestled. The text message would be displayed on the screen if he opened it. The one word that damned them all.

MASADA.

"So we let him find one of the datacards—" Halle began.

Little cut her off. "No."

"But—"

"It's not enough," he said. "Even if the Inspectorate finds the card, they'll still need to catch *us*. This inspector, this Nehru, he's not going to stop until he has us in a cell or our bodies in the morgue." He looked up, meeting each of the women's eyes in turn. "And we'll still have to give him most of the datacards."

"I still think—" Sasha started.

"No, you're *not* thinking. You were there when we made the contingencies. You knew this was an option." He waited, but neither of them spoke. After a moment he looked down. "A few of us might make it, if…"

"If what?"

"If we make the Leaguers believe they caught us all." He sniffed sharply and stepped away from the counter. "Masada means Dan is the ace in the hole. They'll probably get Tibbetts, but they can't very well arrest everyone he's ever talked to. Not when the governor will be crying to get the ports open and travel resumed and they've got enough bodies to fill six morgues."

Sasha chewed her lower lip, then crossed her arms. "Our lives, our souls, our sacred honor…"

"That was the deal when we started in the business." Little felt his stomach tighten. He clenched his belly muscles, willing his gorge to stay down. It wouldn't do to throw up in front of everyone. It wouldn't do to throw up at all. He exhaled slowly. "I'll go first, make a big noise. Maybe that'll be enough."

"Big noise?"

Little smiled. "We're trying to escape, remember? I'll go steal a shuttle."

Sasha touched his hand. He looked down at her pale fingers on top of his. "Ssu-ma could do that. He's already in the aerospace pool."

Little withdrew his hand. "If Kane is the one to shoot me down, maybe he can get away after. And then all of you."

The door to the safehouse apartment—the last safehouse—opened, and Drake walked in. He was wearing surveyman's fatigues that were caked with mud to the waist. He dropped his hard hat on the table by the door and took in the scene in the kitchenette: Little and Feodoreyva inside the cooking area, standing close together, and Ostend standing outside the alcove, hands wrapped around herself. Little could imagine the string of causalities going through Drake's mind.

"I've been shopping," he said, closing the door behind him. Two pistols appeared in his hands as soon as the door closed. He reversed them and offered them butt-first. "Fire-sale prices, even."

Ostend shook her head and walked into one of the bedrooms. Sasha ignored Drake and looked at Little.

Little looked back. Then he stepped around her and took one of the pistols.

25 MARCH 2466

Nehru stood in the small apartment's living room, next to the plastiform coffee table, with his arms crossed behind his back. Behind him a team of infantrymen from the Barter militia were tearing out the walls and stabbing knives into the mattresses. He ignored them, instead letting his mind wash around the room, absorbing details.

They were long gone. No one had entered this apartment for three days.

But did they make it off-world?

No. They hadn't had enough time. They'd left this safehouse before Reyes was dead. Which meant before they knew they had the 'Mech data. Behind him a glass-top coffee table broke with a crash as two soldiers dropped the contents of a drawer on it. Vocaine cleared his throat. Nehru blinked and looked at him.

"We've got people on all the approaches," Vocaine said. The whisker-thin earpiece headset was barely visible. He'd be talking to Bateson, who Nehru knew was just a bit too scared to be in his presence right now.

"Move them," Nehru said. His eyes focused behind Vocaine's bulk on a clock set on a table near the doorway. "Send them to support the team at Ostend's apartment." He sucked in a deep breath. "What are the people at Reyes's flat saying?"

"Nothing."

Nehru looked back at him. "You haven't heard from them?"

Vocaine shook his head. "No—sorry. They haven't found anything. The landlady says she hasn't seen anyone go into Reyes's place before we did." He glanced around at the soldiers steadily demolishing the rooms. "They could be anywhere," he said quietly.

"Yes, they could." Nehru smacked his lips and stepped closer to the general. An infantryman dropped a vase on the floor to shatter before kneeling to pick through the fragments. "We know they *were* here, though. We should be able to guess where they're going *from* here, too."

"We can?"

Nehru nodded. "Is the command post at the port up yet?"

"Two hours," Vocaine said without checking. "Ninety minutes, if we're lucky."

"Let's go." Nehru stepped past the general toward the door. "We've got a lot of sorting to do." If the computers and the specialized sorting software he'd provided could be brought online quickly enough, they might be able to find the needles of the Maskirovka team's faces in the haystacks of Barter's street cameras. His mind was clicking through scenarios.

If…

If they're not already gone.

No flights had left Barter.

They could have driven out.

Why? Barter was the only interstellar port on the planet. All the others had been shut down for years—since the 'Mech operation started. Going to ground at this point only favored the pursuers. Their only chance was to get away with the data.

What if they're smarter than me?

Nehru smiled and started down the stairs toward the waiting car. *Then I lose.*

A private opened the door for him, and he heard Vocaine's heavy footsteps trudging down the extruded stairs.

But I haven't lost yet.

The security guard at the starport departure terminal held up his hand as Hector Little pulled the van up to the curb. Hector toggled his window down and leaned out, already holding up his hand. "I know, I know—the flights are all canceled."

The guard nodded. "So just keep going, buddy."

"The terminal is still open, though, right?"

"Yeah, if you want to sleep on plastic seats and eat rehydrated food that tastes like it was sealed about the time McKenna brought the *Dreadnought* home." The guard leaned around to get a look at Sasha Feodoreyva and Halle Ostend in the back. "Trust me, friend. Go home. Watch the HV. I'm sure it won't be long, and the lines will hold your tickets."

"And the jump series in the next system?" Sasha snapped from the back seat. Her accent was pure Atreus. "Will they hold all those JumpShips so we make our rendezvous?"

The guard smiled. "Now, ma'am, I'm sure every effort will be made—"

"I'm sure too," Sasha snapped. She triggered the door open. "Come along, dear. We're going inside. The moment the port opens, we'll be on the first shuttle off of this hellhole." She slid out, long legs and short skirt. Her skin was pale as ice. Her eyes flashed.

The guard watched her get out, then watched Halle hand out their luggage and step out behind her. Then he looked at Little.

Little shrugged. In the unspoken code between men, it meant *you try and argue with her, pal*. The guard looked at the women, then back at Little. Then he raised his eyebrows and stepped back. Little smiled at him, then leaned the other way and toggled the passenger-side window down.

"I'll just park and be in, honey," he said.

Sasha waved a hand and kept moving, marching through the sliding doors. Halle followed behind her, head down, both hands behind her on the toggle-strap for her luggage. The very image of a quiet child following her imperious mother.

Little toggled both the windows up and checked his rear monitors for traffic. A moment later he accelerated into the thin flow of cars and taxis. He watched the rear monitor with half an eye, until the guard tried to stop the next vehicle.

He smiled. Maybe he'd make such a ruckus the two women might make orbit, after all.

Maybe.

Sasha Feodoreyva watched the van pull away from the corner of her eye while she pretended to sneer at the departure boards. Every line was marked canceled, but the port terminal was still crowded with people doing exactly as she'd told the inept guard they were doing: trying to wait out the emergency and get the first flights out.

Halle stepped closer behind her. "I've seen two guards already," she said, barely above a whisper. "Weapons will not be a problem."

Sasha didn't let her grin show. Instead she made a small signal of assent with her fingers and sneered in the other direction. All they had to do was wait for Little's distraction to open the port. The van was already gone.

So was the man driving it.

Motorcycle-mounted police blocked all the side streets as Nehru's small convoy entered the starport. He ignored the quiet chatter of Vocaine speaking into his headset. His mind was sorting details, trying to fit pieces together, seeing what fit and what didn't. He was trying to stay out of his subconscious's way as much as possible while he was, well... conscious. His eyes flicked over to the window, watching the traffic. Even when the port was closed—it was on every news channel, in a crawl on every HV footer, and posted on every board—people still tried to get around the restrictions. Nehru smiled absently. *People are predictable.*

A brown-painted van was waiting to turn into the parking garage. The yellow blinker strobed barely inside Nehru's awareness. He looked at it, not really seeing it, and sighed.

Where are you?

A compact three-wheeler pulled up behind the van as Little climbed out. He locked the doors and then dropped the remote on the stained ferrocrete. It might go off if he stepped on it.

Nicholas Drake grinned at him from the trike's driver seat, then leaned over and slid the passenger door over. Little climbed in, and the little machine jerked into motion with the drone of electric motors.

"Inconspicuous," Little observed, eyeing the cramped passenger compartment. Drake chuckled and slid into the exit lane. "Goodies in the boot?"

"Yep."

Little grunted. "Good."

A minute later, they were through the checkpoint and on the interstate highway back toward Barter. Drake signaled and took the first exit, following the signs for Crandall Field— the Barter Militia side of the starport—but drove right past the entry gate. Gray-and purple-clad MPs in second-class uniforms stood at the head of the queue of vehicles waiting to get inside, checking IDs and datacards. Little watched them as they passed, but none appeared to look up. If they were on alert—more alerted than the port being closed, anyway—it wasn't apparent. In the Confederation there'd have been a squad of armored vehicles just inside the gate with turrets buttoned and guns trained. Just in case.

Just in case means just in time, Little thought. He smiled again. *I haven't thought about that line since the Farm.* His fingers were rubbing the knuckles of his other hand without him thinking about it. Then he realized what they were doing.

"Through the fence?" he asked.

Drake grunted. "May as well." The driver glanced at him with a wry grin. "Give 'em what they expect." He cycled the trike into a lower gear as it started up the low rise of an overpass. The road crossed one of the taxiways for air-breathing aircraft.

"You got word to Tibbetts and Kane?"

"I did."

"Good." Little rubbed his kneecaps where they rested nearly at the dashboard. "Good."

Drake let the trike idle down the other side of the overpass. "Hector..."

Little chuckled. "It's the smart move."

"I know it is." Drake's voice was as even as wet sand. "I—I think I should do it, is all."

"I was the last person to see Halle outside," Little said. It didn't require much thought to work the logic out. He'd already played the sequences through in his mind for hours. A lifetime's worth of hours. "They'll get my face in a bit, if they don't have it already."

"It's worth it," Drake said after a moment.

Little laughed, a little bark more of surprise than amusement. "I know it is, Nick."

"Yeah." Drake pulled to the side of the road and stopped the trike. "But you should hear it from someone else. It's worth it, what we're doing here. It maybe means life for the Confederation." He held out his hand.

Little took it. "If it means life for Halle or Sasha, it's worth it," he said. "Even you, I guess."

Drake's wry grin returned. He let go of Little's hand, pressed the stud that unlocked the boot with a *thunk*, and pointed past Little's shoulder. "In that case," he said, "get out."

Little looked where he was pointing. A vine was creeping up the military-link fence. Beyond it, across half a kilometer of brush and dead space, was the squat, gray, weather-streaked dome of a shuttle hangar. Little smiled and slid the door open.

Little had barely gotten the bag out of the trunk and slammed the lid when the little three-wheeler accelerated away with a whine. He watched it long enough to see Drake's hand stick out the window, middle finger raised. Then it was around a curve and gone.

He smiled as he walked toward the fence.

**BARTER STARPORT
XANTHE III
FREE WORLDS LEAGUE
22 MARCH 2466**

Fyodor Danilov was in the control tower when the alarm sounded. He stood up from the solitaire game on his console and looked out the ferroglass windows with bar-Danan and everyone else. A shuttle was taxiing toward the runway. It was a civilian job, something like a *Traveler*-class mail boat. Danilov was too far away to tell the difference, and all the binoculars were taken.

"Who is that?" Bar-Danan demanded.

"No one is scheduled," Danilov said without checking. Of course no one was scheduled. The port was *closed*. As soon as he said it he felt like an idiot. Maybe he'd be able to tell someone what color the sky was, too.

"Alert Crandall," bar-Danan said. He glanced at Danilov. "It's not like we can do anything here."

"Do you think—?"

"I think you should alert Crandall Field," bar-Danan said. "And then, yeah. Maybe wake up the militia pilots. If he gets off the ground we might have to send someone after him."

Danilov turned away from the window and the shuttle, and picked up his headset. His voice was urgent, earnest even. He was shouting at the corporal on the other end of the phone. He was sure he sounded like a civilian puke caught in the middle of an emergency. That was okay.

No one would know the tension in his voice wasn't panic. No one would know it was the tension of man watching a friend—*a brother*—going out to get killed on purpose.

Vocaine was shouting into his headset. Nehru watched red spots form on his florid face, watched the beads of sweat well up on his forehead. In a moment, the armpits of his uniform would be wet. He tuned out the big general's words after the first couple—the most important. Anything he said after "Stop that shuttle!" was just detail Nehru didn't care about.

"Too easy," Nehru murmured.

"Easy, hell," Vocaine said, suddenly standing next to him, watching the monitor. "We grounded all the planes, remember? If he gets off the ground, it'll be orbit or transit before we catch up. If then. In space he can be a rock, and we'll never find him."

Nehru blinked. *There's no pursuit*. He looked past Vocaine and speared a finger at a commo tech. "Contact the field CO. Block the field. Trucks, tanks, I don't care. Tell him I want fighters in the air as soon as possible." He looked back at the monitor. The shuttle was turning toward the runway—still several minutes away, but it could have been light years. *Damn it. DAMN it. I've never been so stup—*

"Sir!" Nehru looked. One of the technicians at the face-recognition stations was standing, waving at him. "We've got a match!"

Nehru glanced back at the shuttle on the screen, then at the tech. The need to *know* overcame him. He stalked down the narrow aisle, behind technicians who were already hunched over screens. The technician smiled like a child who'd just been patted on the head and stepped back, pointing.

Two images were on the screen. One was a grainy 2D surveillance still from a traffic camera. It showed a woman, clearly Halle Ostend, walking with her arm through the elbow of a taller man. He was half-twisted, looking at something behind him. And, coincidentally, directly at the camera. The second image was an identification photo from the Barter traffic database. The name underneath it was Hector Little.

A sudden roar went up from the other end of the room. Nehru flinched back and looked. The staffers around Vocaine—and the general—were on their feet, watching the monitor, with arms upraised and fists clenched. While he watched, another roar—*approval*, his mind told him—erupted. Nehru flinched, thinking to run back down the alley behind the technicians and see what they were seeing. Then he looked down.

He stabbed a control. The left-hand security image disappeared. Another control. A graph of something appeared. He snarled and slapped the keyboard with the palm of his hand. A help icon appeared, smiling the same smarmy smile IT geeks had been programming as a sick joke for a thousand years. Nehru jerked back.

"Make this—I need—*the monitor*, woman!" The technician blinked and reached past him, toggling a switch. The shuttle appeared on the runway tarmac, accelerating. The camera was unsteady, shaking as it followed it. Nehru frowned.

The camera zoomed out. On the runway in front of the shuttle appeared the bulk of an emergency sprayer truck. The lights were all on. The ladder-arm that reached up to spray deicer or fire-retardant foam over an aircraft was raised, like an arm trying to catch a ball. The truck was obviously going full-out. While Nehru watched, a man bailed out of the passenger side of the cab, heavy fire coat flapping like a cape. He hit the tarmac with a *crunch* that was soundless but no less sickening and disappeared into the wash of heat and disturbed air behind the shuttle. The shuttle angled slightly to the left, trying to get around. One of the wingtips stuttered. It had almost enough lift.

The driver of the truck heeled the wheel over, sending the truck angling to the shuttle's landing gear at the last second. Nehru saw the truck start to flip onto its side—

—saw the shuttle's nose landing gear bend as it struck the thick torso of the truck—

—saw the nose come down in sparks—

—a flash of light—

—the walls of the hangar they'd appropriated shook.

Nehru looked down toward Vocaine. Every man around him was screaming, waving their arms. Smiling. Nehru exhaled a breath he hadn't realized he was holding. He elbowed the technician aside and collapsed into the chair, letting his face fall into his palms.

The console beeped. Nehru jerked back. *What did I touch*—?

Another photo was on the screen, overlaying the burning wreck of the shuttle. It was Halle Ostend's face, from her Happen security file. A second photo pulled up next to it. It was a static security camera, looking over the shoulder of an attendant of some sort. Nehru frowned. Ostend was standing behind an older, pissed-off looking woman who was haranguing the attendant. She was clutching the come-along strap of a luggage set.

Nehru lurched to his feet. "Vocaine!" His voice didn't get more than two meters past the cheering. He looked at the general, still stuck in the middle of the celebrating officers. Then he looked back down at the screen. The timestamp on the image was barely an hour old. "*VOCAINE!*"

Nothing.

Another beep. He barely heard it. The image of Ostend at the airport terminal repeated itself, but this time it was centered on the woman doing the complaining. Then a second security image popped up, dated three weeks ago. It was the haughty woman and Hector Little, at a cafe somewhere in Barter. A moment later another window opened, showing another Barter ID photo. Sasha Feodoreyva.

Nehru tried to swallow. He couldn't. He looked at Vocaine. Nothing. He looked around. The chair. He picked up the chair he'd been sitting in and spun, slamming the wheeled feet against the thin metal of the wall. The technician dropped to her backside, screaming and holding up her hand. The entire wall shook as he slammed the chair against it again and again. The shouting died down. Nehru kept slamming the chair, until he was conscious of the silence. He dropped the chair.

"Sir!?" Vocaine shouted. He was shouldering his way through the people struck motionless at the sight of the Inspectorate officer—the cool, collected, never-has-a-moment-of-not-eating-your-ass Inspectorate officer—having a breakdown.

Nehru pointed at the screen. His chest heaved. Vocaine reached him, eyes drawn together in worry. He looked where Nehru was pointing.

"Terminal," Nehru gasped. "They're in. The terminal!"

Vocaine frowned at the screen. He looked from the screen to Nehru then back to the screen. He whispered, "Buddha's balls."

Nehru gasped for air, unable to speak but screaming in his mind.

Vocaine stood. He looked at Nehru, nodded once, and spun. "Captain Mallory!" he bellowed, striding back the way he'd come. "Get me the sergeant of the guard!"

Nehru looked back at the images of the two women, overlaying the still-burning wreck of the shuttle. His lungs felt like they were going to explode. "Too easy," he whispered. Then he lurched after Vocaine.

When Halle came out of the lavatory, it took her a second to find Sasha. The tall woman was standing among a crowd of people at one of the four-meter-tall ferroglass windows, holding her hands over her mouth in shock.

Halle frowned. She hadn't known Sasha Feodoreyva could *feel* shock—but then she realized all the other women around her had the same expression. They were all looking at something. Halle walked over, keeping a careful distance.

She had to. People may have seen the blond woman enter the lavatory, but a brunette had come out. She'd darkened her exposed skin, and brown contacts obscured her eyes. Shaped pads rubbed at her gums when she clenched her teeth, but they pushed the outline of her cheeks out. No one who wasn't an expert would see the blond Halle in the new one—unless she ruined it by going right up to Sasha and talking.

A pall of smoke was rising from behind a low building. The runway to the left was scattered with burning patches. Halle stopped. *Hector.* She looked around for the security guards, but most of them were along the windows, too. Halle walked over to one.

"What happened?" she asked. Her accent was backwoods Sierra, to go with the clothes she'd changed into: rustic leathers and homespun. "I was in the can."

"Crash," the guard said, without looking. "Looks like a shuttle was trying to get off, and a fire truck got in the way."

"That's horrible," Halle said. She craned her neck, trying to see past the guard. That's what a girl from Sierra would do. "Was anyone hurt?"

The guard looked at her in disbelief. "You don't see the fires, lady?" He rolled his eyes and looked back at the runway.

Halle made a moue and glanced toward Sasha. The older woman had lowered her hands to her chest. She waggled her ring and pinky finger a bit.

Halle glanced down at the pistol buckled to the security guard's belt.

You bet I'll stay close to the gun.

Vocaine had turned even redder. Nehru watched him listen to his headset as the infantrymen around him geared up. Purple-flashed body armor clacked against each other, while the angry buzz of stun rifles being charged permeated every low-amplitude sound.

Vocaine slammed his fist into the wall. "I don't *care* what you want, Captain. You will alert your guards. You will tell them to be on the lookout for the two women whose images I just forwarded you. You will tell them to arrest the women on sight, and consider them very dangerous. And you will not, under any circumstances, allow them to destroy any of their own possessions." He listened for a moment, eyes on Nehru. "No. Every person in that terminal is expendable." Listened.

"*Yes*, you sack of shit, that includes *you!*" He tore the headset out of his ear and flung it across the room.

For a moment Nehru saw the man who'd been appointed general officer of the 'Mech program on Xanthe. Then he flicked his eyes to the side and brought his attention back.

"A massacre would be bad," he murmured.

"No as bad as that data getting off-world," Vocaine blurted. "Or them destroying it before we can confirm—"

"Sir!"

Both Nehru and Vocaine spun. The building shook as a screaming sound reached through the concrete walls of the terminal. Nehru clawed for the nearest communicators—a guard nearby had one on his shoulder—and shouted.

"Fighters! Now, get the fighters up!"

A gasp rippled through the crowd an instant before Sasha Feodoreyva saw it. Another shuttle clawed its way over the wreck of the first, burning vortices through the pillar of smoke and flame, and angled into the sky. Cursing erupted as every security guard in sight clapped a hand over their earbuds. *Someone's just shouted*—Sasha looked back at the shuttle.

Nicholas. Her hand went back to her mouth. Drake had followed Hector Little and used the distraction of his death to steal his own shuttle. *And he's off the ground*. Sasha couldn't help it—she looked over the where Halle had been standing, feeling the smile threaten to break through her famously iron control. *And so what if it does*—

The guard next to Halle was staring at Sasha. He blinked, then looked down at the small screen of his pocket communicator. Then he dropped the comm and slapped his holstered pistol.

"That's her—*urk*!" His shout cut off as Halle's elbow took him in the throat. Sasha knew from experience the sound the guard's hyoid bone had made when it broke. He'd be a couple of minutes dying. Painful minutes.

Halle's hand scooped the pistol out of the falling guard's holster and spun around. Travelers around her yelped and leaped back. One woman—she had to weigh two hundred kilos if she was a gram—just stared at Halle, jaw agape. The pistol came up, slid past the fat woman's nose, and *cracked*. Sasha saw the muzzle flare brush tufts of the fat woman's hair up, but the round tracked true to enter the next guard's forehead. He dropped like a discarded toy. A woman screamed.

The scream jerked Sasha out of her reverie. She sprinted forward, luggage forgotten behind her, toward the dead guard. Halle was running ahead, trying to reach the next corner. Sasha slid on her knees next to the dead guard's body. He'd fallen on his holster. Sasha gripped his shoulder and hauled.

The *bam-bam-bam* of an assault rifle cackled through the concourse. Sasha looked up even as her fingers unsnapped the guard's holster. Halle was falling back, arms outstretched. Her head hit the floor with a *thunk* that Sasha heard from ten meters away. The brunette wig came loose and skittered across the polished floor like a macabre creature. Blood splashed parts of Halle's platinum hair red.

Sasha fired four rounds into the wall past the corner. The pistol's report was short and sharp, and her nose crinkled at the familiar scent of spent gunpowder. With her free hand she reached into a pocket and grabbed a handful of datacards. She reversed the pistol, holding it by the barrel—her fingers burned but she ignored them—and slammed it down on the first datacard, shattering it.

Bam. Another one flattened.

Her mind was filled with a mantra. *They'll find Halle's cards. Mine will be gone. They'll see me destroying them. They'll find hers. They'll think that's it. Hector is dead. Nicholas is in the air. Halle is dead. I'll be dead. That will be enough.*

Bam. Bam.

She looked up. The barrel of an assault rifle poked around the corner at ankle height. A moment later the edge of a combat helmet appeared. *Two datacards left.* She looked down. Her peripheral vision caught the flare of the rifle firing. Two rounds whistled through the air next to her head. *Bam.*

One more card.

Sasha raised the pistol butt—

Nehru stepped carefully around the blood pooling behind the body and picked up the datacard. Several more were smashed to bits of plastic around the woman's body. Vocaine's men had already turned up half a dozen on the other dead woman. The big general was beyond the dead woman's body, kneeling beside the gurney where a medic was treating the gunshot wound in the leg of an obese woman who'd been hit by stray shots. Vocaine said something and stood.

Nehru turned the datacard over in his hand. When Vocaine approached, he brandished it. "Such a small thing, isn't it?" He looked at it. "Have your people confirm the data is on here. I expect those—" he pointed to the other body, "—will prove to be copies."

Vocaine looked at the datacard, then at Nehru. He raised an eyebrow. Nehru handed him the datacard. Vocaine looked down at the tiny card in his meaty palm. "We got it back."

Muted, but still loud, the scream of a fusion-powered aerospace fighter's engine penetrated the concourse's soundproofing. Nehru turned and looked out the window. A pair of militia *Dragonfire* fighters whipped down the runway and hurtled into the sky with the rapidity only a torch fighter could achieve.

"Almost," Nehru whispered.

Then he turned and started walking toward the stairway that would take him to the control tower.

BARTER STARPORT
XANTHE III
FREE WORLDS LEAGUE
22 MARCH 2466

"There's another one!"

Danilov spun around from the display console, half-lurching out of his chair. The red radar dot of the second shuttle was still receding as it gained distance from the starport. A monitor mounted above the window showed a display of the tarmac; a third *Dragonfire* was taxiing past the wreck of the first shuttle. He sat back. The cold pitons of fear that had shot into his stomach at the shout receded a bit. *Not another shuttle.*

Captain bar-Danan slammed his headset down and cursed. "The order's confirmed." He glanced at the roomful of controllers. His eyes settled on Danilov. "Dan, I want you to steer the fighters. The orders are to force it down if possible, shoot it down if not."

Danilov nodded and turned back to his console, dialing for the fighter frequency. Behind him, he heard the door slide open. "Dagger Lead, this is Barter Control. Your target is angels forty and climbing. Bring it back or shoot it down."

Ssu-ma Kane's voice came back. "Roger, Control." His voice was even, just like Danilov's had been. Maybe a bit excited, but that was expected. No one would know the two men were talking about killing a friend.

A woman's voice rose above the hubbub behind him. "*What?*"

Danilov hit the mute button on his headset and twisted around to look. A black-clad officer and a huge man in sweat-stained general-officer's purples stood just inside the door. Captain bar-Danan stood near them, frowning. The woman who'd spoken was half out of her chair. The black-clad officer said something Danilov couldn't hear. He heard the reply.

"You let those animals *shoot* in the concourse?"

The pitons shot back into his stomach.

"We got them," the big general growled. "It's over."

The small, black-clad man held up a hand and pointed out the window. "Almost." Danilov heard. He turned back to face his display. The paired green carets of the *Dragonfire*s of Dagger Flight were closing with the red caret. He watched the distance lessen.

Sasha and Halle were dead.

Ssu-ma Kane grunted as the *Dragonfire*'s thrust shoved him deeper into the padded cockpit seat. His g-suit inflated, pushing blood back up into his torso and head, and the warbling tone of the fire-control computer searching for a lock began to pulse in his ears. He toggled his comm.

"Two, Lead. My shot, over."

"Lead, Two. Roger, your shot."

Kane dialed his radio to transmit on the emergency frequency. "Unidentified shuttle, this is Dagger Flight of two aircraft, approaching from your six o'clock. You have violated a no-fly order. Return to Barter Starport immediately, or we will force you down."

He waited. The *Dragonfire*'s missile launchers cycled and announced their readiness, but the fire control computer was still beeping an intermittent lock. He waited, and then pushed the button to replay his recorded transmission. His mind was in another place.

Drake. It has to be Drake. Kane knew Little would have taken the first shuttle himself on the tiny chance that his sacrifice was enough. He'd been expecting it since Little confirmed Danilov's Masada call. It was the end-all plan, the one that said they were all expendable except for Danilov himself, who they'd been careful to isolate from themselves as much as possible. Drake would have followed Little in and taken advantage of the first shuttle's destruction.

It might have worked. Except for the alert call.

And the fact that with the whole world watching, Kane would have to shoot him down. He looked at his tactical display, eyeing the green icon of Dagger Two. *I'm already halfway to orbit...* There was a datachip in the thigh pocket of his flight suit. It'd be a long haul to the jump point, and a DropShip might catch him, but he could do a Dutchman for part of the ride and keep from broadcasting—okay, he'd be dead, but *the fighter and the chip* would make it... but how would the Liao JumpShip know to pick up the derelict? Would they have shuttles fast enough to catch it and slow it down?

The radio beeped. He toggled the circuit live.

"You might as well go back." Drake. "I'm not turning around, and you're not shooting down a defenseless shuttle in front of God and radar. By now the media will be all over the port."

Kane smiled. "Descend now, or you will be fired upon." *I'm sorry, brother.*

"You can't intimidate—"

Kane triggered his missiles. The flight was off-target, passing several kilometers in front of the shuttle. The shuttle's course didn't waver in the slightest. The reload mechanism made the entire aircraft shiver as a new cassette-round of missiles *chunked* into the launcher.

"Nice warning shot," Drake said.

"The next one eats your exhaust," Kane said. "Turn and descend, shuttle."

"I told you—"

Kane shut off the radio.

A twitch of his hand brought the reticule on the HUD over the shuttle's icon. The launchers in the *Dragonfire*'s wings signaled ready. A tap on his weapons selector brought the two lasers mounted under the fighter's delta-shaped wings hot. He throttled forward, closing the range, and fired.

The lasers struck first, of course, burning away most of the meager anti-meteor armor over the shuttle's aft fuselage. Moments later, even as the wounded shuttle floundered in the thin air, the missiles arrived and pounded it into two pieces.

Kane pulled back on his stick, guiding the *Dragonfire* over the pall of smoke and away from the debris fall, then angled around to come back toward Barter.

Anyone watching would see a professional fighter pilot who'd done his job.

No one could see the small knot of anguish at what his duty required in the core of Ssu-ma Kane's soul.

Nehru watched the red caret blink off of the repeater console and smiled. Around him the control room erupted with cheers, although he knew most of the technicians and controllers had no real idea what they were cheering for. To them it had been an exercise in keeping a no-fly rule enforced; they didn't realize that they might have just saved a vital military advantage over the Capellan Confederation from escaping Xanthe III.

He wasn't about to tell them.

Instead, he turned to Vocaine and gestured the big man closer. "I want the bodies to go back to Happen. And any evidence we recover from the shuttle wrecks."

Vocaine nodded. His face was smiling, but something rubbed Nehru the wrong way. Something that niggled at the edge of his awareness, like a name half-remembered or a task left undone.

His communicator beeped.

Nehru frowned and pulled it out. He'd left strict orders that all communications were to pass through Vocaine. The code displayed was for the technical section. He flipped the comm open and held it to his ear, blocking his other ear with his free hand to keep out the noise of the control room. "Nehru."

"Sir," a female voice said, "we've had more action on the facial recognition."

Nehru smiled. "Excellent. We'll be able to match the last shuttle pilot. Send the pilot's data to Happen. We'll do the after-action there." He looked back at Vocaine.

"Which one's the pilot, sir?"

"What?"

"I've got two more confirmed hits here, sir. Two men." There was a pause. "I'm sending them to your noteputer, sir."

Nehru froze. "Names."

"Nicholas Drake and Edgar Tibbetts, sir."

Nehru closed his eyes. "Damn it."

"Sir?"

"Nothing. Send me the data. Keep looking." He snapped the comm closed and looked up at Vocaine. "It's not over."

Vocaine blinked. He waved an arm at the monitors. "What do you mean, it's not over? We've got half a dozen bodies. Two blown-up shuttles. Handfuls of datacards." He chewed on his lower lip for a second. Nehru watched his eyes flick to the Inspectorate insignia on Nehru's collar and then back to the Inspector's eyes. "How many of these bastards are there?"

Nehru restrained the semi-helpless shrug he felt. "More." He turned back to the local tower commander. "Captain bar-Danan, thank you for your help. Please inform your staff that I appreciate their help as well." The local officer looked up from where he'd been hunched over the back of one of his controller's seats, indicating something with his hand. Bar-Danan nodded and then went back to his perusal.

"Now, General—," Nehru began, but a voice cut him off.

"Captain?" one of the controllers on the end raised his hand. "One of them isn't coming back."

Danilov hated himself.

Captain bar-Danan came to stand behind his chair. Danilov looked up at him, then back down at his console. He pointed. "Dagger Lead, sir. He was headed back, but now he's broken formation and is headed for orbit."

The captain reached past Danilov's shoulder and stabbed the comm switch. "Dagger Lead, Barter Control, over." He waited. Danilov watched the green carets separate. Kane's fighter had broken away from its wingman without alerting the other pilot—and that meant he was far out of weapons range, even if Dagger Two was inclined to shoot down his wingman. The planes were identical—one wasn't going to catch the other.

When next Danilov looked up, there were two more men behind bar-Danan. The black-clad man's nametape read nehru. The general's tag said vocaine. Both of them ignored him, their eyes intent on the two separated green carets.

"Dagger Two, Control. Respond, please."

"You think it's him?" Danilov heard Vocaine ask quietly. *Him? Have they broken Kane's ID already?*

"Control, Dagger Two."

"Two, how read, over?"

"Five-by, Control."

"Two, where's your pal going?"

"No idea, Control. He just took off. He's not answering my comms, either."

Bar-Danan bit back half a curse. He glanced at Vocaine and Nehru, then stared down at Danilov. Danilov met his stare but said nothing. *He might make it. He might—and then I can wait, and there'll be no danger—*

Bar-Danan straightened. "Two, can you get him?"

"Control?"

"Can you catch him? Can you bring him down?"

"Sir—"

"I asked you a question, pilot."

The anger in the pilot's voice was palpable even across the radio. "Sir, his plane is just as fast as mine. Unless he turns, no. I can't catch him."

Bar-Danan closed his eyes, then opened them. "Roger that, Two. Keep on him." He toggled the microphone off and, after shaking his head at Danilov, turned. "Sirs, there's nothing I can do. Perhaps if we'd had high-orbit interceptors standing by—"

Nehru cleared his throat. "If I may, Captain?"

Bar-Danan blinked, then shrugged. "If you can change the laws of gravity, Colonel..."

Nehru smiled, then looked down at Danilov. He had piercing eyes—not colorful, just smart. Eyes that didn't miss things. His voice, when it was directed right at you, was modulated in just a way that you didn't want to say anything against it. "Might I borrow your console?"

Danilov slipped his headset off and stood. "Of course." His mind was racing. *What could he do?* Kane was free. Unless there was a navy ship in orbit he didn't know about. Or some secret flight of Inspectorate super-pilots.

Nehru called up the information on Kane's fighter. He selected the airframe's maintenance designator and copied it to a clipboard, then opened a new communication window. Several keystrokes later—keystrokes that Danilov, who'd worked that console every day for months, couldn't follow—a black-backed, lightning-bolt-and-sword insignia splash screen flashed, and then a small window appeared. Nehru copied the airframe data into the new field and pressed execute. Then he cleared the screen and sat back, crossing his arms. Only the radar tracking screen remained, with its two green carets.

One green caret.

Danilov stared.

"Control!" Dagger Two shouted. "Dagger Two! Dagger Lead just exploded!" There was a pause. "I just checked the recording. No missiles, no other contacts. He just—blew the hell up."

Danilov looked down at the back of Nehru's head. For an instant he saw himself snatching the man's head with both hands and twisting, listening for the *crackle* of bone snapping. He could do it. He was fast enough. The Maskirovka had trained him how to move like that—

He exhaled. There was a datacard in his locker. It had to get off Xanthe.

Had. To.

"Sir," Captain bar-Danan said quietly. "What just happened?"

Nehru stood and straightened his uniform jacket. "The fighter's anti-capture failsafe just activated."

"You mean—"

"I triggered its self-destruct."

Bar-Danan frowned. "That can't be done remotely."

Nehru inclined his head. "It can if you're the Inspectorate." He glanced at Danilov, who stood back and tried to focus on a spot on the wall above his console. The Maskirovka would be very interested in that information, too—assuming he survived to deliver the report.

Captain bar-Danan's mouth worked. "I don't—"

"You don't need to, Captain," General Vocaine broke in. "Any inquiries can be directed to my office at Happen. Or to General Bangs." He looked from bar-Danan to Danilov, then back. "The colonel-inspector was never here."

"Sir—" bar-Danan began.

"Captain," Vocaine growled, but Nehru held up his hand.

"You're concerned about my authority to do such a thing, Captain?" Nehru asked. There was very little more than pro forma question in his tone. "I assure you, it is well within my jurisdiction when treason is suspected. If Tibbetts or Drake had been able to get out of the atmosphere—"

"Tibbetts or Drake?" Bar-Danan looked to Danilov. "Who was flying Dagger Lead?"

"Kane, sir." Out of the corner of his eye, he saw Nehru blink.

"Kane?" Nehru looked at Danilov.

"Ssu-ma Kane, sir," he said. "Flight lieutenant."

"Is that confirmed?"

"I recognized his voice, sir," Danilov said. "We've done a lot of training ops with the boys over at Crandall Field the last few months." He kept his voice level, but his gorge was threatening to rise. He knew what he had to do. The instructors had warned him about this scenario all the way back to the Farm. There was nothing more important than the mission. Nothing. Not friends, not family, not even the love of his life.

Nothing.

Which meant there was nothing else he could do. Not with the Inspectorate itself standing a meter away and his chance to direct suspicion away from himself right there—

"Then one of them flew the shuttle," Nehru said to Vocaine.

"Tibbetts or Drake," Vocaine said.

"Yes—"

Danilov heard his own voice and hated it. "I'm sorry, sir—but Edgar Tibbetts, is that who you mean?"

Nehru looked at him. "How do you know that name?" he snapped.

Captain bar-Danan opened his mouth, but Danilov kept going. "I know him, sir. He works down the hall." He pointed at the hatch. "In the commo room."

Nehru and Vocaine both turned slowly to look where Danilov pointed. Bar-Danan was watching Danilov, a pained look on his face. Not angry, Danilov didn't think. Hurt—but not hurt by Danilov.

That's right, a cold, evaluative, absolutely loathsome part of Danilov's mind said. *Suspect him, not me.*

"Down the hall," Vocaine murmured. "Buddha's balls..."

Nehru knew what adrenaline felt like. He'd felt it often enough—even recently, when Reyes had attacked him in Happen, or when the sniper had shot the guards in front of him. But the feeling he felt now was new. It was adrenaline mixed with fear. Not fear for himself—he'd either be good enough or he wouldn't, and he'd made peace with that decision years ago. What scared him was that he might have made a mistake.

Nobody knew about Kane.

He touched Vocaine's shoulder and pulled him toward the door. "Right now, General," he said. "We're taking him right now." He looked at Captain bar-Danan. "You have a sidearm? Give it to me."

Bar-Danan pulled a black service automatic from his holster and handed it over. Nehru checked it, then looked at Danilov. "The commo room?"

The traffic controller gestured with his chin. "Third door on the left." He swallowed. "There's a sign."

Nehru nodded and turned away. He heard Vocaine behind him. "Keep your people here, Captain." Then he felt rather than saw the reassuring bulk of Vocaine's body behind him. The large general was breathing softly but heavily.

"You should let me, sir," Vocaine said.

Nehru smiled. "Colonels before generals, General." He almost giggled. Another datum filed; he hated the combination of adrenaline and fear. The door to the control room slid open and he stepped through, pistol leveled. The door closed a moment later behind Vocaine. It was child's play to find the third door on the left—they were a meter apart. *That means small rooms.*

The door was unlocked. He touched the stud to open it and led with the pistol.

The first shot took Nehru in the arm. He spun away, crashing into the other side of the door and falling into the corridor. Vocaine rushed forward and bent down to grab him. More shots rang out, reports crashing against the thin metal walls. A wet-sounding *thunk* clashed with the ringing in Nehru's ears, and Vocaine's bulk collapsed on him.

Nehru ignored the pain in his arm and pointed the pistol into the room. He fired six shots, each one punishing his eardrums. Hands gripped his ankles and yanked him back—his last round *whanged* past his ear as it ricocheted from the doorframe.

More shots from inside the room. Nehru looked toward his feet.

Danilov was dragging him backward. The controller's face was a mask—*fear? Excitement?* All the emotions one expected a semi-civilian in his first firefight to show.

Bar-Danan was next to him, struggling with Vocaine's feet. The big general was dead weight. Nehru gestured madly with in his one working arm. The one holding the gun.

"Get out of here," he hissed. "He might—"

Bar-Danan stepped around Vocaine's body and plucked the pistol out of Nehru's hand. He ejected the magazine and replaced it with one from his belt. The expression on his face was set but distant. Nehru frowned. He'd seen that face before—determination. *Stop cataloguing*, his mind told him. *You'll most likely be dead in a minute*—

Danilov knelt and grabbed the hole in Nehru's upper arm. He nearly bit through his lip at the pain. "Hold on, sir," Danilov said. "Medics are coming."

"Bugger the medics," Nehru said. "We need a tac team—"

Reports from bar-Danan's pistol banged against the corridor walls. He was crouched next to the doorframe, his hand extended around the edge. He burned through his entire magazine as fast as he could and leaned back. His hands were replacing the empty magazine as more rounds from inside the room hit the opposite wall.

"Missed him," the captain murmured.

"Just wait—" Nehru gasped.

Bar-Danan slid his hand around and triggered two rounds. Then he pulled his hand back, waiting. Another fusillade of shots hit the far wall. *I wonder what's on the other side of that wall?* Nehru blinked and tried to look down at his arm. First the adrenaline, then the fear, now being shot—what the hell was he thinking about?

The sound of the last shot from inside the room was still bouncing off the walls when bar-Danan stood and swept into the room, leading with the pistol. Nehru opened his mouth to shout—*bam-bam*—and closed it. There were no more shots.

Bar-Danan stepped out of the room, the pistol hanging loosely at his side. "Got him on the reload," he mumbled. Then he sat down. The pistol clattered to the floor.

"Captain?" Danilov asked. His hand shifted on Nehru's arm. The Inspector gasped and nearly wrenched his arm out of the controller's grip. That made the pain worse—

Danilov felt the muscles beneath his fingers relax as Nehru passed out. He looked at bar-Danan, but the captain was still sitting, staring at the floor. He didn't appear hurt—just out of it. *First kill.* Danilov looked down at the Inspector.

I could let him bleed out.

No.

That was the wrong play. He'd be a lot safer as the man who saved him than the man who let him die. Right now the mental image Nehru had of Danilov was a man who helped. Even if the undoubtedly still-running facial recognition matched him with Tibbetts, it would only be here at the port. And Nehru already knew they worked together.

And I fingered him.

I'm the reason he's dead.

But no. His training took over, shuffling that thought into the folder of things thought but not true. He looked down at the sword-and-lightning flash on Nehru's collar. *That's the reason he's dead. The reason they're all dead.* He shifted his grip.

Nehru's eyes fluttered open. "Danilov..."

Danilov leaned closer, trying to hear. "Tell Vocai—" Nehru stopped, and frowned. His head twisted around until he could see Vocaine's body. "Tell the governor. It's over. We got them."

"I will," Danilov said. He forced some earnestness into his voice. "I'll tell them. Rest now, Colonel."

Nehru let his eyes close but stayed conscious—mostly conscious, anyway. His mind was aflame, burning with the pain of his arm and the exultation of completion and the sheer unexpected complexity of the thing. The Maskirovka had been *everywhere*—at Happen and here in Barter. In the militia, as a bloody *pilot* no less. They'd stolen shuttles under military lockdown, and infiltrated the control tower apparatus. And when they were discovered—

—they fought.

Reyes had died fighting. The sniper—*Quinn, hadn't his name been?*—had died fighting. The two women in the concourse. The two shuttle thieves. The fake militia pilot—all of them had died trying to get away with the BattleMech data. They had all *died*. *Killed themselves*, almost. None of their schemes had much of a chance of success. His mind was already turning over the logic for his report—tactics would have to be changed. The Mask had always been brutal and fanatical, but this was a whole new level. To sacrifice an *entire team*—

Danilov's grip shifted on his arm. Fresh pain washed across his awareness, and he surrendered to it.

The whole *team*.

They'd *almost* gotten away with it.

Danilov stepped back as the medics raced out of the lift and knelt next to Nehru. One of them looked at him and reached out, but Danilov held up his hands and shook his head. "I'm fine," he said. The medic ducked toward Nehru. Another one roused bar-Danan.

"I'm okay," the captain said. He pushed himself to his feet, his earlier malaise seemingly forgotten. He looked down at Danilov. "He said it was over, right?" Danilov nodded. Bar-Danan nodded back. "Then I've got a port to open."

"I'll be right behind you," Danilov said. He gestured toward Nehru. "I want—"

Bar-Danan nodded. "When you're done."

When the medic loaded Nehru onto the gurney and into the lift, he went with them. They got out on the concourse level, but he stayed in the elevator. The lockers were on the bottom level.

The datacard was in his locker. With another clean ID.

And enough cash to buy a spot on the first ship off-planet.

THE TRICKSTER

BLAINE LEE PARDOE

**BARGHAUSEN
GRANT'S STATION
THE CLAN HOME WORLDS
10 DECEMBER 2854**

Barghausen was a small settlement on Grant's Station, built by Clan Coyote. The town was dotted with small, sturdy structures built for utility. At the far end was bunkers for munitions, repair, and storage of BattleMechs, walled off in case of accidents. It had been a thriving community in its early years. Clan Coyote's merchant caste had several thriving businesses in the town, including a small chip manufacturing facility. There had been rumors of growth, expansion...that someday Barghausen would be something more than what it was...a large city.

That had changed five years ago, when Clan Jade Falcon had taken the city. Star Commander Corrigan had just become a warrior then, but remembered when the Jade Falcons came and waged a Trial of Possession for the settlement. It was seen as an act of arrogance on the part of the Jade Falcons. They had no interest in Grant's Station at the time, and hadn't expanded their holdings since taking it. They seemed to have chosen Barghausen simply because it was a symbol of the growth and success of Clan Coyote.

Corrigan remembered the shame that came with the defeat of his people and the loss of the town. The Jade Falcons had turned it into Firebase Barghausen. Gone were the plans for growth and expansion. Many businesses had closed under their rule, and much of the lower castes left the city, seeking employment elsewhere on Grant's Station. Yet the town remained as a symbol, a bold splotch of emerald on the map of the planet, a mark of defiance to Clan Coyote. It was the Jade Falcons way of saying, "We can take whatever you have."

That arrogance ends today...

He approached the gate in his new OmniMech—the *Coyotl*. At 40 tons, it was considered a medium class design—deceptive in its appearance. It was something different, something new. Corrigan knew that the new technology; the Omnis, changed everything. *For decades we have been fighting using the same tech. We have improved weapons and ranges, but the core of what we wage war with has remained constant. Now things are different. This is the new standard— and only my people possess it.*

A lone warrior in a pristine green dress uniform, oozing with confidence, stepped forward to stand before his *Coyotl*. Corrigan popped his canopy and removed his neurohelmet, climbing down to face his opponent face-to-face...*as warriors should.*

"I am Star Commander Corrigan of the Clearwater Bloodhouse, of Clan Coyote, divine and inspired amongst the children of Kerensky. I am attached to Alpha Galaxy, the 38th Assault Cluster, with bloodlines that tie us back to the Star League. Whom do I face?"

The Jade Falcon warrior crossed his arms as he spoke. "I am Star Colonel Remagen Pryde, of Delta Galaxy, 1st Falcon Jaegers, and garrison commander for Firebase Barghausen. I speak for Jade Falcons everywhere in the stars, the Clan that will one day stand on Terra. What business does Clan Coyote have here?"

Corrigan glared at his foe. "I come to issue a *batchall* for Barghausen. It was conceived and built by Clan Coyote and will return to our rule. With what forces will you defend this town?"

Remagen Pryde was unshaken. "As a Jade Falcon, I know cunning in the bid is worth just as much as skill on the battlefield." He paused, as if to somehow intimidate. "This tiny town is not worthy of shedding a great deal of precious Jade Falcon blood for. And judging by the size of your BattleMech," he leaned to the side to look at the *Coyotl*, "I believe I will defend this town with two medium BattleMechs and be joined by one of my fellow Jade Falcon warriors…more than a match for your skills and new BattleMech."

Corrigan nodded. "We too are a people that abhor waste. What BattleMechs will you be defending with?"

That question was not part of the typical protocol and caught Remagen off guard for a moment—Corrigan could see it in his face. "What BattleMechs? Why does that matter?"

"It does, and is proper. If you were defending the town, unaugmented, with a weapon, I would ask with what weapon you were choosing to bid appropriately. This is no different."

Still flustered, Pryde replied. "I pilot a *Sentinel*. I will order Kynell of my Bloodhouse to join me in defending the honor of our Clan, and he pilots a *Wyvern*. Together we are more than a match for whatever you may muster."

"Very well, I will bid my Omni and one other," Corrigan replied, glancing back at his new 'Mech with a look of pride. "As defender, the choice of ground goes to you."

Remagen Pryde looked around at the rolling prairies surrounding the protective berms surrounding the munitions bunker at the edge of the town. "The grasses are in need of fertilization; your blood will do fine for that. We fight here, tomorrow, at dawn."

Corrigan nodded. "You have bargained well, Remagen Pryde. But the only blood spilled here tomorrow will be yours."

BARGHAUSEN
GRANT'S STATION
THE CLAN HOME WORLDS
11 DECEMBER 2854

The next morning, Remagen Pryde stood before Kynell as his junior warrior donned his coolant vest. "This new BattleMech—what were the weapons again?"

"I saw jump jet exhausts, a large pulse laser, a small pulse laser, and a short-ranged missile mounting for four. We should assume those are Streak."

Kynell finished the last connection. "So only one long range weapon. Excellent. Given its weight, we can assume it is slow. All we have to do to be victorious is hold our distance and shower them with LRMs and autocannon fire." He shook his head in disbelief. "Coyotes...they are a stubborn people."

"*Aff*, that they are," Remagen replied. *And today that stubbornness will cost them.*

THIRTY MINUTES LATER

Remagen's BattleMech nearly fell over as another extended range PPC blast smashed into his *Sentinel*'s chest, burning away armor and badly searing the fusion reactor housing. Heat flared in his cockpit as he reeled and regained his footing.

How is this possible? He had been tricked. That was the only answer that made sense.

"My target is moving fast on the flank," Kynell called out, his autocannon popping in the microphone's background. "Where are these short-range missiles you spoke of? I am getting hammered with PPC fire and long-range missiles!" His communications system sputtered and crackled under a blast from a particle projection cannon.

Three long-range missiles exploded on Remagen's right side, removing precious chunks of armor there. As he broke into a run, he managed to snap-shoot his autocannon at Star Commander Corrigan's *Coyotl*, peppering it with some rounds, but not nearly enough. *How is it still firing? Where did it get that firepower?*

As he scrambled along the long ridge line, another blast of extended range PPC fire hit him, melting his right arm off and searing deeply into his 'Mech. The gyro pitched hard and he struggled against the sudden, lurching pull. Staggering, Remagen's *Sentinel* fell hard, armor moaning under protest. He tried to rise, but another wave of long-range missiles arced high and roared down on him, savaging his reactor to the point where it auto-scrambled and shut off.

"I am down," he transmitted, looking on his tactical display for Kynell, but unable to see him.

"As am I," came a strained voice. "I may need help extracting from my cockpit."

Deceit, dishonor...that had to be the answer for this loss. "Very well. I will let the Coyote's know they have defeated us... and I wish to meet them to get to the bottom of their shame."

TWENTY MINUTES LATER

The identical pair of Clan Coyote BattleMechs showed some damage, but not nearly as much as Star Colonel Remagen had weathered. At first he thought they were different BattleMechs entirely. The torsos and arms were completely different, outfitted with the deadly missiles and ER PPC's that had devoured them. The amount of damage they had taken was minimal...and their speed.

"You fought well, Star Colonel," Star Commander Corrigan said as he walked from his *Coyotl* toward him.

"You fought with dishonor," Remagen replied.

"I did nothing of the kind."

"That is not the same BattleMech I saw you with yesterday." He pointed to the *Coyotl* as if it were a standing blight on his honor.

"I assure you, it is the same 'Mech."

"Where are your SRMs, your large pulse laser, or your jump jets? No technician crew could have swapped out that hardware so quickly. And if they did, you would have balance issues, targeting control problems. You have used deceit for this victory, and thus the results are null and void."

His words made Corrigan's face harden. "Be mindful of what you say, Star Colonel. I am forced to treat your accusations as the words of an ignorant warrior. This *is* the same BattleMech. Look at the paint scheme, the number on the torso, all the same except for your paltry missile damage."

Remagen did look at the 'Mech but was clearly confused, delighting Corrigan even more. "How is this possible?"

"How we swap out our weapons and reconfigure our Omnis is our secret."

Remagen shook his head. "That technology does not exist. BattleMechs have been the same for centuries. We have improved weapons, *aff*, but not the 'Mechs themselves. Hot-swapping that much hardware cannot be done."

"Until now," Corrigan said with a broadening grin. "Things have changed. Much like your ownership of Barghausen. As Nicholas Kerensky foresaw, not only do we breed better warriors, Clan Coyote has bred a better weapon of war."

He paused to watch the realization wash over his defeated foe. It was better than a defeat from the cockpit, because now, face-to-face, he could witness the shame and defeat on the Star Colonel's face.

"We claim your two antique BattleMechs as *isorla*. You have twenty-six hours to remove yourself from the town. Since there are no other Jade Falcon settlements on Grant's Station, I suggest you retire to the spaceport and make arrangements to be lifted off-world."

"You will pay for this," Remagen said grimly.

Corrigan chuckled. "Not today…nor any time soon, Star Colonel. Return to your nest and inform your flock that the age of the Coyote is at hand."

THE GARZOLINI BUTTES
FOSTER
THE CLAN HOME WORLDS
10 FEBRUARY 2863

Star Captain Tyrilla Heller pulled herself up onto the tallest butte, then rolled over, near exhaustion. While the buttes themselves were not high, the paths for humans to climb them were challenging. Orange colored dust stuck to her sweaty t-shirt and shorts as she looked up into the darkening blue-orange sky over Foster.

The exhaustion was part of her journey, one that had begun four days earlier. A select group of Clan Coyote warriors had come to this place to take part in a Communion, one of their most sacred warrior rituals. She alone had won the right, having fulfilled the other two legs of his spiritual journey. Last year she had taken part in The Hunt, for which she still proudly bore the scars on her right forearm from and a prominent one on the right side of her face. Now she walked on the final leg of her journey. *There is no better place to obtain it than where Khan Dana Kufahl experienced hers—here, on this butte.*

For long minutes, she lay on his back and stared up at the twilight sky that loomed over her, and the blackening blanket of emerging stars. Tyrilla ignored her gnawing hunger for the time being. Part of this journey was to push her body, mind, and soul. Some rare warriors were honored with visions on their Communions, but that was not her goal. *Those seeking that never obtain it.* Cooler night air swirled around her on a low breeze as she finally rolled over and stood, her muscles aching from the long climb.

The butte was far from a flat plateau. Deep ravine-like-cracks ran down to the flatlands of the desert surrounding them. Plants, mostly a variety of inedible sage brush, clustered in areas where Foster's harsh sun would not scorch them. A few jango-trees, twisted and misshapen, dotted the rugged rocks. As she looked it over he tried to picture what it had been like for Khan Kufahl on her vision quest there.

Tyrilla sipped from her water bottle and slowly ate half of an energy bar. She could feel strength come from the intake, and it surprised her, that so little could accomplish so much. *Was it like this for Khan Kufahl as well?*

She spread a simple olive-green blanket out on a flat piece of rock and sat cross-legged. It was a time of reflection, a chance to look back at her life as a warrior. Tyrilla was proud of her accomplishments. She had won her Trial of Position as a Star Captain, defeating three of her fellow warriors—no small task. Her skills with a BattleMech had earned her a chance to pilot one of the new *Coyotl* OmniMechs. The right to pilot such a machine in battle was a great honor in itself.

The OmniMechs had changed Clan Coyote, ushering in a great age of growth and expansion. Only her Clan knew their secrets, and cherished them as the greatest treasure any Clan might have. The OmniMech technology made them powerful...a force to be reckoned with. In the Clans, respect usually came with brute force, with victories. This new technology had delivered both of those. The OmniMechs had also brought allies—the Wolves and Sea Foxes, who had given her people the respect they had long deserved.

The other Clans coveted what the Coyotes had, of course. In annual trials, many of them had attempted to win the technology, but none so far had been successful. What made the technology so compelling was that it allowed a commander to customize his force after bidding to achieve an advantage over an enemy. If someone were coming in with a fast moving Star in a Trial of Possession, the Coyotes could bid a Star of *Coyotl*s and outfit them on-the-fly with jump jets for additional maneuverability. The enemy did not have that opportunity—they had to fight with their fixed BattleTech hardware.

No single breakthrough had made the OmniMech possible, it was dozens of breakthroughs, engineered over more than a decade. Just swapping out weapons required new actuators, connection points, power feeds—all that had to be battle-worthy and durable. The gyro controls, adjusting for the different centers of gravity and shifts due to weapons changes and ammunition expenditures, had taken years to work out. The battlecomputer operating system upgrades were complex, taking into account a variety of weapons configurations. The new generation of XL engines, while a boon to 'Mech technology, added a new layer of complexity.

But Clan Coyote prevailed.

Tyrilla Heller reached up and stroked the necklace she wore on her sweat-soaked neck. The simple leather thong was a gift given every warrior of the Clan. Each victory entitled the warrior to add a bead to signify their achievement. Tyrilla had ten beads on hers. The large green glass one had been made from the shattered ferroglass armor of a Clan Smoke Jaguar warrior that she had fought in a Trial of Possession on Kirin, a hasty and vicious fight. The black bead made of wood symbolized the forest she had fought in against the Ghost Bears. Tyrilla fondled the beads, not even having to look at them to know which one she held in her fingers. *They are a part of me as much as my arms and legs. They are proof of my existence, and will be preserved by my people long after I am gone, and my genes have passed to future generations.*

Nightfall came swiftly on Foster, and there were only a few wisps of clouds to hide the stars. The dark, cold air chilled the sweat on her shirt, but Tyrilla ignored it. She gazed up into the sky for hours, then out into the darkness of the butte.

A black rabbit emerged, poking its head up from behind some stones where it had been hiding. Ebony Hares were common, even in the heights of the buttes. Big, rigid, black ears made them look like large, grounded bats. Tyrilla watched it for long minutes as it seemed to see her, but kept on foraging for its meager meal. *That is right black rabbit, I am no threat to you tonight. You may dine. I am feasting on the darkness.*

Sleep tugged at her, and eventually won the battle with her consciousness. Tyrilla did not remember lying down. All she knew was that when she awoke, the sun was rising. A crust had formed around her eyes, which she brushed away. Her lips were like raisins, and she took a long sip of her dwindling water supply. The Ebony Hare was long gone, leaving only tiny footprints in the orange dust.

The warmth of the sun did not bring new energy as she sat on the blanket. Five days in the desert had taken a toll. Even the screen gel she had put on was fading, and with it came the burns to her already leathery skin. Tyrilla ignored the pain, which was part of a Communion journey. *Pain provides focus and focus provides insights. Pushing one's self made for better warriors.*

By mid-day she was groggy, having sought a meager bit of shade near a rock formation on the plateau. Her head throbbed, and even a long gulp of water did not ease her growing mental fog. For long minutes she would close her eyes and felt as if she were somewhere between being awake and asleep. Time no longer seemed to have meaning, she measured it by the shadows on nearby rocks when she did pry open her eyes.

As the sun set, she spotted a small snake, and her gaze became transfixed on it. It was a transplanted Mechty Adder, orange and tan with tiny black diamonds on its back. Its bite was deadly, but Tyrilla was not afraid. After all, the snake was a few meters away, and she was far too big for it to consume. *We have parity, you and I. We can each kill the other, but do not.*

As a bird landed in the corner of her field of vision, she continued watching the snake, which coiled up, making itself small. *The bird is a predator, it has come to feed on him.* The snake sensed the threat and remained rigid.

The bird walked out cautiously on its spindly long legs, eyeing the snake, cocking its head from side to side to evaluate its intended victim. It moved in closer, but the snake remained rigid, tightly wound in a circle. The bird got close enough to take a cautionary peck at the snake. It did not move or react, as if it were playing dead. Tyrilla was mesmerized by what she was seeing, entranced by the struggle about to take place.

The bird pecked again, harder, with no reaction. It opened its beak wide and drove it at the snake's head. At the same time, the snake sprung out at the bird, biting it. Feathers flew as the snake coiled around the bird and the bird squawked and jabbed at the snake. Blood was in the air between the two, tiny droplets splattering.

The bird slowed—clearly the poison was affecting it—but the snake seemed injured, too. In a last bid for freedom, the bird took to flight, awkward, unbalanced, flapping over the edge of the butte some ten meters away, with the snake still clinging to it. Both animals suddenly plummeted downward, out of sight.

He is a trickster—that snake. He fooled the bird. The hunted became the hunter.

Time passed, and Tyrilla drifted off to sleep again, the show now over. When she awoke, it was sunrise on a new day. She stood, her joints protesting the throbbing at the effort, walking over to where the fight had taken place. There was nothing there, no blood, no stirring of the orange powdery sand. All evidence of the struggle was gone...*if it had been real at all.*

She went to the edge of the butte and looked down, but there was no bird, no snake, nothing but rocks and a hint of vertigo that caused her to pull back. Slowly it dawned on her what she had experienced. *Perhaps it hadn't been there at all...maybe, it had been a vision...*

Drinking the last of her water, her cracked lips protesting, she fumbled for her pack. Inside was a communicator, which she toggled on. "This is Star Captain Tyrilla Heller requesting extraction."

"Very well, we have your signal." replied Anjij Nuyriev, the Loremaster for Clan Coyote. "How was your Communion?"

Tyrilla nodded, though the effort was for her, not for the Loremaster. "Fulfilling," she said, still unsure if she had imagined the animals fighting or if it had happened for real. *Now the true work begins...I must try and figure out what it means.*

**BATTLETECH MAINTAINENCE FACILITY ALPHA
DRENNAN INDUSTRIPLEX
TAMARON
THE CLAN HOME WORLDS
25 FEBRUARY 2863**

Jarrad wore a worker's jumpsuit for the laborer caste of Clan Coyote, but it was merely part of his disguise. For the past four years, the other Clans had been waging Trials of Possession in attempts to win an OmniMech from the Coyotes. For four years, they had all failed. The security around the production facilities where the Omnis were made was nearly impenetrable. *The problem is that we all tried to go to the source, the wellspring where the OmniMechs were made. That was our mistake.*

Jarrad had assumed the guise of Sharandar. Rather than attempt to penetrate the factory facility, he had adopted a new persona, becoming a technician in Clan Coyote. It had taken almost a half-decade of hard work and training, but he'd finally managed to get assigned as a junior technician and armorer on a Star of OmniMechs.

He loathed the lowly tasks associated with his cover, but it was for the glory of Clan Jade Falcon—which was all he clung to. Even in that role, his access to the OmniMechs had been vastly limited to specific tasks. Clan Coyote maintained rigid rules regarding access. Even when they worked on the new XL engines, tarps were put up to block any unauthorized personnel from seeing the internal workings of the OmniMechs.

He was an operative with a mission—obtain the secrets of the OmniMech technology for Clan Jade Falcon. It was deliberately vague. Going this deep undercover took years of preparation to execute. Jarrad had been in a *sibko* most of his life, only to be badly injured and washed out. The Watch had become his new home, his new life. It was as close as he could come to being a warrior again, and he cherished every moment he spent on assignment.

Jarad/Sharandar's mission thus far had not been a complete waste of resources, though many days he felt as if it were. While he had no access to the schematics or software of the OmniMechs, Sharandar had been able to visually see the weapons pod connection system up-close. He had not penetrated the secrets to how it worked entirely, but enough to keep his superiors content with his hand-drawn sketches. While crude, they were foolproof against digital surveillance and monitoring. As was often said in The Watch, the more sophisticated the security, the more subject it is to low-tech solutions. His only proof of success was that he had not been removed or eliminated by either his own people or Clan Coyote. Such was the life of a member of The Watch.

He was working on the menial task of inventorying LRM warheads when he heard, "Sharandar!" called out by the Senior Technician. He paused, forced a thin, dull smile so common in the lower castes, and walked across the 'Mech bay to Rietman, and older technician, highly respected in bays for his vast knowledge.

"What can I do for you, Senior Technician?"

"There is an opening for a technician to certify and work on the *Coyotl* and eventually the new *Warlock* and the *Lupus*. I have submitted your name for consideration."

Excellent! Sharandar allowed some of his excitement to seep through with a broad smile. "I am deeply honored, Senior Technician Rietman! Thank you."

"You have proven meticulous in your work—which is what is needed on the OmniMech program. Being assigned there is a great honor. They still have to complete their security background check on you, but I told them you were one of my best people."

"Thank you again," he said, shaking Rietman's hand. "I will not disappoint your trust."

But my first and only loyalty is to Clan Jade Falcon…

THE FALCON'S NEST
EDEN
THE PENTAGON WORLDS
CLAN SPACE
5 MARCH 2863

Star Commander Kerek Helmer's *Lancelot* was a grim shadow of its former self. Time had taken a toll on the BattleMech. Bends and quirks to the battered internal structure meant some of the armor plates did not interlock correctly, some overlapping, some leaving small gaps. The 'Mech had fought across the Inner Sphere to retake Terra, and with Clan Jade

Falcon to retake the Pentagon Worlds. *There is honor still in this machine, despite her age.*

Combat Trials were all taken seriously—live fire weapons did that for a warrior. This one was more special than others. This was for the opportunity to face Clan Coyote for a Trial of Possession for their coveted OmniMech technology.

The OmniMech was massive technological leap in military technology. It had made Clan Coyote unstoppable for years. Being able to configure a 'Mech for what an enemy could field gave a warrior a great advantage. The Clans had created an annual Trial of Possession for the technology, but thus far no one had won one. Each Clan got a chance to go against the Coyotes for their technology once a year. These Trials determined the order of these challenges.

This year's Trial had come down to Clan Steel Viper and his own Jade Falcons for the first position. Kerek had beaten three other Jade Falcons for the first right to take on Clan Coyote. Now all he had to do was to defeat Star Commander Slynkers Mercer. That challenge was far from secure, despite being fought in the Jade Falcon's honorary arena for such battles—the Falcon's Nest.

Mercer's lumbering *Warhammer IIC* tromped around the open space in the vast Circle of Equals, waiting for the opportunity to strike a devastating blow. The 'Mech was larger than his *Lancelot*, but sacrificed armor for speed. So far Star Commander Kerek had managed to get in several shots from the rock formations he used for cover, his PPC and pair of large lasers melting off a significant amount of armor.

He poked his his head out around the edge of the rock formation in the middle of the Circle, only to be riddled with rock-shrapnel from the short-range missiles which had missed him, but had slammed into the granite above him. *That was close—and Mercer is no fool. She knows where I am.*

He surveyed the tall gray rock formation. Three options existed using it; go right, go left, or go up. Falling back and waiting for the *Warhammer IIC* to emerge was one, but it would leave him in the open. Climbing the rocks was treacherous, but he had mapped out a steep but risky path he could take to the top. *How many warriors have tried that and failed over the years?*

Then again, they are not me.

He started when his communications channel crackled to life. "Give it up, Kerek. You were daring to take a lighter BattleMech, that much I will give you, but you cannot defeat me. Stand down, and you will save yourself further humiliation."

Kerek smiled in his neurohelmet. "If you are so confident, come after me."

"I refuse to play your game."

"That is where you fail," he said, gritting his teeth as he started the difficult climb up the rock formation. "This was never a game."

"You have no hope of defeating me," Mercer countered.

"Hope is not my strategy," he said, twisting a quote his *sibko* instructor from four years earlier. Some rocks slid under his right footpad as he slowly made his way up, almost causing him to lose his balance. He fought the shift of his center of gravity, twisting his torso and moving his arms forward just enough to avoid the fall.

"I will win this Trial, and my people will be the first to go on to be the first to win the secrets of the OmniMechs from the Coyotes this year," Mercer taunted.

Not if I have any say in the matter. Ignoring her words, Kerek climbed further, coming up just under the crest of the formation. He saw a flicker on his tactical display, one only a few meters way—on the other side of the rocks. It was there for a moment, then faded. He knew from previous trials in the Falcon's Nest that the rocks were littered with dense boulders of nickel, enough to obscure fusion reactor signatures.

"You may live long enough to see our Steel Vipers take all the Coyotes have won from them when *we* possess that technology."

The flicker on his screen told Kerek everything he needed to know. Mercer was executing the same tactic in her *Warhammer IIC*, coming right over the top. *Neg...I will get there first and make you pay for it.*

He pushed off hard, rising to the last rock before he could see over the top. Flexing the right leg of the *Lancelot*, he rose up and saw below him, the *Warhammer IIC*, struggling over the rocks.

Got you!

Mercer saw him a moment after he saw her. Leaning back, she hoisted the *Warhammer IIC*'s massive arms up to bring her deadly extended range particle projection cannons in line with him. One flashed, hitting his right torso, melting a splatter of armor into the air that hissed when it landed on the rocks.

Kerek lunged at her headfirst, plowing into her BattleMech with a grinding collision on the side of the rock face. The *Warhammer IIC*, already unbalanced with its arms up, toppled backward, with his *Lancelot* on top of it.

The pair fell onto the rocks, shredding and grinding away armor from the rear of the *Warhammer IIC* on the way down. Kerek's damage indicators flashed yellow from the collision, but he knew Mercer's 'Mech was taking considerably more damage from the fall. The sound of twisting and warping metal stopped when he hit the floor of the Nest and he tumbled off the *Warhammer IIC*.

Kerek got to his feet before Mercer's 'Mech, unloading his three extended range large lasers into it as he darted around the fallen BattleMech. As the massive *Warhammer IIC* struggled to its feet, its PPC arms waving madly for balance, Kerek lined up a shot at the rear of the Steel Viper 'Mech. Its back was a crumpled mass of caved-in armor, with large rents from the fall on the rocks.

His lasers blazed away. One ER large laser missed, hitting a boulder and causing it to explode. The other ER large laser lanced into the *Warhammer IIC*'s damaged backside, making the armor glow crimson as it dug deep.

It wobbled unsteadily as Kerek swung back around, the heat starting to rise in his *Lancelot*. The *Warhammer IIC* unleashed an ER PPC blast at him, but the beam did not coalesce, and merely washed over him in a burst of blue static discharge, a sign that the weapon was damaged. The short-range missiles it fired. however, slammed into his lower torso and legs, each impact blasting away armor as he ran, showering it on the floor of the Nest.

He juked hard to the right, keeping the distance tight between them, making aiming the PPCs challenging as the *Warhammer IIC* also began to turn, keeping its back to the rock formation and walking backward to give him distance. *I know I must have hit her gyro already, now I need to do this the hard way.*

Kerek's large lasers sent crimson beams stabbing into the right torso of the *Warhammer IIC*, burning deep. He followed it with his Streak SRMs, which tore into the already mangled armor on the right side, blasting away at the guts of his foe. There was a rumble from within as the ammo for the SRMs went off—the CASE doors popping and redirecting the venting the blast outward in a plume of orange fire and black smoke. The *Warhammer IIC* staggered a few steps forward, fighting the damage and gravity at the same time. It unleashed its last volley of SRMs into his right arm and leg, quaking his *Lancelot* with each explosion.

Kerek used the imbalance of his foe to his advantage, rushing around the side and managing to get an ER large laser shot deep into the rear armor again. His reward…a plume of white smoke rolling from where the red beam had cut into the assault 'Mech's internals.

Mercer pushed the *Warhammer IIC* to the right, to get some distance, but Kerek kept moving, trying to stay out of the firing arc of the PPCs. His large lasers cut nasty glowing scars along the right arm and torso of the assault 'Mech, sending melting globs of armor sizzling down onto the rocks at its feet.

As if sensing the danger of a battle of attrition, the Steel Viper warrior broke into her own run in the opposite direction. At 100 meters, both of her ER PPCs flashed. The azure beams stabbed at Kerek's *Lancelot*. One hit him in the center torso, slamming him to the side, searing away precious armor. The other beam, no doubt from the damaged weapon, missed by less than a meter, its discharge charring the green paint on his left arm in the process.

Two can play that game... He brought his targeting reticle onto the sloped torso of the *Warhammer IIC* and fired his large lasers again. One emerald beam dug deep into the right torso, while the other blast hit the 'Mech's cockpit canopy. The 80-ton war machine staggered from the hit—he could see the ferroarmored glass was blackened from the strike. Mercer struggled to stay upright, but could not. The ponderous *Warhammer IIC* dropped hard, slamming into the granite ground face-first.

A wave of heat rose in Kerek's cockpit as he ran up to point blank range, aiming his lasers into the torn and blasted rear armor. He fired again, heedless of the heat bloom that nearly roasted him in his cockpit. The beams stabbed deep into the BattleMech's torso, throwing bits out in a spray of hot shrapnel. A wave of heat rose from the hole as one beam sliced into the reactor housing, while the other medium beam hit the gyro, exploding it into dozens of bits of shrapnel that rattled against his own 'Mech.

His tactical display told him the reactor of his foe was offline, but he kept his weapons aimed at the *Warhammer IIC*, just in case it was a ploy.

"Yield," Kerek commanded on the open channel.

"I yield," Mercer replied wearily, coughing into the microphone. "You fought and won with honor."

"Honor is returned," Kerek replied, lifting his weapons.

The Jade Falcon Loremaster's voice boomed in his ears as sweat stung in the coroners of his eyes. "*Seyla,* brothers and sisters! We stand before Jade Falcon and Steel Viper warriors in a Circle of Equals. We have witnessed great skill and battle-prowess. Slynkers Mercer represented her people well, but the victor of this Trial is Kerek Helmer. So we stand together, so we all stand by the results of this contest. *Seyla!*"

A resounding "*Seyla!*" rose from the gathered warriors.

Kerek grinned. *Today the Steel Vipers...soon the Coyotes...*

**JADE FALCON ROOST
EDEN
THE PENTAGON WORLDS
CLAN SPACE
THREE HOURS LATER**

Jade Falcon Khan Natalie Buhallin sat behind her obsidian desk and looked Kerek Helmer up and down carefully. He could feel her taking in every detail about him, silently studying him as he stood before her in his dull green dress uniform. He had met her once before, when he had won his Bloodname, but not since.

"So, you are the warrior that bested your peers...the one that will vie for Clan Coyote's precious OmniMech technology first this year, *quiaff*?"

"Affirmative, my Khan," he replied.

"Are you indeed the best of the best?"

"I am," he said firmly, fighting the urge to grin.

She said nothing for a long moment, just boring into him with her level gaze. "More is at stake here than just winning a Trial of Possession, Kerek. In the last few years, the Coyotes have won Trial after Trial since developing the OmniMech. It has changed the balance of power among our people as nothing has for years. You are not just vying for a new OmniMech, but the technical specifications for them."

"I understand, Khan Buhallin," was all he could offer.

"Do you? If left unchecked, this technology could spell the end of our people. If it were to fall into the hands of other competing Clans, we could be facing extinction over time. Even if we win, it will take time for us to retool this technology for our BattleMechs. Clan Coyote is ascendant because of it, and we cannot allow this to continue.

"We fought Trials with the other Clans for the right to win the OmniMech technology from the Coyotes. You were victorious, meaning we get the first attempt this year. That is testimony to your skills. I need you to appreciate that there is more on the line than your personal honor. Every Jade Falcon is looking to you to break this chain of Clan Coyote victories, to bring parity and balance to our people again. If you fail, it will be another year before we have an opportunity to blunt the Coyotes' onslaught. Or worse, a Clan that follows us may be successful, putting us a year behind.

"You will lead a single Star against Clan Coyote. You will be provided warriors and equipment as you determine. As is the tradition, the Coyotes will field two Stars of their OmniMechs against us. We will tell them what 'Mechs you are fielding, though you will have some discretion as to how they will be equipped."

Two to one odds, with superior equipment. He knew the terms of the fight beforehand, but now that he was leading it, the reality set in on him. *It is a daunting task, but not impossible. Much will depend on our tactics and our weapon load-outs.*

"You are all that stands in their path. It is not just the eyes of your Clan upon you, Kerek, it is all of other Clans as well. ilKhan Khan Zenos Danforth of Clan Burrock will preside over the Trial. No doubt the Coyotes will be prepared for you. They will pit their best warriors against you and your Star. You must win however, even at the risk of your own life. Do you understand?"

"Affirmative—I do. I will not fail the Jade Falcons."

BATTLETECH MAINTAINENCE FACILITY ALPHA
DRENNAN INDUSTRIPLEX
TAMARON
THE CLAN HOME WORLDS
9 MARCH 2863

Star Commander Tyrilla Heller stood before Khan Kevin McTighe, unsure why she had been summoned. The big bay was a pilot plant for assembly of prototype BattleMechs, namely the new OmniMechs.

The security here was the greatest in the Clan home worlds. Most of the guards were Clan Coyote warriors, heavily armored and armed. Beside them were Clan Sea Fox guards. The sight of the Sea Foxes was no surprise to Tyrilla. They had provided invaluable technical and manufacturing assistance to his people. In return, they too had gained the priceless

OmniMechs, albeit in limited number. They and the Wolves were the only true allies to the Coyotes. Not because they coveted the technology the Coyotes possessed, but because they respected her people.

Techs moved around the OmniMechs in their bays, with security guards watching their every move. They seemed oblivious to the observation, something she admired. *They and the engineers are the heart and soul of our OmniMech program. The secrets they are exposed to are worth more than the equipment they work on.*

"Ah, Tyrilla of Bloodhouse Heller," Khan McTighe said. "I am glad you are able to join me."

"I am honored, my Khan," she said, dipping her head slightly.

"Attend me," McTighe said, walking into the bay as if it were a place he frequented. "Behold," he said, gesturing to a 'Mech in one of the bays. "This is the *Lupus*."

Tyrilla's eyes fell on the heavy OmniMech. It was short yet oddly brutish in appearance, with large, boxy shoulder missile racks over lower arms like an old model *Crusader*, though smaller. The legs reminded her of an *Archer*'s, though more forward, with a flared footpad.

"It is a thing of beauty...and death. The *Lupus* is the next of our new OmniMechs. Beyond it is a prototype *Warlock*." He gestured at the assault 'Mech. "We are still working through some of the finer details of its configuration."

This was a new model, one she was not familiar with. The OmniMech had a large, boxy torso, not attractive, but utilitarian. It was top-heavy in her mind, possibly a challenge to pilot. *They are improving on its design...wise and prudent.*

"The *Lupus* and the *Coyotl* will further pave the road to our conquests. Adding the *Warlock* to our *touman* will provide new configurations that will give us greater flexibility in battle."

Tyrilla suppressed her awe of the new OmniMechs. *Truly we will be unstoppable. We have two OmniMech models in use, and another nearly ready. No wonder our enemies loathe and fear us.* "They are impressive, Khan McTighe."

"It is more than that—it is coveted," the Coyote Khan replied. "Our enemies see this technology as the key to our growth and success. They salivate over what it represents—and that makes our enemies dangerous."

"We are more than our OmniMechs," Tyrilla replied.

"*Aff*, we are. We are Clan Coyote. To them, we owe it all to the technology we developed."

Our fellow Clans are short-sighted. "I understand, my Khan."

"You may," McTighe replied, studying her face for a long moment. "Recently I spent some time with Loremaster Anjij Nuyriev. She tells me that you believe you have had a vision."

For a moment, Tyrilla was unsure how to respond. "I saw something during my Communion. What I saw…I do not know for sure what it means." Memories of the trickster—the snake that lured in the bird, came flashing to the forefront of her mind.

The lean Khan flashed a rare smile. "I understand far too well. Once I experienced a vision as well, of faceless monsters stalking me in the darkness. Each time I tried to see them, they moved into the darker shadows. They haunt my nightmares still."

"We each have to process what we have seen in our own way. Anjij has told me you have had difficulty interpreting what you saw. Many *never* learn the true meaning of what they experienced. It is enough for them to have had the vision in the first place. Often that is the trail the Coyote prowls." The Khan paused for a moment, clearly trying to read her face.

Tyrilla nodded. "Thank you for your wisdom on such matters. It helps to know that others have similar difficulties as I do."

"It is my role as Khan to protect the pack. Your vision was not why I summoned you, Tyrilla. I brought you here for another, more pressing reason," Khan McTighe said, planting his fists on his waist. "As you know, every year the other Clans wage Trials of Possession for our OmniMech technology. Every year, we have beaten them."

"*Aff*, I am all too aware," she replied.

"Loremaster Nuyriev and I develop the list of warriors who will represent our people. We believe only the purest of Coyotes should qualify for that right. We do not look to the past, but to those that have been honored by experiencing vision quests recently."

"I was unaware of the selection process, my Khan," Tyrilla said. "I only know of the final Trials."

"As it should be. This year, only two such warriors had visions. You, Tyrilla, and Star Colonel Matthew Nash. The two of you have been honored to experience what only the unsullied and best of our warriors see."

Tyrilla had heard of Matthew Nash. He commanded one of the Clan's elite Striker Clusters with distinction. They were aptly named, piloting mostly assault BattleMechs. Star Colonel Nash had a reputation for ferocity, having won his rank in a melee battle. They called him, "The Cunning Coyote," which told her a great deal about him. "I am pleased to be associated with such a warrior as the Star Colonel."

Khan McTighe's smile flashed again. "I am glad to hear it. You and he will fight each other in a Trial to determine which of you will lead the two Stars that will defend our Clan in the Trial of Possession for our OmniMech technology. There is no greater honor, nor are the stakes as high in any other battle. In a week's time you will fight, and the winner will face the champions of the Jade Falcons."

That gave her resolve. *We do what we must but must do so with honor.* "I will fight to the best of my abilities my Khan, with all of my effort."

"Excellent Tyrilla Heller. You honor your Bloodhouse well, now you must see if you will honor your Clan in the ultimate contest."

BATTLETECH MAINTAINENCE FACILITY ALPHA
DRENNAN INDUSTRIPLEX
TAMARON
THE CLAN HOME WORLDS
15 MARCH 2863

Senior Technician Rietman loomed over Sharandar as he strained to get a better view of the right shoulder actuator on the *Coyotl* 570. Parts were obscured with temporary masking material, others were simply inaccessible.

"You need to adjust the inverter by no less that point-zero-three percent," Rietman advised as he leaned in farther.

"It is difficult work. I could do better if I had greater access, Senior Technician," Sharandar replied as he slowly adjusted the tool.

"Impossible. You should be able to perform the task from there," Rietman replied as he strained further to reach up inside the assembly.

"*Aff*, I can. It would simply be easier if access plate SJ-07 were opened," Sharandar said, adding more strain to his voice.

"You are not cleared to see the technology there," Rietman said curtly.

"Got it," Sharandar said as he retracted his arms and body from the narrow gap under the armpit of the *Coyotl*. He paused to wipe the sweat from his brow.

Reitman slid up and took his place, using his own tool to verify the work. "Perfect alignment, Sharandar."

Sharandar carefully wiped his tool and returned it to its marked slot in the case. Every aspect of their work was based on precision. He had been in many BattleMech repair bays and had never seen one organized on this level. Even the tools had to be returned and accounted for at the end of each shift, each one cleaned before and after use. *There are times when this seems more like a surgical bay than a BattleMech plant.*

Rietman put his hand on his shoulder. "I know you are frustrated with how we have to work. I sympathize with you, I do. It is for security reasons. As you know, we have many layers of security. There are parts of this chassis that even *I* have yet to see. It can be frustrating, but it is necessary."

"I understand the need for scrutiny and security, but it makes matters slow and stressful at times. I simply wish there was a better balance of productivity and security."

Rietman chuckled. "As do I, but that is not likely to change. This technology is valuable. There have been innovations in weapons and 'Mech systems before, but nothing on this scale. The OmniMech changes that. I can foresee an age when the old way of creating BattleMechs is gone! Only the OmniMechs of our Clan will rule Clan Space." His voice rang with pride.

"I appreciate what it represents," *Perhaps more than you can realize.* "It is merely difficult to work this way."

Rietman nodded. "Absolutely, but security is everything. In a decade or so, if we can continue our monopoly on this technology, Clan Coyote will be the most powerful of all of the Clans. We will rule unchallenged, and fulfill Nicholas Kerensky's dream of one day unifying our people." He spoke as if he were a man that was experiencing a religious experience.

Sharandar nodded. "I understand. I am a loyal member of our Clan. Forgive my impatience, Senior Technician. I was simply striving for higher productivity. I would never suggest compromising the future of our people to achieve it." He said the words as if he believed them, but they were acid on his tongue—burning as he spoke them.

"This Omni is very important," Rietman said putting his hand gently on its armored leg. "It is to be one of the ten that will be fielded against the Jade Falcons who are coming to try and wrestle our secrets from us. This will be the 'Mech of Tyrilla Heller, who will command that force. That is why we are fine tuning it the way we are."

So that *is why we have it here!* Sharandar looked at the *Coyotl* with newfound respect. *This will be going into battle against the best of our warriors.* It was a sobering thought, and he did well to conceal his emotions.

The Senior Technician grinned. "We are near the end of the shift. Go and record your calibration. Tonight, if you are free, you may come home with me and eat with my wife and I."

Sharandar flashed a smile. "Thank you for the invitation. I look forward to it."

He glanced back at the *Coyotl*, and the others lined up in their bays beyond it. *The words of Rietman are to be considered as a warning. If not checked soon, Clan Coyote will dominate the other Clans...even my Jade Falcons. Our own Clan has tried to develop the OmniMech technology independently, but they are years away from achieving success.*

His thoughts tore at Jerrod/Sharandar deeply, though he refused to let it show on his face. *The security here is* insurmountable, they have factored in almost everything. What I have been able to learn is so compartmentalized, it is of little value.

There had to be a way to circumvent the Coyotes' security, but thus far he had not figured it out. It was a matter of great stress and pride with him that he had been outfoxed by the Coyotes. *Who would have thought them this ingenious?*

I must find a way to serve the Jade Falcons, no matter what it takes, or the Coyotes will consume us all!

THE KUFAHL GRAND COULEE
FOSTER
THE CLAN HOME WORLDS
26 MARCH 2863

The final Trial for the right to lead the defense of the OmniMech technology took place at one of Clan Coyote's most sacred sites, the Kufahl Grand Coulee. The arid, desert land was filled with deep, dry gullies that would flash-flood then quickly run dry, rolling hills covered with various forms of cacti and flammable scrub brush, all framed by a ring of plateaued hills. It was a large Circle of Equals, with the observing Coyote warriors taking position on the plateaus, since it gave them a wide view of the entire coulee.

As Tyrilla stepped through a canyon pass into the immense landscape, she was struck by its stark beauty. The brilliant blue sky with wisps of white clouds seemed to frame the setting more like a painting than a place where she may be killed. In other words, it was perfect. *It is the ultimate expression of Clan Coyote, nature and machine, merged together in harmony.*

Tyrilla knew that somewhere, kilometers away, Star Colonel Matthew Nash was entering the coulee as well. Nash not only piloted a *Coyotl* like her own, but he brought something else as well, his reputation. From what she had learned, he was brutally efficient in his style of fighting. Star Colonel Nash was not the kind of person that let emotions come into play during a battle. Instead, he fought with cold calculation, attempting to defeat his enemies in the most economical way possible. If he did get rattled, he never showed it. No bragging, no ego oozed from his cockpit, unlike many warriors she knew. *I will not waste time trying to goad him into actions that could give me an advantage. Such efforts would be a waste.*

On her far right, Tyrella saw a small disk rise from one of the plateaus and move out over the middle of the Kufahl Grand Coulee. It had a small safety rail surrounding it, and was only large enough for two people to stand on it. A crystal-clear and penetrating voice, that of Loremaster Anjij Nuyriev, rang in her earpieces.

"Bloodnamed of Clan Coyote, heed my words as *rede*. We are about to witness two warriors who will vie for the right to lead the defense of our Clan against the first of the Clans to come for our prized technology," she said from the hovering platform.

"Both come to us having experienced visions and the hunt. Both come from illustrious bloodlines—Nash and Heller. Both have demonstrated themselves to me and our Khan as warriors worthy to protect our den from the raiders that come to steal our technology. *Seyla!*"

"*Seyla!*" echoed the voices of the two dozen warriors that stood witness on the plateaus around them. Their chant of the word gave her strength. The meaning of the word was not lost on her, "So shall it be!"

"Star Commander Tyrilla Heller will face Star Colonel Matthew Nash. They do not fight each other, they fight to protect all of us like the pack leaders that they are. We honor them by witnessing this contest, this test of skills and battle prowess. We grant them our support and watchful eyes, observing their honor. We listen to them push themselves to their limits and beyond. We are the Coyotes!"

"*Seyla!*" The chorus sounded again. This time Tyrilla joined in.

"As was ordained by Nicholas Kerensky, this Trial shall commence. Matthew Nash and Tyrilla Heller, you may begin, knowing that your pack is watching you and giving you its protection."

Tyrilla pushed her *Coyotl* out into the Grand Coulee, immediately dropping into a deep dry gully. She had configured her OmniMech with a large pulse laser, two racks of Streak short-range missiles, a torso-mounted small pulse laser, and jump jets. The configuration was, she hoped, the opposite of Star Colonel Nash. His swift and brutal efficiency told her he was likely to choose the primary configuration for his *Coyotl,* with an emphasis on long range firepower—LRMs and an extended range PPC being the core of its firepower. *He will want to defeat me before I can get close enough to do serious damage.*

The gully was almost deep enough to hide her OmniMech as she moved. *If I was Nash, I would get to high ground, attempt to get an angle to attack me at range.*

A few moments later, she came to a shallow point in the ravine and eyed it carefully...here more of her 'Mech would be visible. She sprinted across the opening as a bright white and bluish flash slammed into her *Coyotl*'s left side. It was a glancing hit, but still melted away armor, leaving what was left blackened and gnarled.

Reaching the far side of the shallow area, where she had cover, Tyrilla's breath was ragged, and she saw yellow warning lights on her damage display. The good news was that she had tracked where the shot had come from, off to her right. *I can ill afford to use this tactic again to narrow the odds.* Pulling up her tactical display, she saw a rock formation in the same direction the blast had come from. *That is where he is likely at—high, with cover.*

She spotted a dense growth of brush; low trees, thick with snaking branches that looked tormented in the heat and desolation of the coulee. It was enough to give her good cover and to move up along his flank. From there, another rocky mound would allow her to get closer.

Tyrilla swung her *Coyotl* into the copse, emerging from the gully into a wave of long-range missiles. Only three found their mark, hitting her legs. As she moved into the dense brush, another flash of PPC fire flared at her, missing, but igniting some of the nearby trees.

She saw Nash's *Coyotl* that time, emerging from the top of the rocks where she had expected him to be. Not waiting for a weapons lock tone, Tyrilla fired her large pulse laser. The weapon throbbed with each pulse, sending a spray of bright green beams at the Star Colonel's Omni. It was enough to make him turn away, giving her a chance to sprint toward the closer rock formation.

She maneuvered her *Coyotl* swiftly, but was still followed with another barrage of long-range missiles. Four blasted the armor in her legs as she reached the rocky outcropping. Only massing 40 tons, *Coyotl*s were not built to weather much damage. Speed and firepower were their primary components.

Assuming he had not shifted, she knew he was within the range of her short-range missiles, but the key for her was to avoid any further damage on her left side, where the PPC had savaged her armor. She was sure that chance would come. *He is used to fighting with assault BattleMechs in his Strikers. He will come for me. It is only a matter of which direction he will attack from.*

Rather than move out from the flank of the rocks, she pedaled her jump jets to life, rising slowly over the orange and brown rocks. She rose up and to the right, catching Nash's *Coyotl* on the move, exposed. As he spun to face her, she waited for weapons lock and the moment it sounded, fired everything she had.

Her large pulse laser tore into his OmniMech's upper body with red pulses of coherent light. Her Streak missiles passed his in mid-air between them, with twice as many raining down on his Omni. The incoming fire rattled her right side and arm as she began her descent. His PPC flashed, but missed, but his medium pulse laser burned nasty short black streaks in her right leg as she dropped back down.

Her trained mind knew she could ill-afford such exchanges. *It will turn this Trial into one of attrition. I need more of an edge.* Having seen where he was moving, she swung around her own rock formation, keeping it between them. The key would be getting in close and fast. The worst part was the Star Commander would know that as well.

Tyrilla girded herself for the charge. She broke her *Coyotl* into a full run, with Nash's long-range missiles swarming around her like a kicked hive of bees. Explosions from the impacting warheads rattled her *Coyotl* hard, two finding a gap in her left side armor, chewing into her Endo Steel structure. Tyrilla ignored it and firing her jump jets, rising into the air high enough to riposte with her pulse laser and Streak missiles as Nash's medium pulse laser flash-melted armor on her left leg.

Nash reeled under the attack, the laser melting away what was left of his center torso armor and leaving a tell-tale smoke plume from the damage deep inside his OmniMech.

Tyrilla landed hard, one of her jump jets flashing crimson on the damage display, indicating it had been turned to worthless slag in the attack. Gritting her teeth, she rushed toward where she presumed Nash was moving. Out of the corner of her eye, she spied the floating circular platform on which Loremaster Nuyriev no doubt hovered.

Her opponent surprised her, his PPC destroying what was left of her right leg's armor and turning her knee actuator into a solid, non-moving chunk of metal. She staggered, almost falling over, but compensated, her head throbbing inside her neurohelmet as she fought gravity, momentum, and a changing center of gravity.

Whipping around to face his new position, her SRMs roared from their racks, five hitting his right arm, turning the PPC into a smoldering piece of slag hanging uselessly from the *Coyotl*'s battered torso. The other Streaks had dug into where his center torso had been, erupting deep within his OmniMech. She saw flickers of orange and yellow explosions from within as his spray of long-range missiles missed, filling the air over her head.

Limping rapidly forward, Tyrilla fired her large pulse laser again, hitting the *Coyotl*'s left leg at the hip, sending bits of his actuator spraying into the air as molten metal.

Nash wheeled in place, peppering her with his medium pulse laser—shredding what little armor was left on her left side. One of her SRM launchers flickered red on the damage display for a moment, then went solid crimson. "*Katay!*" she cursed, her jaw aching from constant flexing.

Tyrilla staggered on her bad leg as Nash did the same. She fired her large laser as he sprayed her with his LRMs. The laser savaged his left arm, turning it into a limp, worthless piece of twisted metal. His salvo of LRMs blasted her already damaged leg low, returning the favor on her ankle. *If I move, I risk falling, and I will not do that, not with my leg so mangled.*

Nash's medium pulse laser missed her by less than a meter, one errant beam stabbing into her armored ferroglass and leaving a blackened mark where it had been deflected. She unleashed her small pulse laser in her melted torso, sending thin green bursts into his cockpit—tit for tat.

Nash twisted as the laser seared his canopy...and it was too much to compensate for on his damaged leg. His *Coyotl* toppled over onto a boulder, destroying what was left of his wrecked limb, twisting it backward and skyward as the OmniMech went face-first on the coulee floor. Sand flew up from the fall as Tyrilla struggled to keep her weapons locked onto Nash and remain upright.

"Stand down, Star Colonel," she said.

To his credit, he ignored her and tried to right himself, learning the full damage to his leg in the process. As she drifted her targeting reticle onto the prone *Coyotl*, her communications system crackled to life.

"I stand down," Star Colonel Matthew Nash said in a strained voice.

Good! She felt her body quake slightly as it tried to shake off the rush of adrenaline from the Trial. It was still a mental effort to keep her own battered *Coyotl* upright.

Then came the deep voice of Loremaster Nuyriev. "*Seyla*, Coyotes of the Great Pack! A victor has risen from the ashes and sweat of battle. Both warriors fought with honor, but in the *rede* of our people, the better has risen from this contest—Star Captain Tyrilla Heller. Rejoice that our champion has emerged, ready to protect our pack from our lesser that come to raid the den!"

"*Seyla!*" chanted the witnesses to the Circle of Equals.

Still shaking slightly, she nodded. *This is not the end, but the beginning.*

In her ear, she heard the voice of Star Colonel Nash. "You did well, Tyrilla Heller. You are the first warrior to defeat me in a Trial in five years, which says a great deal about you. When you are done defeating the Jade Falcons, there is a place for you in my Strikers."

"Thank you, Star Colonel," she said wearily. "One battle at a time, if you please. I need you to fight at my side as we fend off the Jade Falcons."

There was a pause. "So it shall be," he said in a low tone.

AUXILARY TECHNICIAN BAYS
TRISTEN
FOSTER
THE CLAN HOME WORLDS
12 APRIL 2863

"We need to finish our work on 570," Senior Technician Rietman said. "She needs to go the paint shop this afternoon. There is still some work to be done on 572 as well."

The ten OmniMechs slated for the Trials had been brought to Foster, where they stood in a secured 'Mech bay. Clan Coyote had spared no expenses in fitting out the facility, duplicating the prep-bays on Tamaron. They had arranged for rapid transport of the precious cargo as well, to ensure that the Techs could ensure the Omnis were in peak working order.

Sharandar nodded. Word of the challenge against his people, the Jade Falcons, was the talk of the technicians that had been perfecting every detail of the *Coyotl*s for their upcoming Trial of Possession.

"I should be finished in an hour or so," he said. "I am waiting for Kaitlin to finish his work."

"I will be done in an hour," Kaitlin said from his position on the gantry on the topside of the *Coyotl's* shoulder actuator.

"The good news is we will be getting a much-needed break after all the hours of work we have put in," Rietman said as he walked up to where Sharandar lay on his back to look up at the actuator assembly.

"What do you mean?"

"Our crew will be rotated out once the Trial is finished. It is standard procedure. It provides us with a large number of technicians that are familiar with the OmniMechs."

Stravag! If I am redeployed, I will not be able to fulfill my mission! Sharandar extracted himself to look over at the Senior Technician. "Are there no exceptions? I enjoy working on the OmniMechs, and I still have much to learn."

Rietman shook his head. "It is a standard procedure. We are here to serve," he said, uttering motto of the technician caste.

"We are here to serve," Sharandar repeated instinctively. "I will miss this work."

"You may get rotated back in, though it will be a year or two before such an opportunity presents itself. With the recommendation I will give you, I have no doubt you will be working on OmniMechs again. You are a thoughtful worker with good attention to detail, Sharandar. You have earned several pips on your record for your work here. There is always good work for technicians of your caliber." With those words, Rietman started to walk away.

"As you say, Senior Technician. I had hoped to do more." *My rotation ends my usefulness in the Watch. I have failed the Jade Falcons.*

For long moments he stared up into the shoulder actuator. *I barely scratched the surface in terms of knowledge about this technology. If we lose our Trial of Possession, it will be another year before we get another chance. Another year of Clan Coyote dominance. That is intolerable!*

There must be a way! As he stared up into the dark cavity of the *Coyotl*, Sharandar's mind changed its focus. *If I cannot learn or steal this technology, perhaps there is a way I can ensure that my people will win.* He eyed *Coyotl*s 570 and 572, both of which were still in the bays. *It is worth the risk...*

He slid out. "Senior Technician, it will be a few minutes before I can begin. Perhaps we can get some coffee together?"

Rietman paused. "Excellent. You know how I like it. Meet me in the break room."

Sharandar went to his toolkit and retrieved the tiny case he had concealed there. It was a Watch toolkit of sorts, small, easy to conceal. Security focused on the personnel and the

OmniMechs, but rarely on the tools themselves. Smuggling it in had been risky, but worth it.

An hour later he returned to the gantry. "Where is the Senior Technician?" Kaitlin asked.

"He felt ill and is in the bathroom," Sharandar said, sliding his hands in his pockets. "Are you wrapped up?"

"Affirmative," Kaitlin said. "She is all yours."

Yes, she is...and so is her mate.

**TRISTEN
FOSTER
THE CLAN HOME WORLDS
12 APRIL 2863**

Tyrilla Heller assembled her nine warriors around the holotable in the tactical operations room in Tristen, some 30 kilometers from the site of the upcoming Trial. They had trained several times together, and in two days would be defending the most prized assets of their people. Every warrior there understood the burden they faced, despite outnumbering their foes by a two-to-one margin.

"The Jade Falcon commander, a Star Commander Kerek Helmer, has sent us his force composition." Tyrilla brought up the 'Mech files on the table. "A *Conjurer*, a *Warhammer IIC*, a *Thug*, a *King Crab*, and a *Vapor Eagle*."

"I am surprised by the *Thug* and *King Crab*," Star Colonel Nash said. "They are older models. *Aff*, they are likely the Royal versions, but I would have expected something more from this Star Commander."

Star Captain Julie Clearwater weighed in. "We must assume they have changed their configurations in some manner."

"*Aff*," Tyrilla replied. "Even so, the Jade Falcons are nothing if not consistent in their approach to these Trials. Every time they have fought us, their forces rush in to try and engage at optimal ranges."

"Up close and personal," Star Colonel Nash added.

"Correct. It is part of their doctrine and they will, no doubt, try it again." Tyrilla rotated through the Jade Falcon 'Mechs until she reached the assault class. "That *King Crab* is slow. It is devastating when it gets in close with those large caliber autocannons, but it is ponderous. The *Thug* will win no races either. As such, I have chosen configurations for our Omnis that factor that in."

"They may have mass on us, but we have speed. Speed is armor for our Omnis," Star Captain Ramses Koga said. "That, and we have numbers. We will need to keep moving, get to their flanks and rear."

While Ramses could feel an advantage, Tyrilla could not afford that. "Do not let our numbers or technology make you overconfident. The reason we bid so many to protect our technology is because of its value. The Jade Falcons know this. They each have to take out two of us to be victorious, and we have all had similar results in our Trials of Position—as have they. We cannot rely just on our technology to win, your skills will separate our victory from defeat."

There were solemn nods from around the holotable as she activated it. "Alright then, let us discuss the best way to strip these Falcons of their wings."

TEMPER
FOSTER
THE CLAN HOME WORLDS
12 APRIL 2863

Temper was a small mining town that had been temporarily ceded to the Jade Falcons as their staging area for the upcoming Trial. Clan Coyote had been gracious in that effort, flying the Jade Falcon banner in honor of their guests. Star Commander Kerek Helmer had seen the rolled-up Steel Viper banner leaning against the wall, not far from his own Clan's. *They are confident that we will lose, and are prepared for the next Clan to come.*

He assembled his four warriors in the portable command dome that served as his tactical center. These were the best of the Jade Falcons *touman*; he had been given his choice of warriors, and had been bold in his selection. Star Colonel Claw Hazen had fought in the last trial against the Coyotes, and had done remarkably well. Star Captain Sinn Roshak had a reputation for timing, knowing when to strike and then striking hard. Star Colonel Sandra Chrichell was a seasoned leader with a reputation for patience—sometimes a rarity with Jade Falcon warriors. Star Captain Klaus Buckenburger rounded out their small force; a warrior known for his ferocity in Trials, with a long list of those that had opposed him now remembered only by their codexes.

"It is good to see all of you. We have three days to prepare for this fight. I have taken the liberty of making some changes to your BattleMech configurations. This has been done to add to our long-range strike capabilities as well as increase some of our armor. On top of that, it will throw off our Coyote opponents."

Sandra Chrichell spoke up. "The *King Crab* you have me piloting has replaced one autocannon with an extended range PPC."

"*Aff*, it allowed me to increase your attack range, drop some ammo, and add to your armor," Kerek replied. Chrichell nodded at that.

"What is our strategy, Kerek?" Sinn Roshak asked.

"In the last few Trials, our warriors have followed our typical doctrine of rapid advance and medium to close range engagement. In one case, they opened the fight into a grand melee by grouping fire on targets. Those approaches play to the advantages of the *Coyotl* OmniMechs. It also means the Coyotes will be expecting similar tactics.

"I refuse to play the game they expect. We will maintain fire discipline, each of us only targeting a single foe in battle. We will maintain far ranges, allowing us to whittle down our enemies while they advance. It will frustrate them at first, then they will attempt to rush in and close with us. We will then deny them that strategy by executing a retrograde. They have speed on their side, but by the time they get close, we should be able to engage and defeat our initial targets. Then they will either engage us by trying to mass firepower, or will move into close range and seek to flank us. By that time, the numbers should be more even, giving us the advantage. All we have to do is destroy two foes each."

Star Colonel Hazen cleared his throat. "These Omnis are fast and powerful. It is not simply a matter of tonnage versus tonnage."

"Correct," Kerek said. "We will throw them off by frustrating them. The reconfigured BattleMechs will add to their confusion. This is a fight for their minds as much as their 'Mechs. Next, let us study the terrain where we will defeat Clan Coyote."

Those words brought grins from the gathered Falcons.

**THE KUFAHL GRAND COULEE
FOSTER
THE CLAN HOME WORLDS
15 APRIL 2863**

IlKahn Zenos Danforth was an imposing figure. Tyrilla could see his battle experience represented by scars on his hands, neck, and forehead. The Clan Burrock ilKhan's dress uniform was utilitarian, dark leather with armored blast plates over his muscular chest. His chiseled face bore an expression of grim solace. She appreciated that. Tyrilla was well aware of the gravity of this Trial, and it seemed the ilKhan was, too.

Next to her stood Kerek Helmer of Clan Jade Falcon. Like her, Kerek wore his MechWarrior togs—his green, hers khaki. She glanced sideways at him, sizing up her foe. He was stout, with thick leg muscles. His light blue eyes were fixed solely on the ilKhan.

Off to her left stood her nine Coyote warriors. Next to Kerek, a half-step back and to his right, was a shorter row of Jade Falcons. Seeing them did not intimidate her; instead, it filled her with deep resolve. *This is beyond the honor of Clan Coyote...this is about the future of our people and our place among the Clans. I cannot fail today.*

The ilKhan surveyed the gathered warriors of the two Clans as if they were being judged. When he spoke, his voice was deep, penetrating. "I stand before you as ilKhan of the Clans. We are gathered this day to stand witness as equals to Clan Jade Falcon's Trial of Possession for the OmniMech technology of Clan Coyote." He paused for a moment, letting the weight of his words echo out over the small butte where the warriors had assembled.

"Star Commander Kerek Helmer, a Bloodnamed warrior of Clan Jade Falcon, do you and your warriors stand ready to conduct this Trial?"

"*Aff*, ilKhan," he barked.

Danforth turned to her, his eyes boring in as if they were targeting reticles. "Tyrilla Heller, a Bloodnamed warrior of Clan Coyote, do you and your warriors stand ready to conduct this Trial?"

"*Aff*, ilKhan," she replied crisply, lacking the boom of Kerek's voice, but containing no less conviction.

"*Seyla*!" the ilKhan replied. "Very well. Retire to your BattleMechs while we, as honored witnesses, assume our position in the Circle of Equals. Your prowess will determine which of your Clans stands triumphant."

Tyrilla turned as the ilKhan started away. She stood only three meters from Kerek. He turned to face her as well. "You will fail today."

She chuckled at his attempt to goad her. "The day is young, and words alone will not give you victory, Jade Falcon." She spun and headed for the hover transport to take her to her *Coyotl*.

Fifteen minutes later, she stood in front of her new *Coyotl*, its hull number 570 stood out on the tan and brown streaked camouflage. Fresh from the pilot factory floor, she could not help but feel a swell of pride as she climbed up the OmniMech and into the cockpit.

There was a smell here, just before she put on her neurohelmet—the pristine smell of a new 'Mech. Older ones stank of coolant, burned metal, and worse. *How can I fail in such a machine?* She moved through her security protocol maneuvers with her Omni's arms and felt the surge as the reactor kicked onto full pow r.

Star Commander Kerek Helmer stood before his *Conjurer* and grinned at the improvements. He had swapped out the Streak SRMs and ammo and dropped the large pulse laser for an ER large laser. The Streak missiles were only useful at close range, and he wanted to fight the Coyotes at distance. The longer range was in anticipation of his Coyote foe mounting an extended range PPC. He was not going to make the mistake of the last warriors in the same Trials of Possession. *We can hit farther out, hopefully negating those pesky extended range PPCs they are likely to mount.*

Facing two times as many enemies as he fielded was not daunting, but it was far from encouraging. When he reached the cockpit hatch, he looked down at the light green paint, patterned with squares of olive drab, black, and dark green on the armor plates. Simple and effective. While not best for the desert, it was pure Jade Falcon. *Defiance counts, let this Tyrilla see who we represent, who we fight for. Besides, camouflage is nearly worthless with BattleMechs.*

As he climbed into the cockpit, he was reassured by the aroma that stung his nostrils. This *Conjurer* was pristine, fresh off of the assembly line, fully tested and ready to fight. It smelled unlike other BattleMechs which carried the hints of those that had fought in them before. While Jade Falcons, by nature, were not superstitious like the Nova Cats, there was a sense of destiny in this *Conjurer* that could not be denied. Raising the arms up and down in a specific pattern, the battlecomputer and reactor came online, and the controls lit up before him. The low dull throbbing of the fusion reactor was reassuring and strangely comforting.

Helmer could feel the eyes of his entire Clan upon him. *If we fail, other Clans will follow us to challenge to Clan Coyote. I will have failed my people, and the other Clans will have a chance to seize this technology before us. Instead of facing one Clan with this OmniMech technology, the Jade Falcons could be facing two.* He knew the fate of those before that had tried and lost. There was nothing they could do to regain honor short of their deaths in battle.

The stain of such losses will not be upon me. I will *be victorious.*

**TRISTEN
FOSTER
THE CLAN HOME WORLDS
16 APRIL 2863**

Technician Sharandar disappeared as his temporary home went up in a roar of flames. He had been assigned an apartment in Tristen while the final prep had been done on the OmniMechs.

Jarrad, the Jade Falcon Watch operative, however, grinned in a coffee shop three blocks away as fire engines roared past. A black tornado of smoke twisted into the sky over the city, marking where his life for the last few years was being burned to ashes. *You are already too late, the true crime has already happened.*

Once the Trial was over, they were to be transported back to Tamaron, and that was something he had to be avoid at all costs. There might be questions, agonizing questions, inquiries, a search for wrongdoing would likely be launched. He could have no part of that. As such it had been necessary to torch the entire apartment building, so that his death would be recorded as "one of many victims." He had even provided a body, a member of the Coyote Bandit Caste he had killed, brought to the apartment, and dressed in his clothes.

Aff, *innocent people had to die, but it was necessary for the greater good.* Any other fake death would have prompted more of an investigation by the Coyotes, and his true identity may be uncovered. *If you are making an omelet, you have to break a few eggs.*

He was proud of himself, having found a solution to his mission before being reassigned. *I beat Clan Coyote's security, no small task. I succeeded where others failed and completed my mission, regardless of the sacrifice.*

He cradled a warm drink in his hands, mentally patting himself on the back. Sharandar sipped his Zazu latte as an ambulance raced past the coffee shop window, heading toward the inferno. Now, all that was left was to book passage on a Jade Falcon merchant vessel and return home.

THE KUFAHL GRAND COULEE
FOSTER
THE CLAN HOME WORLDS

"Kerek Helmer and Tyrilla Heller, we stand as a Circle of Equal warriors, ensuring that the ultimate judgement of this contest is settled fairly, in a test of arms. The eyes of your people are on you. Let this Trial commence!"

IlKahn Danforth's voice boomed in Tyrilla's ears as she broke her *Coyotl* into a run perpendicular to the Star of Jade Falcons somewhere in the distance. The 'Mech handled perfectly as she shot out onto the Grand Coulee.

Her long-range sensors had not detected Star Commander Helmer yet, but she knew where she wanted to go—a thick grove of old-growth jango-trees. They would provide some cover and give her a good position to snipe from. It was three kilometers away and she leaned into the sprint as her *Coyotl* picked up speed.

Her two Stars of warriors were also moving out, maintaining a steady pace, but not rushing in. *The Jade Falcons will do that for us.* After a minute or two she wondered *where are they?*

"Coyote Actual to all Coyotes, call out any sensor readings."

"I have one, a *Thug*—Royal configuration," called out Matthew Nash. "Relaying signal." Her tactical display showed his target. She saw a new red blip on her tactical display, a *Conjurer*, according to her battlecomputer. It was fast—not as fast as her *Coyotl*—but fast enough. Instantly she knew it was Star Colonel Kerek Helmer's ride. It was angling for a boulder field that snaked through the middle of the coulee, with deep gullies not far from where she was heading. *He is not closing range.* That struck her as odd. *Are they holding back for some reason?*

As she approached the jango-tree woods, other crimson dots showed up on her tactical display, all at extreme ranges. Suddenly a bright flash stabbed past her cockpit canopy. *A laser shot!* It was Kerek. *Impossible—the* Conjurer *does not mount extended range...damn!*

"They are not closing," Julie Clearwater said. "I am being hit with long-range missile fire."

Tyrilla's mind, trained from birth on strategy and tactics, immediately grasped the situation. "They have outfitted their 'Mechs with extended range weaponry. We need to close the gap with them. Begin to close now!"

Tyrilla caught a glimpse of Kerek's green *Conjurer* in the distance, rising out of a shallow wash. She swung her targeting reticle onto it and fired just as it dropped into a gully. Her extended range PPC flashed bright blue-white, sending molten armor drops flying into the air. Tyrilla had hit his left leg, blackening the armor there. Her breathing increased as she plowed into the growth of trees.

A bright crimson beam flashed from the boulder field, hitting her left arm. The laser strike left a meter-long scar, smoking from the armor melted there. She winced at the hit, realizing her choice of ground may not be suited to her Omni's strengths. *Given where he has gone to ground, these trees are of little use to me.* Her mind immediately switched tactics. *Speed, that is the key.*

Running through the thick trees, another enemy laser fired, missing her by centimeters, setting several branches ablaze in the process. She broke free of the wooded area, getting a target lock as she did.

Tyrilla unleashed her long-range missiles and ER PPC. The missiles twisted in the air, plowing into the green *Conjurer* and sending bits of armor flying into the rocks around it. Her PPC missed the running Jade Falcon, the shot slamming into a boulder and obliterating it.

"They are falling back, not closing with us," Ramses Koga said. "Star Colonel Nash, watch that clearing."

In the corner of her eye, Tyrilla saw two brilliant flashes of bluish-white PPC energy race from the far end of the coulee.

"I just lost my left arm," came a frustrated response from Nash.

"We need to close with them," Tyrilla snapped. "Rush them now!"

"Star Captain Angus Kautz is down," replied Julie Clearwater. "They are adhering to honorable engagement tactics."

Stravag! They are not fighting like the Jade Falcons before them. Tyrilla focused on Kerek again. His green BattleMech dove for cover as she swung wide in a long, running arc. His ER large laser flashed again, this time the beam hit her legs mid-stride, wobbling her for a millisecond before she regained balance. Her jaw clenched as she kept her targeting reticle in the area where the shot had come from.

The green *Conjurer* rose, and she unleashed her ER PPC again. The flash of white and azure energy slammed into the Falcon 'Mech, filling the air with the splatter of red-hot melted armor. She grinned until a return blast came from the ER medium lasers of her foe.

One slender green beam seared her right torso, another bore in on her *Coyotl*'s chest. The sudden loss of armor made her lean awkwardly forward. Tyrilla regained her stride, loosing another ten long-range missiles at the *Conjurer* as she moved in closer to engage with it.

A warning light flickered on her right shoulder actuator. *What? Not possible—I took no damage near there!* The conflicting information between what she could see from her cockpit, her damage warning lights, and her damage indicators was confusing. *Katay! That is where my PPC is.*

She moved behind a rocky outgrowth and tried the actuator. The targeting reticle could not move, it was as if it was frozen. *Not now...I need that weapon!* The right arm was frozen at the shoulder, so aiming it required contorting the *Coyotl. The laser blast must have severed some connection.*

"I am down," Ramses Koga said.

"As am I," said Star Captain Clarice Hoffman. "That *Thug* is weakened. Someone do the honor of finishing it off."

"*Seyla!*" Star Commander Phyllus Jerricho called out. "I have avenged you Clarice!"

"They are still falling back," Julie Clearwater said.

The battle was now beyond her coordination—it had turned into a series of mini-fights between each combatant. Her tactical display showed the Jade Falcons were taking damage, but the contest was far too close for her liking.

She glimpsed the *Warhammer IIC* of Star Captain Sinn Roshak in the distance. One ER PPC hung limp, smoking from missile hits, which gave her some hope.

The *Conjurer* was no longer drifting back, as if Kerek could sense the damage she had taken. The Jade Falcon 'Mech emerged as she rounded the cover of her rocks. Their shots passed each other in mid-air between the warriors. Her Streak short range missiles locked on and pummeled the *Conjurer*'s right arm, sending fragments of armor plating thudding into the orange and brown dust.

The *Conjurer's* right arm ER large laser raked across her torso, burning through the remaining armor and furrowing into her reactor shielding. A ripple of heat rose from the floor. Kerek's ER medium lasers flashed at her as well, one searing into the armored ferroglass of her cockpit. The discharge was so intense she felt the skin on her arm burn as if it were exposed to the sun for hours.

Tyrilla ignored the pain, twisting hard. She fired her LRMs once more at the Jade Falcon. They arced high in the air over the rising dust of the coulee, then plunged down, setting off explosions all over her enemy.

The heat rose even higher in her cockpit, proof of the damage indicator on her fusion reactor...and smoke drifted around her exterior canopy glass from the holes in her OmniMech. Kerek began to close on her and she kept her target lock on him, now unleashing her short-range missiles.

Her Streak missile barrage blasted the twisted armor on his left leg, the explosions exposing myomer muscles and their actuators. She brought her medium pulse laser to bear, its brilliant green bursts of deadly energy tore into his cockpit and the lower body of the *Conjurer*. For a moment, the Jade Falcon was obscured by the smoke of the explosions as she shifted, starting to pick up speed again.

"I am down," Julie Clearwater said. "As is the Jade Falcon *Warhammer*."

Tyrilla's eyes flicked to her display. Of the Jade Falcons, only Kerek's *Conjurer* and the *King Crab* remained, as did herself and two more of her *Coyotl*s. *Three to two...victory is in our grasp.*

Kerek burst through the smoke, limping on the mangled knee of his left, leg, but still coming at her. She swung hard to the left, hoping to put some distance between them, waiting for the sounds of the missiles reloading.

The bright red blast from his ER large laser tore at her left torso, melting a glowing hole deep inside. His pair of medium lasers threw emerald beams at her direction. One missed by less than two meters, but the other stabbed into her already damaged left leg, blowing the limb off from the knee down.

At a full run, the loss was catastrophic, sending her *Coyotl* plowing into the sandy floor and tossing Tyrilla hard against her restraining straps. She heard a *snap* inside her chest, and knew something had broken...likely a rib. Metal groaned and protested the fall and her damage indicators everywhere flickered from amber to crimson. Then came the pain from her broken rib—hot, nauseating, strangely focusing. *Stravag!*

She tried to use her *Coyotl*'s crippled right arm to roll over and stand, but it refused to move. Her eyes darted to the tactical display and saw the last of the *Coyotl*s, that of Star Captain Darius Topol, charge head on into the Jade Falcon *King Crab*. The reactors of both 'Mechs flickered off.

It is just Kerek Helmer and me.

Tyrilla used her left arm to roll over just as Kerek let go with another wave of laser fire. Her reactor warning lights flared and a radiation warning flickered from the hit. Her gyro pitch went out of alignment—and she felt a surge in her brain of feedback from the damage. She did not want to throw up in her neurohelmet, so she popped the protective faceplate.

Sitting up, she managed to get a faint target lock from her prone position and unleashed her last remaining operating weapon, her Streak SRMs. Three locked onto the Jade Falcon *Conjurer*, exploding all over the BattleMech. It remained unshaken by the explosions, as if Kerek were deliberately shrugging off the damage.

"Stand down," Kerek said, moving to flank her as she struggled to rise. "I do not wish to kill someone obviously so skilled…but I will."

"*Neg!*" she cursed as bile rose in her mouth. She rocked the *Coyotl* hard, but it felt as if she were only doing more damage in the process. "I would rather die than suffer defeat!" Those words were not in anger, but an expression of her soul.

"That is a choice," Kerek replied.

There was a flash of bright crimson laser fire down on her and a scream filled her ears—her own. As her mind reeled with waves of agony, everything Tyrilla knew went black.

Star Commander Kerek Helmer stood before ilKahn Zenos Danforth, his twisted and mangled *Conjurer* listing to one side behind him. His body was soaked with sweat, and his coolant vest hung limp on him as he dipped his head.

"Kerek of the Bloodhouse Helmer of Clan Jade Falcon, you have defeated your opponent, and have thus proven yourself worthy of the challenge you faced. Clan Coyote will provide an OmniMech and the technical specifications of this technology to the Jade Falcons. So shall we stand, until we all shall fall. *Seyla!*"

The replied "*seyla*" was far from enthusiastic from the Coyote warriors behind the ilKhan. Kerek could see their anger and frustration, but it meant nothing to him. *I won this contest fairly and justly, according to the ways of our people. If you have any issue with my victory, take it up with Nicholas Kerensky.*

Several of the Jade Falcons present stepped forward, including Khan Natalie Buhallin. "You have served the Jade Falcons well, Kerek Helmer. Your name will be remembered in our Remembrance as the one that brought this technology from the jaws of the Coyotes to our Clan," she said, resting her hand on his shoulder.

"I did my duty, my Khan," he said, glancing off as the hover ambulance sped out to where Tyrilla Heller had been defeated.

"And for that, you shall be honored," Khan Buhallin replied.

COUTT HOSPITAL
FOSTER
THE CLAN HOME WORLDS
16 MAY 2863

Tyrilla glared down at the soft, pink skin of her regrown right arm. Its muscles were still being trained and developed. At first, it had been difficult to lift a glass of water. Now, with rehabilitation, it became stronger each day. While a part of her knew the arm would one day look as normal as the one she had lost, she hated it. Every time she looked down and saw the fresh, new skin, it represented something she loathed—defeat. It was a permanent reminder of what had happened. *I lost an arm, but my people lost their technological advantage.*

For days, she had wished she had died in that cockpit. She had even contemplated suicide, an act scorned by the warrior caste. Death seemed like a welcome release compared to the shame she had to bear. When she had tried, they had medicated her, and in time the urge seemed to fade.

Her broken hip and ribs were almost healed, thanks to the bone-knitters, though slight pain nagged each motion she made. Tyrilla still limped slightly as well, yet another reminder of her defeat. There were other warriors in the hospital ward, but when they saw her, their faces went from pained to angry. Some turned away from her entirely rather than pass her in the hallway.

I am *dezgra*—tainted. It had been earned. When she had awakened two days later in the hospital, she had asked that her *Coyotl* be checked. *That shoulder actuator should not have failed. It has to be a design flaw of some sort.* None seemed to take her warnings seriously, and her words had been disregarded. *They think I am trying to excuse what happened, to somehow explain away why I was defeated.*

The final indignation came when her orders arrived. She had been assigned to a *solamha* garrison unit on a Coyote settlement on Londerholm. *Sent into exile...fitting, given my defeat.* She had wadded up the order papers and thrown them away. *Tomorrow I ship out, and will likely never have a chance to prove myself in battle again. What could I ever accomplish that could erase this black mark?*

Leaning back on her bed, she stared up at the flat white ceiling and thought back to her vision on the butte. *What good was it? The trickster...the snake that lured in the bird. Is that something I experienced, or is it something yet to come?*

A knock sounded at her doorway, making Tyrilla looked over to the entrance. Standing there in his warrior jumpsuit was Matthew Nash.

"May I come in?"

At a loss for words, Tyrilla nodded and he entered, closing the door behind him. "I hear you are mending," the Star Colonel said.

"Physically, *aff*," she replied.

Nash approached to stand alongside her bed. "I heard you were going to be sent to Londerholm, a *solamha* garrison. No BattleMechs or tanks, just an infantry unit."

"Fitting," she said. "I failed my people."

"*Neg*, perhaps you did not," Nash replied.

"What do you mean?"

"The saKhan asked me to head up an inquiry into the Trial while you were recovering. We reviewed the battleROMs and sensor data. We conducted it in secret. Your arm seized up in battle, do you recall that?"

"*Aff*."

"The Jade Falcons took one *Coyotl* as *isorla*, Ramses Koga's, as it was the least damaged. Yours was left behind, which allowed us to perform a detailed analysis of it."

"And what did you find?"

"There was burn damage on the actuator."

"I assumed it had suffered some damage, as it was not operational."

"There should not have been any damage there at all. It was a reinforced wire harness that provided feedback to the battlecomputer to allow for actuator control and coordination. It was burned inside the armor, which had suffered no damage during the Trial. We were unable to determine how it could have been damaged during the fight."

"So how was it damaged?"

"We do not know for certain. There are...theories, but that is all."

"It was *not* my fault, *quiaff*?"

"*Aff.* My inquiry found the loss of your primary weapon to be due to mechanical failure, Star Commander, not Mechwarrior error," he assured her.

For a long moment she said nothing. "What happened?" Tyrilla finally asked.

Her query caused the Star Colonel's eyebrows to rise. "There are two possibilities. One, the damage happened through some fluke that defies all simulations, that somehow damaged that small wire harness. Two, it could have been sabotage. The damage was consistent with a burn, but there are minute chemical traces there that could indicate a slow-acting acid—one that would have been accelerated by heat."

"Sabotage?"

"It is a possibility. We have not been able to determine who performed the act. One of the technicians assigned to your OmniMech died in an apartment fire. As he was only a technician, his body was disposed of before anyone could validate that it was indeed him. At the time, it was seen as just an unfortunate fire.

"His Senior Technician vouched for him and his record was impeccable. Review of security footage showed him working on your OmniMech, but that was his job. The other technicians are all being interrogated, but thus far we have not been able to determine any additional information that supports the theory of sabotage."

"We can not let this stand," Tyrilla said firmly. "We should take the evidence to the ilKhan. If it was sabotage, the Jade Falcons must be held to account."

"With no one to accuse, and a lack of physical evidence beyond our theory, we cannot invalidate the Trial. They could easily refute our theory and claim the damage came from battle—they would not have to prove it. Also, there are concerns that if we did reveal our findings, it would expose a breach in our security measures that others might try and exploit. Now is not the time for us to show weakness in the eyes of the other Clans."

A shadow of dejection fell over Tyrilla. "So they walk away with one of our prized OmniMechs? That does not feel honorable or ust."

Nash pulled up a seat next to her bed and sat down. "Our monopoly of this technology would come to an end would sooner or later. Every Clan was attempting their own crash program to copy what we accomplished. In a week or so, the Steel Vipers are coming for their Trial of Possession. Khan McTighe feels that contesting this, without any real proof, may actually injure our honor. The results of the Trial stand. The Jade Falcons won."

Tyrilla's entire body sagged on the bed. "And my honor is the price of this secret."

Nash nodded. "We all make sacrifices for the Clan. That starts when we are in *sibkos*. Few are ever called upon to make one as public and damaging as yours, but *aff*, it is a secret you cannot share. That does not mean, however, that the Coyote cannot be compassionate. We protect our pack. That is why I have come here."

She frowned. "I do not understand."

"When I learned of your orders, I convinced the other members of the inquiry that they were in error. You should not be punished for the acts of another. They agreed. As such, I am rescinding your orders to Londerholm. I have come to take you with me."

"With you?" Tyrilla asked.

"Yes. I told you when you defeated me that I would offer you a place in my Strikers. I will honor that."

For the first time since the Trial, she allowed herself to smile. "I cannot thank you enough, Star Colonel."

"It will not be easy. We cannot discuss our theory to anyone, not until we can prove who is behind it. Your name will be known, but not in a good way. You will face resentment and anger from others. You will have to rise up and overcome their misconceptions about you.

"I believe you to be a warrior great enough to do so."

Tyrilla nodded. "I will not fail your trust, Star Colonel." She held back the tears glimmering in her eyes.

Matthew Nash nodded. "I know you will not, Star Captain."

JADE FALCON WATCH COMMAND
EDEN
THE PENTAGON WORLDS
CLAN SPACE
25 JUNE 2863

Jarrad stood in the office of the Commanding Officer of the Watch, Star Colonel Stanislav Bang-Chu. The older man's face was etched with deep wrinkles and a half-dozen scars—likely earned in battles before Jarrad had been conceived. Star Colonel Bang-Chu glared at him as his gaze lifted from the report.

Jarrad could not help feeling proud. *It is rare that someone in the Watch contributes as much as I have.* Still, it appeared there was no happiness on the face of the Star Colonel, only what looked like disdain.

"So, you attempted sabotage on two of the *Coyotl*s used in the Trial of Possession, *quiaff*?" he finally asked Jarrad in a gravelly voice.

"Affirmative," he said trying to suppress his grin. "On one I placed a heat-sensitive packet that held a corrosive used in etching parts in the shop. The packet protected the acid until the actuator was used a great deal. After it gets warm, the coating melts away, allowing the acid to do its work. On the other I was able to adjust the targeting and tracking system using a small magnet so that it was off by two percent; not enough to alert the warrior, but perhaps enough to cause a missed shot or two.

"From what I saw of the footage of the Trial, it worked exactly as I had planned, at least on Star Colonel Tyrilla Heller's *Coyotl*. The arm seized at the shoulder actuator, right where I put my little surprise."

As he finished, he finally flashed a grin. *I am a hero to my people and to the other Clans who will benefit from my actions.*

Stanislav Bang-Chu only offered scornfulness in his expression. "You are proud of what you did, this devious sabotage."

"I am. I served my Clan the best way I could."

"Do you know what you have done?" The old man's voice was deep and angry.

"I do not understand. I ensured that our warrior would secure the OmniMech technology—"

"You came out of the warrior breeding program!" Bang-Chu slashed a hand through the air. "There is *nothing* honorable in sabotage. You have tainted a true warrior's victory. Not only that, by performing this act, you have dragged the honor of the Jade Falcons into the mud."

"I only thought that—"

"*Silence*!" roared Bang-Chu. He paused, drawing a long breath. "Did you *think* of what would happen if this sabotage was found by Clan Coyote? You would be putting my own honor at risk for allowing you on such an assignment. The Coyotes would be in a position to challenge the results of the Trial, and their grounds for that challenge would be solid. You risked the honor of your entire people to achieve a goal we never assigned you."

Anger washed over his pride. "My mission was to ensure that the Jade Falcons obtained the OmniMech technical specifications. I did that."

"This is our greatest victory as a Clan. We did something no other Clan had done. Your actions—" Bang-Chu said through gritted teeth, "—have tainted me and our Clan."

He tapped button on his desk, and two sentries entered the office, laser rifles at the ready. Suddenly, the gravity of the situation became all too clear for Jarrad.

"We cannot risk this information ever being discovered," Bang-Chu said, tapping the delete key on his report. "We have been fortunate thus far that the Coyotes have not dug deeper into this matter, but that day may yet come. If they do not, you remain a loose end. If they do, you are a liability, a witness that links us to your dishonorable act. Either way," he said, rising to his feet. "Your services are no longer required by your people."

The Star Colonel pulled out his pistol, then rose, walked around the desk and handed it to Jarrad. It was a dead weight in his hands. His eyes rose to the old man's, and he saw the blazing contempt there. *How could I have misjudged this so poorly?*

"Sir, it is...possible that my acts did not have an impact on what happened," he said attempting to evade the rapidly spiraling situation. "While I suspect it was my sabotage, that actuator may have been damaged in battle. There is no way to know for sure unless we had that OmniMech to evaluate."

"Which we do not...the Coyotes do. At this point, it no longer matters if your acts altered the battle, the fact that you did them at all is enough to warrant my decision."

Jarrad's mind went blank with panic. *I did what was right! I did what I had to to ensure my people secured the OmniMech technology. How can this be happening? I should be treated as a hero!*

"Normally, I would simply have you terminated," the old man said, leaning in close enough for Jarrad to smell the coffee on his breath. "But your actions *may* have allowed us to obtain that technical information. So, rather than a death in the night or a firing squad; you will be allowed to retain some modicum of honor by killing yourself."

He started toward the door. "And be quick about it, I have much work to do."

Jarrad stood trembling, clutching the gun. Slowly, he raised it to his temple. "For Clan Jade Falcon…"

BATTLETECH GLOSSARY

Clan military unit designations are used throughout this book:
 Point: 1 'Mech or 5 infantry
 Star: 5 'Mechs or 25 infantry
 Binary: 2 Stars
 Trinary: 3 Stars
 Cluster: 4—5 Binaries/Trinaries
 Galaxy: 3-5 Clusters
 Nova: 1 'Mech Star and 1 infantry Star
 Supernova: 1 'Mech Binary and 2 infantry Stars

ABTAKHA

An *abtakha* is a captured warrior who is adopted into his new Clan as a warrior.

AUTOCANNON

This is a rapid-fire, auto-loading weapon. Light autocannons range from 30 to 90 millimeter (mm), and heavy autocannons may be from 80 to 120mm or more. They fire high-speed streams of high-explosive, armor-piercing shells.

BATCHALL

The *batchall* is the ritual by which Clan warriors issue combat challenges. Though the type of challenge varies, most begin with the challenger identifying themselves, stating the prize of the contest, and requesting that the defender identify the forces at their disposal. The defender also has the right to name the location of the trial. The two sides then bid for what forces will participate in the contest. The subcommander who bids to fight with the number of forces wins the right and responsibility to make the attack. The defender may increase the stakes by demanding a prize of equal or lesser value if they wish.

BATTLEMECH

BattleMechs are the most powerful war machines ever built. First developed by Terran scientists and engineers, these huge vehicles are faster, more mobile, better-armored and more heavily armed than any twentieth-century tank. Ten to twelve meters tall and equipped with particle projection cannons, lasers, rapid-fire autocannon and missiles, they pack enough firepower to flatten anything but another BattleMech. A small fusion reactor provides virtually unlimited power, and BattleMechs can be adapted to fight in environments ranging from sun-baked deserts to subzero arctic icefields.

BLOODNAME

A Bloodname is the surname associated with a Bloodright, descended from one of the 800 warriors who stood with Nicholas Kerensky to form the Clans. A warrior must win the use of a Bloodname in a Trial of Bloodright. Only Bloodnamed warriors may sit on Clan Councils or hold the post of Loremaster, Khan, or ilKhan, and only the genetic material from the Bloodnamed is used in the warrior caste eugenics program.

BONDCORD

A woven bracelet worn by bondsmen who has been captured and claimed by a Clan member. Warrior-caste bondsmen wear a three-strand bondcord on their right wrists, with the color and patterning of the cords signifying the Clan and unit responsible for the warrior's capture. The cords represent integrity, fidelity, and prowess. The bondholder may cut each strand as he or she feels the bondsman demonstrates the associated quality. According to tradition, when the final cord is severed, the bondsman is considered a free member of his or her new Clan and adopted into the Warrior caste. Each Clan follows this tradition to varying degrees. For example, Clan Wolf accepts nearly all worthy individuals regardless of their past, while Clan Smoke Jaguar generally chose to adopt only trueborn warriors.

BONDSMAN

A bondsman is a prisoner held in a form of indentured servitude until released or accepted into the Clan. Most often, bondsmen are captured warriors who fulfill roles in the laborer or technician castes. Their status is represented by a woven bondcord, and they are obliged by honor and tradition to work for their captors to the best of their abilities.

CASTE

The Clans are divided into five castes: warrior, scientist, merchant, technician, and laborer, in descending order of influence. Each has many subcastes based on specialized skills. The warrior caste is largely the product of the artificial breeding program; those candidates who fail their Trial of Position are assigned to the scientist or technician caste, giving those castes a significant concentration of trueborn members. Most of the civilian castes are made up of the results of scientist-decreed arranged marriages within the castes.

The children of all castes undergo intensive scrutiny during their schooling to determine the caste for which they are best suited, though most end up in the same caste as their parents. This process allows children born to members of civilian castes to enter training to become warriors, though they belong to the less-prestigious ranks of the freeborn.

CIRCLE OF EQUALS

The area in which a trial takes place is known as the Circle of Equals. It ranges in size from a few dozen feet for personal combat to tens of miles for large-scale trials. Though traditionally a circle, the area can be any shape.

CRUSADER

A Crusader is a Clansman who espouses the invasion of the Inner Sphere and the re-establishment of the Star League by military force. Most Crusaders are contemptuous of the people of the Inner Sphere, whom they view as barbarians, and of freeborns within their own Clans.

DEZGRA

Any disgraced individual or unit is known as *dezgra*. Disgrace may come through refusing orders, failing in an assigned task, acting dishonorably, or demonstrating cowardice.

DROPSHIPS

Because interstellar JumpShips must avoid entering the heart of a solar system, they must "dock" in space at a considerable distance from a system's inhabited worlds. DropShips were developed for interplanetary travel. As the name implies, a DropShip is attached to hardpoints on the JumpShip's drive core, later to be dropped from the parent vessel after in-system entry. Though incapable of FTL travel, DropShips are highly maneuverable, well-armed and sufficiently aerodynamic to take off from and land on a planetary surface. The journey from the jump point to the inhabited worlds of a system usually requires a normal-space journey of several days or weeks, depending on the type of star.

FREEBIRTH

Freebirth is a Clan epithet used by trueborn members of the warrior caste to express disgust or frustration. For one trueborn to use this curse to refer to another trueborn is considered a mortal insult.

FREEBORN

An individual conceived and born by natural means is referred to as freeborn. Its emphasis on the artificial breeding program allows Clan society to view such individuals as second-class citizens.

HEGIRA

Hegira is the rite by which a defeated foe may withdraw from the field of battle without further combat and with no further loss of honor.

ISORLA

The spoils of battle, including bondsmen, claimed by the victorious warriors is called *isorla*.

JUMPSHIPS

Interstellar travel is accomplished via JumpShips, first developed in the twenty-second century. These somewhat ungainly vessels consist of a long, thin drive core and a sail resembling an enormous parasol, which can extend up to a kilometer in width. The ship is named for its ability to "jump" instantaneously across vast distances of space. After making its jump, the ship cannot travel until it has recharged by gathering up more solar energy.

The JumpShip's enormous sail is constructed from a special metal that absorbs vast quantities of electromagnetic energy from the nearest star. When it has soaked up enough energy, the sail transfers it to the drive core, which converts it into a space-twisting field. An instant later, the ship arrives at the next jump point, a distance of up to thirty light-years. This field is known as hyperspace, and its discovery opened to mankind the gateway to the stars.

JumpShips never land on planets. Interplanetary travel is carried out by DropShips, vessels that are attached to the JumpShip until arrival at the jump point.

KHAN (kaKhan, saKhan)

Each Clan Council elects two of its number as Khans, who serve as rulers of the Clan and its representatives on the Grand Council. Traditionally, these individuals are the best warriors in the Clan, but in practice many Clans instead elect their most skilled politicians. The senior Khan, sometimes referred to as the kaKhan, acts as the head of the Clan, overseeing relationships between castes and Clans. The junior Khan, known as the saKhan, acts as the Clan's warlord. The senior Khan decides the exact distribution of tasks, and may assign the saKhan additional or different duties.

The term "kaKhan" is considered archaic, and is rarely used.

LASER

An acronym for "Light Amplification through Stimulated Emission of Radiation." When used as a weapon, the laser damages the target by concentrating extreme heat onto a small area. BattleMech lasers are designated as small, medium or large. Lasers are also available as shoulder-fired weapons operating from a portable backpack power unit. Certain range-finders and targeting equipment also employ low-level lasers.

LRM
This is an abbreviation for "Long-Range Missile," an indirect-fire missile with a high-explosive warhead.

POSSESSION, TRIAL OF
A Trial of Possession resolves disputes between two parties over ownership or control. This can include equipment, territory, or even genetic material. The traditional *batchall* forms the core of the trial in order to encourage the participants to resolve the dispute with minimal use of force.

REMEMBRANCE, THE
The Remembrance is an ongoing heroic saga that describes Clan history from the time of the Exodus to the present day. Each Clan maintains its own version, reflecting its opinions and perceptions of events. Inclusion in The Remembrance is one of the highest honors possible for a member of the Clans. All Clan warriors can recite passages from The Remembrance from memory, and written copies of the book are among the few nontechnical books allowed in Clan society. These books are usually lavishly illustrated in a fashion similar to the illuminated manuscripts and Bibles of the medieval period. Warriors frequently paint passages of The Remembrance on the sides of their OmniMechs, fighters, and battle armor.

SEYLA
Seyla is a ritual response in Clan ceremonies. The origin of this phrase is unknown, though it may come from the Biblical notation "selah," thought to be a musical notation or a reference to contemplation.

SRM
This is the abbreviation for "Short-Range Missile," a direct-trajectory missile with high-explosive or armor-piercing explosive warheads. They have a range of less than one kilometer and are only reliably accurate at ranges of less than 300 meters. They are more powerful, however, than LRMs.

SUCCESSOR LORDS
After the fall of the first Star League, the remaining members of the High Council each asserted his or her right to become First Lord. Their star empires became known as the Successor States and the rulers as Successor Lords. The Clan Invasion temporarily interrupted centuries of warfare known as the Succession Wars, which first began in 2786.

SURAT
A Clan epithet, alluding to the rodent of the same name, which disparages an individual's genetic heritage. As such, it is one of the most vulgar and offensive epithets among the Clans.

TOUMAN
The fighting arm of a Clan is known as the touman.

TROTHKIN
Used formally, *trothkin* refers to members of an extended sibko. It is more commonly used to denote members of a gathering, and warriors also frequently use it when addressing someone they consider a peer.

TRUEBORN/TRUEBIRTH
A warrior born of the Clan's artificial breeding program is known as a trueborn. In less formal situations, the Clans use the term truebirth.

WARDEN
A Warden is a Clansman who believes that the Clans were established to guard the Inner Sphere from outside threats rather than to conquer it and re-establish the Star League by force. Most Wardens were opposed to the recent invasion of the Inner Sphere.

ZELLBRIGEN
Zellbrigen is the body of rules governing duels. These rules dictate that such actions are one-on-one engagements, and that any warriors not immediately challenged should stay out of the battle until an opponent is free.

Once a Clan warrior engages a foe, no other warriors on his or her side may target that foe, even if it means allowing the death of the Clan warrior. Interfering in a duel by attacking a foe that is already engaged constitutes a major breach of honor, and usually results in loss of rank. Such action also opens the battle to a melee.

BATTLETECH ERAS

The *BattleTech* universe is a living, vibrant entity that grows each year as more sourcebooks and fiction are published. A dynamic universe, its setting and characters evolve over time within a highly detailed continuity framework, bringing everything to life in a way a static game universe cannot match.

To help quickly and easily convey the timeline of the universe—and to allow a player to easily "plug in" a given novel or sourcebook—we've divided *BattleTech* into six major eras.

STAR LEAGUE
(Present–2780)

Ian Cameron, ruler of the Terran Hegemony, concludes decades of tireless effort with the creation of the Star League, a political and military alliance between all Great Houses and the Hegemony. Star League armed forces immediately launch the Reunification War, forcing the Periphery realms to join. For the next two centuries, humanity experiences a golden age across the thousand light-years of human-occupied space known as the Inner Sphere. It also sees the creation of the most powerful military in human history.

(This era also covers the centuries before the founding of the Star League in 2571, most notably the Age of War.)

SUCCESSION WARS
(2781–3049)

Every last member of First Lord Richard Cameron's family is killed during a coup launched by Stefan Amaris. Following the thirteen-year war to unseat him, the rulers of each of the five Great Houses disband the Star League. General Aleksandr Kerensky departs with eighty percent of the Star League Defense Force beyond known space and the Inner Sphere collapses into centuries of warfare known as the Succession Wars that will eventually result in a massive loss of technology across most worlds.

CLAN INVASION
(3050–3061)

A mysterious invading force strikes the coreward region of the Inner Sphere. The invaders, called the Clans, are descendants of Kerensky's SLDF troops, forged into a society dedicated to becoming the greatest fighting force in history. With vastly superior technology and warriors, the Clans conquer world after world. Eventually this outside threat will forge a new Star League, something hundreds of years of warfare failed to accomplish. In addition, the Clans will act as a catalyst for a technological renaissance.

CIVIL WAR
(3062–3067)

The Clan threat is eventually lessened with the complete destruction of a Clan. With that massive external threat apparently neutralized, internal conflicts explode around the Inner Sphere. House Liao conquers its former Commonality, the St. Ives Compact; a rebellion of military units belonging to House Kurita sparks a war with their powerful border enemy, Clan Ghost Bear; the fabulously powerful Federated Commonwealth of House Steiner and House Davion collapses into five long years of bitter civil war.

JIHAD
(3067–3080)

Following the Federated Commonwealth Civil War, the leaders of the Great Houses meet and disband the new Star League, declaring it a sham. The pseudo-religious Word of Blake—a splinter group of ComStar, the protectors and controllers of interstellar communication—launch the Jihad: an interstellar war that pits every faction against each other and even against themselves, as weapons of mass destruction are used for the first time in centuries while new and frightening technologies are also unleashed.

DARK AGE
(3081-3150)

Under the guidance of Devlin Stone, the Republic of the Sphere is born at the heart of the Inner Sphere following the Jihad. One of the more extensive periods of peace begins to break out as the 32nd century dawns. The factions, to one degree or another, embrace disarmament, and the massive armies of the Succession Wars begin to fade. However, in 3132 eighty percent of interstellar communications collapses, throwing the universe into chaos. Wars erupt almost immediately, and the factions begin rebuilding their armies.

ILCLAN
(3151-present)

The once-invulnerable Republic of the Sphere lies in ruins, torn apart by the Great Houses and the Clans as they wage war against each other on a scale not seen in nearly a century. Mercenaries flourish once more, selling their might to the highest bidder. As Fortress Republic collapses, the Clans race toward Terra to claim their long-denied birthright and create a supreme authority that will fulfill the dream of Aleksandr Kerensky and rule the Inner Sphere by any means necessary: The ilClan.

LOOKING FOR MORE HARD HITTING BATTLETECH FICTION?

WE'LL GET YOU RIGHT BACK INTO THE BATTLE!

Catalyst Game Labs brings you the very best in *BattleTech* fiction, available at most ebook retailers, including Amazon, Apple Books, Kobo, Barnes & Noble, and more!

NOVELS

1. *Decision at Thunder Rift* by William H. Keith Jr.
2. *Mercenary's Star* by William H. Keith Jr.
3. *The Price of Glory* by William H. Keith, Jr.
4. *Warrior: En Garde* by Michael A. Stackpole
5. *Warrior: Riposte* by Michael A. Stackpole
6. *Warrior: Coupé* by Michael A. Stackpole
7. Wolves on the Border by Robert N. Charrette
8. *Heir to the Dragon* by Robert N. Charrette
9. *Lethal Heritage* (The Blood of Kerensky, Volume 1) by Michael A. Stackpole
10. *Blood Legacy* (The Blood of Kerensky, Volume 2) by Michael A. Stackpole
11. *Lost Destiny* (The Blood of Kerensky, Volume 3) by Michael A. Stackpole
12. *Way of the Clans* (Legend of the Jade Phoenix, Volume 1) by Robert Thurston
13. *Bloodname* (Legend of the Jade Phoenix, Volume 2) by Robert Thurston
14. *Falcon Guard* (Legend of the Jade Phoenix, Volume 3) by Robert Thurston
15. *Wolf Pack* by Robert N. Charrette
16. *Main Event* by James D. Long
17. *Natural Selection* by Michael A. Stackpole
18. *Assumption of Risk* by Michael A. Stackpole
19. *Blood of Heroes* by Andrew Keith
20. *Close Quarters* by Victor Milán
21. *Far Country* by Peter L. Rice
22. *D.R.T.* by James D. Long
23. *Tactics of Duty* by William H. Keith
24. *Bred for War* by Michael A. Stackpole
25. *I Am Jade Falcon* by Robert Thurston
26. *Highlander Gambit* by Blaine Lee Pardoe
27. *Hearts of Chaos* by Victor Milán
28. *Operation Excalibur* by William H. Keith
29. *Malicious Intent* by Michael A. Stackpole
30. *Black Dragon* by Victor Milán
31. *Impetus of War* by Blaine Lee Pardoe
32. *Double-Blind* by Loren L. Coleman
33. *Binding Force* by Loren L. Coleman
34. *Exodus Road* (Twilight of the Clans, Volume 1) by Blaine Lee Pardoe
35. *Grave Covenant* ((Twilight of the Clans, Volume 2) by Michael A. Stackpole
36. *The Hunters* (Twilight of the Clans, Volume 3) by Thomas S. Gressman
37. *Freebirth* (Twilight of the Clans, Volume 4) by Robert Thurston

38. *Sword and Fire* (Twilight of the Clans, Volume 5) by Thomas S. Gressman
39. *Shadows of War* (Twilight of the Clans, Volume 6) by Thomas S. Gressman
40. *Prince of Havoc* (Twilight of the Clans, Volume 7) by Michael A. Stackpole
41. *Falcon Rising* (Twilight of the Clans, Volume 8) by Robert Thurston
42. *Threads of Ambition* (The Capellan Solution, Book 1) by Loren L. Coleman
43. *The Killing Fields* (The Capellan Solution, Book 2) by Loren L. Coleman
44. *Dagger Point* by Thomas S. Gressman
45. *Ghost of Winter* by Stephen Kenson
46. *Roar of Honor* by Blaine Lee Pardoe
47. *By Blood Betrayed* by Blaine Lee Pardoe and Mel Odom
48. *Illusions of Victory* by Loren L. Coleman
49. *Flashpoint* by Loren L. Coleman
50. *Measure of a Hero* by Blaine Lee Pardoe
51. *Path of Glory* by Randall N. Bills
52. *Test of Vengeance* by Bryan Nystul
53. *Patriots and Tyrants* by Loren L. Coleman
54. *Call of Duty* by Blaine Lee Pardoe
55. *Initiation to War* by Robert N. Charrette
56. *The Dying Time* by Thomas S. Gressman
57. *Storms of Fate* by Loren L. Coleman
58. *Imminent Crisis* by Randall N. Bills
59. *Operation Audacity* by Blaine Lee Pardoe
60. *Endgame* by Loren L. Coleman
61. *A Bonfire of Worlds* by Steven Mohan, Jr.
62. *Ghost War* by Michael A. Stackpole
63. *A Call to Arms* by Loren L. Coleman
64. *The Ruins of Power* by Robert E. Vardeman
65. *A Bonfire of Worlds* by Steven Mohan, Jr.
66. *Isle of the Blessed* by Steven Mohan, Jr.
67. *Embers of War* by Jason Schmetzer
68. *Betrayal of Ideals* by Blaine Lee Pardoe
69. *Forever Faithful* by Blaine Lee Pardoe
70. *Kell Hounds Ascendant* by Michael A. Stackpole
71. *Redemption Rift* by Jason Schmetzer
72. *Grey Watch Protocol* (*The Highlander Covenant, Book One*) by Michael J. Ciaravella
73. *Honor's Gauntlet* by Bryan Young
74. *Icons of War* by Craig A. Reed, Jr.
75. *Children of Kerensky* by Blaine Lee Pardoe
76. *Hour of the Wolf* by Blaine Lee Pardoe
77. *Fall From Glory* (*Founding of the Clans, Book One*) by Randall N. Bills
78. *Paid in Blood* (*The Highlander Covenant, Book Two*) by Michael J. Ciaravella

YOUNG ADULT NOVELS

1. *The Nellus Academy Incident* by Jennifer Brozek
2. *Iron Dawn* (*Rogue Academy, Book 1*) by Jennifer Brozek
3. *Ghost Hour* (*Rogue Academy, Book 2*) by Jennifer Brozek

OMNIBUSES

1. *The Gray Death Legion Trilogy* by William H. Keith, Jr.

NOVELLAS/SHORT STORIES
1. *Lion's Roar* by Steven Mohan, Jr.
2. *Sniper* by Jason Schmetzer
3. *Eclipse* by Jason Schmetzer
4. *Hector* by Jason Schmetzer
5. *The Frost Advances (Operation Ice Storm, Part 1)* by Jason Schmetzer
6. *The Winds of Spring (Operation Ice Storm, Part 2)* by Jason Schmetzer
7. *Instrument of Destruction (Ghost Bear's Lament, Part 1)* by Steven Mohan, Jr.
8. *The Fading Call of Glory (Ghost Bear's Lament, Part 2)* by Steven Mohan, Jr.
9. *Vengeance* by Jason Schmetzer
10. *A Splinter of Hope* by Philip A. Lee
11. *The Anvil* by Blaine Lee Pardoe
12. *A Splinter of Hope/The Anvil* (omnibus)
13. *Not the Way the Smart Money Bets (Kell Hounds Ascendant #1)* by Michael A. Stackpole
14. *A Tiny Spot of Rebellion (Kell Hounds Ascendant #2)* by Michael A. Stackpole
15. *A Clever Bit of Fiction (Kell Hounds Ascendant #3)* by Michael A. Stackpole
16. *Break-Away (Proliferation Cycle #1)* by Ilsa J. Bick
17. *Prometheus Unbound (Proliferation Cycle #2)* by Herbert A. Beas II
18. *Nothing Ventured (Proliferation Cycle #3)* by Christoffer Trossen
19. *Fall Down Seven Times, Get Up Eight (Proliferation Cycle #4)* by Randall N. Bills
20. *A Dish Served Cold (Proliferation Cycle #5)* by Chris Hartford and Jason M. Hardy
21. *The Spider Dances (Proliferation Cycle #6)* by Jason Schmetzer
22. *Shell Games* by Jason Schmetzer
23. *Divided We Fall* by Blaine Lee Pardoe
24. *The Hunt for Jardine (Forgotten Worlds, Part One)* by Herbert A. Beas II
25. *Rock of the Republic* by Blaine Lee Pardoe
26. *Finding Jardine (Forgotten Worlds, Part Two)* by Herbert A. Beas II
27. *The Trickster (Proliferation Cycle #7)* by Blaine Lee Pardoe

ANTHOLOGIES
1. *The Corps (BattleCorps Anthology, Volume 1)* edited by Loren. L. Coleman
2. *First Strike (BattleCorps Anthology, Volume 2)* edited by Loren L. Coleman
3. *Weapons Free (BattleCorps Anthology, Volume 3)* edited by Jason Schmetzer
4. *Onslaught: Tales from the Clan Invasion* edited by Jason Schmetzer
5. *Edge of the Storm* by Jason Schmetzer
6. *Fire for Effect (BattleCorps Anthology, Volume 4)* edited by Jason Schmetzer
7. *Chaos Born (Chaos Irregulars, Book 1)* by Kevin Killiany
8. *Chaos Formed (Chaos Irregulars, Book 2)* by Kevin Killiany
9. *Counterattack (BattleCorps Anthology, Volume 5)* edited by Jason Schmetzer
10. *Front Lines (BattleCorps Anthology Volume 6)* edited by Jason Schmetzer and Philip A. Lee
11. *Legacy* edited by John Helfers and Philip A. Lee
12. *Kill Zone (BattleCorps Anthology Volume 7)* edited by Philip A. Lee
13. *Gray Markets (A BattleCorps Anthology)*, edited by Jason Schmetzer and Philip A. Lee
14. *Slack Tide (A BattleCorps Anthology)*, edited by Jason Schmetzer and Philip A. Lee
15. *The Battle of Tukayyid* edited by John Helfers
16. *The Mercenary Life* by Randall N. Bills

MAGAZINES
1. *Shrapnel Issues #01–#04*

Made in the USA
Monee, IL
13 September 2024

2c3232e7-9c1f-467d-abb3-991e9a5007e7R01